PSY

Emma Curtis was born in Brighton and now lives in London with her husband. After raising two children and working various jobs, her fascination with the darker side of domestic life inspired her to start writing psychological suspense thrillers. She has published seven previous novels: *One Little Mistake*, *When I Find You*, *The Night You Left*, *Keep Her Quiet*, *Invite Me In*, *The Babysitter* and *The Commuter*.

Praise for *Emma Curtis*

'Loved it, couldn't stop reading. Emma Curtis is a genius!' – Andrea Mara

'Complex, clever plotting and empathetic characters. Emma Curtis gets better and better!' – Jane Shemilt

'Curtis is a smart writer, who has come up with another "just one more chapter" thriller' – *Telegraph*

'Stylish, dark, hugely addictive and so twisty, *The Commuter* is an exhilarating high-speed ride from beginning to end. Her best yet!' – Claire Douglas

'Addictive, page-turning thriller writing. Once you've reached the end, you'll want to start all over again just to marvel at how it was done.' – B. P. Walter

'Emma Curtis is a master of suspense.' – Jenny Knight

'A pacy, unputdownable thriller that is completely addictive. It had everything I want from a psych thriller, and I inhaled it in a few days.' – Emily Freud

'Full of secrets, lies, and the dark side of suburbia.' – *Heat*

'A compulsive read that'll get under your skin and keep you guessing.' – Gilly Macmillan

'A seductive, well-written story ... had me riveted.' – Jane Corry

'A tense thriller.' – *Woman's Own*

'A perceptive and engaging account of the powerful forces unleashed by motherhood.' – *Daily Mail*

'A brilliant book of unforgettable characters harbouring unforgivable secrets.' – Amy McCulloch

'Effectively tugs at the reader's sympathies.' – *Literary Review*

'A powerhouse of a novel in which character, motive and murder are deftly woven into a tense and compelling psychological drama. It's clever and it haunts.' – Elizabeth Buchan

'Captivating, original, and full of chilling twists!' – Lauren North

'A masterclass in psych suspense writing.' – Nicola Rayner

Also by Emma Curtis

One Little Mistake
When I Find You
The Night You Left
Keep Her Quiet
Invite Me In
The Babysitter
The Commuter

THE
PSYCHIATRIST

EMMA CURTIS

CORVUS

First published in paperback in Great Britain in 2025 by Corvus,
an imprint of Atlantic Books Ltd.

3   5   7   9   10   8   6   4   2

A CIP catalogue record for this book is available from the British Library.

Paperback ISBN: 978 1 80546 357 3
E-book ISBN: 978 1 80546 358 0

Printed and bound by CPI (UK) Ltd, Croydon CR0 4YY

Corvus
An imprint of Atlantic Books Ltd
Ormond House
26–27 Boswell Street
London
WC1N 3JZ

www.atlantic-books.co.uk

Product safety EU representative: Authorised Rep
Compliance Ltd., Ground Floor, 71 Lower Baggot Street,
Dublin, D02 P593, Ireland. www.arccompliance.com

MIX
Paper | Supporting
responsible forestry
FSC® C013604
FSC
www.fsc.org

You know who you are
But you don't know who you wanna be.
So, baby girl, go right ahead
And take your confusion and delusions out on me.

D.I.G.B.Y., 'Leave me Alone'
Lyrics by Dexter Coleridge and George Farr

PART ONE

Chapter 1

THE PSYCHIATRIST

I'm looking at Ben Clarkson's lowered head and I have the unpleasant sensation that I've failed, and that he knows it as well as I do. He sits with his hands clasped between his thighs, his dirty-blonde hair hiding his expression.

'You've come a long way, Ben. I have confidence in your ability to maintain your progress.' I feel the weakness in my words as he lifts his blue eyes to my face. There's an element of disdain there.

'Yeah.'

As is sometimes the way with people with bipolar presentation, Ben is volatile and hard to predict. He has the arrogance of a young man who thinks he's cleverer than his psychiatrist. All my patients are challenging or they wouldn't be here, but there is an unsettling quality to Ben, something I can't put my finger on. Only that he knows it and uses it. Even when he's being charming, I've sensed a latent hostility, a desire to dominate. People living with the disorder can experience periods of overconfidence or impulsivity during manic episodes, which can present as trying to have the upper hand, but I'm not convinced that is the case with Ben. After all, he hasn't had a manic episode in the weeks I've been treating him.

'Are you worried that you aren't ready to manage your treatment plan on your own?' I ask.

'What do you think?' he says, arching an eyebrow.

He often does this, throws my questions back at me. I don't think he realises how much I can read from that. A shield batting off the arrows.

'You've worked hard to develop strategies that can help stabilise your mood and prevent episodes.' I smile at him. 'You've got this.'

'Thank you for believing in me.'

I detect a note of insincerity. It mirrors my own. What has happened here? Why haven't I been able to get through to this man?

'It doesn't matter what I believe. You have to believe in yourself.' I struggle on, itching to be rid of him. He makes me nervous. He has from the off. 'You have the tools to manage your symptoms and you can recognise the early signs of a relapse in time to put your strategies in place. You know this is true.'

We've discussed his safety plan. If he's troubled, he will talk to his parents, who for all their faults have always made sure he has professional help, and if that proves insufficient, he'll come back to see me. I doubt he will. Fleetingly, I realise I'll miss the flashes of savage humour that have enlivened our sessions.

'Okay, Ben?' I say when he doesn't answer.

There's the glimmer of a smile as he nods.

Ben seemed lost when I met him. Coming here has given him a routine and stability he lacked, so of course there will be a sense of abandonment. Diagnosed a year ago, his condition has dominated his life since his early teens. His family situation – he's the only child of a diplomat – hasn't helped. His father is two years into a three-year stint in Nigeria, and before that they lived in Dubai and Cairo. Sent to boarding school in England at the age of eight, moving to a London day school for sixth form and then university while his parents lived abroad, Ben gives the impression of being self-sufficient but somehow is not. There's a vulnerability that his combative personality masks until you get close enough to see the chinks. He is a man of contradictions.

I can't help feeling that Mr and Mrs Clarkson have been selfish. It seems extraordinary to leave a vulnerable young person unanchored. He's rattled around London on his own since he was sixteen, living in a studio flat in central London during school holidays, subsisting on takeaways and occasional visits to the homes of family friends. Plenty of money and zero attention.

No wonder he unravelled. While his mother clearly worries about her son enough to have got in touch with me, she's happier to throw money at his problems than interrupt her glamorous life to fly over and offer emotional support. But who am I to judge? I'm not a parent.

'Why did you go into psychiatry?' Ben asks. 'Why not general practice, or surgery?'

I don't mind answering that. It's a valid question. 'Because I learnt a long time ago that bodies are often made unwell by minds. That's where I wanted to be. Teaching people to manage their mental illness can have a profound effect on their physical health. And vice versa. It's a very close link.'

'Do you always succeed?' He looks into my eyes, and I blink.

'Not always, no. It's an imperfect art. You can never really eradicate mental pain, but you can make it hurt less; you can make it manageable by putting the patient in charge of it.' It feels good explaining it to him, like he's a potential student of the discipline rather than a consumer of it. 'Often when people come to me they've lost all sense of control. Their mental anguish has taken the reins and their life is no longer their own. I believe in dealing with the symptoms first by getting the medication right, then working on the causes. Essentially, I aim to stop patients like you spiralling out of reach before you can be helped.'

He nods slowly, eyes on my face, appearing impressed by my eloquence. In truth, I feel a bit of a fraud. I haven't been qualified long and I'm still under supervision, still have to feign the confidence I lack, still sometimes wonder what gives me the right to diagnose patients' mental and behavioural disorders, still feel like I'm getting away with it. So far I have, hopefully because I'm better than I think I am, but at times I've had the distinct feeling that Ben, in particular, sees through me.

'Does helping people give you a sense of power?'

'That's an odd question.' And a manipulative one, I silently add.

'I'm curious.'

'All right. Not power so much as achievement. I try not to be self-congratulatory, but sometimes when I see a patient turn their life around, then absolutely, it's a powerful feeling. But that's different from having a sense of power.'

'Do you think you've succeeded with me?'

I roll the question over in my mind. 'I hope so.'

'But you're not sure.'

'No. But then a sense of certainty is something I want to give *you*, not that I need you to give me.' Certainty is a state of being I work towards my patients attaining, even though it's a tough one to achieve. I want them to believe they have the ability to manage their condition, that their lives are worth something, that their medication works, that they have learnt the techniques that will help them function better, even thrive. 'That would be a shameful state of affairs.'

I am breaching professional boundaries here and need to wrap this up before it gets any worse. I get to my feet to indicate that our session is over and Ben follows suit. He's considerably taller than me.

'Do you feel shame about me?' he asks.

'Does unsettling women give you a sense of power?' Oh Christ. I should not have said that. This is more about me than him. I can feel a blush warming my cheeks.

'You think I'm deliberately unsettling you?'

'I do. You're a young man, but not too young to know precisely what you're doing.'

'It isn't deliberate, and I'm sorry if I've unsettled you. I didn't mean to. And it doesn't give me a sense of power to discover that I have.'

I attempt to claw back my dignity. 'I didn't say you'd succeeded, just that I believe it's what you're trying to do.'

Ben grins. 'Touché. I get scared of things, scared of myself sometimes. Is that normal?'

'It's something we all do at one time or another.'

'I thought you psychiatrists would be immune.'

I think of the heath at night, of the black depths of the river. 'I'm not immune. I doubt anyone is, even psychiatrists.' I move past him to the door and have an odd feeling that he was about to put his hand out to touch me. I'm over-aware of his physicality. Not attracted, more switched on to him. Fight or flight. 'If you ever feel like stopping taking your medication, get in touch with the practice.'

He hesitates, evidently disappointed. 'I will.'

'Good luck, Mr Clarkson.'

'Thank you, Dr Geddes.'

He offers his hand, and I take it automatically. It's the first time we've touched, and I feel it in my chest, like a portent of danger. He starts towards the door, then turns back.

'I'm not your patient any more, am I?'

'No, Ben,' I respond, half smiling. 'You're not. Go and get on with the rest of your life.'

He's barely listening. 'Then I just want to say . . . you're beautiful.'

I keep my face blank as he leaves, my training kicking in. I expected a challenging final statement from Ben, but not this.

The receptionist says goodbye, the door to the street closes. I release my breath.

My face is set as I sit down to update my session notes. I put on my reading glasses, take the cassette from the Dictaphone and label it. I haven't got round to replacing the tape recorder I bought when I was a student with a modern digital version. My next appointment is in ten minutes. There can be no sense that I've been thrown off kilter.

*

I'm lost in my thoughts as I walk down Griffiths Lane on my way home. I must have done something to make Ben think his words would be welcome. Or did he do it simply to prove a point? *I can unsettle you if I want to.* I grimace. There have been times when I've sensed I've amused him, so perhaps he likes to play mind games with authority. I'll talk to my supervisor later.

I walk into Sainsbury's Local and see him, as though I've conjured him up. He has his back to me and hasn't seen me as he carries a basket containing milk, bread, bananas and a pizza up the cleaning products aisle. I step backwards, bumping into a shop assistant loading packets of biscuits onto the shelf beside me.

'Sorry,' I mutter, and scuttle away, into fruit and veg. I wait, heart thumping, until I see him leave, then make my own purchases and go home.

I acknowledge that it was stupid to take on a patient who lives so close to me, but at the time, the only thing that registered was the odd coincidence of him renting one of the flats in the converted house in Gladwell Grove where Daniel and I began our married life. Before Ben's time, but does he know that? How could he? I dismiss the thought as not worth worrying about. He won't be in Alverley for ever. He'll move on once his tenancy is up for renewal.

Chapter 2

LORNA

'I don't know anyone here,' Matt whispers.

'Stop grumbling,' Lorna says.

'I'll stop grumbling if you stop totting up every penny they've spent on this place. I can practically see your brain working.'

Lorna chuckles.

The Coleridges' housewarming feels more like one of the swanky charity galas she goes to for work from time to time. The house and garden have been dressed in fairy lights, so that when you first arrive you feel as though you've walked into a romcom, waiters weave around the guests bearing trays of champagne and canapés, while a quartet of young women in black denim and cowboy boots play a medley of classical greats and instrumental versions of pop anthems. Exquisite floral displays in hues of cinder rose and olive green designed by Thistledown, the expensive florist on Griffiths Lane, grace the surfaces. It's all completely over the top, but Lorna has to give her friend points for using local businesses.

Her friend. How good that sounds.

She's glad she dressed up, since everyone here has

dusted off their finery. Her midnight-blue satin dress is stitched on the bias. It skims her body when she's still and undulates like water when she moves. Earlier in the day she squeezed in a blow-dry.

The Coleridges have invited all their new neighbours from Gladwell Grove, with the addition of a handful of non-residents, including her and Matt. Lorna follows Elise with her eyes. Their hostess illuminates the room even when she doesn't try. Lorna wishes she could relax. She and Matt have as much right to be here as anyone else. More, in fact. She knocks back her champagne, for courage. She should not feel in any way inferior to these people.

When rumours that the former lead singer of D.I.G.B.Y. had bought in Alverley swirled through the community, Lorna knew all about it already, because she worked for Chetham & Church, a local independent estate agent. She got to know Elise and has seen the house at various stages of its development, but this is Matt's first glimpse. He's been blatantly examining the finely turned banisters and architraves. She can tell from his subdued expression that he's impressed. Elise Coleridge is from Sweden, although you wouldn't guess it from her auburn hair, and Dexter is from Liverpool, so their tastes differ widely, but since Dexter has zero interest in interior decoration, this heady mixture of understated glamour and *hygge* is one hundred per cent Elise. She used to be in musical theatre, appearing in *Cats*, *Phantom*, *Les Mis*, *Cabaret*, among others, before retiring at the age of thirty-three to raise Noah. In Lorna's mind, she sprinkles fairy dust wherever she goes.

Lorna recognises several familiar faces: people she's helped secure houses for, women who put her through the wringer. Property negotiating, when it means literally *everything* to the house hunter to be in the right street, is a nightmare, and Gladwell Grove is very much the right street. And position counts too. The most coveted houses are in the Alverley Park area, preferably backing onto the heath, a thousand acres of common land bordered to the south by the River Bute, a tributary of the Thames, by the less salubrious Alverley High Street to the west and by East Alverley . . . well, to the east. Almost as important is to be at the end of Gladwell Grove furthest from the Baslow Estate, a relic of 1960s council housing now seventy-five per cent in private hands.

It never ceases to amaze Lorna how pushy and down-right rude her clients can be once they've set their sights on *the one*, but it keeps her in work, and far from resenting the challenges, she relishes them. She wonders if they'll acknowledge her this evening or pretend not to recognise her. If anyone has the cheek to ask what she's doing here, she has her answer primed, her courage bolstered by the knowledge that she is here because she is Elise's chosen friend while this lot have been invited simply because they live in Gladwell Grove and Elise owes them a party. If asked the question, she plans to say, 'Oh, I wouldn't have missed it for the world. Elise is such a good friend.'

Not that she's a social climber or anything.

'Half an hour,' Matt grumbles, turning his mouth into her hair.

She jerks away from him. 'I hope you're joking. That would be so rude.'

She glances at Dexter. He doesn't look any more relaxed than she is. She sympathises. These aren't his people. Too conventional. She hasn't told him they've crossed paths before or what the circumstances were. She's only told Matt and Amy the bare minimum: that she met him after he'd played a gig at her university and had a drink with him and his bandmates in the student bar before they jumped in their minibus and vanished into the night. Too much time has passed, and she'd hate him to think she wants something. It's no big deal. She hadn't exactly been a vestal virgin. They had been young, adrenaline-fuelled, drunk and horny. He probably has no recollection of that night. She imagines having to explain it, and cringes. It was a youthful indiscretion that did no one any harm.

Lorna suppresses a grimace. There was some harm, wasn't there? There is embarrassment and there is humiliating mortification. They are two very different things. If she'd simply been embarrassed, she'd have told her friends, had a laugh about it, but she never has.

It doesn't matter. What matters is that Dexter knows her by name, has a smile ready for her if he meets her in his house, a bit of banter. His greeting is sometimes accompanied by a touch that lingers. It's pure friendliness, of course. In fact, she's witnessed him doing it this evening as he works the room. Kiss-kiss, hand on back. Some people are more physical than others and she really should not read anything into it.

The clink of metal on glass silences the room. Their hosts are about to speak. Bloody hell, they're glamorous, Lorna thinks, with a pang of envy.

13

Chapter 3

LORNA

'Welcome to our home,' Dexter says.

Heads swivel, conversations cease, the trickle of chatter from those too distracted to hear is shushed, and guests form a semicircle around their hosts, glasses of Dom Perignon in hand. A sense of excitement ripples through the room. Dexter, who until tonight has been merely a face briefly glimpsed by a lucky few, is now a human being.

Thin as a rake, his hair still thick, though salted with grey, he is an inch or so shorter than Matt, making him just over six foot. His smile is slow, he has a habit of running his fingers through his hair so that it spikes, and he speaks with a Liverpool accent largely unaffected by the years he's spent away from the city. To Lorna, who feels a frisson every time he walks into the room, he is a dream made flesh, blood and bone.

'Elise and I are dead grateful to you all for coming,' he says. 'Because we know how much we've pissed you off.'

The laughter is nervous. People don't feel secure, don't know if they're being mocked.

'Yeah, I know what you're thinking. A glass of champagne doesn't make up for a year of disruption, dust, noise, all that shit. Have two glasses. Knock yourselves out. Truly, we are sorry. One hundred per cent. But it's done now, and you're our guests, and Elise and I are made up to see you here.'

Matt nudges Lorna, but she ignores him. He finds the whole concept of the Coleridges faintly ridiculous. These people are A-listers, but who gives a shit? They walk all over everyone and are repulsively entitled. She's told him it isn't like that. He doesn't know them like she does, hasn't sat at their kitchen table feeding pasta to three-year-old Noah or seen Elise weep over the death of their cat.

Was it really a year ago that she'd wandered round 55 Gladwell Grove with Elise, practically melting with envy? Elise loved talking about little Noah, the Tasmanian devil of a toddler who accompanied her on one of her visits. Lorna, almost as in love with Elise as she was with the house, assured her that Noah's behaviour was nothing out of the ordinary. She told wildly exaggerated tales of other nightmare tots and a friendship was born. Lorna is one of the few local mums prepared to tolerate him rampaging round their house.

And then there's Dexter. No longer a pop star, he has segued into acting, but is still mostly famous for having been the frontman of a once feted but now defunct boy band.

D.I.G.B.Y. stands for Dexter, Ivo, George, Brendan and Yann. Their anthems were a soundtrack to the roller coaster of Lorna's youth. The song 'Tell It My Way' meant more to her than she could have possibly communicated to her friends at the time. That lyric, *If I could look in your eyes, if I could tell you I know, that I've been here before, would you open your door?*, never failed to bring a lump to her throat. Dexter Coleridge, cupping the microphone close to his mouth, heavy eyelids lowered, shoulders hunched, back contorted into a question mark, voice husky, had spoken to her and her alone.

Which had led to the incident that changed the course of her life.

Nowadays, saying hi like he's just any other person is a thrill beyond her wildest imaginings. As far as she's concerned, what happened doesn't matter. She's over it, happily married, moved on. She can put it out of her mind for the sake of her friendship with his wife.

Dexter's burgeoning career as an actor means he's home at odd times, so you never know when he'll appear, which has added a sense of anticipation to Lorna's visits. He's a man in constant motion, so it isn't as if he's sat down at the table with her for a nice long chat. He comes in, jokes with the little boys, wraps a careless arm round Elise, grabs something to eat from the fridge and leaves them. It's as though a whirlwind has passed through the room, and her.

'We've got a kid, yeah.' Dexter is getting into his stride now. 'Noah. Some of you will have met him. When I was a kid, we used to play out in the street. I've still got those mates – well, except for the ones who developed drug habits.' He acknowledges the nervous chuckle from his guests with a wink. 'But yeah, some of them are fine and they've got my back, you know. And I want the kids here to have Noah's back, and for Noah to have theirs. That's what putting down roots is all about. That's what growing up is all about.'

'Is he going to cry?' Matt whispers in her ear.

'Shh.' Lorna is irritated. Why can't he take this seriously? More to the point, why can't he take *Dexter* seriously? The man is doing his best to make amends, for the sake of his child. What is there to laugh at in that?

'I know you're curious. I know you'd love to see what it's all about, so with the exception of the top floor, where Noah is sleeping, we will give guided tours throughout the evening. We're proud of what we've achieved here. Nah, that's a lie. I'm proud of what the wife has achieved, because I've basically done sod-all. Elise has fantastic taste, and yeah, she, like, vetoed literally all of my suggestions. So if you're expecting tiger-skin carpets, mirrored ceilings and purple walls, I'm sorry, but you're gonna be disappointed. Apart from my man cave.' He grins. 'You guys know what I'm talking about, right?'

Matt rolls his eyes. He has a workshop in the garden. A proper workshop for a proper man, with a table saw, a jigsaw, a circular saw and other essential items Lorna can't remember the names of, and a drawing board he'll sit hunched over late into the night when he has a commission. Anyway, he has the lot. They built it when they moved in and it takes up half the garden. The neighbours kicked up a stink, but it was all within permitted development. Dexter has a fridge freezer, a massive TV, an entertainment centre, a wood-burning stove and a couple of reclining chairs.

'I expect you're wondering what this gorgeous woman sees in me.'

'He is definitely going to cry,' Matt whispers.

'Will you shut up.'

17

'I expect you're thinking, what's a princess like Elise doing with a lout like Dexter Coleridge? I know I'd be thinking the same, 'cos she's the business, isn't she? She's—'

'Okay, darling. That's enough.' Elise puts her hand over his mouth. 'Finished?'

'Finished,' Dexter mumbles.

This time the laughter is heartfelt. There's a sense among the guests that they are co-conspirators in the lives of these people.

Elise releases him. 'Thank you for coming to our house this evening; for giving us a chance. Please enjoy yourselves. We feel nothing but warmth and love for our new neighbours and hope more than anything to become part of your community. Dexter might be famous, but he's just a silly bloke, like any other. He's a dad, he's greedy, he likes a beer, he farts in bed, he shouts at the telly. Normal, like you. He has a good heart. Be kind to him.'

Elise's English is perfect, due to the fifteen years she's spent here and her time on the stage. If it wasn't for a subtle inflection from time to time, no one would know she was foreign. Her voice has a melodic quality, as if she's learnt intonation through song. Eliza Doolittle, Lorna thinks. *The rain in Spain.*

Goodwill flows with the expensive champagne. Moments later, Elise is surrounded by glossy women, and Lorna's feeling of proprietorship over her fades and her confidence slips.

Elise will be absorbed into Gladwell Grove, sins against peace and quiet forgiven. She has a whole other life: the music industry and theatre relationships built up over years. Lorna can never be part of that. She reminds herself of what Elise is doing for Amy, giving Lorna's starstruck fifteen-year-old daughter free singing lessons. Elise, who is a vocal coach these days and whose clients are the stars of stage and screen, made the offer after chatting to Amy. Lorna had been annoyed at first. She wasn't sure she liked the idea of her daughter becoming close to Elise, but this isn't a competition.

Elise approaches, swaying like a model in her sheer, sparkling dress, her face lit up.

'Lorna! Lorna! It's so good to see you, my lovely friend. And Matt. Thank you for joining us this evening.' She wraps her slender arms around them, and Lorna feels Matt's antipathy and ironic eye-rolling melt away. 'You beautiful people,' Elise says. 'Now, Matt, I can't believe you haven't met Dexter yet. I'll introduce you. No. Wait. First I'll show you round the house. Lorna, you come too. You are part of it.'

Lorna blushes, pleased with the compliment.

Chapter 4

THE PSYCHIATRIST

My split-level flat is on the sixth floor of the Baslow Estate and has an amazing view over the heath. On a clear day you can even catch glimpses of the river through gaps between the trees on the far side. From the front walkway I can survey the houses and gardens of Gladwell Grove. I still wonder how I ended up here, at the edge of wealth, looking over it rather than being a part of it. I could have been, had things worked out differently.

Mum and Dad can't understand why I chose the flat, but it was a compulsion. Even with my training and experience, I couldn't reason or counsel myself out of what was, at best, a puzzling decision. I was reeling from the break-up of my marriage to Daniel and bought it not because I couldn't afford anywhere else, but because of the views. They were my yin and yang: Gladwell Grove with its unhappy, clamouring memories against the calm serenity of the heath.

I'll do well when I come to sell it, because two bedrooms with a balcony and the proximity of green space have become much sought after since the pandemic, plus the 1960s buildings are now described by estate agents as possessing retro chic, but emotionally . . . I don't know.

Daniel wasn't rich and famous when we met. I was in my third year studying medicine at Southampton University, and he was studying English literature and philosophy. I had seen him in the drama department's production of *Look Back in Anger*, playing the role of Jimmy Porter. A mutual friend introduced us. We were together for six years before we married. By then I was working three days a week in the NHS and two in a private practice, paying the rent on the flat in Gladwell Grove while Daniel worked his way up through pub theatres and rep. When he could, he earnt money bartending or tutoring primary school students for the eleven-plus. I made the mistake once of suggesting he do a teaching qualification, just in case the acting didn't pan out. He hit the roof. But it wasn't that that broke us.

When I first started going out with Daniel, I'd said – in passing, because it's a subject you don't want to get into with a new love interest – that I didn't want children. I said it again when we moved in together, and he shrugged and told me he was cool with that. I said it again when he asked me to marry him, and he told me I was enough. But it turns out that wasn't true, it turns out he never took me seriously, that he thought hormones and my body clock would change me, that at some point in my thirties I would get broody. When I realised this, because of an off-the-cuff comment of his when his best friend became a father, I felt a chill descend. I hadn't expected to have this conversation because I thought it was understood and that he was happy with the status quo. But he'd heard what he wanted to hear and blocked out the rest. We were on different pages, and as soon as we realised this, the foundations of our relation-ship were brutally stripped away.

Months passed while we tried to make the marriage work, then one day Daniel told me there was someone else and she was pregnant. He was sorry, he cared deeply for me and always would, but he had to be true to himself. He wanted and needed to be a father. So that was that. He checks in on me from time to time, though less so since they've had their second baby. He's moved on and I should do the same.

I expect Daniel's parents are deliriously happy now they have their grandchildren. I wonder sometimes if I could have coped, for his sake. I would have loved my child, but it would have always been there, my well-documented reluctance. And Daniel would have been disappointed in me for not sharing his enthusiasm. My mother-in-law told me I was selfish and self-obsessed. Perhaps I was, though frankly I'm tired of hearing that about women who choose not to have children. Perhaps I am. It doesn't mean I never wonder what my children would have been like, that I don't occasionally feel their absence. These ghost children nudge me from time to time. I let them be.

As for future relationships, I've made a ragged-edged peace with that. I'll never believe a man who says they're fine with not having kids, even if they genuinely think they're telling the truth, so I don't expect to find a permanent partner.

My settlement was small, reflecting Daniel's precarious income, and six months after we divorced, he got his big break. Now he's constantly on TV, has a film coming out this summer and lives in a smart house on Richmond Hill with his wife and kids.

*

I'm not myself today. Ben sensed that and used it. I don't understand why I can't brush his remark off like I do any other stupid man who thinks I'm there for the taking.

Perhaps it was spontaneous. I don't think so, though. He's been pretty consistent in his attempts to needle me. It's never felt like an innocent overstepping, but I didn't want to draw attention or give him the satisfaction of knowing he'd got to me. Was it a battle all along? I should have addressed the issue, not swept it under the carpet.

This was always going to be a difficult day. I just need to get through the evening. Then it's done for another year.

I rarely take the lift, counting using the stairs as my daily cardio, but today I feel washed out, so I do. I leave through the reinforced glass doors onto the walkway and am greeted outside my front door by Dylan, my black and white tom. He slinks around my legs, purring. I scoop him up and hold him to my cheek. He allows me a few seconds of his undivided attention, then springs to the floor, and I let myself in.

There's a mirror hanging in the hall, the one I use to check my appearance as I leave. I stand in front of it now and examine my face. Despite everything, today I have felt beautiful. It's a weird thing, that however inappropriate the message and the messenger, a compliment still has a profound effect on the way we see ourselves. Until we confront the reality. I'm not beautiful. I'm well groomed, and if I make an effort and put on mascara and lipstick, I'd go so far as to describe myself as pretty. The big brown eyes help, as do the decent bone structure and good teeth, but I don't have a particularly generous mouth, and my nose is a little short.

Dylan meows from the kitchen door.

'Give me a chance.'

I shrug at my reflection, tug the scrunchie out of my hair and pull it over my wrist, then give in to my cat's increasingly forceful blandishments. Trying not to breathe as I tear open a sachet and the pungent, meaty smell hits my olfactory nerves, I squeeze chicken chunks into Dylan's bowl and carry it through the sitting room to the balcony. Then I fetch myself a glass of wine, and while he eats, noisily guzzling, I lean against the brick balustrade and gaze out over the heath. I drink slowly, appreciatively, letting the wine go to work on my tense muscles. I am not an alcoholic; I just have a particular day when drowning my sorrows is justified and necessary. I hate anniversaries, resent having this yearly reminder of my mistakes. In so many ways, I am lucky: I enjoy my job, I'm healthy, and if I want to sell this flat and move away, there's no one stopping me. I'm glad I'm divorced. I should never have got married in the first place.

'I can't complain,' I tell Dylan. 'And you shouldn't either.'

My phone rings, and I brace as I go back inside, knowing who it will be.

'How are you, darling?'

Mum has developed a quiver in her voice, even though she's only fifty-eight. She's had it tough, with a diagnosis of multiple sclerosis coming after years of mysterious symptoms, from chronic fatigue to nerve pain and sleeplessness. She has periods of respite, but it's becoming harder to cope.

'Good. What about you? How are the muscle spasms?'

She'd been overtired last week. My brother had come to stay with his current partner. Mum would have pulled out all the stops for them.

'Easing. But it's you I'm worried about.'

'I'm fine, Mum. Really. I'd rather not talk about it.'

She sighs, disappointed, and starts to tell me what they've been up to. I zone out. What am I supposed to do? Cry for her satisfaction? Things went wrong. I fucked up. Life's a bitch. I put my phone on speaker, lay it on the counter and refill my glass.

It really doesn't matter how much 'work' you do on yourself, it doesn't matter how much you know about the human mind; when it comes to our own problems, a psychiatrist can fail as much as the next man or woman. I have failed, because I can't move on. In many ways I don't even want to.

Dylan has finished eating. He comes and sits close to my foot. Daniel gave him to me for my birthday, three months before he moved out. He's always been thoughtful.

Later, I sit down at the table, pull my laptop towards me. I have a desk in the smaller bedroom upstairs, but I prefer it down here. I open the search engine, the last resort for the lonely and the absolute last action I'd suggest to my patients. Do not search for the people who've hurt you, do not search for the person you once were. I type 'D'. My fingers hover over the keys, then I backspace. There is nothing to be gained except soul destruction from wandering down that rabbit hole.

Thirty-four years old and feeling like forty-four. I'm tired, irritable and unhappy, while trying to look and behave the opposite. I really must make an effort to find some joy in life. I'm instantly reminded of Ben telling me I'm beautiful. Angry, I tip the glass clumsily to my lips and slosh a little wine down my chin.

Chapter 5

LORNA

'My husband doesn't exercise,' Elise tells Matt when he asks her why they don't have a swimming pool in the basement. 'Also, I detest the smell of chlorine on my skin.'

Matt flushes.

Lorna knows the truth, because Elise told her. Dexter has never learnt to swim. Something he witnessed on a family holiday when he was little made him resistant, and his parents didn't care enough to push. There was no money for luxuries like private lessons.

'This space is where I work. My clients can sing as loudly as they like. We don't disturb anyone down here. It's where I teach your stepdaughter, actually.'

'I call Amy my daughter,' Matt says.

'I didn't know that.' Her eyes glow as she looks at him. 'You are such a great dad.'

Lorna smiles. They've hit it off. Elise will remember the conversation. She may even tell Dexter about it. It means they're proper friends.

They complete their tour with a peek into Noah's playroom, then Elise escorts them back into the throng of guests and leaves them to fend for themselves, which at this point Matt is happy to do. It's Lorna who's ready to go home.

She watches Matt move easily between groups, the chip on his shoulder soothed by Elise's flattering attention. The men don't have the same hang-ups and insecurities as the women; they don't care that he isn't a Gladwell Grove resident, they just like him.

The vicar is here. Lorna had no idea that Elise was religious, and after thinking about it for precisely two seconds, she feels a little hurt that her friend hasn't shared her faith. In the next instant she wonders whether perhaps she ought to start going to church, then dismisses the idea, distracted by the frown on the face of a woman who is obviously trying to place her. Lorna throws her shoulders back and approaches.

'It's Sophie Meadows, isn't it? I'm Lorna Chilcott. We met when you bought your house. I hope you're enjoying living here.'

'Oh, yes.' Sophie, whose husband is a hedge fund manager, looks disconcerted, but she recovers nicely. 'It's a lovely community, and we're so happy to welcome Elise and Dexter. I presume you handled the sale?'

'I did.'

'It was a wreck, wasn't it? But still, so expensive. I cannot believe it went for seven million. We bought ours for five. Do you remember?'

'I do,' Lorna says. 'You've done extremely well.'

Sophie launches into everyone's favourite obsession, the local property market, and Lorna, even though she'd sooner talk about anything else, encourages her because it means she has someone to talk to. She can see Matt out of the corner of her eye, chatting to a man in a stripy shirt and chinos. Another City type, she guesses. They mostly are in Gladwell Grove. There are some exceptions. Dexter and Elise, obviously. Number 37 belongs to two elderly sisters, Eileen and Ann Brooker. They're a local institution. Eileen used to be the headmistress of Holmewood High, where Amy goes to school, and Ann was a lawyer. Lorna hasn't seen the pair out and about together for some time. Then there's the house opposite, which was converted into four flats in the 1980s. She's sold all of them since she's worked for Chetham & Church.

'Where's your little boy going in September?' Sophie asks.

'Alverley School, hopefully,' Lorna says. 'We hear about places on Tuesday.'

'Sounds nail-biting.'

'It is.'

'Best of luck. Alfie's going to Fairlands. He passed the assessment with flying colours, thank goodness.'

'Well done him.' Lorna is familiar with the varying admission requirements of the local independent schools. Fairlands tests the kids at the age of two. She doesn't like the practice.

'You can't blame them,' Sophie witters on, possibly sensing disapproval. 'The fees are extortionate, so parents' expectations are going to be high. And they offer an awful lot in terms of clubs and sports and getting involved. It's full-on, so they want the children who can cope with that, not the shy, retiring kind, or the hyperactive ones. Apparently—' she lowers her voice '—they get told they're not Fairlands material.'

That sounds awful, but Lorna doesn't say so. Diplomacy is called for if she wants to sell this woman's house down the line. 'It has a very good reputation.'

Sophie puts her hand on Lorna's arm and says with a kindness she reads as condescension, 'And so does Alverley School. I know a couple of mums who've been to tribunal after their children weren't offered places, and even then, they were left out in the cold. What's your backup plan?'

'We don't have one. We just want Jack at Alverley, with the friends he's made at nursery.'

Sophie looks at her shrewdly. 'Small children cope with change. I'd imagine this is more about you wanting to be with the friends *you've* made. Oh, Elise,' she coos, stretching out an arm as Elise glides by. 'We were talking about schools. Noah's down for Fairlands, isn't he?'

'We haven't decided yet,' Elise says.

'Is there a problem?' Lorna asks.

'Oh, no. It's just that neither of us went to fee-paying schools. It depends on Noah, really.'

'Yes. In the end, you do what's right for your kids,' Sophie says.

Elise peels away. Lorna is sorry to see her go. She wants to dig deeper. Only a couple of days ago, Elise was eulogising Fairlands. What's happened in between? It's a little concerning if she's considering Alverley, because Gladwell Grove is closer to the school than Matt and Lorna's road, Bramcote Avenue. She's not sure what she'll do if Jack doesn't get his place. She doesn't want him to go to Northcliff. It's much bigger, three-form entry instead of two, and most of the kids who go there live in East Alverley. Not that she's a snob, but like Sophie said, you want the best for your child, and East Alverley is a rough area. She doesn't know anyone who's sending their child there.

She mutters something about needing the loo and makes her way into the hall, where there are already three people queuing. Because she knows the house so well, she feels justified in slipping off her shoes and nipping upstairs to use one of the four alternatives, choosing the family bathroom with its cream polished marble floor, walk-in shower and clawfoot bath. There's an expensive Jo Malone diffuser on the windowsill and a trailing green plant in a stone tub hanging by chains from the ceiling in the corner of the room.

Glancing at her watch, she sees that it's almost eleven. Oh Lord. She didn't mean to stay so late. She takes her phone out of her clutch and guiltily messages Amy.

All well? Will be back very soon.

Amy messages back. *Fine. Reading in bed*.

As she walks across the soft-pile carpet and down the stairs, she's met by Dexter and promptly loses the power of speech.

Chapter 6

LORNA

'Having a good time?' Dexter asks.

'It's a lovely party.' She hopes he didn't notice her momentary loss of control.

'You've been so supportive of Elise. I'm dead grateful to you.'

Lorna flushes happily. 'Elise is wonderful. I love her.'

'You're the only genuine friend we've made. The rest of that lot...' he jerks his chin in the direction of the sitting room, 'Those people, I'm like, fuck, they're from a different planet.'

'You're not regretting the move?'

People like the Coleridges can afford to be fickle. Money facilitates whims.

'Nah. We've done it for the kid. And the prices. Did the wife tell you what happened?'

Lorna nods. She knows he was sued for plagiarism and lost the case, and has been left with a compensation bill running into millions.

'Only money, right?' Dexter says. 'But when you grow up without it, it's important.'

'I know,' she agrees.

'This lot understand money. How to make it. How to keep it. I didn't get much of an education, but I'm not too proud to learn.'

'Be careful who you learn off. There are sharks out there.'

'You're not kidding.'

'But you're happy with the area?' Does she sound needy? If she does, he doesn't appear to notice.

'Pretty much. Where we were before, our neighbours were like us but with older kids, and I could see what was happening to them. Acting like they were gods. Drinking, doing drugs. Turning into a waste of space. We don't want that for Noah. We want ordinary.'

'Ordinary but wealthy.'

He laughs, and she glows.

'Yep. I worked hard for this gaff. You're from West Kirby, aren't you? One of those roads near the golf club.'

Her eyes widen. 'How on earth do you know that?'

'The way you talk. Soft and posh.'

Lorna grew up in a detached Arts and Crafts house within a stone's throw of the Royal Liverpool. West Kirby and the area where Dexter is from are worlds apart. He might as well have been from Planet Zog. She would never have bumped into him under normal circumstances.

'I had a girlfriend from Eddisbury Road when I was fifteen. Talked just like you.' When Lorna raises her eyebrows, he grins. 'Her family hated me. That little toerag from Toxteth. I need a fag,' he says. There's something brutal in his voice, a vestige of his past. It's sexy. 'Wanna keep me company?'

There doesn't seem any reason not to, except she's

enjoying herself a little too much and desperately hoping Matt won't come looking for her.

It's chilly, but there's a heater on the patio. Lorna watches the guests through the windows. Everything carries a golden sparkle. Wealth. Dexter lights his cigarette with a shiny black lighter and takes a long, appreciative drag.

'I didn't know you smoked,' Lorna says.

'I try not to,' he says, holding his cigarette away from her and blowing a stream of smoke over his shoulder. 'But coming outside for a fag keeps me calm. I'm where Noah gets his temper from. Not Elise.'

'That's honest.'

He shrugs.

'I'm sorry about what you went through,' she says. 'It seems so unfair.'

'The plagiarism thing? Occupational hazard. I'm not going to lie: it's made a dent, but I still make more money than that twat.'

Lorna laughs. 'Yes. I'm not a fan.'

He glares at her, but he's smiling through it. 'You'd better not be. So do you get back to Liverpool much?'

'Weddings and funerals. What about you?'

'Same. Oh, I went and spoke at my old school. An alumni thing. Inspire the kids.'

'I'm sure you did.'

He laughs. 'It's a grammar school. Fucking miracle I got in. It wasn't as if I grafted or my parents could afford tutors.'

'So you were one of those annoying kids who didn't do a stroke of work and passed exams with flying colours.'

He smirks. 'Guilty.'

'Why didn't you finish your education?'

She knows, because she is a fan, that apart from Brendan, who is a couple of years older than the other band members and achieved four A levels, none of them had been educated beyond their GCSEs.

'Because I was a plonker. Anyway, you know the story. I met Ivo, Yann and George at school. And Brendan was a mate of Ivo's big brother. Let myself be washed along by the current.'

He looks so sad, she has to ask. 'Do you ever regret it? If you were that clever, it must be frustrating.'

'Not really. I use my brain every day. That's why, in spite of the court case, I can still afford this house and that wife of mine.'

That last comment strikes a jarring note. 'I still can't understand why you chose to live here. It must be stultifying for someone like you.'

'Someone like me?' He grins wolfishly.

The air smells of blossom now that he's finished his cigarette and discarded the butt. The atmosphere is soft and pliant, the background music, the chatter and chink of glasses, like a love song. She doesn't know where to look, so she tries that thing of looking at the bridge of his nose, but still gets caught by his eyes. They are hooded and brown, slightly weary, with crow's feet and dark shadows.

'Someone who's lived the life you have.'

'Drink and drugs and rock and roll?'

'Your words, not mine.'

'I've misbehaved, sure. Perhaps this is my punishment.'

I was part of that misbehaviour, Lorna thinks, then says,

'A jail sentence in a middle-class suburb?'

'My mum would've loved it.'

She can see he's serious and feels bad for mocking Mrs Coleridge's aspirations.

'I only want what's best for the boy,' he says. 'I looked into the future and saw him going off the rails. There's more control here, a sense that there are consequences for your actions. Know what I mean?'

'I do,' Lorna says, thinking: not for everyone. 'It isn't a question of curtain twitchers, or judgy neighbours, although there is that. It's more a sense that you're part of a whole and that what you do affects the community, that you have responsibility for the well-being of others.'

'Exactly,' Dexter says, the surprise evident in his voice. After a pause, he adds a non-sequitur. 'Did you ever go to the Raz?'

Lorna chuckles. 'I led a sheltered life. I wasn't allowed to go to nightclubs.'

'Where did you and your mates hang out on a Saturday night, then?'

'Mostly in each other's houses.'

'Sweet.'

'Do you miss the city?'

'A little. I used to go to the Walker Gallery. Just stand there and look at the pictures. Didn't tell my mates. They'd have ripped the piss out of me. But I loved those paintings, especially the ones that told a story. Still do,' he adds wistfully.

'*And When Did You Last See Your Father?*'

'Yeah, that one. I loved the Pre-Raphaelites too, those women.'

Lorna pictures Elise's rippling auburn hair and pale skin. 'Elise,' she says.

'Yeah. Got myself a living, breathing painting.'

'When I was a child,' Lorna says, again ignoring the odd note, 'my gran used to take me. I was fascinated by the guy kicking the dog.'

'*Isabella.*'

'That's right. Then when I heard the story behind it, the love between Isabella and her brothers' apprentice, I was obsessed with it.'

'Classic bit of rough.'

'Don't say that. The poor boy ended up with his head in a flowerpot.'

' "They could not, sure, beneath the same roof sleep. But to each other dream, and nightly weep." Shit poem.'

His gruff voice, with its Liverpool lilt, is beautiful. Lorna instantly recalls his hands cupped around the microphone, his eyes searching hers through a fringe dripping with sweat. The hairs stand up on the back of her neck, and it's only partly due to the chill.

'It is, isn't it? I've heard better lyrics from a D.I.G.B.Y. song.'

Dexter bursts out laughing, a rich sound that lingers in the air. 'Which is your favourite?'

She doesn't have to think. '*If I could look in your eyes, if I could tell you I know, that I've been here before, would you open your door?*' She gazes down at her feet.

Another silence, then Dexter coughs. 'And that only got to number four.'

'Number three,' she says, then inwardly berates herself. He's going to think she's obsessed with him. 'Sorry. Sorry. I sound like your *number one* fan.'

36

'Terrifying,' he agrees with a wink. 'So what about that girl of yours?'

She's ashamed to feel irritated that he's brought Amy into the conversation. 'It's so lovely of Elise to encourage her. The lessons are the highlight of Amy's week. She's desperate to be a pop star.'

'They all are at that age,' Dexter says. 'She'll grow out of it.'

'I don't know. Have you heard her sing?'

'No. I don't disturb the wife when she's working.'

Lorna wants to make up for her mean-spiritedness towards her daughter. 'She has an amazing voice, and she's got the looks,' she gushes. 'Pete – my ex-husband – is a musician. Amy takes after him.'

'I'm sure your genes had something to do with it.'

Nervous, she responds with a self-deprecating laugh – she really wasn't fishing for compliments – and glances through the window. 'We'd better go back inside. Your guests will be wondering where you are.'

'I couldn't give a flying fuck.'

Then he leans forward and kisses her on the lips. It's a soft, exploratory kiss, a kiss that says: we understand each other, don't we? Something long repressed bursts into life. His hands are on her lower back, warm and bony through the satin; he draws her against him and mutters, 'You turn me on.'

Lorna giggles, but she pushes back. He looks like a disappointed little boy. A little boy who stinks of booze.

'We shouldn't,' she says, touching his cheek. He twists his head to kiss her hand, and she pulls it away. 'I made that mistake before. I can't make it again.'

He frowns. 'What do you mean?'

She smiles to dispel a sense that she bears him any rancour. 'It's nothing. It happened so long ago. Fifteen years. I met you when D.I.G.B.Y. played a gig at my university.' This is a mistake. Too late now – his eyebrows have risen. She blushes deeply. 'We bumped into each other backstage, and well, one thing led to another.'

'Pardon?' His expression has cooled somewhat.

'We flirted and then we . . . um . . . fell on each other.'

'You're not going to dob me in, are you?'

Lorna laughs out loud, even though her stomach is full of butterflies. 'No! I've never told anyone. I never will. It was a consensual act between adults.'

'Because the last thing I need is to be dragged across the coals for sexually assaulting you.' He isn't being funny now.

'You didn't.' She wishes she could unsay it, is desperate to claw the moment back, but she's spoilt it.

'You know about George, right?' Dexter mutters. Everyone knows that George Farr has been accused of groping a fifteen-year-old fan. The woman, now in her late twenties, is making a real meal of it. And so she should, Lorna thinks. George was renowned back in the day. 'It's shit.'

She nods, unwilling to get into an argument about it and alienate him further. George is his friend; of course he's going to believe him.

'Fifteen years ago?' he says. 'I was twenty. It was right before we went massive.'

'Yes. It was the Student Union's finest moment.'

'I'm trying to remember you.' His gaze sweeps her face and figure in a way that makes her want to run and hide.

Then he points at her, his fingertip so close to her clavicle she draws in a breath.

'Got it. Manchester Uni. The girl in the crowd. I did this thing I thought you had to do to get laid: you know, pick out a girl, hold her gaze, sing to her.' He laughs. 'Christ, what a plonker. And then we left the stage and there you were, looking all shy and excited. We went back to my hotel with the lads, didn't we? You said you were studying maths and it blew my mind. Someone brought vodka. Ivo had Ecstasy.' He smiles ruefully. 'I eventually passed out.'

And the rest, Lorna thinks. She feels a wave of bitterness. He came out of it unscathed, clearly never gave her a second thought. Just another groupie. But they had talked all night and there had been such a strong connection. Nothing had come close to that before. She'd been on dates but had never felt what she did with Dexter, not only weak-kneed with lust, but feeling as though she'd found her soulmate and that he had found his in her. She had felt loved and safe despite only knowing him a matter of hours. When he said goodbye, he had held her face in his hands, looked deep into her eyes and told her exactly what she wanted to hear. *We'll see each other again, yeah? Promise.*

She believed it, until it became brutally clear that he'd forgotten her. Dexter's star rose and she faded. And yet all these years later, she still occasionally plays his music. When Amy was little, she had played it all the time, before Matt came along. Masochism. And now she's sitting here shooting the breeze and the feelings are rushing back, powerful enough to rock her world. Dexter, she realises, is a destructive force, a disrupter. Why is she drawn to that?

She doesn't say any of this. Instead, she says, 'These things happen,' like she does when she's comforting her children, when she's making other people feel better. 'We were young and pissed.' She won't tell him that she finally said yes to a date with Pete after waiting in vain for Dexter to come back for her. She won't tell him she got pregnant by Pete, that she kept the baby and dropped out of her course, that she meant to go back and complete her maths degree but never did, that she never reached her full potential. Those were her decisions, not his.

They're both quiet for a moment, Lorna's head full of thoughts. And Dexter's ... She can't be sure.

'Did you think I was a slut?'

He coughs so hard she has to pat his back. 'No, I didn't. We talked for quite a while, didn't we? Put the world to rights. I remember the event, even if I eventually forgot about you. Nothing like that had happened to me before. We were relative newcomers, and it was so good. We laughed and made out. That's what stayed with me. The laughter and genuine liking. I'm sorry I never got in touch, but life went mad.' He peers at her through the dim light. 'I'm sorry about just now. I shouldn't have done that. Elise and I, we had a row before the party.'

'You don't have to explain,' Lorna says. 'I understand.'

He takes her hand and, with a curious formality, lifts it to his lips. 'We have a bond, don't we?'

She blushes. 'We're expat Liverpudlians, so we're bound to.'

'Elise hates it when I'm too Scouse. She thinks if she can lose her Swedish accent, I should be able to lose my Scouse one.'

40

'But she wanted to,' Lorna says. 'You don't. Come on. We'd better go in.'

They stroll through the enormous kitchen, where the caterers are packing up, and into the hall. Out of instinct, Lorna ducks into the cloakroom. She doesn't want to be seen with Dexter after what has been a long absence. A good fifteen minutes. It felt as though he was looking for a connection, perhaps to fill some gap in his life. This man had reached for the stars and caught them; caught Elise, caught the big house in the expensive area and the flash car, but essentially he's a lost boy, and he thinks he's found what he's searching for in her. She must not fail him. She remembers his hand sliding down her back, but best of all, he feels an affinity with her. She examines her face in the mirror. He kissed her. And Elise criticises him for being who he is. Lorna's new best friend needs to be careful, or she'll push her husband away.

Chapter 7

THE PSYCHIATRIST

Lured by noises from the street, I refresh my glass of wine, take it out onto the walkway and lean against the balustrade. In Gladwell Grove, a woman calls a cheery goodbye. Someone else crosses the road; a man lets himself into the flats. It's busy down there. Maybe someone's having a party. There was a time, when I was married, when Daniel and I might have been invited, but I don't see anyone from those days. It's remarkable how quickly I was dropped after the divorce.

My thoughts return to the events of the day. After all his failed attempts, Ben has finally got to me. I suppose I should be grateful he waited until he was about to leave.

Grateful?

Why did I use that word? If it wasn't a deliberate attempt to get under my skin just for the satisfaction of seeing me blush, there has to be something I did to make him think it would be acceptable to me to hear that. And it isn't the way I dress. I invariably wear a grey suit with a white buttoned-up shirt.

It doesn't take much for a man to fixate on a woman, whether she's aware of him sexually or not, and vice versa.

And it shames me to admit it even to myself, but something inside me responded.

I should get a life. It's what my supervisor advised when I spoke to her after the call with Mum, although she didn't put it that way, reminding me that small events can snowball into full-blown fantasies if there's a large enough void for them to fill. I feel better about what happened having spoken to her, but also chastised. I behaved unprofessionally.

Human feelings are nothing to be ashamed of. The shock of connection can be strong, but it's fleeting. To understand that is to be able to control it. I'm not worried Ben will take me up on my offer to see him if he needs me, but if he does, I have the right to refuse a patient if I think it's not in their best interests to be treated by me.

Dylan purrs and rubs his head against my shin. 'Bedtime,' I say, stroking the length of his body as he arches under my hand. 'Thank God.'

In my dream, the rapping is someone banging on the hull of a boat. My berth is cramped, barely room enough for my mattress, the darkly varnished tongue-and-groove ceiling so close to my face I can smell it. The rapping stops for a few seconds, then starts again, and this time I open my eyes wide. The numbers on the digital clock are out of focus. I blink and they briefly resolve into 02:03. I am not on a boat; I am in my bedroom, and my head hurts.

No one knocks on my door, least of all at night. Occasionally new residents have done so, confused about which floor they're on. As for my sixth-floor neighbours, I doubt any of them would do something so alarming unless the place was on fire.

The knocking starts again. I fumble for the light switch, pull my dressing gown on over my pyjama shorts and T-shirt, do up the sash and go downstairs to the kitchen. I grab the edge of the sink, lean over it and pull up the blind, and a pale face with a thatch of messy hair juts into view.

I scream and lurch backwards.

'Dr Geddes? It's me. It's Ben.'

'Ben! For God's sake. You scared the life out of me.' I open the window a crack. 'What the hell are you doing here?'

His long coat is open over the clothes he was wearing earlier. In the sickly glow of the lights that illuminate the walkway, he looks unkempt. 'I need to talk to you.'

'How did you get my address?'

'I saw you in Griffiths Lane earlier and followed you.'

That jolts me. 'And you waited until two in the morning to bang on my door?'

'I was working up the courage.'

'Are you drunk?'

He droops, then eyes me through his fringe. 'I've had a beer.'

'Then if you're not drunk or high, you must know that what you're doing is inappropriate.' I maintain a firm grip on myself, on my voice. I need to sound sober, authoritative and reassuring. Angry and confused young men often react well to boundaries. It's what they wanted from their parents and didn't get. On the other hand, sometimes they lash out. 'Your behaviour is making me uncomfortable.'

'I didn't know what else to do.'

'Go home. Get some sleep.'

'You don't understand.'

'Believe me, I do.'

'What do you mean?' he says.

I ignore the question. It was a stupid thing for me to say. 'Come on, Ben. You know this is wrong. You're going to wake up in the morning and feel a fool if you don't go home now.'

A small voice says: what if this is real? What if in sending him home I'm letting him down?

When I was still in training, but seeing patients, one of them, a forty-three-year-old father of two, threw himself in front of a train. The shock derailed me for a while. I still think about him. What if Ben . . .

My head feels squeezed, my stomach nauseous. I crave a sugar and caffeine hit. Why has he come? It's almost as though he knows what day it is. Or was, yesterday.

'I can give you a website for a service you can access. There's always someone there. They're called Talk Now. They're very good. I promise it'll help.'

He screws up his face. 'Don't do this to me. Please don't.'

'I understand what you're going through, but coming here is not the right thing to do. If you really need to talk to me, then make an appointment.'

Ben whacks his palms against the glass, and I jump, my hand flying to my heart. 'You said you would help me!'

'I want to, and I'm trying to.'

'You don't give a shit.' He turns away and I think he's leaving, then he spins on his heel and shouts, 'You're the same as everyone else.'

From below, a male voice bellows, 'Will you shut the fuck up before I call the police!'

Ben gives me a hard look. Then he turns to the balcony, pulls himself up onto the wall and crouches there, one hand on the pillar, looking like a vampire waiting to swoop on its prey.

Chapter 8

THE PSYCHIATRIST

'Ben. Be sensible. Get down from there.'

If he hears me, he doesn't show it. I hesitate. I am in no condition to counsel a man teetering on a wall six floors above concrete. I should fetch my phone from beside the bed and call the emergency services. On the other hand, if he jumps while I do so, I'll never forgive myself. It's a horrible dilemma, but in the end, urgency trumps good practice. I pull back the bolt and open the door.

'I'm going to jump.'

'No, you're not. I'm going to step over to you and we're going to talk some more. Do you mind if I approach you?' I'm shaking so hard it's impossible for my voice not to quiver. 'Ben?'

'You can come.'

I cross the walkway and stand beside him. He jerks, and I grab his arm. Something in me shifts. I am no longer his doctor; I'm a fellow traveller in his world, burdened by the instinct to save, to protect, to avert disaster.

'I don't know how to be,' he says desperately.

'You do know, because we've talked about it. Come in out of the cold. I'll make you a hot drink.' His arm is rigid.

47

I'll remember this for ever, this feeling that a life might end right here, right now. And it will be my fault. I cannot risk that. 'Ben.'

I feel a tentative loosening in his muscles and stop breathing. Seconds go by, before he says, 'Okay.' And my breath heaves out of me in a rush.

He climbs down and stands with his head hanging, like a child. I feel an overwhelming urge to wrap my arms around him.

'Come on then,' I say, trying to lighten the atmosphere. 'I'm getting cold.'

At that moment, my neighbour opens her door and pokes her head out. 'Everything all right, dear?'

I turn my back on Ben and step over to her quickly. 'Everything's fine, Breda. I'm sorry to have worried you. He's my brother.' I force a wry smile. 'Too much to drink.' I'm not sure if Ben heard me. I hope not. I shouldn't have lied in front of him. It makes us co-conspirators.

Breda looks sceptical, but she wants to go back to bed so she doesn't ask any more questions. 'If you're sure . . .'

'I am.'

She shrugs and closes the door.

'Nosy old bag,' Ben says.

I bridle. 'Nosy neighbours aren't the end of the world. She looks after my cat when I go away, and we're keyholders for each other.'

'Sorry,' he says. 'I didn't mean to be disrespectful.'

'I'm going to call the crisis team. I can't let you go back to your flat on your own tonight.'

Ben looks horrified. 'No, please don't do that. I'm fine, I swear. I was just . . .'

'You were just what?' I study his face. 'Was this a wind-up?'

'No. It was real, I just don't need any intervention. You're enough. I want to talk to you, that's all. I promise I won't go off on one again.'

I sigh and open the door. It appears that once you've crossed boundaries, it's hard to go back. As Ben steps into my flat, both my gut and my professional expertise scream that this is the wrong thing to do, that I may well pay a high price.

Chapter 9

THE PSYCHIATRIST

I show Ben into the sitting room and go to the kitchen to make us both a ginger tea. I pour myself a generous measure of brandy, which I drink while the kettle is boiling. Hair of the dog. My stomach is tense. I've crossed so many lines, ripped up the code of conduct. Why didn't I call the emergency services despite Ben's assurances? Is it because I'm curious? Attracted to him? God, no. I lean against the wall and press my fingers against my face. I'm tired, but that is no excuse. I could lose my job over this.

I need to remove the personal element and start thinking rationally. For instance, what did I miss during our sessions? What was Ben hiding? All psychiatric patients hide parts of themselves from their doctors. All shed some layers and retain others. It gives them a measure of control when they feel the power has been stripped from them. Should I have insisted on keeping him on? It's not as if I'd 'cured' him or expected to. That isn't how it works with bipolar disorder. I did not see this coming, but I can see the implications for myself, and for him, if I make another mistake. I'll allow him the space to talk, then I'll do what I should have done when he turned up outside the flat and call the crisis team.

When I join him, he's sitting straight-backed on the sofa, hands imprisoned between his thighs, staring at his knees. His presence feels larger than it did in my consulting room.

He raises his head as I set our mugs down on the table.

'Do you have a biscuit or anything? I'm starving.'

Of course he is. I try to cultivate a maternal attitude. Young males and low blood sugar are not a marriage made in heaven. He needs food and reassurance.

'Let's avoid sugar, shall we? I'll make you some toast and butter.'

When I return, Ben is on his feet, inspecting the book-shelves containing my collection of contemporary and classic novels. My psychiatry books are upstairs.

'You have some good books there,' he says, sensing my presence.

I indicate the table. I'm not falling for a crass attempt to get under my skin. He sits back down and I put the plate of buttered toast in front of him.

'Right,' I say, once he's wolfed it down. 'You have my full attention.'

He clears his throat. 'What I said in your office, I appreciate I was out of order. I meant it, though. I still mean it, and I'm not sorry I said it. I've never met anyone like you before. My other therapists were just scratching the surface. You're the first to get into my head.'

'What you said was about my physical appearance, not my skill as your therapist,' I remind him.

'I'm sorry.'

'I'm doing a job, Ben. There's nothing personal, and you mustn't think there is.'

'I'm not stupid,' he says sharply. 'I know how easy it is to fixate on someone who seems to get it when you're low. But what I'm trying to say is it's more than that. I see you.' His voice is a caress, making the syllables sound so seductive. 'When I said you were beautiful, you blushed.'

'It's best to forget that happened, don't you think?' He has got to go. I feel like I'm going to drop where I'm standing, and if truth be told, I'm a little scared of him. I don't understand what all this is about; I can't predict the outcome.

'Forget? Do you really think that's possible?'

I suddenly cannot speak. Ben pushes his fingers into his brow, then rises from the sofa. He goes to the door to the balcony and unlocks it.

'What're you doing?' I spring up and grab his wrist. His heat almost floors me.

He thumps the glass with the side of his fist. 'I need some air.'

'Then I'll open a window. You're not going outside.'

'I'm not going to jump, if that's what you think.'

'I'm more worried about you pissing off my neighbours.' My voice sounds weird. Slurred. I should not have had that brandy. Stupid.

Ben has dropped into a crouch, locking his hands behind his neck. I lower myself to his level. He lifts his head and meets my eyes. I can't tear my gaze from his. It's agony, and I shuffle backwards, falling onto my bottom. I scramble up and immediately feel giddy. Ben grabs my elbow.

'Hey. Are you okay?'

'Fine.' I blink. I don't feel fine, but I'm not saying any more.

Something in his face stops me telling him to leave, like any sensible woman would. He is six inches taller than me and isn't made of pipe cleaners. I feel weak and unsteady, and when he reaches for me again, I melt into his arms. I don't want to. I want him to go. I want to fall into bed and sleep it off before I get myself into any more trouble. His arms are so strong, feel so good.

'You're tired,' he says, helping me into the hall and up the stairs, his arm around my waist.

He gently lowers me onto the bed, unties my sash and slides the dressing gown off my shoulders. I sink into the pillows. He lifts my feet, swivels me around and covers me with the duvet. My mind has been invaded by warm cotton wool. The room shifts unpleasantly. Ben whispers something, his breath hot in my ear. I think it's my name. Then his lips are on my neck, a hand sliding under my T-shirt. My mouth is trying to form a *no*, and I make some kind of noise, but it gets lost in that hazy no-man's-land between awake and asleep. It might not have been a noise at all.

Chapter 10

LORNA

'Oh God,' Lorna groans. 'Really?'

She doesn't mean to be grumpy, but she's dehydrated, and a memory keeps flicking on and off like a strobe. She rarely has more than one small glass of wine in the evening these days. Last night, probably out of nervousness, she drank three glasses of champagne, and on not much food either, just those impossibly delicate canapés.

'Feeling rough?' Matt says, as Jack wriggles out of his arms and onto the bed.

'Just a little.' She lets Jack crawl under the duvet and snuggle up against her. 'Why have you woken me up?'

'Sorry, love. The Boltons want me to refix the larder unit to the wall. Apparently it's listing slightly. I'll only be a few hours. Back by lunch, I promise.'

'Couldn't they wait till Monday?'

Matt moves to the window and opens the curtains a crack, and Lorna squints as the light hits her face. She is overwhelmed by a sickening wave of guilt. Dexter kissed her, and she allowed it, even welcomed it, when she should have slapped him down. What had she been thinking, betraying her husband like that? Not to mention taking

54

such an enormous risk. They could have been seen. She feels a frisson as the heat rises up her neck. She pulls up the duvet to cover it. The only thing that comforts her is the thought that she hadn't been deluded all those years ago. It was just a case of wrong place, wrong time. They met too early. Things got out of hand. She lost her mind and, well, shit happens. But now it's all right because he is attracted to her and he does care. And from some of the things he said, or the way he said them, actually, she doesn't think all is as rosy as it seems between him and Elise. They protest too much about their love for each other.

'They have family coming over at one.'

'They must have a very judgy family,' she says grumpily.

'Don't be like that. These are wealthy people. They like things perfect.'

'They like to snap their fingers and see you come running.'

He frowns, offended, and she regrets it.

'Sorry.'

'We need my clients to be happy,' he says, 'if they're going to recommend me to their friends.'

'I know.'

'Plus, for my own satisfaction, I want to be confident I've done a perfect job. If I leave now, I'll be there by nine. An hour tops to make sure everything's done. I'll be back before you know it. Do you want me to get Amy up to help you?'

'Mummy!'

'In a minute, darling.' She ruffles Jack's hair. 'Let her sleep in. I think she said she was going into central London with friends later. She'll have put her alarm on.'

'Right.' He looks anxious. 'If you're sure.'

'I'm sure. Go on. The sooner you leave, the sooner you'll be back. Me and Jack can have a quiet morning together.'

Her mind drifts again. Perhaps she could pretend it was a dream. Because you don't do that to a friend, do you? If anything did happen, it was simply her teenage self muscling in on her present self for a few, admittedly high-octane and sexually charged, seconds. Dexter had been drinking. She had been drinking. End of.

But it isn't end of... because the kiss came after the connection. It wasn't a drunken, out-of-context snog; it was the result of something keenly felt, if disguised. She mustn't go there. Dexter might be discontented in his marriage, but Lorna is emphatically not. Married life isn't perfect, but she and Matt are very happy.

'We'll be fine.'

Amy is smiling, but she sounds bored. Which annoys but nonetheless reassures Lorna. She's meeting Lily and they're heading to Oxford Street to visit the massive Primark, which is apparently an all-day event. Lorna doesn't anticipate seeing her daughter before teatime. She worries, because the girls are only fifteen, but she was out and about in Liverpool at that age, so having warned her about pickpockets, she refrains from cautioning her to cross the roads carefully.

As soon as Amy has left, she calls Elise, thanking her effusively for the evening.

'How are you feeling?'

'Fine,' Elise says. 'Just tired. I didn't drink too much. I kept putting my glass down and losing it.'

Lorna smiles. 'Pity I didn't lose mine. Matt's had to go and see clients and Amy's gone out with her friend, so it's just me and Jack and my head.'

'Really? Clara's out too.' Clara is Elise's live-in nanny. 'And Dexter's at a rehearsal. I don't know how he does it. He drank a lot, but he was up this morning, bouncing round the house with Noah. So now Noah is overexcited and I don't have the energy to do anything. Come round. We can take the boys to the playground and wear them out. Please,' Elise adds. 'Just for a couple of hours. I'll go mad otherwise.'

Lorna relents. It feels good to be needed by Elise. 'Okay. Just don't expect scintillating conversation.'

She dashes into the bathroom and does her make-up. Jack follows her every move.

'Pretty,' he says, and she winks at him, her blusher brush flicking across her cheeks. He holds out his hand, clenching and unclenching his fingers.

'What's one plus two?' she asks.

He lifts up his fingers and counts, his brow furrowed. 'Free!'

'Well done.' Pleased, she hands him the brush with a flourish. He's already showing signs of having inherited her affinity with numbers. Amy not so much.

Chapter 11

THE PSYCHIATRIST

There is a hand on my thigh, its weight and heat spreading through my skin into the muscle and fat beneath. There is a leg bent into mine, a knee, a shin making contact. There is breathing that has nothing to do with me. It's a deep-sleep breath that tickles my neck. I can smell him, that sleepy, stale mixture that is at once seductive and repulsive. I shuffle to make some space. I remove the hand. I was dreaming just now, but I already cannot remember what the dream was about, only that I was not where I was meant to be. One of those sorts of dreams. My mouth is dry, I feel sick, my head aches and I am desperate to pee. All these things need dealing with, but there is a man in my bed. Ben. My patient, who last night threatened to throw himself off my sixth-storey balcony. I'm overwhelmed with horror and shame. What have I done?

I twist round and examine his face, his long lashes and dusting of sandy stubble. I try to remember, but the moments before I slept are foggy. Did I agree to this? What led up to it? Gingerly I run my fingertips between my legs. My skin is sticky.

Shit.

He grunts, and I freeze as his toe finds my shin.

'Morning, gorgeous.'

He smiles drowsily, touching my face, and I flick his hand away. I feel panic. Nothing is making sense. This is not me. I swing my legs off the bed and my head swims. How much did I drink? A couple of glasses of wine before I went to bed. A slosh or two of brandy after the shock of finding Ben on my doorstep.

'Whatever happened, it was a mistake,' I manage. 'I'm sorry.'

There's only been one episode before this when I've been so blind drunk I've remembered nothing in the morning. That was after moving out of the flat in Gladwell Grove into this place and realising with a shock that I was on my own for the first time in over a decade, that I had lost the man I loved and that my friends, most of whom were either pregnant or discussing it, would incrementally withdraw from my orbit. I went out with a sympathetic male friend, who I haven't seen since, and drank myself stupid.

'If you can't remember,' Ben says, 'then perhaps we could try it sober. And you don't have to be sorry, you were amazing.' He places his hand on my hip and tries to draw me towards him.

'Don't you dare,' I snap, wriggling out of his grasp and jumping up. My head swims and I nearly topple over. I get to the door, where my dressing gown is hanging from a hook, steady myself and put it on, knotting the sash. 'And I'm apologising for crossing the line with a patient, not for my performance.'

Dylan saunters in, looks startled to see a male human

in my bed and winds himself around my legs, meowing plaintively.

'I'm not your patient any more.'

'It makes no difference whether you're still my patient or not. You came to me for help last night, and I . . . I . . .'

'Had sex with me. It isn't a problem.'

'Of course it is. I've done the worst possible thing. I could be struck off.'

'No one's going to know, because I won't tell them.'

I wrap my arms around my body. 'You won't?'

'I won't.'

That puts me in his power, and I don't like that. He stands up, and I take a step back, unsure.

'Hey,' he says with a crooked smile. 'Just a friendly hug.'

And because he's promised not to tell, I allow it. I try not to breathe in his scent as he pulls me against him and rests his chin on my head. It makes me wonder why I don't recognise the feeling of his arms around me.

'Can I ask about the scars?' he murmurs.

I panic. 'No.'

'I need a piss.' He lets me go and wanders out of the bedroom. Once he's gone, I remove the dressing gown and throw on a pair of sweatpants, bra and baggy shirt.

How could he think he was entitled to ask that question?

He comes back in and I ignore him. I take my turn in the bathroom, propping my sore head in my hands as I pee. I trace the scars with the tips of my fingers. They are mine. When Daniel first saw them, he was horrified. We were in my student bedroom. I cried for an hour, and we ended up not having sex that first time. I avoided him for the next two weeks, but he was persistent, and he was kind. He told me they were a chapter in my life written into my skin. Time to turn the page.

I sit there longer than is necessary, then pull myself together. I need to be sensible. There is a delicate path to tread here. Ben is a troubled young man. I'm ten years older and also screwed up, but he needn't know that. It's up to me to make it clear that there is no relationship, that what happened last night was a huge mistake and won't happen again. I'm appalled, actually, but there's nothing I can do except behave with dignity.

I go down to the kitchen, bang the kettle onto its stand and flick down the switch. There are two wine glasses upturned on the drainer. Did we drink together? I remember finishing one bottle before he arrived and putting the empty one in the recycling bin. I have no recollection of opening a fresh one and find it hard to believe that I would have offered Ben a drink. I check the fridge. There it is, half empty. I remember I made us both ginger tea, but the mugs have been washed, dried and put back in the cupboard.

Ben appears, a towel around his waist, his hair tousled and wet. His half-naked body feels like an assault. He appears entirely oblivious to my dismay. To him this is apparently perfectly normal.

'Did I open a bottle of wine last night?' I ask. I have no recollection at all. As far as I'm concerned, there was the tea and that was it.

'Well, technically I opened it. But the bottle was yours.'

'Whose suggestion was it?'

He shrugs. 'I don't remember. Bit hung-over, to tell you the truth. I don't remember much, apart from the sex.

Please don't worry. I'm just so grateful to you. I couldn't have wished for a better partner for my first time.'

My jaw slackens. 'Your first time? Ben, for Christ's sake. You never told me you hadn't had sex before.'

'You knew I'd never been in a long-term relationship.'

'That's a very different thing. You've never ... You're twenty-three. You've been to university.'

'I don't mean I've never been intimate with a woman. I have. Just not penetration. I'm a Catholic. I've been saving myself for my future wife.'

I can't get my head round this. 'So why did you break your vow? I don't believe I'm so irresistible you'd act against your core beliefs.'

'A man has his tipping point.' He smiles ruefully. 'Okay. We were ... appreciating each other. Up until now it's been girls from church, and we all understood. But I hadn't told you and it seemed like a bad time to make that announcement. You were unbelievable. I didn't want to kill an incredible moment. I literally couldn't. And when you got on top—'

My hand shoots up, like a traffic cop. 'Stop. Please.'

He pinches his lips together, but he's smiling.

I am not smiling, not even a little bit. 'This is a disaster.'

'It doesn't have to be. What's done is done. I'd do it again right now if you'd let me. And there's always confession.'

Is he joking? This cannot be happening. How could I have behaved like that? I try to remember, but don't get further than crouching next to him in the sitting room. How did we get from that point to this? Ben puts his hand on my back. I shake him off.

'What are you so scared of? I've told you I'm not going to

tell anyone. I want to be with you. I have from the moment I first saw you.'

I find my voice. 'Ben! Stop it. I'm much older than you. I'm ... I was your psychiatrist. Whatever happened last night, it's not going to happen again.'

To my horror, he drops to his knees and puts his arms around my thighs, pressing his lips to my crotch.

'Don't!'

He leans back, surprised and a little hurt. 'If that's what you want.'

'It is.'

His Adam's apple lifts and falls. He gets to his feet and says, rather formally, 'Then I'll respect your wishes. I think you're wrong, but I understand why you're scared and why you think it's impossible. I know you'd have to be much braver than me, you have a lot more to lose. But I want you to know that I adore you. You can trust me. Last night was beyond my wildest dreams. I won't betray you.'

I watch from the safety of the walkway as he leaves the block of flats. He waves then strolls away, hands deep in his pockets, whistling a tune. I don't understand what just happened. I go back into the flat, close the door, lean against it.

'Hell, hell, hell. What were you thinking?'

Dylan wanders out from the kitchen and studies me with his green-gold eyes.

'Don't look at me like that.'

Chapter 12

LORNA

Outside Elise's house, Lorna picks Jack up so that he can ring the bell.

'It's Jack!' he squeaks into the intercom, and then squirms to be let down as the gates slide on their runners. The front door opens and Noah charges towards them.

'Mamma says we can watch cartoons,' he says, puffed up with importance.

From the doorway, Elise smiles at Lorna. 'When you've had a play, Noah. Sorry. I literally don't have the energy to go for a walk. I'll take him out with Dexter later. Do you mind?'

'Not at all.'

It's a relief. Lorna's head is still banging and the prospect of keeping Jack, and possibly other random children, safe from Noah while not allowing Elise to see that's what she's doing is not enticing. Far better to be in a situation she has more control over.

The Coleridges' kitchen caused some marital tension. Matt would have given his eye teeth to have designed and built it. He'd asked Lorna to put him forward to her new friend, but she hadn't done so, not because she didn't think he was capable – he was more than capable – but because she understood that if Elise had someone else in mind, which it turned out she did, the embarrassment it caused would have spelt the end of a friendship that Lorna wanted to continue. So she told Matt that she'd found out by chatting to the Coleridges' architect that they were going with the chap who had designed the kitchen for their Primrose Hill house, and who had since become a friend.

Settled on the sofa in the spacious kitchen-cum-dining-room, Elise yawns and apologises for being no fun. Outside, in the enormous, expensively landscaped garden with its tasteful wooden playhouse, Noah and Jack are fighting. Lorna's not certain if it's serious or a game but keeps an eye on it just in case.

'Don't worry. It's enough that Jack's occupied,' she says. 'You don't have to entertain me.' There's a yelp from Jack. Lorna flinches. 'Perhaps I'd better check on them.'

She wanders into the garden and has a chat with the boys about sharing, making sure that Noah doesn't feel singled out, despite being clearly in the wrong. Jack objects, but she distracts them both with a suggestion for a new game. She'll make it up to him later. When she comes back inside, Elise is sound asleep. She looks beautiful, reclined on the long pale sofa, her auburn hair spilling over a plush olive-green cushion. Lorna glances at the boys. They're ignoring each other. Noah's bottom lip is jutting out impressively. She rolls her eyes and goes back out.

'Would you like to watch a film?'

'Yes!'

They choose *The Lion King*, and Lorna puts mugs of milk and plates of carrot sticks and raisins in front of them and leaves them to it. For something to do, she calls Matt, but he doesn't pick up. Elise's gentle snoring is beginning to get on her nerves. She slips off her shoes, pads upstairs and wanders into the master bedroom. The view of the heath is stunning. There are binoculars on the windowsill. She picks them up and looks through them, panning across the heath. Birdwatching or people-watching? Probably both. She would. She focuses on a couple jogging together flanked by two lean fox Labradors.

The room is luxurious, with carpet her feet sink into and a vast, sumptuous bed. She's pleased to see it hasn't been made this morning. Elise isn't perfect after all. Curious, she opens the drawers in the bedside cabinets. Dexter's contains a pair of reading glasses, a Kindle and a packet of prescription sleeping pills; Elise's holds over-the-counter sleeping pills, a novel in Swedish and a lubricant. And something wrapped in a velvet pouch. Lorna raises her eyebrows, thinking it must be a sex toy, but when she picks it up, it's heavy. She rolls back the neck and touches the mother-of-pearl-encrusted grip of a gun. She murmurs, 'Wow,' then draws it out carefully and rests it on her hand. The barrel and trigger are made from engraved steel. It's a pretty weapon, designed for a handbag. She puts it back quickly and closes the drawer.

The shirt Dexter was wearing last night is puddled on the carpet in the corner of the room. Lorna scoops it up and holds it to her nose, and her breath shortens.

There's no sound from the playroom apart from the strains of 'I Just Can't Wait to Be King', and no movement from the kitchen. Still holding the shirt against her mouth and nose, she backs into the bedroom and softly closes the door. Something shifts inside her, causing a delicious tension. She can't possibly … Yes, she can. It'll only take a second. She climbs into Dexter's side of the bed and unzips her jeans, thinking about the kiss, the cigarette taste in his mouth, the beer on his lips, the tension that felt like a storm was about to break. She imagines him roughly taking her and tucks her fingers inside her knickers.

Chapter 13

THE PSYCHIATRIST

'I'll see you in a week's time, Daisy. Take care of yourself.'

This morning's session has gone well. I have a couple of teenage patients and enjoy that side of my work more than dealing with adults. Once you get through to them, they are more honest, more brutal even. And they're not in the slightest bit interested in me.

Someone knocks as I'm updating Daisy's records. I call, 'Come in,' and glance up. It's the practice manager. I greet her with a smile. She closes the door behind her. For some reason that feels ominous.

I like Belle. We're not bosom buddies, but we occasionally go for a drink after work. Like me, she's divorced and has no children. She's also, like me, very private. I have no idea what she gets up to at the weekend or in the evenings.

'Can I have a word?'

'Sure.' I remove my fingers from the keyboard.

Belle doesn't sit down, which is mildly worrying. She stands about three feet from the edge of my desk with her arms folded and says the words every doctor dreads. 'There's been a complaint.'

I frown. 'Really? Who from?'

'Mr Clarkson.'

My stomach drops. 'Ben Clarkson has made a complaint about me?' I don't want to ask, but of course I have to. 'What is he saying I've done?'

'He's complained that you lured him into your flat, plied him with alcohol and had sex with him.' Belle keeps her tone neutral, but she can't hide her curiosity.

'That's not what happened at all. He banged on my door at two in the morning, then threatened to jump off the balcony if I didn't let him in. He was in a terrible state. What was I supposed to do?'

'Call the crisis team or the emergency services. That might have been a good place to start.'

'I'd have had to get my phone. By that time, anything could have happened. I didn't want to leave him.'

'Did you call them once you had him safe inside?'

I flush. 'No, I didn't. He seemed to have calmed down. I made him a ginger tea and something to eat. Has he contacted the GMC?'

'Not yet, as far as I know. But I have, of course, advised him to do so.'

I drop my head and chew my lip, staring at my keyboard until the letters blur. He asked me to trust him.

'Did you have sex with him?' Belle asks.

I could lie. It's his word against mine. But what if he took photos when I was asleep? I imagine myself sprawled naked on the sheets and my stomach turns to stone. If he can do this to me, after promising never to breathe a word, I wouldn't put it past him.

'I don't remember any of it, but I woke up in the morning and it was obvious what had happened.'

'You don't remember?' Belle frowns. 'How much had you drunk?'

'A couple of glasses of wine in the evening before he came round. Ben told me I opened another bottle, but I don't remember that part. I can't believe I would have let him drink, because he's on medication, but there was an opened bottle in my fridge, so I assume he helped himself without asking me. I would have said no.'

'Anything else.'

'I might have had some brandy.'

Belle looks aghast. 'For heaven's sake. Why would you do that?'

'Because he'd scared the shit out of me.' My voice rises. 'He was sitting on my wall, threatening to throw himself six floors onto solid concrete. I was shaking from the stress. I needed it.'

'You had sex with a vulnerable patient. The fact that you were too drunk to remember and he was over the age of consent is meaningless. Did you put brandy in his drink?'

'No! Of course not.'

'He said you did, that he could taste it.'

'That is simply not true.'

I can't think straight. I know I drank too much, so much that I ceased to think about ethics, consequences and my own safety, but I'm certain I didn't give him anything.

Belle sighs. 'I gave you your first job. I took a chance on you because I liked you, but you've crossed a line. I'm suspending you as of now. Katy will cancel your appointments for the next two weeks. After that, depending on the outcome, we'll review.'

'Can't you let me explain?'

'Not now, no. Go home. An NHS trust lawyer will be in touch. In the meantime, I must advise you not to try and contact Mr Clarkson. If you do, I'll be forced to terminate your employment. I suggest you seek advice.'

Chapter 14

THE PSYCHIATRIST

I shut down my computer, gather my belongings and swap my boots for trainers, then hesitate before placing the boots under the desk. I only go ahead and leave them there because not to do so would imply a belief that I won't be coming back. There's an old cloth tote, a souvenir from some conference or other, hanging forgotten under my coat on the hook beside the door. I transfer the cassettes containing my sessions with Ben into it from the drawer.

If there are clues to his behaviour, they'll be there. I take a last look at my office, open the door and come face to face with Belle.

'What's in the bag?'

In reception, Katy's focus on her screen is fierce.

'Bits and pieces from my desk. Nothing that doesn't belong to me.'

'Can you open it, please?'

'This isn't an airport. I'm not obliged to show you the contents of my bags.'

Belle waits, mouth pursed. I roll my eyes and hold it open. She reaches in, takes out a cassette and reads the label.

'You can't remove these from the building.'

'They're mine. I can do what I like with them.'

'I don't think you understand how serious this is. They are evidence.'

'They belong to me.'

'Nevertheless,' Belle says, 'you will be leaving them here or this will end in your dismissal. We value you. Please don't push me.'

I hand the bag over, practically shoving it at her.

She shoots me a look in which I detect triumph. 'I hope you understand this isn't personal. We need to investigate so we can help you.'

'You just don't want the practice embarrassed.'

'I don't mind admitting that. We have a reputation to maintain. But it also behoves me to make sure you're treated fairly. I'm not throwing you to the wolves.'

'Aren't you?'

The door to the street opens. Belle and I stand in silence, and I wonder whether the patient, a man in his forties, feels the charged atmosphere. If he does, he doesn't show it, walking past us and straight up to the desk with a friendly greeting for Katy.

'I'll be in touch,' Belle says.

I turn on my heel and leave, barely reacting when Katy calls out a goodbye.

Two months ago, I was mugged on the heath. My assailant grabbed my bag and the pretty pale green wireless earbuds that had been a Christmas present to myself, pushed me over and ran off. His face was covered by a grey scarf and he was wearing a black woolly hat. He must have been cross when he opened the bag and didn't find my phone, which was in my pocket, but thankfully he didn't return. Still shaking from shock, I contacted my bank and reported the incident to the police. I didn't realise I was crying until a passing dog-walker asked if I was okay and insisted on escorting me off the heath. We parted company on Gladwell Grove. An act of kindness for which I will for ever be grateful.

It was a peculiarly nasty incident. I'm normally confident about walking across the heath in the early evening, but, not having children, I hadn't taken into account that it was February half-term and there were far fewer people around.

My handbag was returned to me at the weekend – minus my charge cards, which I'd stopped before they could be used – by a group of fifteen-year-old girls who found my business card among my things and called me. Thankfully my keys were there. I have a spare car fob, but I'd had to get my neighbour to hand over her copy of my door key.

At the time, I thought I handled it well. I didn't make a fuss. I'd lost nothing but my dignity, after all. But even two months later, I can smell his stale breath. If I shut my eyes, I can see the hairs on his wrist and the tattoo of an eagle in flight on the back of his hand. I can feel how broad and powerful he was, his chest and thigh pressed against me as he held me and pulled the leather strap of my bag over my head. What's happened since last night makes me feel as though I've been mugged all over again.

Walking across the heath now feels like an act of defiance.

Why would Ben deliberately paint me as a sexual predator? Yes, there's something suspect about a thirty-four-year-old psychiatrist sleeping with her twenty-three-year-old patient, but what's happened simply does not feel like something the Ben Clarkson I've got to know would do – run squealing to the authorities because he's been seduced. It makes me want to reassess every conversation I've ever had with him. I wish I had those tapes.

I wonder if I remind him of his mother; if in getting my full attention, he was finally getting hers, then punishing her. Is that what this is actually about? An Oedipal thing? Having got what he desired, is he now filled with self-disgust and wanting to lash out.

'Pop psychology,' I mutter. 'You can do better.'

I cup my hand over my mouth and swear under my breath. The bastard. Why hadn't I thought... Because in the morning, he had been so charming and sweet I'd been lulled by it, had never even considered. He spiked my drink. Of course he did. And I, like a fool, showered. Not that it would make a difference. It's not as if he's going to say he lied about having sex. I should never have put myself in such a dangerous situation. It was badly judged. Whatever the truth of it, this will always be my fault. There was a power imbalance, although it doesn't feel like it. It will be held against me.

I hear footsteps and tense. I can't see anyone because the path bends round tall, billowing brambles, but they're getting closer. I whip my phone out of my bag and open my emails, dropping my head to hide my red face. My eyes blur when I see there's one from a lawyer. I wince. That was quick.

The footsteps stop, and I look up in time to see Ben turn and stride back the way he came.

'Wait!' I shout. 'Ben. Hang on!'

Ridiculously, he starts to jog away from me. 'Ben!' I break into a run. I'm nearly out of puff as we round the bend.

Ben turns on his heel and holds up his phone. 'I'm recording you, so leave me the fuck alone or I'll send it to the police and report you for harassment.'

I draw a breath in through my teeth, hands on my hips. 'Then record this, you little prick. You spiked my drink. You did it when I was making your toast. That's why I was muddled in the morning, why I couldn't remember. Did you plan it all along? I bet you weren't even a virgin.' This time it feels good to be unprofessional. Like I'm bursting into colour and sound.

'You're mad.' He turns and walks away.

When I get home, I strip the bed, crying with frustration and rage, and put the sheet into one of the vacuum bags I keep my wool jumpers in in the winter. I put my pyjama bottoms in as well, then seal the bag and stash it in the back of my wardrobe. After that, I shower again, scrubbing my body until it stings.

Chapter 15

LORNA

Lorna cannot sit still. She doesn't expect the email from the local authority to arrive before nine, but she's so nervous she can barely breathe. She clunks around getting breakfast together, grateful to Amy for distracting Jack. This must be how politicians feel on the eve of an election. Jack has to get his place at Alverley School. The alternative simply doesn't bear thinking about. It's why she insisted they buy this house, because for no other reason would she have chosen what is basically a box. It's an infill building, one of three where there had once been two large Victorian houses before they were destroyed during the Blitz. It was the only way they could afford to live in the right catchment. She tells herself, and others, that it possesses a certain retro chic, but it doesn't really.

'Mum?' Amy says.

'Sorry, darling. I was miles away.'

'Don't forget I've got singing this evening.'

'I haven't forgotten.'

'With Noah's mummy,' Jack says.

'That's right, Jack.'

'Can I see Noah?'

'Not this time, darling.'

Noah isn't in nursery all day, five days a week, like Jack is. He goes for three mornings to a different, much more expensive nursery, to help him socialise and get him ready for the transition to primary school. Jack is picked up from nursery at 3.30 by Miriam, a youthful grandmother who stays until Lorna gets home. She's company for Amy too.

Lucky Elise to have the luxury of organising her own hours. Lorna needs to work, and besides, she's never relied on a man. She also loves her job. She gets a buzz from wielding her powers of persuasion, getting buyers to focus on what's important and not be distracted by the irrelevant: the colour of the front door, for instance. It's unbelievable what people will complain about, especially the wealthy.

'What are you going to do at nursery today, Jack?' Amy asks.

Jack screws up his face. 'First, there's break. Then there's lunch. Then there's playtime. Then there's circle time. Then home time.'

'Ah.' Amy gets up and wrings a cloth out under the tap. She uses it to clean Jack's face and hands. 'What about lessons?'

'I will do reading.'

Thank God for Amy.

'Call me as soon as you hear,' Matt says. He's dropping Jack off on the way to work today.

Lorna nods mutely, and to her surprise, Amy hugs her. She doesn't get many hugs from her daughter these days; far too uncool. The hug goes on for a long time, long enough for her to worry. Is her anxiety that obvious? She feels a rush of guilt. She mustn't pass on her fears to her children.

'Chill, okay, Mum.'

Lorna resists the urge to cling to her. 'I'll do my best.'

It's here. Lorna's heart lurches nauseatingly. She takes a deep breath and clicks.

Unfortunately . . .

Alternative schools . . . Northcliff Primary.

Waiting list . . .

Oh God, no. She sits back, stunned. Not getting into Alverley has always been a possibility, but she's never seriously thought there'd be a problem. She just assumed, and she's let poor little Jack assume it too. He'll be devastated when he learns he's not going to the same school as his pals. He's been so excited about starting.

She can't tell her friends the awful truth. Not until she's processed it. Her phone pings. Already? She glances down, expecting the message to be from Jules, or even Raisa – but it's from Elise. She probably wants to know if there's been any news. Elise is endlessly curious about Lorna's life.

Noah has been offered a place at Alverley School! Isn't that fantastic!

No! She immediately hits the call icon.

'Lorna! It's brilliant news, isn't it?'

'Not for me.'

Elise gasps in surprise. 'Jack hasn't been offered a place? Oh no. That's awful.'

'I thought Noah was going to Fairlands. I thought it was all decided.'

'In the end, Dexter and I agreed it would be better for him to mix with a more diverse crowd. Not just the kids of wealthy parents. It'll be better for him in the long run.'

'So you're definitely accepting the place?' It isn't Elise's fault, and yet Lorna is furious. It feels personal.

'Yes. Are you all right?'

'No, I am not. We can't afford Fairlands, so if Jack doesn't go to Alverley, he has to go to a school that won't suit him.' Lorna can't help herself. 'You can afford to go private. We can't. And yet you've chosen not to, just because of some stupid principle. Why would you do that?'

'Lorna,' Elise says gently. 'It isn't my fault Jack has missed out. I'm sure there are others in the same boat.'

'Jack might be top of the waiting list. He might have missed out because of Noah.'

Elise's tone turns frosty. 'It certainly isn't Noah's fault.'

'No. Sorry. I didn't mean that. Please change your mind, Elise. Getting Jack into Alverley School means everything to us. You have choices Matt and I simply don't have.'

'You're not thinking rationally. Me rejecting the offer does not mean Jack gets a place.' Her voice has become slower, like she is holding on to her patience.

Lorna swallows back a retort. The last thing she wants is to alienate the Coleridges.

'Sorry. I actually think I'm going to have a nervous breakdown. I shouldn't have taken it out on you. Please don't say anything to Amy.' Her daughter would be mortified.

After Elise has graciously forgiven her, Lorna leaves Jules a message. She can't face the others yet.

Jack didn't get his place. Will speak later. Trying to get my head round it.

Oh no! Jules pings back.

She stares out of the window. She'd already had a chat to James about tweaking her hours so that a couple of days a week she could do the school run with her friends, their kids trotting along beside them, proudly carrying their book bags, wearing those sweet red tracksuits with the Alverley School crest on the front. Then the walk back, without the children, perhaps detouring to Nettles Café on Griffiths Lane for a coffee and half an hour or so of delicious gossip about the other mums and the teaching staff before dashing to the office. Northcliff is in the other direction. She doesn't know anyone round there and it just wouldn't work with her job. There'd simply be no time. And she can't complain about her allocated school, because she'll be called a snob.

Elise and her ilk – the ones who can afford to go private but like to flaunt their social consciences by taking up precious places in state-maintained primary schools when everyone knows they'll remove their boys after Year 3 and send them to an expensive prep school to rub off the rough corners and see them through to the thirteen-plus – are thoughtless and selfish. There's even a name for it: state till eight.

Chapter 16

THE PSYCHIATRIST

'I don't believe it.'

I scowl as I stare at my monitor. *Access denied*. So this is how it's going to be: not only suspended, but not allowed to update work or read records written by me about my patients. If the lawyers can see my reports and listen to the cassettes, then I should have access too. It's only fair.

I glance down at Dylan. 'If I need a lawyer, they'll have to share them anyway. They know that.'

He doesn't comment.

I email Belle. She replies ten minutes later, crisply explaining that it's a temporary measure until things are sorted out. She finishes by hoping I'm well and getting some rest. Since I barely slept last night, I don't bother replying.

Five minutes later, a new email comes in, this time from Katy, informing me that a meeting has been set up with the lawyers at two p.m. today, at their offices.

No notice. No apology for any inconvenience. The coldness hurts. Does she too believe I seduced my patient? I go to pick up the phone, but change my mind. What's the point? I don't want to put her in a difficult position, and asking for her support would be akin to demanding she take sides. The time for that may come, but not now. Now, I have to put my story to the lawyer and hope I'm believed.

Chapter 17

THE PSYCHIATRIST

'How are you feeling?' asks Jeremy Osborne. The lawyer is a middle-aged man with grey hair, plump features, a generous mouth and bright blue eyes. There's something of the talk-show host about him.

'I'm great,' I lie. I have kept myself going with regular infusions of caffeine and ultra-processed food. I was terrified of bumping into Ben again when I left the safety of my flat, avoiding most of Griffiths Lane, doglegging down the side streets to reach the station and checking nervously up and down the platform.

'This is a difficult time for you, I'm sure.'

'It is.' I smile, trying not to look defensive.

Jeremy sits down, picks up his pen, pulls a pad of paper towards him and dates it. 'Okay. Let's get started. And please don't worry. I'm not the enemy. I'm here to listen to your side of the story.'

I begin with the comment Ben made before he left my office and end with me waking up in the morning in a state of confusion. 'I honestly didn't know what had happened,' I say. 'He told me the details. He could have said anything and I'd have believed him. I had no reason not to.'

'What were you wearing when you let him in?'

'Sorry?'

He's scribbling, but he glances up. 'Pyjamas, nightdress? Dressing gown?'

'I wear pyjama bottoms and a T-shirt in bed.' I flush. 'But I put on a dressing gown. It's pale blue cotton.' That detail matters to me. I want him to know I don't waft around my flat in a lacy peignoir.

'Do you often invite men home?'

I meet his eyes. 'I didn't invite Ben.'

'Can you answer the question, please.'

I roll my eyes. 'Occasionally.'

'Where do you meet them?'

'That has literally nothing to do with what's happened. What I do with my body and who I do it with is my business. I did not invite Ben in because I wanted to have sex with him. I invited him in because I was genuinely concerned, and even then I was reluctant. My intention was to calm him down and call the crisis team.'

'Why didn't you do so?'

'I didn't dare take my eyes off him, even for the few seconds it would have taken to run and get my phone. Even if he didn't jump, I was worried he would topple off. I didn't know whether he had been drinking or had taken drugs; I instinctively knew I had to stay and maintain contact.'

I explain about the ginger tea and toast, and Jeremy leans forward.

'Why didn't you call while you were doing that, since he was safely in your care?'

'Because he begged me not to. I agreed because I needed him to know he could trust me.'

He puts down his pencil and rests his chin on his knuckles as he contemplates me. 'You do see how this looks?'

'Of course I do. I woke up in the morning to find Ben in my flat, happy as Larry, making me coffee, treating me like a princess, telling me how great I'd been.' I take a deep breath. 'It felt all wrong. Contradictory. He'd made a remark about finding me attractive at the end of his last session.' I swallow hard. 'I believe he spiked my drink.'

Jeremy gives me a sad smile. It's clear he pities me. 'You're a thirty-four-year-old woman in a position of authority and trust. He's a twenty-three-year-old patient with mental health issues. He came to you for help. You can sleep with whom you choose, with few repercussions. What it will look like to a jury is that you chose him.'

'A jury?'

'If he presses charges. He hasn't done so yet, but you need to be ready.'

I stare at him. Is he really not even going to give my suspicions the time of day?

'My main concern is for the practice. If this gets out, it could do serious harm. They don't need that kind of notoriety.'

'I'm certain he drugged me. Is that too much for you to entertain? Even in this climate?' My voice is too loud, too insistent, as though I think he's stupid. I sense him bristle, but it can't be helped. 'Why else would I have woken up with missing memories? I remember nothing after he put me to bed.' The words dry in my mouth. I've lied about that up until now. I told Belle my last memory was being in the sitting room with him. Too late. 'You have to believe me.'

86

'It doesn't matter if I believe what you say or not, Dr Geddes. It depends entirely on how far Mr Clarkson wishes to take this. If he doesn't go to the police, I can only imagine he made the complaint for financial gain.'

'That's extortion.'

'It is. But sometimes extortion works.'

I sit back, screwing up my face. 'And if I report him?'

'I wouldn't advise it. You can't prove anything, and it's likely to backfire. You know perfectly well someone in therapy cannot give consent. They may think they're consenting, but they aren't. As their therapist, you are the one holding all the power. Even if the first move comes from them, it is still your responsibility.'

'Ben was no longer my patient. We'd had our final session.'

'That's not going to wash, I'm afraid.' Jeremy places his hands palms down on the desk. 'Let's move on. I've had a chance to listen to the recordings of your sessions with Mr Clarkson, and—'

'There's nothing in there I could possibly be ashamed of.'

'What I was going to ask was why you attempted to remove them from the building.'

'I'd have thought that was obvious. I wanted to listen to them to see if I could find any clue as to why Ben has done this to me.'

'Fair enough. There is one conversation I found concerning.'

'Right,' I say warily.

'It's thirty-five minutes into your fourth session.'

He presses play on my Dictaphone. Ben's voice gives me a nasty jolt.

'I'm scared.'

'Of what?'

'I'm lonely and it's going to get worse. I won't be able to have a lasting relationship because I frighten people off. I'll end up alone, no kids, nothing.'

I remember this conversation, how uncomfortable I felt, how I realised afterwards I had handled it badly.

'You're thinking a long way ahead.'

'Don't you?'

'This isn't about what I think. This is about you.'

'But you understand, don't you? Because you're lonely too.'

There's a hesitation. The scars on my inner thighs tickle. *'Ben, you don't know anything about me.'*

'It takes one to know one.'

On the recording, I cough.

'Can you switch it off, please?'

'Not yet.' Jeremy shakes his head, and I am forced to listen to myself trying to retrieve control of the situation.

'Let's take this one step at a time. Addressing your issues now will help you navigate life into the future. The fact that you're here, that you're able to voice your fears, that you can be honest about yourself is a great sign. You're making progress.'

'I'm sorry. I disconcerted you back there. I didn't mean to. I'm not analysing you or anything creepy. It's just that I have a radar for other lost souls.'

'I'm not . . . Look, it's fine. Can we move on?'

Jeremy clicks the Dictaphone off. I itch to grab it from him, but he puts it into a drawer and turns the key. 'He got under your skin.' It's a statement, not a question.

I rub at a small mole below my ear.

'If he'd been less attractive to you – a much older man,

or a woman, say – do you think you'd have sounded like you do here?' He taps the machine.

'No. I think they'd have disconcerted me too, just in a different way. I'm not a robot.'

Out in the street, I take two long breaths. I'm unlikely to be protected. If Ben Clarkson decides to escalate, and God forbid the case goes to court, the practice won't back me. Belle is already unreachable.

My head is bursting. I remember the day he walked into my office, the tiny jolt I got when he smiled and said hello. It surprised me, flustered me, made my manner cooler when I addressed him. Then I started the session and the unease I felt receded. Ben Clarkson was just another patient. He talked about the episodes of bipolar disorder that had devastated his life over the last few years. He saw them as a cycle. Hyper-manic, wonderful company, taking too much on, running out of steam, crashing, then raging fury, scattering friends and family. The anger had consumed him, become like a second state of being, another person. And then when that was burnt out, there was the long journey through shame and depression. Medication helped, but what he really wanted was to be able to wrest back control of his own personality. He didn't want to stop taking the pills; he simply wanted to feel powerful again, not weak and dependent. I understood that lack of power only too well.

Did he sense it was more than professional empathy from me? It isn't uncommon for people who have been through years of therapy to go into the profession. It makes me vulnerable, and it turns out that he is the type to prey on that.

Bottom line: should I have seen it coming? Possibly. Yes. He is an appealing character. Someone you want to help despite knowing they are capable of doing you harm.

So did I always know? No. I refuse to believe I could be so unprofessional. Ben is a clever liar.

I am not naïve. If I press charges, he will do the same, and there's no way I can win. I didn't say anything about my drink being spiked until after he made the complaint. I haven't used the word *rape*.

I walk to Griffiths Lane, pick up my coat from the dry-cleaner's and buy over-the-counter sleeping pills from the chemist.

Fuck Ben Clarkson. He thought he'd won the lottery when his fingers found my scars. But he must have already sensed I was broken, or why did he do all that? Why did he behave like a cat with a wounded bird?

Chapter 18

ELISE

'What was that all about?' Dexter asks, wandering into the kitchen. His hair is mussed and he smells of sleep. When he isn't working, it isn't unusual for him to stay in bed until ten or eleven. Once Elise would have stayed there with him, but those lazy days of drowsing, making love and reading are long gone. Despite her irritation and hurt, she musters a smile at the sight of her husband.

'Nothing.'

'It didn't sound like nothing.' Dexter ruffles Noah's hair, so that it resembles his own, then opens the fridge and peers in. Elise often wonders what it is he expects to find, beyond the usual. There's a half-finished tub of yoghurt. He takes it out, lifts the lid and sniffs its contents. 'This okay to eat?' He's already scraping it into a bowl.

'It's fine,' Elise says.

He takes granola out of the larder cupboard and adds a liberal helping to the yoghurt, then stirs in a spoonful of cheap store-brand honey. He's still the poor boy from Toxteth at heart. Elise bought a twenty-pound jar of manuka once, and he went mad. So sweet. These days she keeps her honey hidden behind the tins of tomatoes.

91

'So,' he says. 'Spill.'

'Okay.' She hugs her dressing gown round her. The disagreement with Lorna has left her feeling exposed, like a peeled banana. She shouldn't feel like the bad person, but she does. 'Jack didn't get a place at Alverley School, and because Noah did, Lorna is blaming me.'

'She's fucking what?'

'Dex!'

'Sorry. But honestly, are you kidding me? That's mental.'

Elise gets up and goes to the door. She shouts Clara's name.

'Coming.' Clara thumps downstairs. For a slender woman, she is remarkably noisy. 'Do you need me to take him?'

'Yes please.' Elise waits for the nanny to coax her son out of the room, before saying, 'It wasn't very nice.'

'I don't trust her.'

This jars rather than making her feel better. 'I didn't know you had an opinion about her.'

'I don't. It just feels like she's taken you over.'

'That is an opinion.'

'Can you not pick apart every word I say?'

'Sorry, but taken me over? Do you mean like a cult?'

He scrapes his fingers across his scalp. 'Hey, I'm not the enemy here. She's wormed her way into your life through our kid. You don't know her particularly well, and yet she's round here all the time. I can't move for bumping into her.'

'Don't exaggerate.' Elise laughs, but it's a nervous reaction. She's beginning to feel defensive. After all, she chose Lorna Chilcott as a friend, so what he says makes her feel shitty. 'She only comes round when I invite her. Do you think I'm that weak?'

'I think you're fantastic. But that woman is taking advantage. Now we're settled here and you're making new friends, you might want to distance yourself. I'm glad Noah and Jack won't be at the same school. It's healthier.'

'Why is it healthier? That's not logical. Noah behaves better when he's with Jack.'

Dexter shrugs.

'The school thing is mad here. Sophie Meadows told me. She said securing a place in the school of your choice is up there with divorce. It drives women crazy, it makes men angry and aggressive, it ends friendships. I don't want to end my friendship with Lorna.'

'That won't happen. There's too much riding on it for her.'

'It must be exhausting to be so cynical, my love.' Elise goes to him, draping her hands around his neck. 'We've got what we wanted. Noah will be going to a good school, where they are legally bound to address his needs. My friend is upset and I don't like it, but I'm not cutting her off just because I caught her at a low moment.'

Dexter huffs. 'She was out of order.'

'Stop it. I can choose my own friends, and if I want Lorna around, that's my business. The Gladwell Grove lot are only interested in me because I'm rich, I'm married to you and I live in this street. Lorna is different. And she apologised. That's good enough for me.'

She can tell he's still in a bad mood when he goes upstairs to shower. It's in the set of his jaw. She doesn't like to push, because she's experienced Dexter in a rage and it is not a pretty sight, but that does not mean she has to be the one to roll over every time they disagree. The trouble is, she loves him more than he loves her. There is always that imbalance in a relationship. How can there not be? Dexter professes to worship her, and sometimes she even believes him. Even so, worshipping one woman doesn't preclude him from worshipping another. There have been at least two since they've been together, maybe more. She has learnt to pick her battles. In which case, why has she dug her heels in over Lorna Chilcott? She sighs. Perhaps she's just feeling bloody-minded. Perhaps tomorrow she won't care about Lorna's feelings at all.

She feels very lonely all of a sudden. She has many friends, but not a proper best friend, one she can laugh and cry with, who knows her through and through. Lorna is the closest she's come in a long time.

A day spent with her clients Hannah Chase and Maria Kowleska, getting them ready for their roles in a musical version of *Cold Comfort Farm*, does much to soothe Elise. Lorna will come round. Perhaps once she's got over her prejudices she'll realise that the school she's been offered is as good as Alverley. Elise will make sure she doesn't feel alienated from the community here. She understands, as one coming from another country, that this is what it will feel like for a while at the new school, but Lorna will settle down because Jack will.

She is concerned about Amy. It's been so much fun training the girl, seeing her develop. She doesn't want to let her down by quarrelling with her mum so that she feels duty-bound to drop the classes. Amy is a good little singer;

94

not the most fantastic voice ever, but if her aim is pop rather than musical theatre, she stands as good a chance as anyone. In a year or two, who knows? She has that mixture of surly adolescent confidence and vulnerability that is appealing.

'Mamma!' A blue crayon flies across the room.

'Don't throw your crayons, sweetheart. Come on, you haven't done the tree yet. Do you have a green?'

'I don't like trees.'

'Everyone likes trees.'

'I don't. I want Amy.'

'Amy will be here in a minute. You can say hi, then you can watch TV until bedtime.'

She checks the clock again. She has time to call Lorna, maybe suggest a glass of wine. No. Tomorrow is soon enough.

What stopped her telling Lorna that she had no choice but to accept the place for Noah? Should she explain? It might make her more sympathetic. On the other hand, this is about Noah, his self-esteem. People chat, and she doesn't want anyone to find out that Fairlands withdrew their offer after a conversation with the manager of Noah's nursery. He is only three, for God's sake. You'd think they'd have been falling over themselves to get Dexter Coleridge's son. But apparently they have 'a duty to the other families'. Stupid school with its stupid policies, only wanting perfect, cream-of-the-crop kids. And she's never liked that manager.

'Patronising bitch.' She glances at her son. He's oblivious.

The doorbell rings.

'Amy!' Noah slips off his chair and charges to the front door, his solid little body bouncing. He reaches for the latch, but he's too short, thank goodness. Elise pushes the button to open the gate.

Amy beams as she hurries past their cars and scoops him up. 'Hello, gorgeous little man!' Then she smiles at Elise, as natural and excited as ever. Evidently she hasn't spoken to her mum yet.

Chapter 19

LORNA

Jack zooms his wind-up shark through the bubbles, his face flushed, his damp hair in a Tintin peak. Lorna glances at her watch. Twenty past six. Amy should be home any minute. Good. She can read Jack his story this evening. She's feeling broken by the school news and the row with Elise, and it's a huge effort not to show it. She behaved like a madwoman, and that's going to be hard to wind back from. She sincerely hopes Amy never finds out.

Earlier she'd phoned the admissions officer. Two years ago she'd secured a very nice house in a great location for Victoria Caudle and her family. Victoria confirmed what she'd suspected: that Jack was at the top of the waiting list. If it hadn't been for Elise, he would most definitely have been offered a place. 'You can appeal,' she said. 'But you're unlikely to succeed. We're already at capacity.'

It's true, their countryside-close-to-the-city paradise has been discovered recently – a feature in the property pages of a broadsheet hasn't helped, with people moving here from more built-up areas. Good for business and house prices, but not so good for entry into Alverley Park's oversubscribed primary school.

'Best to wait a couple of years,' Victoria added. 'There's always movement in Year 2 and 3.'

Lorna is grateful she didn't have to face the school gates today. She couldn't have stood it. Everyone congratulating each other, commiserating with her, telling her Northcliff is fine. It's far from fine. It reputedly can't retain its staff, and if the rumours are true, which they often are, last year a seven-year-old boy was caught with a kitchen knife in his book bag. She twists round, pressing her face into the towel. Jack mustn't see her upset. It isn't fair on him. She picks up the shark and dives it down to his feet. 'Oh no. He's nibbling your toes!'

Jack squeals with laughter and splashes so hard she gets wet.

'Out you get.'

Amy should be back by now. If she's late, which some-times happens because she likes to linger with Elise, then it's bad form of Elise to encourage her, today of all days. Unless she's getting back at Lorna by being extra nice to her daughter? Lorna wraps a large fluffy towel around her son and rubs him dry. Elise wouldn't stoop to that.

Was it really only last Friday that Dexter kissed her? Was it only Saturday that she held his shirt to her nose and—

'Mummy! Ow!'

She's rubbing Jack's head too hard. 'Sorry, darling.'

Where is Amy? She picks her phone up off the side of the basin and types out a message. *Are you on your way home? Xx*

She puts Jack down on the floor and pulls out the plug, then tweaks his pyjamas off the towel heater, where they've been warming, and checks her phone. Nothing. But that's all right, isn't it? Amy turns her phone off during sessions with Elise. That's sacrosanct. Not even sound off. Off off. Focus is all. She's probably forgotten to switch it back on. It's unlike her, because she and her friends find it necessary to be in constant touch, but Elise has probably filled her head with sparkling dreams. Lucky girl to have that opportunity.

Has she lost Elise? Accusing her of being out of touch, too rich to understand the problems lesser mortals face, was not clever. The idea distresses her almost as much as the possibility of Jack starting at Northcliff in September. She decides then and there that she'll call Elise and clear the air as soon as Amy gets home. She's behaved badly and she's ready to admit it.

It's ten to seven. She calls Amy again, but it goes straight to voicemail. Of course it does. Amy will be too busy having deep and meaningful conversations with Elise Coleridge. Getting anything personal out of her daughter since she reached adolescence is like getting blood from a stone. Lorna does her best to keep the lines of communication open, offering to drive her places so they can have conversations in the car, showing she's listening and that she cares. It's tough enough parenting a teen without being shut out. Lorna is convinced Amy tells Elise things during those Tuesday-evening lessons that she doesn't tell her, because she comes back lighter and happier, as if she's unloaded a sack of stones at the Swedish woman's feet. Elise, with her glamour and Zen-like calm, has tamed Amy. As Amy's boring, naggy mother, Lorna cannot compete.

She reminds herself that all is not perfect in the Coleridge household. After all, Elise has not succeeded in taming her son, and her husband has a secret.

'Story,' Jack says, squatting beside his bookshelves. He pulls out one about a frog and brings it to his bed. 'Get under the duvet, Mummy.'

Lorna does as she's told. There's nothing like a snuggle with her son to make her feel better. She reads the story, does the voices, then they have their goodnight chat. At the end of it, her anxiety has abated.

By the time she hears the key in the lock, her worries have crept back. She isn't anxious enough to start the potentially embarrassing process of calling round Amy's friends, but she does keep nipping upstairs to peer at the street from her bedroom window. She exhales a sigh of relief and rolls the tension out of her shoulders. She won't get cross because she doesn't want Amy stomping upstairs and slamming her bedroom door. But it's Matt who walks in, looking weary, not Amy. She checks the time again. Seven fifteen. That isn't right.

Matt drops his keys on the kitchen table and kisses her.

'How are you feeling?' he asks.

'I'm all right.' They'd talked it through earlier, though Lorna didn't mention the spat with Elise. She's too ashamed. 'Amy hasn't come back from Elise's. The lesson finished over an hour ago. She's ignored all my messages, and she's not answering her phone.'

'Perhaps they got talking.'

'Not for this long. Elise will be putting Noah to bed.'

Matt glances at his watch. 'She'll be back soon. She'll be getting hungry.'

Lorna has an odd feeling. When she looks at Matt, she can see he feels it too, that shift in your belly when your body accepts a fact before your mind does. She's right to be worried.

'I'll ring Elise.'

Chapter 20

LORNA

'How are you?' Elise's tone is wary, but Lorna expected that.

'Uh . . . I'm fine. I was wondering, is Amy still with you? Could you ask her to come home?'

'Amy isn't here, Lorna. She left ages ago.'

Lorna's blood runs cold. She tries to keep her voice steady. Matt is watching her. 'What time did she leave?'

'About five forty-five,' Elise says.

'But that's . . . Why did she leave so early?'

The long pause makes Lorna frown.

'She was a little upset,' Elise says eventually.

'Why?'

'It was nothing really.'

Matt signals to Lorna to put her phone on speaker, then leans over. 'Elise, this is Matt. Can you tell me exactly what happened?'

'I'm sure Amy will be back any minute.'

'I don't give a shit. If she left before the end of your session, there must have been something wrong. She lives for those lessons.'

'Okay then. I'm afraid my husband told her a few home

102

truths about her chances of succeeding in the music industry.'

'He did what?'

'He was trying to manage her expectations. He doesn't think she has what it takes, and decided it was better for her to know now than put years of work into it and be disappointed. I'm very sorry. I've told him he should not have done that.'

'Your husband is a cunt.'

Lorna winces and shakes her head at him, mouthing, *No*.

'Excuse me,' Matt says. 'I shouldn't have said that.' Then he raises his eyebrows at Lorna and mouths, *Okay?*

But Elise has hung up.

While Matt combs the streets in his battered white van, Lorna calls Miriam, who says she saw Amy briefly and describes what she was wearing when she left for her singing lesson. Then she tries the mother of Lily, one of Amy's best friends. When Amy was at primary school, Lorna knew exactly who her daughter's friends were. Nowadays she picks up clues, but allegiances change, and she's not sure who is in favour with who at any given time.

Lily's mother hands the phone straight over to her daughter.

'Hi,' Lily says. 'I don't know where Amy is. She has singing on Tuesdays, doesn't she?'

'Yes, I just thought she might have gone to see a friend afterwards. Could you ask her to call me immediately if she gets in touch?'

'Sure. Have you tried Maya?'

'No. Can you give me her number, and the numbers of any other friends she might have gone to?'

'I'll have to ask them if they mind first.'

Oh God.

'Lorna.' Lily's mother has taken back the phone. 'I have a list of numbers. I'll email it to you. Please don't worry too much. I'm sure Amy's perfectly safe.'

Lorna works through the telephone numbers Lily's mother sends over, but no one has any idea where Amy is and they all sound genuinely surprised. She leaves her laptop, moves to the window and scans the street again. Scaffolding has gone up on a house further down. The owners are on the pavement looking up at it, the woman with her arms crossed around her pregnant belly, the man pointing at something. Lorna negotiated the sale but hasn't bumped into them yet. She didn't tell them she lives in the road, so there'll be a moment of confusion when they do meet. It won't be the first time. She decided years ago that that isn't something you share with potential buyers.

Matt's van turns into the road and she narrows her eyes, fingers gripping the sill. But there is no one in the passenger seat. He gets out, shoulders slumped as he looks up at the house, obviously hoping that Amy has come home while he's been out, knowing it's a false hope because Lorna would have called. Her heart bleeds for him.

She rushes into the hall and opens the door before he can get his key in the lock. 'I don't think she's with a friend.'

Matt breathes out heavily. 'We should call the police.'

*

'Amy Christina Chilcott...Fifteen...Uh.' Matt looks at Lorna, hovering nearby. He cups his hand over the receiver. 'When did she leave Elise's, love?'

'About five forty-five.'

'Around five forty-five from 55 Gladwell Grove...No, not a friend – well, a friend of my wife's...Elise Coleridge. She's been giving Amy singing lessons. Something upset her and she went off in a huff...I doubt it. Amy isn't like that...' Matt bristles. 'Of course we've tried her phone ...Yes, we've checked her bedroom and contacted her friends...'

He turns to Lorna after ending the call. 'They're saying give it an hour. Apparently, most teenagers who have been reported missing turn up.'

'Most?'

Lorna is sorry she said it, because Matt pales. She puts her arms around him and draws him against her. He's stiff with tension, but after a second, he returns the hug with force.

'I'm going out again,' he says. 'I'll drive around for a bit.'

Lorna switches on the lights in Amy's bedroom, closes the curtains and sits down at the cluttered desk. There's nothing particularly personal here, but then what teenager would leave something personal in full view? She opens a drawer and finds a couple of phone chargers, some pens and colouring pencils. A ruler, highlighters and Post-it notes. Another is stuffed with sheets of paper.

It's eight o'clock. They would normally have eaten by now and Amy would be on her phone or reading a book. Her laptop is closed, her book, spine cracked, face-down on her bedside table. Lorna knows the code to the laptop because that was the agreement when they bought it. She checks Amy's emails but finds nothing dubious, and her internet history only turns up fashion and celebrity gossip sites, and homework research. No chat rooms.

She flicks through the papers and finds a sheet filled with sketches. Amy is good at sketching portraits, her powers of observation acute. Lorna has no trouble recognising her subjects: Jack, herself, Matt, Lily.

Dexter.

There are three drawings of his face. She's caught his expression in a few brisk strokes: his dry humour, the slightly wicked curl of his lips, that look in his eyes – direct, questioning. And something more, something almost sexually challenging. Does Amy have a crush? There is nothing unusual about that, except that she was in his house this evening and hasn't been seen for over two hours. Lorna folds the sheet of paper and slides it into the back pocket of her jeans. Obviously the sketches are copied from photos Amy must have found online, but still, she's captured something about him: the way his intensity draws you in. His animal magnetism.

At nine, they call the police back and insist they take action.

Chapter 21

LORNA

Matt's eyes are red, his skin ashen, and he's unshaven. He hasn't looked like this since the night Jack was born. 'If anything's happened to her,' he whispers.

'Nothing's happened. Amy is sensible. She's had a shock and she doesn't want to face anyone. Maybe she's embarrassed. She was so certain that knowing the Coleridges would be her big break.' Lorna is convincing no one, least of all herself. 'She had dreams and she . . .' She falters.

'She what?' Matt says, jerking his head up.

'I think she may have had a crush on Dexter.'

It feels strange to say his name, the words physically affecting her mouth. Until this happened, she'd been thinking of little else but him. And now. Well, what? Did she misread the situation? Has Dexter been trying to get to Amy through her? She doesn't believe that.

'You're fucking kidding me. He's old enough to be her father.'

'He's charismatic and famous, Matt. She's at an impressionable age. And here. I found this.' She takes Amy's sketches out of her pocket and shows them to him. Her hands are trembling. What struck her when she first saw the drawings of Dexter, and strikes her even more powerfully now, is his eyes, the way he's looking straight at the artist. This is precisely the way he looked at her when they were alone in his garden. As if she was the only girl in the world.

Matt scrutinises the drawings, then looks up. 'You don't think something happened there, do you?'

'They're never alone together. She has her session with Elise, then she comes straight home. This is coming from Amy, not Dexter. He barely knows she exists.'

'Until now.'

She hesitates. The man who kissed her in the darkened garden, who shared things about himself, who comes from the same town as her, is not interested in pubescent girls. She knows how people's minds work, though, the imaginative leaps they make, and prays Amy comes home before the gossip and insinuation start to surge.

'You told the operator your daughter had been having a singing lesson.' Police Constable Dutton glances down at her notes. The older of the two female constables by a good ten years, she has an air of brisk efficiency that Lorna finds reassuring. 'At 55 Gladwell Grove.'

It's almost eleven o'clock, but Lorna isn't tired. She's running on adrenaline. The constables arrived fifteen minutes ago, anticipating her fears with a barrage of reassuring statistics. Seventy-nine per cent of children are found within twenty-four hours and ninety per cent within two days. Less than two per cent are still missing after a week.

Answering their questions for risk assessment has a calming effect. It's like working through a medical assessment form at a practitioner's: any heart disease? Epilepsy? Diabetes. No. No. No.

Afterwards, PC Dutton explained that Amy was low to medium risk. She didn't have mental health or medical issues or a habit of running away, she wasn't being bullied and had never committed a crime. Lorna and Matt were happily married and there was no drug or alcohol abuse in the home. The fact that they haven't been able to contact her by phone, and that she does, in theory, have two addresses, if they count Pete's, pushes her closer to medium risk.

The change in the officer's expression is infinitesimal, and all the more powerful for it. Lorna's stomach feels strangely cold.

'So Amy is your stepdaughter,' Dutton says to Matt.

'She is. I've been in her life since she was six. We have a great relationship.'

'Could Amy have gone to her birth father?' asks the younger officer, PC Carter.

'I doubt it. He lives in Devon,' Lorna says.

'Perhaps call him just in case?'

'Now?'

The officer nods. Lorna takes out her phone, scrolls through her contacts and taps Pete's mobile number.

'Lorna!' Pete sounds like he's outside, tramping through long grass. What is he doing out so late? She doesn't ask.

'Have you heard from Amy today?'

'No. should I have?'

'She hasn't come home.'

'Oh God. Lorna, I'm sorry. She hasn't called here. Is there anything I can do? Do you want me to come up?'

'No. No, you don't have to do that.' Pete arriving in his beaten-up ex-army jeep belching fumes is one thing she can happily do without. 'Just keep your phone on and call me if she gets in touch.'

'You must be worried sick.'

'Yes. I am. Sorry, I have to go.'

'Lorna—'

She cuts him off. 'She's not there.'

'Tell them what happened earlier,' Matt says.

She takes a breath and nods. 'Amy left her singing lesson early because she was upset, but her teacher didn't think to tell me.' The thought of how cavalierly her daughter's pain was treated enrages her. Managing her expectations. God. She gives the two constables the gist of what Elise said. PC Carter looks sympathetic; Dutton moves on with her questions without so much as a nod of understanding.

'The full name of the singing teacher?'

'Elise Coleridge.' They'd find out soon enough, so she might as well put them in the picture. 'She's married to Dexter Coleridge.'

PC Carter raises heavily made-up eyebrows. 'And he is?'

'He used to be the lead singer of a band called D.I.G.B.Y.'

'Oh yeah, I've heard of them. So this guy's wife gives singing lessons. Surely they don't need the money.'

'No, not at all. Elise used to be in musical theatre and now she's a vocal coach. She doesn't work because she has to; she works because she's passionate about it. And she doesn't charge us for Amy's classes. We're good friends.' Heat suffuses Lorna's face and she stops talking abruptly. Why is she leaping to Elise's defence when she's so angry with her?

110

'Do you know what was said?'

'Yes. Dexter told Amy she didn't have what it took to be a successful singer. It was Amy's dream, and he crushed it.'

'I can see how that would have caused her distress,' PC Carter says. 'She's probably hiding somewhere, nursing her wounds. She'll calm down, though, Mrs Chilcott, and come home.'

Lorna sniffs.

'Apart from the lessons, does Amy see much of the Coleridges socially?' Dutton asks.

'No.'

'Do they have kids?'

'Just one. A three-year-old boy.'

'Does Amy babysit for them?'

Lorna gathers herself, understanding what Dutton is fishing for. Any sign that Dexter has an unhealthy interest in teenage girls. 'No. They have a live-in nanny.'

'Does she talk about Dexter Coleridge at all?' PC Carter asks.

'Not really. It's Elise she talks about.' The sketches are burning a hole in her pocket and Matt keeps looking at her. He's waiting for her to produce them.

'Mr Chilcott?'

'No.'

'Has she ever been on her own with him?'

'Not as far as I know,' Lorna says.

Matt's face darkens, but he shrugs. 'If she has, she's never told us.'

'What about the heath?' Dutton asks after a pause. 'Could she have gone there to walk off her mood?'

111

Lorna stares at her, horrified.

'We don't allow her there on her own,' Matt says, reaching for Lorna's hand. 'There's rarely any trouble – well, you'd know more about that than us – but it's better to err on the safe side.'

'What's the relationship like between yourself and your daughter?' Dutton asks Lorna.

'Very good. Warm.'

'Were there any problems between the two of you? I have teenagers; I know how it can be.'

'Not problems. She pushed my buttons occasionally, and I pushed hers. Normal mother–daughter stuff.'

'What about today?'

'No,' Lorna says firmly. 'Everything was fine. She was looking forward to her singing lesson. That always puts her in a good mood.'

'And what about you, Mr Chilcott?'

'Same deal as my wife. Bit of button-pushing. The teenage years are a roller coaster, but I don't think we've argued in a while. We're not that kind of family.'

'What kind of family is that?'

'The kind who yell at each other.'

'So you repress your anger?'

'No,' Matt says with studied patience. 'We talk about things. If Amy's upset, she tells me. We're pals.'

'All teenagers keep secrets from their parents, don't they?'

'If she does, I don't know about them. That's the nature of secrets. She has a good appetite, lovely friends, does her homework on time and is a wonderful big sister to Jack. I couldn't ask for a better daughter.'

Lorna's heart breaks for him. 'Amy is perceptive. She knew I was worried about something this morning. We were waiting to hear if our son had been offered a place at our preferred school.' She pauses, feeling for the right words. She still hasn't processed this. 'Amy knew I was anxious about it. She hugged me.'

'Was that unusual?'

Was it? 'Er . . . no,' she stammers. 'I . . . I don't think so. She probably felt bad for being carefree when I was so anxious.'

Lorna's phone rings, but it isn't Amy, it's Lily's mother, wanting to know if there's been any news. She gets rid of her quickly.

'Would it be okay if we have a look at Amy's bedroom?' Dutton asks.

Lorna is flooded with guilt. She shouldn't have poked through Amy's things. She certainly shouldn't have re-moved the drawings. Too late now. If she admits to it, she'll look guilty of something. Protecting a paedophile. The words slither into her mind. She almost gasps out loud. Dexter is not that. Never that.

'Yes, of course,' Matt says. 'If you could be quiet, though. Our son is asleep in the bedroom below Amy's. Darling, perhaps you should show the officers Amy's drawings.'

Wrong-footed, she fumbles for them, her face flaming. She nearly rips the page as she tugs it out of her pocket. She smooths out the creases and hands it to Carter. 'Sorry. I forgot all about this.'

The officers don't comment, and she gabbles on. 'I found it among Amy's things.' She indicates three of the studies. 'These are of Dexter.'

Dutton inspects them, then takes an evidence bag out of her pocket and drops the page in. 'Thank you.'

Matt leads them upstairs and stays with them while Lorna paces. Hungry, she cuts a slice of cheese from the pack of Cheddar in the fridge and tries to eat it, but her throat constricts and she starts to cry.

The staircase creaks. She wipes her eyes and drinks some water from the tap, turning as Carter walks in carrying Amy's laptop.

'We'll talk to Mr and Mrs Coleridge now,' the officer says. 'Obviously, if Amy reappears in the meantime, call me.' She hands Lorna a card. 'I'm sure she'll come home soon.'

Once they've gone, Matt slides down the wall and bangs his fists against his forehead. 'This can't be happening.'

'I'm sure she's—'

'Don't say that! You're not sure, and neither are they. All I know is that my daughter went round to the Coleridges' this evening and hasn't been seen since she left their house.' He lifts his head. '*If* she left their house.' He pushes himself up and grabs his keys.

'Where're you going?'

'To Gladwell Grove.'

She clutches his arm. 'Don't be ridiculous, Matt. Those officers aren't going to let you be there while they interview them. Don't make things worse.'

The words *for yourself* hang in the air. Matt stares at her. 'How could I? They already suspect me.'

'Is that why you brought up the drawings?'

He nods. 'Sorry. I could just feel them sizing me up. As far as they're concerned, if anything has happened to Amy, it's most likely going to be someone in the family. Do you know how horrible that is? I just don't want to be the only guy they're looking at.'

He rubs aggressively at his face, and Lorna reaches up and takes his hands, pulling them away. He leans forward and presses his forehead against hers.

'They know you were out on a job,' she says. 'They'll check that stacks up, and it will.'

He hesitates before answering.

'What?' Lorna says.

'Nothing. It doesn't matter. Even if I have a watertight alibi, everyone else will think I had something to do with it.'

'You're a good man and a fantastic father. You've done nothing wrong.'

'What if someone's hurt her?'

She replays the hug from this morning, feels Amy's slender arms around her neck, her cheek pressed close. *Chill, okay, Mum.*

A tear runs down her cheek. Lorna has never felt chillier.

Chapter 22

THE PSYCHIATRIST

I may not have my notes or my recordings of Ben's sessions, but there is a lot I remember about them. I pour myself a glass of wine, open my laptop and create a new document entitled *BEN CLARKSON*. I close my eyes, picture the door to my consulting room opening, see the young man with the scruffy hair and anxious smile step inside, and begin to type. Jeremy Osborne has listened to the cassettes, while I haven't been able to refresh my memory. What I need to help him understand is how it felt to be in the room with Ben.

The things I remember most clearly are the things that reflect badly on me, like when something I said disappointed him, or my feelings of guilt when he got angry. Of course it isn't verbatim, but once I start, the memories come thick and fast, especially when I don't try to massage my own responses. Gradually I see a pattern. A steady drip-drip of behaviours – holding my gaze too long, deliberately avoiding my gaze, showing vulnerability by fighting against it – that led to that final comment. *You're beautiful*. Even though I didn't realise it, Ben was manipulating me. I don't think he planned it, I think that at some point, early on in our acquaintance, something in me triggered something in him, and not in a good way.

I stop typing and put my head in my hands.

Dylan is standing inside the doorway, staring at me, green-gold eyes unblinking, head lowered, back hunched.

'What's up?'

I pat my thigh, willing to offer my lap if he needs comfort, but he slips beyond me to the far side of the room and crouches between the TV and the curtains. That's not like him. I click my fingers, but he doesn't come.

My glass is empty. I refill it with the velvety Merlot I bought earlier, then sit back and stare at my screen. Seconds later, the lights go out, my screen goes dark and the flat shuts down like a factory at the end of the day. Bewildered, I tap stupidly at my keyboard, then push my chair back and feel my way to the coat cupboard, where the fuse box lives.

I push aside coats and jackets to find it and flick the main switch back up. The lights come on. I check the fridge freezer is still working, then turn my laptop back on. It hums into life. I key in my password and wait with some anxiety, breathing a sigh of relief when I see that all I've lost is the last sentence. I save the document again for good measure.

It's eleven p.m. by the time I'm satisfied that I've done enough. I open a new email to Jeremy Osborne and attach the document with a terse message.

In the absence of my notes and recordings, this is a record
of what I recall of incidences during my sessions with Ben
Clarkson that would have been cause for concern and
which I feel I navigated properly and with propriety. Given
that you have already listened to the cassettes, I hope
that once you have read this and understood my feelings
and motivations, you will agree that I have behaved
with professionalism throughout. If he has, on occasion,
managed to get

The lights go out again. This time I feel a tiny flutter of
fear. I go to the cupboard and flick the switch back up.

under my skin, I certainly did not encourage him to think
I was interested in him romantically. I would be grateful
if you could contact me when you've had a chance to
read this.

Despite the wine, I have enough sense to know that it's
invariably better to sleep on important emails before sending them. It can wait till morning.

Dylan, in the corner of the room, twitches his tail. I'm
not surprised he's on edge. The electric outages have made
me nervous too. I'll call an electrician in the morning.

I'm about to minimise my email page when another
memory jumps in. The time Ben sat in silence for a quarter
of an hour and I thought he'd fallen asleep. I'd coughed and
he hadn't opened his eyes. I got up and gently nudged his
shoulder, saying his name, and he'd startled and grabbed
me by the wrist, his grip so hard I'd cried out. How could I
have forgotten that? He apologised and we moved on, but

118

it had felt like he was ready to strike. Like a snake. I remove the document from the email, add that story and reattach it, then minimise the screen.

Dylan's cat flap opens and closes. The absence of my cat fills me with self-pity. The flat feels empty and I feel very alone.

Chapter 23

THE PSYCHIATRIST

I'm woken by Dylan pummelling my shoulder. I open my eyes and stare groggily into the dimly lit room. The curtains filter the sunlight shining through the gaps at the edges of the blackout blinds.

I roll over, feel for my reading glasses and put them on askew. Eight ten. God. I sit up and fling the duvet to one side, dislodging the cat. He looks affronted as he leaps off the bed and pads away. I step into the shower, then remember, as the jet of hot water hits me, that I don't have a job to go to because I've been suspended. There is no hurry; there is all the time in the world, thanks to Ben-bloody-Clarkson.

I munch a slice of buttered toast and honey while I read the news on my iPad and scroll through reels on my phone, but those activities soon pall. I wash the plate, dry it and put it away, then pour myself another cup of coffee. Thank goodness I had the sense not to send the email. Nothing written late at night, slightly pissed, should be seen by anyone other than the author. I'll use it as an aide-memoire next time I'm forced to defend myself to Jeremy and Belle.

Dylan meows round my shins. I shake dry cat food into his bowl and replenish his water. My phone rings as I'm washing my hands. I dry them quickly on a tea towel and reach for it.

'What the hell were you thinking?' Jeremy Osborne booms down the line.

'Hang on. What?'

'It's bad enough emailing me in the middle of the night, but to cc Belle Needham and Ben's mother – I mean, the damage you've done to yourself, not to mention the reputation of the clinic . . . I'll do what I can to mitigate, but I can't promise you won't get struck off.'

'Wait.' I flounder. 'I don't . . . What email?'

'The first thing you need to do is issue an apology. And sound like you mean it. You were drunk. You've been under a lot of strain. You didn't mean to write or send it. You were upset by the accusation and were trying to put things straight in your mind. You are very, very sorry for the distress you've caused.'

'I don't know what you're talking about.' I move into the sitting room and tap my laptop keyboard. The screen lights up and opens on my Gmail account. I glance at the bottom bar. There is nothing minimised. With growing horror, I click on *Sent*. And there it is. My late-night scrawlings have gone to Jeremy, to Belle and to Georgina Clarkson. My stomach sinks like a stone.

'But I didn't send it. I decided to sleep on it.'

Beside me the empty bottle of Merlot stands like an accusation. My glass is stained with a translucent blush darkening to a dry pool at the bottom of the bowl.

My voice wavers. 'Have you spoken to either of them?'

'Not yet. I wanted to get your side of things first. I have to say, I'm astonished by this.'

I frown. That's a bit over the top. 'There's nothing in there that isn't true. I stand by every word.'

In the brief silence, I can almost hear Jeremy wince. 'Perhaps you'd better reread it and refresh your memory before you say that. I'm going to call the others now. In the meantime, start working on that apology.' He pauses. 'You're going to need it.'

I slump back in the chair and push the mouse around, then click on the document attached to my email. As I read, my eyes widen and I sit bolt upright. I push back my chair, slam the laptop shut and run upstairs to the bathroom, where I dry-heave into the toilet. Only when the heat has left my face do I risk coming back downstairs and peeking again.

It starts innocuously enough, but within three lines the words take on a life of their own, as if hands other than mine have attacked the keyboard, bashing out a stream of discontent, delusion, misery, anger, misplaced arrogance and petty spite. If I was reading it in my professional capacity, I'd describe it as the drunken late-night ravings of a deeply unhappy and traumatised narcissist. My words literally spew vitriol and paranoia. What were supposed to be notes on conversations between me and Ben segue into complaints about my current situation. Sentences like *Why would I touch him?*

You have the cheek to assume that because I'm divorced and childless, I'm desperate.

How dare you believe that little shit over me. But then it's always the same. I've never been believed.

122

As for you, Belle, you're a self-important nobody who gets her kicks by playing power games. If anyone's desperate, it's you.

And Georgina Clarkson. You are the biggest bitch of all. What kind of mother are you, leaving your son on his own while you waft around pretending you're something you're not? I know your type. You like to be a big fish in a small pond. No wonder Ben is riddled with problems. You've been a crap mother. And you thought you could pay to put him right. Well let me tell you, money has fuck-all to do with it. Money makes things worse. Do you understand how much damage you've done? Do you fuck. Too wrapped up in yourself.

And on, and on. Pages of it. One thousand four hundred and nineteen words. I recognise some of the conversations and incidents from Ben's sessions, but where I've detailed an exchange, I've then gone into a blizzard of self-justifying brain splurge. Last night I sat at my desk and worked my way through a bottle of wine. And had a full-on, intercontinental, nuclear-level self-destructive rant.

When I close the document, I notice I have a new email. It's from Belle. I open it with a sick feeling in my stomach. She tells me in no uncertain terms to consider myself fired. If I attempt to attach myself to another practice, she will personally make sure they know everything about me. At that, I finally break and burst into tears. Despite being the only person here, I lock myself in the bathroom. The woman I meet in the mirror is blotchy-skinned and red-eyed. Not deranged, just sad and lost.

I went into this business because it felt like the right thing to do. The counselled often end up counselling. We survivors get a taste for it. We believe we have a special insight into the mindsets of our fellow human beings. We draw out feelings from our patients, and in return for their utterances, we fill the spaces their words have left with strategies and pills.

My career is over. I crawl into bed. I don't want to see people; I don't want to have to talk to anyone or deal with anything except mine and Dylan's immediate needs. I shut down my laptop and switch off my phone. I need to lie low, but it's more than hiding away; I want to obliterate everything for a little while – twenty-four hours, a day or two at the most – and get my head straight. I don't even want to dream, because with dreams comes guilt. But dreams I cannot escape. And they are bad. I wake with a start, lurching up and crying out. People have crawled out of the closet I keep them in. They've told me they are coming.

I cannot believe what I've done, and yet the evidence is on my computer, on Jeremy's, Belle's and Georgina Clarkson's as well. And who knows? Perhaps Georgina has shared it with Ben. Or her friends. Last night I lost all judgement, all my dignity, all my credibility as an adult and a professional. What a mess. I think about my ex-husband, with his new wife and longed-for babies, in his smart house with his car parked on the forecourt. He has succeeded in life, where I have failed. I switch my phone back on, taking it into the sitting room and curling up on the sofa. All I want is to hear his voice. It only rings once.

'Hi, you've reached Daniel's phone. I'm not able to take your call. Leave a message and I'll get back to you.'

Ding.

It isn't the first time I've done this. He never calls back.

Chapter 24

ELISE

Elise pushes open the bedroom door with her elbow, goes in and sets a cup of tea down beside Dexter. She crosses to the window. Their bedroom looks out over a walled garden onto the acres of heath beyond. The proximity to nature is one of the reasons she chose this house; it reminds her of the island where she grew up, the long walks she'd take with her father. He knew the names of all the wildflowers and insects. The heath is a designated Site of Special Scientific Interest, known for the diversity of its flora and fauna. A heath fritillary, a butterfly with brown and orange wings edged in white, once on the brink of extinction, has been spotted.

She wonders if Amy is out there. Perhaps she has been found, and in her relief, Lorna hasn't thought to call Elise. She's in her bad books anyway. Last night before they went to bed, she and Dexter saw a torch beam moving in the darkness and wondered if it was Lorna and her husband.

It's cold this morning, an unseasonal April frost creating a fairy-tale landscape. Elise turns to look at Dexter, who is still fast asleep. She loves him so much, even if he is an arsehole sometimes.

Yesterday's chat with the two policewomen was un-nerving. The Chilcotts have been telling tales – though who can blame them? But these things can escalate quick-ly, and Dexter is a celebrity. The taller officer, the one who appeared to be in charge – Elise cannot recall her name – was impatient, the slimmer one with the startling eye-brows wide-eyed as she took in the opulence of the house. Elise and Dexter played down the incident, saying it was a stupid, tactless remark on Dexter's part and that Elise had done her best to reassure Amy before she left them. When Dexter admitted to leaving the house to 'drive around for a while', there was an infinitesimal pause.

'Babe?' Dexter grunts. He is propping himself up on his elbows, sleepy-eyed.

'Sorry. I didn't mean to wake you.'

'It's fine. Any word on the kid?'

'No.' She speaks sharply, and Dexter's face falls.

'It isn't our fault if something happened after she left us.'

'No, but . . .' Elise catches something out of the corner of her eye and goes back to the window, sees a group of uniformed officers conferring. 'There are police out there. They look like they're about to start searching.' The group disperses, leaving the main path and following the maze of tracks trampled through the trees and undergrowth.

'Really?' Wide awake now, Dexter gets out of bed and joins her at the window. 'We should go down and help.'

Elise bites her lip, frowning. 'I don't think that's a good idea.'

'What do you mean? I can't sit here twiddling my thumbs.'

'Don't be stupid, Dex. Someone will recognise you. The

press are going to turn up as soon as they're tipped off.' She puts a hand on his chest. 'We'll wait, see what happens.'

'I hope she's okay. It's fucking creepy out there at night. You get some dodgy types hanging around.'

'Don't,' Elise says.

From his bedroom Noah shouts, 'Mamma!' and seconds later she hears Clara's door open.

'I'm going downstairs. You get a shower.'

But Dexter isn't listening, he's still gazing out of the window.

Chapter 25

LORNA

Lorna feels as though she's dissolving. The police have found Amy's beanie; the pink one with the cream pom-pom Lorna bought her for Christmas two years previously. It's wet. They show her the spot where it was found, behind a fallen tree on a bed of decaying leaves close to but hidden from the path. Did Amy come here to cool off after Dexter's insensitive comments? Lorna can easily imagine her staying out because she felt humiliated. It's hard for anyone, let alone a teenager, to deal with shame around the people who love her.

She reaches for Matt's hand. He doesn't attempt to talk to her. His presence is all the comfort he can give. Unless they are very lucky, this is the start of a protracted nightmare, the long, slow devastation of their lives.

James has told her not to come into work until she feels able to. He and Catherine from lettings can cover her appointments between them. When she called her friend Jules in distress, Jules rushed round and picked Jack up, still in his pyjamas. Jules's daughter, Amelie, is a gentle little thing, a far cry from Noah Coleridge and a much more sensible friend. Lorna feels guilty for neglecting them for Elise and Noah. Jules hasn't said anything, but it's obvious she feels hurt.

'What'll happen now?' Matt asks PC Carter. Lorna hasn't been able to trust herself to speak.

'We'll continue searching. You should go home in case Amy turns up. We have plenty of feet on the ground. If we find anything else, we'll contact you.'

'Darling, you go,' Matt says to Lorna, adding, 'It's all right if I stay, isn't it?'

'That's up to you, Mr Chilcott.'

Lorna glances around, breathes deeply, sees her breath leave her mouth in a billow of mist. 'I . . .' she starts, then falters, her eyes widening as Matt cups her cheeks with his hands and wipes under her eyes with the pads of his thumbs. She hadn't realised tears were falling.

'Go,' he says. 'You wouldn't want her to turn up and find no one there, would you?'

She walks along the path feeling a thousand years old, her shoulders hunched forward, steps a little unsteady. The cold nips her hands even though they're in her pockets. She didn't spare the time to search for her gloves. A policeman guarding the entrance to the alleyway nods briefly before letting her pass. Without a second's thought, she turns right and walks up to the gates of number 55. She jabs her finger against the bell.

'Yeah, who is it?' Dexter's voice says.

She finds her voice. 'It's Lorna Chilcott. Can you let me in, please?'

The intercom buzzes. Lorna passes through the sliding

gate and crosses the forecourt as the door swings open. The creamy luxury and vastness of Elise's house is, as always, an assault to the senses. The familiar scent of her favourite orange blossom diffuser, the perfect lighting, the limestone floor and sweep of stairs – it all makes Lorna suddenly, inappropriately yearn.

Elise is effortlessly chic in black leggings, a huge, roll-neck cream sweater and flip-flops, Dexter scruffy in low-slung jeans, T-shirt and leather slip-ons. Tattoos climb his arms. A winding tree, a scorpion, a guitar, the ink saturating his skin. Lorna pulls her eyes away and tries to speak, but once again the words don't come, just sensations of panic, catastrophe, disaster.

Upstairs, muted by soft furnishings and hardwood doors, Noah is having a paddy, his frustration exploding into anger. Lorna understands; she feels something similar building in the space between her shoulder blades, a suppressed frustration and fury.

Elise takes her in her arms. Lorna stiffens. 'We thought . . . We weren't sure what the police were doing on the heath. They are searching for Amy?'

'Yes.' Lorna wills Elise to let her go.

'Come into the kitchen.' Elise releases her. 'You're frozen. I'll make you a hot drink. Have you had anything to eat?'

Lorna doesn't answer. Noah is still yelling. Somewhere upstairs a door opens – 'Let me go! I hate you! Mamma . . .' – then closes again.

'My God,' Elise says. 'Sorry. I'll just run up and calm him down. He isn't great in the morning.' She swivels abruptly towards her husband. 'Pour Lorna a coffee.' And then she's gone, feet barely making a sound on the lushly carpeted stairs.

Lorna silently follows Dexter into the back of the house. She watches him pick up the cafetière and pour steaming coffee into a plain white mug. Elise told her with a wink that the china is from IKEA. Why does she keep noticing these stupid details?

'I don't want a coffee,' she says.

'No?' He had been about to hand it to her, but he sets it down on the side. He looks like he wishes he was anywhere but here, in this room. 'Are you okay?'

'Am I okay?' She looks down at her trembling hands and thinks about it. Her breath is coming hard. She lifts her gaze to his face. Something about it lights a touchpaper. It detonates the bomb inside her. Noah is bawling, trying to explain his grievances, his reedy voice getting under her skin. 'No, I am not fucking okay. It's your fault Amy is missing. Your fault if she's hurt. I will never forgive you if anything's happened to her. How could you?'

'That isn't fair.'

'Not fair? I'll give you fair.' She pushes him, her hands on his chest, but he's already leaning against the counter, so she's blocked. She breaks down, curling her hands into fists, all control gone as her shoulders shake and her chest convulses. Dexter hesitates, then folds his arms around her.

'Hey.' He awkwardly pats her back. Her wet face is pressed against his chest. The T-shirt doesn't smell clean, more like he's slept in it. His heart beats against her cheekbone. 'They'll find her,' he says. 'Come on, love. You're from the north. You're stronger than this.'

Lorna chokes on a laugh swollen with tears. She pulls away from him and wipes her eyes on the back on her hand. 'Sorry.'

'Don't apologise. I get it.' He grips her shoulders and stoops to look directly into her eyes. 'I admire you, Lorna. You're brave and strong and I'm here for you, okay?'

It feels like he's going to kiss her, the thread between them is so taut, so tense. Overwhelmed, she stammers something, but then they hear Elise approaching and he lets her go.

'Hey,' Elise says gently. 'Sit down, Lorna. We can talk.'

'Sorry. I need to get home.' Lorna doesn't know what to do with her hands, so she traps them under her arms.

'You will let me know ...' Elise allows the sentence to trail off. *If there's good news or bad?* is not a question anyone wants to respond to. Lorna's misery, held at bay for a moment, washes back in.

'I've got to go,' she blurts.

When Elise walks Lorna out of the main gate, there's a police car parked outside the flats opposite. Lorna stops and stares, her mind thrashing through possibilities.

Could Amy have been tempted inside after she left the Coleridges'? Perhaps she was crying and one of the residents spoke to her in the street. Perhaps they've spoken previously, bumping into each other before or after Amy's singing lesson. Lorna tries to picture the group who came to Elise and Dexter's housewarming. There were several young men among them. She wants to march across the road, to demand answers, but she knows that she would be hustled away, treated like she's the one in the wrong.

The policeman who'd been at the entrance to the alley-way has left his post. She wonders why, then sees that he's at the other end talking to a dog-walker. She's about to cross the road to get to her car when Dexter catches her up. He's thrown on a jacket.

'I need to say something,' he says.

Her spirits soar, then drop in a lurch that nearly floors her. She presses the fob; the locks click and the wing mirrors turn, like hands opening in supplication.

'I saw Matt.'

She swings round. 'What?'

'About ten minutes after Amy left, parked in Griffiths Lane.'

She frowns. 'What was he doing?'

'Nothing. Just sitting there.'

'Why didn't you say something before?'

'I've only just remembered.'

She hears a step and turns. Matt is hurrying up the alley. He stops short when he sees her.

'Why are you still here? I thought you were going home.'

'I—'

'I was just telling your wife,' Dexter interrupts, 'that I saw you in your car, in Griffiths Lane, around the time Amy went missing.'

Matt glares at him. 'What has that got to do with you?'

'Quite a lot, if I'm honest,' Dexter says coolly. 'As someone in the public eye, I'm going to bear the brunt of the media attention. I don't see why you should be off the hook. You're her stepdad. You have a lot of explaining to do.'

'Fuck you.'

Lorna is startled. Matt is not an aggressive man. She searches his face. The strain he's under shows in the deepening lines on his brow, the tension in his jaw. Dexter is being horrible, but he has a point. Matt knows that. Like it or not, his relationship to Amy will make a difference in the eyes of the police, and the public. It's why he sought to shift the focus to Dexter by making her produce the sketches.

'Hey. I get it, mate,' Dexter says, his voice even. 'I'd be the same if it was my daughter. I'm not making excuses. I didn't judge the situation as well as I should have. I want to help.'

Matt's face is puce, his eyes popping. Lorna is terrified he's going to have a heart attack. 'I'm not your mate and I don't want your help. You were the one who called my daughter talentless and let her leave your house distressed. And if you saw me, *mate*, I'd like to know what you were doing out and about when my daughter vanished?'

'Elise ticked me off about my behaviour. I'm not at my best when I'm pissed off, so I took myself out of the situation – anger management, you know? I drove around until I'd cooled off. The police know about it.'

'Why didn't you tell me you were there?' Lorna asks Matt.

'I was going to.' His voice is sullen.

She doesn't believe him. She turns to Dexter. 'Perhaps you'd better go.'

Dexter responds by patting her arm reassuringly. It feels electric.

Matt launches himself at him. 'Don't you dare touch my wife.'

'Stop it! For God's sake.' Lorna gets between the pair of

them, pushing Matt away. She can feel the trembling deep in his chest. Dexter shrugs, then strolls back up the street, and Lorna hates herself for wanting him. She makes up for the thought by pulling a rigid Matt into her arms and holding him until he stops shaking.

Chapter 26

LORNA

They are home before Lorna can bring herself to speak. 'You told me you were still at work. Why did you lie?' Her surprise is genuine. Matt is a good man with a strong moral compass. She is sick with anxiety, staring into his eyes, willing him to have a decent excuse. Not a woman; something else, something he's ashamed of but she can take on board, maybe even laugh at when all this is over, when Amy has come home.

Matt picks up a Stanley tape measure from the kitchen counter and fiddles with it, drawing the tape in and out. She wants to scream at him to stop.

'I was going to tell you, but you were so worried about Amy, I decided to leave it for a better time.'

'A better time?' she says in disbelief. 'What better time could there be?'

'I'm sorry. I don't know what else to say.'

'Try.' She reaches for his hand and stills it, then prises the tape measure from his curled fingers and adds it to the collection of random small tools and stubby pencils that routinely drift in from his workshop.

Her mind scrolls through their female friends. Jules or Raisa? Unlikely. Someone else then. A client, maybe? He's a good-looking guy.

'I'll tell you,' he says. 'Just don't knee-jerk.'

'I'm listening.'

'Carolina, the client, made a pass at me.'

Okay, so she was right. It's still a shock.

'And?'

'And what?'

'Oh for God's sake, Matt. Were you tempted?'

'No, of course I wasn't,' he explodes. 'What do you think I am?'

'Is she attractive?'

'Yeah. You could say that.'

'So what? She flashed her cleavage? Asked you to inspect the wardrobe in her bedroom?'

Matt rolls his eyes, clearly finding the whole thing excruciating. 'Does it really matter what she did? The point is, I dealt with it badly.'

'I want to know.'

'Right. Well, she straight-up asked me.'

'Asked you what?'

He flinches. 'To have sex with her.'

'What did you say?'

'I mumbled something about having to go. I said sorry a lot.' His neck reddens. 'She apologised for getting the wrong idea and asked me if I was going to come back and finish the job.'

'And you said?'

'That I would be back. I had to get out of there.'

'So why not come straight home?'

137

'It's a long time since anything like that's happened to me. I needed to figure out how I gave her the idea that I might be open to ... well, you know.'

This would be hilarious if she wasn't in a state of acute anxiety. The irate wife and the penitent husband. 'Did you flirt with her?'

'I may have done, when I was trying to get the job. But I was just laying on the charm so she'd pick me.'

'You realise the police are bound to find out?'

He sighs. 'Give me Dutton's number. I'll call and explain.'

Lorna extracts PC Dutton's card from her bag. She holds it between her finger and thumb and doesn't let it go when Matt tries to take it.

'You promise it's the truth.'

'Darling, you know it is. You know me. I love you. Nothing is more important than our family.'

She leaves the room while he makes the call. She doesn't want to listen to him squirm, possibly even massage the truth to make himself look less bad. It's easy to imagine how it happened, how Matt might have brightened whenever Carolina came into the room; the banter. There is no way he didn't fancy her a bit. Lorna is used to believing that he has never looked at another woman, that he is as in love with her now as he was when they first met, but perhaps she's been deluding herself.

She thinks about the way Dexter gazed into her eyes at the housewarming, the way he held her when she was so angry and upset earlier, and shivers. Then she dissolves into tears again. Amy is missing. It's as though a tsunami is racing towards them and all they can do is wait for it to hit, and the hit will be the worst possible news. News that until now has always been about some other desperate couple's child.

Body found.

Don't think it. Please don't think it. But she can't help it. Two men, two scenarios.

What if Dexter saw Amy wandering around looking upset and wanted to apologise. He slowed his car and drove along beside her, window open, trying to talk her down. Perhaps she took evasive action by running onto the heath, and he stopped the car and went after her and they argued . . .

And then there's Matt, who has been shown to have lied. Lorna can imagine a scenario where Amy stormed out of 55 Gladwell Grove and for some reason headed to Griffiths Lane instead of home. She might have seen Matt parked at the side of the road, or he saw her. She got in and told him what had happened and cried on his shoulder. And then . . . No. She refuses to let her mind explore any further. It's vile to even think of Matt that way. He's explained. There has to be trust between them or everything will fall apart.

Chapter 27

THE PSYCHIATRIST

I don't think my flat has ever been so clean. Still in shock after Jeremy Osborne's call this morning, I've tidied and vacuumed and tackled the bathroom and kitchen. I've wiped inside the units and reorganised my fridge. As the day has dragged by, I've found things to do that I've never done before, like vacuum the top edge of the curtains and polish the light switches. I've swept the balcony and evicted the spider whose presence I've been tolerating for weeks. Last on my list is the cupboard under the stairs. It bothers me; the fuse going like that, and on the night I destroyed what was left of my credibility. I've been wondering if the stress of what had happened at work, the horror of not being believed by Belle, caused me to sleep-walk to my computer, write that load of garbage and send it. It just doesn't ring true.

I open the cupboard door and run my hands across my coats. The smartest is the cashmere and lambswool one I wear for work events, where I need to look groomed. It's long, coffee-coloured, with a velvet collar and a belt, and it cost a small fortune. I heave an armful of coats off the rail, carry them to the sitting room and dump them on the sofa.

The velvet-collared coat I take upstairs to lay flat over the spare-room bed. Smoothing it out, my eye is caught by a stray hair on one of the sleeves. The hair is blonde, so not one of mine, and certainly not Dylan's. My brain races to make sense of this.

The only other person who has been in my flat recently is Ben, and I remember taking his coat and hanging it over the banister. No way would I have put it in the cupboard, not when I expected him to leave any minute. It would have looked weird if I had. And even if he'd hung it in the cupboard himself, this particular coat wasn't there. I'd taken it to the dry-cleaner's a week ago, because I won't wear it again before winter. I picked it up yesterday. The implications make me let out my breath in a rush. Was he in the cupboard, messing about with the fuse box, while I wrote? Was he right there, wedged into the smallest space, while I flicked the switches? No wonder Dylan was spooked. I have so many questions. How long was he there for, and how the hell did he get in? Why would he do that, except to scare me? Was he planning to rape me again? What stopped him? Curiosity? Yes. That'll be it. He wanted to see what I'd spent hours typing. It's quiet up here, away from traffic noise. He would have been able to hear the tap of the keyboard. I imagine him opening the cupboard door, listening for signs I was awake, then creeping into the sitting room, opening my laptop and finding the email and document minimised. He'd have pulled out the chair and sat down. I picture him rolling up his sleeves and flexing his fingers. He'll have enjoyed every second.

I take an envelope from the desk drawer in the spare room, carefully pick the hair off the sleeve and drop it in, looking up at a sound from outside. Dylan screeching his displeasure. My cat is no pushover and has been known to get into spats with the local felines. I find him on the walkway, having a face-off with an exotic creature new to the estate. Its thick grey fur is charged with electricity.

'Right then, you two,' I say. 'Who started it?'

Dylan doesn't flinch, but his rival does, backing off and running to the far end, tail held high. Dylan nudges me with his head and meows plaintively.

'Yeah, yeah. Don't look at me like that. I don't believe you're entirely innocent.'

I'm about to go back in when movement in Gladwell Grove catches my attention. There's a jeep with its back doors open parked outside one of the houses. The flats, in fact. A tenant is either moving in or out. Then a man appears, and my nerves crackle. It's Ben. He's carrying a box, which he loads into the back.

My eyes widen. Ben is leaving Gladwell Grove. Before I can even consider what I'm doing, I scoot inside and pull on my trainers. I fly down the stairs and across the car park, hitting the street at full pelt just as Ben closes the jeep's doors and goes back inside, presumably for a last check.

When he reappears, he takes one look at me, still gasping for breath, and tuts. 'You're a mess.'

'Sorry.' I roll my eyes, 'Should I have prettied myself up for you?'

'Does anyone else know what a total bitch you are?' He delivers the line like he's expecting applause.

'What were you doing in my flat last night?'

'I've been nowhere near it.'

'You're lying. You were hiding in my coat cupboard.'

There is a dangerous light in his eyes. 'You're deranged.'

'Ben. I found one of your hairs on a coat sleeve.'

'Don't be ridiculous. It could be anyone's. And even if it is, no one's questioning that I've been in your flat and your bed. You hung my coat in your cupboard. The hair could have got transferred from mine to one of yours.'

'Except the coat came from the dry-cleaner's yesterday. I haven't washed my sheet and duvet cover from the night you drugged and raped me. Did you think I would? The police only have to compare the DNA.'

Ben gives me a smile that oozes contempt. 'That's a bit desperate, don't you think? I expect my hair was on the pillow and you kept it in case you needed it. No one's going to believe you.'

'I'll take that risk. I don't have much more to lose, thanks to you.'

He is standing with his legs apart, hands on hips, his face animated with triumph and aggression. 'You are nothing,' he hisses. 'I can do what I like, when I like. You may think you've seen the last of me, but I'll be watching you. I'll never let you go.'

Something distracts me, the sound of electronic gates opening on their sliders. I turn, and my mouth drops open.

A woman walks out pushing a buggy with a small boy in it. She's immaculate, and clearly very wealthy, or she wouldn't live in this street or that particular house, and for a moment there . . . for a moment . . .

While I'm distracted, Ben gets into the jeep and slams the door. I bang on the window and pull at the handle, but he accelerates away faster than I expected and I lose my grip. I cry out as I stumble back, grasping the wrought-iron gate to steady myself, but it swings open and I fall, whacking my hip and embedding grit into the palm of my hand. Slowing at the corner, he stretches his arm out of the window and gives me an ironically cheery wave.

'Everything okay?' the woman calls as she hurries across the road.

'Fine. I'm fine. Just tripped.' I struggle to my feet, brushing the dust from my clothes, flinching at the stains on my sweatpants.

'Do you need help? There's a shelter in East Alverley if you're . . . if you're in trouble. I can call an Uber for you.'

'I'm not homeless,' I say, appalled.

'No, I meant . . . It's for victims of abuse. That man . . .' She's tying herself in knots.

'It's okay. I can manage.'

The woman narrows her eyes. 'Do I know you?'

'I don't think so, no.'

'But I do. Didn't you used to . . .' She hesitates, then leans over the pushchair, adjusting the little boy's straps to hide her embarrassment. 'Well, nice to meet you.'

I say nothing as I turn away, and then feel mean because she stopped to help and I was ungracious. It's too late to rectify that. She's almost at the end of the road. I don't recognise her, but then the affluent young mothers round here all look the same to me.

Someone moves in the first-floor window of the flats. On impulse, I walk back up the path and ring the bell. Footsteps pound downstairs. The front door is opened by a clean-shaven young man wearing a smart shirt, scruffy jeans and leather slippers.

'Are you the psychiatrist?' he asks.

'I used to be,' I say, surprised into honesty.

Chapter 28

THE PSYCHIATRIST

Ben's ex-flatmate folds a piece of kitchen towel, runs warm water over it and hands it to me. I dab my palm, removing the grit.

'I bet that stings,' he says. His name, he told me a few minutes ago, is Tom.

Tom comes from Buckinghamshire, although his dad is from Ireland. He works for HSBC. Loves rugby. He has an open, friendly face and likes to chat.

'Did you know he'd be moving out today?'

'Ah. No. He's kind of left us in the lurch.'

When I walked through the front door, it was a shock. I lived in this house for two years. I spent the entirety of my marriage to Daniel here, picked our post up off the same mat. Daniel used to carry his bike up the stairs, occasionally scuffing the wall with the handlebars. The marks are still there. The only flats in a street of incredibly expensive houses, I used to imagine we were resented for lowering the tone with our stack of four doorbells, four sets of each category of bin, rarely swept front and regular turnover of tenants.

I glance at Tom. He's leaning against the counter. 'Do

you mind if I ask you what he was like to live with?'

'Mmm.' Tom considers the question. 'He was quiet and tidy. The perfect flatmate.'

There is something in his tone, a hint that Ben is someone you need to be wary of. 'You didn't like him.'

'Not especially. You felt you were on trial with Ben. Not about whether you were nice or not, more like were you useful to him or not. I came under the *or not* category. We got along... It's hard to explain. I don't think Ben feels attachment to other people, but he has no trouble with women.'

'He had girlfriends?'

'Depends on what you mean by that. He went out with girls, but he never brought one back here. Not as far as I know, anyway.'

'Did he stay over with them?'

Tom thought for a moment. 'No, I don't think he spent a single night away, unless it happened the times I went home.' He's still young enough to consider his parents' house his home. That's sweet. 'He never talked about it if he did. He's either a gentleman or he doesn't care. I'm not sure he cares about much.'

'Probably a good thing in his business. Being cut-throat, I mean.'

'Security? I suppose you could say that.'

'Oh. I thought he worked in finance.'

'Nah-ah.' Tom seems delighted to know something I don't. 'He runs a rent-a-muscle outfit – an agency for security guys, bouncers, bodyguards. That kind of thing.'

Wow. One more thing about my patient that wasn't true. 'Do you know the name of the company?'

147

'Not got a clue.'

'Or where it is?'

'Uh . . . no. South London? I don't think he ever told me.'

'Would you mind if I take a quick peek in his room?'

Tom's smile slips. I've gone too far. Even good-natured people-pleasers have their limits. 'Why?'

'There might be a clue to where he works.'

'He obviously doesn't want you to find him, or he'd have told you where he was.'

'No, I know. But I'm worried about him.' I pause. 'Why did you ask me if I was the psychiatrist? I could have been anyone.'

'Because he pointed out where you lived. He said you were watching him. Is he paranoid? Is that why he was seeing you?'

'You know I can't answer that. Look, do you mind? I won't touch anything.'

Tom shrugs. 'I guess it's nothing to do with me. Knock yourself out. His is the room on the other side of the hall.'

Chapter 29

THE PSYCHIATRIST

Ben's room is clean and orderly, the chair pushed under the desk, the cupboard doors closed. I glance out of the window onto the side return. Our dining room was directly above this, so the view is the same and nothing has changed. It's still a neglected space with the same weeds pushing up between the same cracks in the concrete. Nothing to feel nostalgic for, especially since we didn't have access to the garden; we used the heath when we wanted to get out.

I pull out the stationery drawer under Ben's desk. Not even a forgotten biro. Underneath that, in the filing cabinet, the hanging folders have also been emptied, but when I slide them aside, I find a forgotten invoice. On it is the name of a company, Vigour Security, and an address in Croydon.

Later that day, I stuff the bag containing my bed linen into a tote and make my way to the police station. When I state my business, that I'm here to report a sexual assault, I'm asked if I'd prefer a female officer, and I say I would. I'm asked if I'm injured, and when I say I'm not, I'm told to wait until someone appropriate becomes available. Ten minutes later, I follow PC Innes down a corridor and enter an interview room. I take a seat and remind myself that I'm not here because I've done something bad, I'm here because someone has done something bad to me. I tell her everything I remember about that evening, ending with Ben's accusation and my conviction that he spiked my drink.

'Since then, I believe he's been stalking me.' I hand her the envelope containing his hair and explain about the fuse going in the coat cupboard and my belief that he was there for at least part of that night. To all of this she listens attentively. Finally I pull the tote bag off the back of the chair and put it on the table between us. 'This is the sheet from my bed. It has Ben Clarkson's DNA on it. If you compare it with the hair, that means he's been in my flat since he assaulted me.'

'Are you okay?' she asks.

I look into her eyes, expecting scepticism, but the look she returns is frank and sympathetic. 'I'm coping.'

'Did he use protection?'

'I'm not sure, but I don't think so. There was stickiness between my legs. And nothing in the bin, though I suppose he could have flushed a condom down the loo.' I feel a wave of visceral disgust, heat sweeping my body.

'You should see a doctor. Just in case. Are you worried about pregnancy?'

'No, I'm on the pill.'

'Ah, so you're in a relationship?'

'No. I take precautions because I occasionally use online dating sites and I want to be in control. I make sure the man uses a condom, but I don't one hundred per cent trust them. The condoms, I mean.'

'Understandable.' Innes taps her fingers on the table. 'Dr Geddes, how did Ben get in? Presumably he didn't force entry or you'd have reported it immediately.'

'I haven't worked that out yet.' Something in her face stops me going on. The sympathy is beginning to look forced. 'What does that mean?'

'I beg your pardon?'

'You grimaced. I am telling the truth.'

'I apologise. I didn't mean to. I'm very sorry you've been through this and I want you to know that I'll do my best.' She pauses, and I wait for the qualification. 'But you need to understand how hard it is to make a rape charge stick, especially when, as in your case, an accusation has already been made against you. It could be perceived as trying to evade the consequences of your actions, or even revenge. Body fluids on a sheet do not prove rape, only that Ben Clarkson was in your bed. If you press charges, it's unlikely the CPS will allow it to go to court. They don't have a great record on rape charges at the best of times. In your circumstances, as someone in a position of power over a vulnerable young man, your chances of getting what you want are vanishingly slight.' She nudges the tote with the sheet in it towards me. 'I know this is not what you wanted to hear, and I'm very sorry. Talk to a lawyer. I can give you contact details if you don't have one. Take some time to think and come back to me if you want to pursue this. If that's the case, I'll do the best I can.'

'What if he does it again, to someone else?'

'There is nothing I can do about that without proof he raped you, and as he isn't denying having sex with you, that is going to be next-to-impossible to obtain.' She must have seen something in my expression, because she narrows her eyes and adds, 'I hope you're not intending to approach Mr Clarkson.'

'Absolutely not.'

'Because that would be extremely unwise.'

Chapter 30

LORNA

Another night without Amy has nearly killed her. Lying in bed, remembering the time when it was just the two of them, silent tears rolled down her cheeks. She thought Matt was asleep, but he rolled over and drew her into the crook of his body. She put up with it for barely a minute before gently pushing him away. It was kind, but it was also oppressive. She got up for a while, and when she was ready to try to sleep again, it was Amy's bed she fell into, dropping off sometime after four and waking when Matt started moving around. Together they'd silently got Jack up, fed and dressed and dropped him off at nursery.

Now she's waiting for Matt in the police station while he's questioned. Waiting and wondering, jerking her head up every time the door to the back offices opens.

He comes out after an hour, looking pale and frayed. Keith, Jules's lawyer husband, is with him. Lorna is so relieved when she learns he hasn't been charged that she bursts into tears.

'What happens now?' she asks.

Matt doesn't speak, so Keith fills her in.

'You wait. There's nothing else you can do. I would

advise you to keep out of the way, though.' He pauses. 'Don't join the search or even hang around on the edges. Perpetrators are well known to return to the scene of their crime.'

Matt looks at him in disgust and Keith raises his palms. 'I'm saying it for your own good. People will naturally be suspicious. Don't give them cause.'

Back at the house, they don't speak to each other. There doesn't seem any point. What would they even say? Matt switches on the radio, and Lorna goes upstairs to Amy's bedroom. She crawls back into the bed and pulls the pillow into her arms.

Why did she get involved with the Coleridges? She should have anticipated that nothing good could come of it. They are out of her league. Seduced by the friendship, she didn't for one minute consider that people who can afford to blow seven million on a family home and a further million renovating it do not live on the same planet as normal people. Elise made friends with Lorna because she was lonely, a Rapunzel figure in her ivory tower. But she blithely betrayed Lorna's trust, taking up a precious place at Alverley School, a place that by rights belongs to Jack.

And then there's the problem of Dexter. Yesterday when he held her and comforted her, something passed between them, a silent acknowledgement that they *saw* each other. She closes her eyes and allows herself to be borne into a daydream where Dexter finds Amy, alive but weak, carries her into the house and lays her on the sofa. Matt isn't there and Elise is absent from the picture too; it's just Lorna trembling with relief in Dexter's arms while

154

Amy sleeps on, oblivious, sirens blaring as the emergency services close in.

She brusquely flings the pillow aside and gets up. She does not need these treacherous feelings, this conflict. She needs the steadiness of Matt, not the tumbling rockfall of an affair with Dexter. She should not have reminded him they'd had sex after that gig. It was a dangerous thing to do because it makes her vulnerable.

Her phone rings, and she almost drops it when she sees it's Elise.

'Yes?'

'I don't know whether they've told you, but there are divers in the lake . . . Lorna? Are you okay.'

Lorna has sat down hard. 'I heard you,' she manages. 'Thank you for letting me know.'

She runs downstairs and puts on her coat and trainers. Matt comes out of the kitchen.

'Where're you going?'

'Elise called. She says there are divers in the lake.' She chokes on the words. 'If Amy is pulled out, I want to be there. I want to be the one to hold her.'

'What about what Keith said?'

'I don't give a shit.' She shouts the words, and Matt takes a step back, shocked.

'Then I'm coming with you.'

It's called a lake, but it's more of a large pond, the size of a public swimming pool and loosely kidney-shaped, a man-made feature from Victorian times with reeds thronging its banks and weathered wooden jetties for walkers to inhale nature from. This area of the heath is curated but no

155

less beautiful for it. Lorna and Matt watch the police team from a distance, trying not to be conspicuous, sunglasses and woolly hats disguising them. Lorna is barely holding it together, imagining a fist punching out of the water, like they do on TV. That shout. Her breath shortens.

Beside her, Matt swears. She turns to see what he's looking at. Dexter and Elise are striding along the path. Elise squints at them, unsure, then raises her hand and waves.

'Are they mad?' Matt says.

'It'll be down to Elise.'

There's no way Dexter would choose to do this. He looks utterly miserable, his hands shoved deep in the pockets of his jacket, his head hunched between his shoulders. He must be so conflicted, hating her for dragging him into this mess but wanting her as well. She feels that way too, hating and wanting at the same time. It isn't love, she tells herself. Just a powerful animal urge.

Elise hurries up to her and hugs her, ignoring the stiffness in Lorna's body. Dexter and Matt behave like a couple of tomcats. Their hostility is palpable. She imagines the angry hiss, the slash of a paw.

'We thought you might need support,' Elise says.

Dexter is looking at her. Lorna can feel it. She pulls her gaze from Elise and frowns at him, wanting to convey a strong message. *Please do not stare at me like that.* But he returns her frown with a look of such profound sympathy and understanding that she almost cracks.

'Photographers,' Elise says sharply.

The press have temporarily abandoned their positions round the lake and are taking pictures of the two couples.

Elise links her arm through Matt's and walks away, leaving Lorna alone with Dexter. Is this deliberate? Be seen and photographed supporting the poor Chilcotts. She hopes not, but knows they'll be hyper-aware of the optics. Someone in Dexter's position wouldn't show his face if he was guilty.

'Lorna,' Dexter says. 'I—'

'It can't happen.' Surely he has the sense to know that things can't go any further between them? 'I'm so sorry, Dexter, but I have to put my family first.'

His brows lift against the hem of his beanie. He looks bewildered. 'What're you on about?'

She goes pink. Has she got it wrong? 'Nothing.'

'No,' he says. 'Tell me what you meant.'

'We kissed. At your housewarming.'

He is visibly taken aback. 'If we did, I was off my trolley.'

She shakes her head. 'We talked for ages.' She stares at him in dismay. 'And yesterday, the way you held me and looked at me.' She feels like she's losing her grip. 'What you said to me.'

'Jesus. I didn't mean . . . I just felt sorry for you.' He pulls off the beanie and scratches his head, his hair tufting up under his restless fingers, then he shudders. 'Christ in heaven, what is wrong with you? Your daughter is missing.' He strides away from her, muttering, 'Stupid cow,' leaving her standing there wanting to vomit.

In the next second, she hears a shout and whirls round. A diver has surfaced, hand raised. Lorna sinks to her knees with a cry of anguish. Dexter comes running back.

'It might not be Amy,' he says.

Matt, who has arrived at her side with Elise, drops

down beside her and takes her in his arms, rocking her against him.

'I think we should leave,' Dexter says.

Matt rounds on him. 'This is your fault.'

'That is unfair,' Elise says. 'You cannot put this on us.'

'You want to bet?'

'Lorna,' Elise says gently. 'We'll go, because we're obviously not welcome, but I want you to know that I'm here if you need me.'

Out in the lake, two divers are towing something towards the bank. Lorna pushes Matt away and jumps up, but he grasps her wrist, pulling her back.

'You can't go crashing into this. They know we're here. They'll come to us.'

'She's my daughter!' Lorna screams, clawing at his hands. 'Let go of me!'

He gets to his feet and pins her against him so tightly she cannot move except to batter his shoulder with her head. His heart is racing as fast as hers, his breath shallow. She howls into his chest. And then he lets go of her.

'Oh Christ,' he breathes.

They've lifted the body out of the water. The scene-of-crime team converge around it. Lorna and Matt start to run. They're caught by four officers. Held by strong arms, Lorna strains, yelling at them to let her go.

Chapter 31

THE PSYCHIATRIST

Leaving East Croydon station, I take out my phone and check directions on the map. It's only a ten-minute walk to the offices of Vigour Security. I could do with it being further, and consider a coffee at Boxpark, because I'm in no hurry for my next encounter with Ben. But I'm here now. I need to do this. I wait for a tram to move on, then cross the road and head down a side street.

I've asked myself the same question over and over again. Why is Ben Clarkson targeting me like this? Is it personal, or was I simply in the wrong place at the wrong time? Is this just the way he gets his kicks?

Ben's jeep is parked to the side of a modest Victorian industrial building on two floors. The brick exterior is emblazoned with graffiti. There's no light on downstairs, but upstairs someone is in. There are buttons on the door, but it hasn't been closed properly so I'm able to enter without announcing my presence. A grubby flight of stairs, painted with grey floor paint, leads up to a small landing with two doors leading off it. One is clearly a toilet; the other has a glass panel through which I can see two men. I recognise Ben even though he has his back to me. He's seated at a desk. The other guy, also with his back to me, is standing with his legs apart, his arms crossed, studying a table of names and addresses ruled in blue marker pen on a whiteboard.

It's taken me an hour and a half to get here and I am desperately, inconveniently, in need of a pee.

I use the toilet, then wash my hands and shake them before blotting them on the back of my jeans. I don't use the hand dryer in case they hear it; I'd rather enter the room on my own terms. As I turn to go, the door opens and I'm confronted by Ben's colleague, already unzipping his fly. He zips it back up and crosses his arms, and I see that he has a tattoo of an eagle on the back of his hand. I keep very still, but inside I am freaking out, my heart jumping so hard I'm scared it's going to crack my ribcage. I've seen that tattoo before: on the hand of the man who mugged me on the heath.

'Here to see the boss?' he asks, raising an eyebrow. He is smirking as he steps closer, blocking my exit.

'Yes. Sorry. I needed to nip in here first.'

I am so scared; even more so than when he attacked me on the heath. That incident happened so quickly there was no time to feel fear. The rush of blood is loud in my ears. My desire to confront Ben has gone, replaced by an urgent need to get out of this place.

He waits a moment, staring at me in an unnerving way, then moves to one side with a shrug. He continues to stare as I walk out and reach for the other door. I make as though to push it open, then throw myself down the stairs and into the street. He comes after me, but he doesn't follow for long, his need to relieve himself presumably getting the better of him. By the time I reach the station, I have a stitch that folds me double outside the barriers. I grip my waist and slap my debit card on the reader, then turn to see Ben sprinting towards me. I push through the barrier and run to a guard.

'Clapham Junction?'

'Platform 1,' he says, nodding to the left.

I dart down the slope. My train is already there. I won't look back. There's no point. I reach the platform and jump on, willing the doors to close behind me. Ben charges towards the train, but he's too late. Apoplectic with fury, he slams his hand against the moving window and practically snarls at me as I collapse breathless onto a seat. As my fear abates, I chide myself: I should have stopped and demanded answers, not panicked. Still, I've linked him to the man who mugged me. That's got to count for something, if only to confirm that he had me in his sights before the day we met. If that smug bastard thought he could upend my life and disappear, he now knows it's not that easy.

Chapter 32

LORNA

'It isn't Amy,' PC Carter says. 'By the looks of it, the deceased has been in the water for several months. And it's an older person. I'm sorry you had to go through that.'

Lorna feels her body's workings with an unfamiliar intensity, so much so that it's almost as though she could switch each vital organ off at will. Perhaps if it had been Amy she would have done. Whoever it is, she's sorry they ended up this way, but she can't waste precious energy on them. She tries Amy's phone again. Nothing.

She and Matt trudge home. She collapses onto the sofa and pulls the woollen throw over her. Now that the upsurge of panic and euphoria has evaporated, she remembers what she said to Dexter, and how he responded, and breaks out in a cold sweat.

She looks up to see a camera trained on her from the street. Startled, she screams and runs through the kitchen and into the garden, bursting into Matt's workshop.

'There's someone taking pictures.'

'Fuck. Did you close the curtains?'

'No. I was too shocked. Can you?'

He grunts his assent. Lorna follows him into the house

162

and waits, twitching, in the kitchen. When he reappears, he gives a despairing shrug. She both wishes he'd stay with her and hopes he won't. He doesn't. He gives her shoulder a squeeze and goes back out to the workshop, and she opens her laptop. In these circumstances, when they're the ones in the news, it's as painful as eavesdropping and as foolish, but she cannot help it. Amy's name is all over social media, and now both Dexter Coleridge and Matt Chilcott are trending. So are the words *fifteen years old* and *stepdaughter*. The mood has turned and Matt is the evil one, Dexter the saint. His acolytes, women of Lorna's age, have come out of the woodwork in their legions to defend him and shit all over her husband.

She was his stepdaughter ffs. Did no one see that coming?
Should be castrated.
Shades of Billie-Jo Jenkins?
What's he done with the body?
LOL. Buried under the patio?

It's a free-for-all toxic dump on Matt, the nicest guy she's ever met. She hopes he's not doing the same as her. He's never been near social media, but still . . . If he has any sense, he'll be losing himself in his work.

She scrolls down. A tweet with a link directs her to an article in the MailOnline.

MISSING AMY: STEPFATHER
LIED ABOUT HIS ALIBI

Matt Chilcott (38), who married Amy's mother when
Amy was seven years old, has admitted to investigating

officers that he was not at work when Amy was last seen, leaving the house of former D.I.G.B.Y. lead singer Dexter Coleridge.

Who would have leaked this? She grimaces. It could only have been Dexter and Elise. Or more likely Dexter's PR machine rolling into the mess. Shifting the focus from their golden goose onto the stepfather.

Before turning his hand to carpentry, Chilcott was a secondary school teacher. He left teaching citing stress, but sources who knew him at the time say there was trouble with a pupil who accused him of inappropriate behaviour. The teenager retracted her accusation when it was proven that she had never been alone with him. There is no suggestion that Chilcott has been sexually abusing his stepdaughter . . .

Who do they mean by 'sources'? Matt's ex-colleagues? Other parents? Lorna stares at the screen until the words blur. The absolute fucking bastards. And the journalists. They know what they're doing, smearing a man's name before he's charged with anything. They want to get it said before he's exonerated because it sells copies. It's disgusting.

Poor Matt, to have those things about himself raked up, things long buried. He was wrongly accused by a petulant schoolgirl. It happened several years before she met him, and he'd told her when they first got together, wanting her to find out from him rather than some shit-stirring so-called friend. It puts him in an appalling position. People won't listen; they'll just want to bring him down. No wonder he didn't tell the truth about his whereabouts. He knew this would come up.

Miriam messages her at three, saying that she's very sorry, but she has a tummy bug and can't pick Jack up from nursery. Paranoid, Lorna wonders is if she's lying, if the truth is that Miriam believes what's being said about Matt. No, surely not.

She'll ask Jules to help. Her finger hovers over her friend's name. She leaves the phone on the table and goes into the front room, peeking through the curtains. There are journalists milling around. A gathering of sharks waiting for prey. And she's hiding behind her curtains like she's ashamed. She'll go and pick Jack up herself. If she leaves early enough, she can call for Raisa and Jules on the way. Their presence will give her courage. She hasn't heard from Raisa since before all this kicked off. She'll apologise, clear the air. Raisa will understand.

Raisa's husband tells her, his neck reddening, that Raisa has already left. Lorna knows he's lying. Beyond him the kitchen door is closed, which it never is. She can feel Raisa hiding behind it.

'Sorry,' he mutters, then briefly pulls his lips between his teeth. 'You'll see her in the playground, I expect.'

She doesn't want to go through this again, so she messages Jules to tell her she's on her way, and when she gets there, her friend is waiting for her at the door.

'Courage, darling,' Jules says. 'Everyone knows Matt hasn't done anything wrong.'

Lorna will take anything that will stop her tipping into the abyss, so she nods mutely and they set off, Jules close enough that their shoulders brush from time to time.

At the nursery gates, an eager press is being held at bay by the manager. You really wouldn't want to argue with Mrs Bayliss. She can show her claws in defence of her little realm when she needs to. She can't stop the journalists talking to the parents, though, and Lorna shrinks when she sees how many are happy to do so.

She spots Raisa talking to another mother by the door and realises, with a shudder of guilt, that she was wrong about her. She catches her eye, but Raisa looks away.

'Everyone's staring,' she says to Jules.

'Ignore them. You can't blame them for being curious. It's all anyone is talking about.'

Not to me, Lorna thinks. A lot of them had joined the search on the heath. They don't approach her now.

'Can you tell us how you feel about the allegations made against your husband?' a journalist asks.

'Fuck off, why don't you,' Jules says.

'Nice language outside a nursery school, love.'

They scoop up their children and leave the school premises, Lorna tight-lipped. She can feel the burn of eyes on her, but she won't look up or round. She keeps going, pushchair wheels rattling over the pavement, Jules trotting to keep up with her.

'Do you want to come in?' Jules asks when they reach her front door.

'No. But thank you for walking with me. Not everyone would.'

166

'Well, I'm not everyone. Let me know if you want me to take Jack in in the morning. Be strong.'

How can she be strong when she feels like a dead man walking? Her life has collapsed, her beloved daughter gone for two nights now. She has tried not to imagine what might be happening to Amy, what kind of person she might be with, but it's all there, in the back of her mind. The terror gnaws at her minute by minute, hour by hour. She is losing everything that means anything to her. Amy's absence has pulled away the foundations that under-pinned her life. She feels exposed, and can only guess how much more agonising this must be for her husband. This is the end of their warm, happy, safe little life, and the begin-ning of something more dangerous than they can ever hope to deal with.

As she turns into Bramcote Avenue, the first thing she sees is the journalists. The second is the figure walking towards her on the opposite side of the road.

She stops in her tracks, unable to breathe, narrowing her eyes to squint through the sudden hot brim of tears.

'Mummy, Amy!' Jack yells, pulling frantically at his safety harness. 'Mummy, out!'

If it's possible for the world to slow down, then Lorna experiences it in that moment. Even a pigeon taking off from the pavement seems lethargic.

The girl has a baseball cap pulled down hard on her head, but it didn't fool her little brother and can't disguise her from Lorna. She knows Amy's gait, the way she keeps one hand in her pocket, the other clutching the strap of her bag. She knows those down-at-heel Doc Martens. She waits, still not wanting to believe it in case this is a trick of the brain, a brain that so desperately wants it to be her daughter, more desperately than she has ever wanted anything in her entire life. Then, gripping the pushchair handles, she starts to run.

Chapter 33

LORNA

Everything seems to happen at once. Lorna is running; the journalists, alerted, switch direction and jog towards her daughter. Amy stops short, her mouth hanging open. Lorna shouts at them to get out of her way, manoeuvring the pushchair like she's on a shopping trolley challenge, Jack still fighting with his harness.

Holding onto the pushchair with one hand, she wraps an arm protectively around Amy and shows the press pack the flat of her palm. 'Give us space,' she says fiercely. 'Leave us alone.'

Amy buries her head in Lorna's shoulder, the baseball cap scratching her neck. Lorna smells an unfamiliar shampoo in her daughter's hair, an unfamiliar soap on her skin. It feels like there are voices everywhere, ricocheting off the parked cars, the terraced houses. A confusion of sound that resolves into one name.

'Amy!'

Then the questions start coming.

'Amy, where have you been?'

'Have you been held against your will?'

'Was it a man, Amy?'

'Are you hurt?'

'Do you know how much trouble you've caused? Your stepdad's been hung out to dry.'

Amy is whimpering. She grabs Lorna's hand, something she hasn't done in years. Her hands are slimmer and smaller than Lorna's; Lorna recognises the shape of them, the bones beneath the soft skin, and breathes out a sigh as her daughter's heat mingles with hers. She reluctantly detaches herself, sets her chin and marches the last few yards, her door key held ready between her fingers as she leans over Jack. She thrusts Amy into the house, then slams the door behind them. Jack raises his arms and kicks to be let out. Amy unclips his harness and pulls him into her arms. He grabs hold of her hair.

'Oh my God,' she says, looking at Lorna over Jack's head. 'I'm so sorry.'

'It doesn't matter. Honestly, darling, I'm just relieved you're back.' Lorna's smile is so wide it hurts her face. She is about to ask Amy if she wants a bath, because that's the kind of thing you do with someone who's returned from God knows where, then thinks: forensics. Better wait until she's sure no one's touched her. She looks okay physically, and she's not falling apart, but that doesn't mean nothing's happened.

'Are you ...' She hesitates. 'I mean, are you hurt? Did anyone ...'

'No,' Amy says, flushing. 'I'm fine.'

'Okay. The police will ask you, though.'

Amy's face tightens. 'It's horrible what they've been saying about Dad.'

170

'I know. But that's what happens these days. You'd better go and see him. He's been in bits.'

'Can you come with me?' Amy pleads.

Her mum shakes her head. 'You need to do this yourself. Be brave.'

'Where is he?'

'In his workshop.' She sees Amy falter and smiles encouragingly. 'Here, let me take Jack.'

Amy hands over her little brother and Lorna sets him on the ground.

'Mummy!'

'Yes, sweetie.'

'Amy came home.'

'She did, didn't she.' She crouches down and takes his hands. 'Mummy's happy. Are you happy too?'

Jack nods vigorously. 'Can I have a biscuit?'

Chapter 34

AMY

Her fingers rub at the pendant Daddy Pete gave her for her thirteenth birthday, a little gold disc about the size of her thumbnail with *The world is your oyster* engraved on it. She'd planned to come back tomorrow, but she'd failed to take into account how swiftly the situation would spiral out of control. Plus she'd been miserable on her own in Lily's grandmother's flat. It was so depressing. The power was off and there was no internet, and it smelt weird and pungent because the old lady had died in her bed and lain in it for two days before anyone noticed. Amy slept on the sofa. And Lily hadn't been able to come over, when she'd said she definitely would. Two nights was more than enough. She'd begun to question what she was doing, worrying everyone like that, and had to remind herself that Dexter had deliberately humiliated her, and it was her mother's fault, smarming round Elise, using Amy to worm herself into the Coleridges' life. It was creepy. It was also embarrassing when Amy babysat Amelie for Jules and Keith. They were obviously confused and hurt by Lorna's behaviour and said stuff that hinted at it. It was like they thought her mum had decided she was too good for them

172

because she was pals with celebrities. They all needed to learn a bit of humility. She didn't mean Matt to be dragged into it in this horrible way, though. He's done nothing wrong.

Anyway, the house clearance people are booked for Friday, so she wouldn't even have had a sofa after that.

Her dad's workshop is at the side of the garden, brick-built and about twenty foot long with a wooden door and two windows. Roses and honeysuckle cover its west-facing wall. Before he and her mum got married, her mum sold their pretty little worker's cottage in Hanwell and Matt sold his flat in Kennington. Amy had to move schools, but she hadn't much minded because she'd had her eye blacked by another pupil.

She has never bothered knocking on his workshop door before, always sure of her welcome. For once, she does, but he doesn't hear her. He's listening to music. Noughties stuff. She pushes the door open. Inside, it smells of wood and oil. He has his back to her, hunched over drawings with his pencil and ruler, the Streets playing 'Dry Your Eyes'. It's one of their favourite songs. They know all the words and normally she'd have sung along. The fact that her father is listening to it makes her feel even worse.

If she'd expected him to react like her mum, she's dis-appointed. Not just disappointed, scared. The shock on his face, the colour draining from his skin, his hand tightening around his stubby pencil while the veins in his neck stand out keep her glued to the threshold.

'I . . . I'm sorry I worried you,' she says. 'I . . . um. I didn't realise how bad it would be. I came home when I saw what they were saying about you.'

He doesn't move at first, then he puts the pencil down on the rough wooden shelf beside him, as though it's a weapon he's scared of using.

'Do you have any conception of what I've been through?'

'Er . . . yes.'

'Really?' He slaps his hand down on his drawings to emphasise his words. 'My name has been dragged through the mud, Amy. I've been called a paedophile, suspected of molesting you, murdering you. How could you be so stupid? You must have known what would happen.'

'I didn't. I'm sorry, Dad. I was upset.'

'Because some guy says you don't have enough talent? What you do when that happens is you work harder and prove them wrong. You do not waltz off in an almighty strop and leave your family churning around in a vast vat of shit. These have been the worst days of my entire life, of your mother's life too. How could you?'

'I didn't . . . I wasn't . . .' She wrings her hands. She'd expected a huge bear hug, not this cold heat.

'I hope it was worth it. Fuck!'

She flinches at the shout. 'I didn't mean for this to happen!'

'Well it did. Your coming back changes nothing. All that stuff on the internet, it's not going to go away. That is what is going to come up when people search for my name. When clients google me. *Paedo.* Do you think the truth is going to wipe that word from their minds? And just because you couldn't take a bit of criticism.'

She's disintegrating, tears pouring down her cheeks. She can't bear it. She *is* upset, extremely upset, but now he's making her excuses sound trivial, making her feel like an entitled brat. Is that what everyone is going to think? Her life is over.

'Oh God, come here.' He pulls her into his arms and hugs her so tightly she thinks she's going to break. 'I've been so worried. I thought . . . All those stories you hear, people saying they never thought it could happen to them. I thought it had happened to us. To you.'

'I'm sorry. I'm so sorry.'

He loosens his grip on her and looks straight into her face. 'Why, Amy? Was it something your mother and I did? I just want to understand.'

'No.' Still blubbing, Amy bawls the first thing to come to mind, the thing she'd hinted at to Lily, the only thing that will make her situation less brutal. 'He touched me.'

Her dad goes very still. 'Say that again.'

'Dexter touched me.'

'Are you telling the truth?'

She nods, choking on her tears.

'Amy,' Matt says sharply. He takes her shoulder and shakes it – and then her mum comes in.

Chapter 35

LORNA

Lorna slides a protective arm around her daughter's waist. Amy turns into her, sobbing, while Lorna glares at Matt, mouthing, *What have you said to her?*

He responds with an infinitesimal shake of his head. 'Where's Jack?'

'Watching *Bluey*. I can't leave him long. Tell me what's going on.'

Matt turns to Amy. 'Tell your mother what you just told me.'

Amy closes her eyes when she speaks. 'Dexter touched me.'

'But you said you were okay.'

'I don't mean while I was gone,' she responds with genuine horror. 'When I was at their house.'

'Oh.' Lorna seems to deflate. 'Touched you in what way?' Hold on, she thinks. Hold on. Do not overreact.

'He touched my breast.'

'Deliberately, or did he just brush you by mistake?'

'He rubbed his thumb over it.' Amy demonstrates rather than say the word *nipple* to her parents. 'I panicked and pushed him away. I told him to fuck off. I think that's why

176

he said I was crap when Elise came back in, because he was angry with me for rejecting him. I'm so sorry. I was always going to come back. I just needed some time alone. It was the wrong thing to do and really, really stupid, but I was in such a mess, and so ashamed.'

'You shouldn't feel ashamed. It wasn't your fault.'

'But I was wearing a tight top. And make-up. And he's always been a bit flirty with me.'

'Flirty?' Lorna doesn't miss Amy's sneaky glance. Assessing her mother. But for what? For sympathy and understanding, or for the level of her gullibility? Something isn't right. When has Dexter had the opportunity? As far as she knows, from what both Elise and Amy have said, Dexter hasn't been present at the singing lessons. 'I don't understand. Why did Elise leave the room?'

'That's what I'd like to know,' Matt says.

Amy sniffs. 'She went upstairs to talk to someone. The lady next door complaining about noise, I think. Dexter had come to get her because he couldn't deal with it. She was irritated about that.'

'Whose suggestion was it that Dexter stay in the room with you?' Matt's voice is cool, but Lorna can feel the restraint behind his question.

'His. He said he'd listen to me sing while she was gone.'

'I'll kill him.'

'Dad!'

'Okay, let's all calm down,' Lorna says. 'First things first, I'm going to call the police and let them know you're safe.'

PC Carter arrives half an hour later, bustling in with an air of authority Lorna hasn't see in her before. Perhaps she's

177

just delighted to be putting this to bed, or it's the prospect of reading Amy a lecture about wasting police time. Maybe it's simply because her sterner colleague isn't with her. They sit round the kitchen table, Amy drooping, Matt ramrod straight, his face betraying his bewilderment. Dexter or no Dexter, how could Amy do this to them?

'Right, Amy. I think you'd better tell me what happened, don't you?'

Lorna squeezes Amy's hand. 'Go on, darling.'

Amy explains, faltering. She refuses to name Lily; this was agreed with Lorna and Matt beforehand. She doesn't want to get her friend into trouble. Lorna is not happy with this, but there is little she can do. When Amy gets to the part where Dexter assaults her, she yawns. Lorna knows her daughter and this worries her. When she yawns in that particular way, while she's talking, it generally means she's either being evasive or a little economical with the truth.

On the other hand, she could just be tired.

'Amy, this is serious. A man's reputation and freedom are at stake. Are you sure he touched you deliberately, that it wasn't accidental?'

Amy's voice is small, but her words are clear. 'Dexter touched me, like I said. Why don't you believe me? Is it because he's rich and famous?'

'Amy.' There's a warning in Matt's voice.

'Sorry,' she says sulkily. 'I'm just tired. And I want a bath.'

'I'm sure you do, Amy,' Carter soothes. 'And I'm almost finished here. While ultimately it's the CPS's decision whether to press charges, they will take your views into account if you don't want to go any further with it. You needn't make a decision right now – I'm sure you and your parents need time to discuss this – but sooner rather than later. Shall we say tomorrow by midday?'

'What do you think?' Matt says. 'Do you believe her?'

They face each other across the kitchen table. This feels like one of those tiny shifts in the atmosphere, like the flap of a butterfly's wing. How they respond to the situation they now find themselves in will dictate the rest of their lives.

Lorna shakes off her thoughts. She's stressed and overthinking. 'Sometimes teenagers can build things out of proportion, and obviously I don't want Dexter to be wrongly accused if it was an accident, but if Amy wants to take it further, I'll support her, and so should you.'

'Why wouldn't I?'

She looks at him askance. 'Because you're not one hundred per cent sure.'

'And you are? You didn't answer my question. Do you believe her?'

She thinks about the way Dexter reacted when she told him there couldn't be anything between them, and inwardly winces. The derision in his voice. It was uncalled for. Maybe he does prefer young girls and Elise is simply camouflage. He needn't have humiliated her, though. She doesn't think she's ever hated anyone more than she hates Dexter Coleridge.

'I do.'

Matt rocks his head back and groans. 'What a fucking nightmare.' He pushes his chair away from the table and gets up. 'Well, if you're sure, then of course I'm behind you both.'

179

Chapter 36

THE PSYCHIATRIST

By the time I get back from Croydon, my euphoria has drained and I'm beginning to think more clearly. The man who mugged me works for Ben. Does that mean Ben arranged the attack? He must have. The alternative is too much of a coincidence. What did he have to gain? My phone? It has my life on it. Possibly, but even so it's password-protected. Perhaps he'd seen me around and become obsessed with me and used his associate to shake my confidence before walking into my life as a patient. Too weird. Money? Was it the beginning of a romance con? Hardly. If he already knew where I lived, then he knew I wasn't rich.

What else was in my bag? Oh no.

How could I have been so stupid? I drop my head into my hands. Carter asked me how Ben got into my flat on the night he hid there. Here's my answer. He paid that man to steal my bag and get my front door key copied. That has to be it.

I call an emergency locksmith, who offers me his services in an hour and a half. Not wanting to go home in the meantime, I set off along the river. The path is lush with greenery, the air soft. Birds are singing. I don't feel nervous, at least not until I hear the whistling. The sound raises the hairs on the back of my neck. It reminds me of the tune Ben whistled as he walked away from my flat that morning. And there's something else, something I barely acknowledged at the time. Although I can't pin it down, I recognise the melody.

My shoulders tense as the whistler gains on me. I whirl round and wait for him. I was right. It is Ben. This is not going to be like the last time I confronted him on a deserted path. I'm not going to lose my temper again. It's what he wants.

'You know you shouldn't be here,' I say.

When people transfer the emotions and energies around sexual obsession to hatred in order to ease the humiliation of rejection, that manufactured hatred can be much more extreme than it would be towards someone they've taken a violent dislike to on sight. The body does strange things to the mind, and vice versa.

'I'm just walking, getting some fresh air, like you.'

'Have you been taking your medication?'

He steps closer and I step back. 'I don't need it.' He cocks his head. 'Are you scared of me?'

'No.'

'Liar.' He reaches out and pushes his fingers through my hair, and I gasp and bat his arm away.

'Do not touch me.'

Ben laughs. 'How did you find out where I work?'

'Your flatmate.'

'Good old Tom. Why are you stalking me?'

'I'm not stalking you. I'm gathering information.'

'Because the police won't do it for you?'

I don't answer.

'Why is it that you can't cope with being in the wrong, Dr Geddes?'

I answer with a question of my own. 'Why is the man who attacked me on the heath two months ago working for you?'

'What man? I have no idea what you're talking about.'

'This is how you want to play it, is it? Fits, I suppose. You've been lying to me from the beginning.'

'You know fuck-all about me.'

'You paid that man to steal my bag and copy my door key. That's the truth, isn't it?'

He's silent.

'I'm assuming you knew who I was before you booked an appointment? Either you deliberately targeted me, or you simply decided to ruin my life on a whim. In the light of what I've discovered today, I'd say it was the former. You've destroyed my reputation, got me fired and humiliated me. I'd like to know why.'

He sighs. 'You're a fantasist.'

'I don't think so. You had my keys copied and used them to enter my flat. You spiked my drink and raped me.'

'Rubbish. We had consensual sex, though I admit it was a silly mistake. I didn't come with the intention of sleeping with you.'

'A silly mistake to have sex without using protection.'

'I don't carry condoms. You know that.'

'You could have asked me,' I sneer. 'I keep some in my bedside cabinet.'

'It didn't occur to me. I was drunk, you were there and you were hot. I agree it was wrong, but you should have put

182

a stop to it, or insisted I used a condom and told me where to find them.'

'Not if I was unconscious.'

'You weren't.'

'Do I need to get myself checked for STDs?'

Ben looks revolted. 'No, you do not.'

I raise my eyebrows.

'Do what you like,' he says. 'If it'll give you peace of mind. You have trust issues, and I don't know about the men you sleep with, but perhaps you should be more picky.'

'I don't believe a word you say.'

'That's your prerogative. But I think my narrative is a little more convincing, don't you? I went to you for help when I was having a manic episode, triggered by the end of our sessions. I didn't realise you'd been obsessed with me from the moment I walked into your consulting room, because you were professional enough to hide it. You plied me with alcohol and seduced me.'

I don't feel very professional when I step forward and poke my finger against his clavicle. 'You know what, Ben. You're a creep. I would not have slept with you. Not in a million years.'

'Wouldn't you? Then why are you touching me now?'

I drop my hand as if his skin has burnt me, and he laughs unkindly.

'Do not come near me again,' I spit. 'Do you understand? Or I'll report you for harassment.'

'Now that's an idea. I wonder if turning up at someone's place of work uninvited, when you've been expressly told not to approach them, counts as harassment.'

I walk away. He follows and grabs my arm, swinging me

183

round to face him. A lean middle-aged man jogs towards us in shorts and a T-shirt. I open my mouth to cry for help, but Ben grabs me by the shoulders and kisses me hard, his teeth grinding against mine. He moves one hand to the back of my head, the other to the small of my back. I can't scream, I can't move, and within seconds the jogger has passed us. I can hear him panting. Ben clamps his hand across my mouth and keeps it there until the man is out of earshot.

I wipe his saliva from my mouth. 'You are disgusting.'

'You asked for it, Dr Geddes. Whatever happens now is your own damn fault. I could crush you like a beetle.'

I stare straight into his blue eyes. 'You already have.'

'Ah, no. Your little legs are still wriggling. Google yourself later, Dr Geddes.'

'What?'

An elderly couple appear around the bend with a dachshund. They're followed by a cyclist, who startles them by ringing his bell too late and swerving round them. The couple tut.

'Why is everyone so rude these days?' the woman asks.

Ben laughs good-naturedly. 'Next time use your elbows. A swift jab should do the trick.'

When they continue on their way, I run. I don't look back and I avert my gaze from the river. I sense Ben watching, still smiling, my departure enhancing his excitement and anticipation, and I know that in his narrow world view, I am the puppet and he is the one yanking my strings.

I call the number Innes gave me and leave a message on her voicemail.

'This is Amy Geddes. I want to press charges against Ben Clarkson. Please call me back.'

Whether I get anywhere or not, I'm still going to make life difficult for him.

PART TWO

Chapter 37

DEXTER

FORMER POP STAR CHARGED WITH SEXUAL ASSAULT

Former pop star Dexter Coleridge (38) has been charged with the sexual assault of a minor. Coleridge was today arrested at his nine-million-pound home in desirable Alverley Park. He was later released on bail. Teen runaway Amy Chilcott (15) has accused him of making a crude sexual advance. Mr Coleridge maintains his innocence.

Mr Coleridge's wife, vocal coach Elise Coleridge (36), a former star of West End musicals, was giving a singing lesson to Miss Chilcott when she was called out of the studio to deal with a neighbourly dispute. While she was out of the room, Mr Coleridge joined the teenager in the basement studio. The pair were alone for five or six minutes, and in that time Miss Chilcott alleges that Coleridge gave her advice on breathing, then touched her diaphragm and the lower part of her ribcage to guide her, before raising a hand to her breast. She has explained that she ran away because she was traumatised and ashamed.

Matt Chilcott (38), who is no longer suspected of wrongdoing with regards to his stepdaughter, is said to be deeply upset by the media storm and has not been available for comment. Sources close to the family say he has expressed relief at the return of his stepdaughter and is taking legal advice. Mrs Susan Eastman, a neighbour of the Coleridges', spoke to our reporter. 'They have a pair of binoculars in their bedroom. As a mother of teenage girls, I find that deeply troubling.'

Dexter faces his lawyer across the kitchen table, his hands steepled against his forehead. Lawrence Cohen is, as ever, immaculately dressed in a single-breasted grey suit, his hair cropped short, his beard and moustache neatly trimmed.

'She's doing it to save face,' Dexter says. This is a total mindfuck. He feels beleaguered, is losing friends and running out of options. What has shocked him is how quickly everyone has turned. No one wants to believe him. There's a difference between that and not believing, and it makes it more frustrating, more anger-inducing. He's keeping calm, but at a cost. He's going to blow a fuse at some point. 'If you ask me, when her stepdad was getting called a paedophile, she panicked. Then the shit hit the fan and she started lying. She's a starstruck teenager with a pretty face. People look at her big brown eyes and they look at my mug, and guess whose side they're on.'

'We can fight this,' Lawrence reassures him. 'If Amy broadcasts lies about you, that is defamation and you would be entitled to take her to court. This would result in years of stress that could impact both Amy's mental health and the family's well-being. There's a good chance her parents will persuade her to back off rather than allow her to put herself through that.'

Dexter rubs his frown lines with his middle finger. They feel more pronounced. 'There's something else. Lorna Chilcott.'

'What about her?'

'Years ago I met her hanging around after one of our sets. I slept with her then forgot all about her.'

'That is unfortunate,' Lawrence says drily.

'Yeah, well it doesn't end there. We had a party at our house for the neighbours. Lorna was there. We got talking and I kissed her.'

'For God's sake, Dexter, what is wrong with you?'

'I have a strong sex drive. What do you want me to do? Get chemically castrated? And Elise, since Noah was born . . . Look, I'm the kind of guy who needs sex regularly and often. I'd have sex every day given half a chance. I know life's not like that, but these days I'm lucky if I get it once a week.' Lawrence raises his eyebrows and Dexter musters a smile. 'I've never been a great fan of wanking.'

'I'd advise you not to say any of that in court. So, has Mrs Chilcott made trouble over this?'

Dexter shrugs. 'She read too much into it. She came on to me a few days later – when her kid was missing, for fuck's sake. I told her I wasn't interested. I admit I haven't always been faithful to Elise, but I love her. Any affairs I've had have been one-night stands, two nights at the most, when I've been working abroad, and really not since I gave up DJing. I'm not interested in Lorna Chilcott. She's the wife's friend; or she was until her daughter started telling porky pies.'

191

'If Lorna insinuates that you weren't interested in her because Amy was your target, you'll come across as even less sympathetic.'

'Lorna's pissed off with me because she's embarrassed.'

'Let's hope she remains embarrassed then. Listen, it's not all bad. Nothing dodgy has been found on your computer.'

'That's because there *is* nothing dodgy!'

Lawrence lifts his hand and Dexter slumps back.

'Amy has no messages from you and you have none from her. The story is that you upset her, she overreacted then lied because she felt humiliated and didn't want to be in more trouble than she already was. You've done nothing worse than crush a young girl's dreams.'

'But she's saying I touched her up, then told her she couldn't sing because she rejected my advances. Even if the jury rule in my favour, how is that ever going to go away? This is going to be like George, isn't it?'

Lawrence sighs. 'Let's hope not.'

Chapter 38

ELISE

'It was unprovoked,' the nursery manager says, after Elise asks the question. 'Noah bit Christian and then threw a tantrum. He was out of control.'

'Unprovoked according to who?' Elise asks.

'To Christian and the member of staff on duty.'

'And what has my son said?'

'Noah has refused to speak. The best thing you can do is take him home and settle him down. No doubt he'll tell you what happened when he's ready.'

'And what if it turns out your staff member missed something and in fact he *was* provoked?'

'Then we will look at it again.'

'Noah isn't usually this quiet. If he's in trouble, he gets voluble. He would defend himself.'

'Nothing has been said to make him feel guilty, I assure you. We've simply told him that biting is not allowed and asked him to say something that will make Christian feel better. Which he's refused to do. We've also had a chat about other ways of venting our feelings. If he's not speaking, I'd imagine it's because he knows it was wrong but isn't ready to admit it. He's a July baby, young for his year.

I would suggest you keep him at home until he's ready for school. Perhaps even consider deferring his place at Alverley until next year.'

Elise lifts her head. 'What exactly are you saying?'

The nursery manager coughs. 'I am terribly sorry for what you're going through, Mrs Coleridge, but I'm afraid I have to request that you do not bring Noah back this term.'

'You're suspending a three-year-old?'

'Our parents are obviously concerned about the effect on their children, given what's been going on. The adverse publicity, you know.'

'You mean my husband being arrested for something he didn't do? That's what this is about? I cannot believe it. I will report you to the governing body.'

'That's your right. I should tell you that this decision has come after a meeting with our chair of governors, but by all means report me. Mrs Coleridge, I wish only the best for Noah. Perhaps over the summer you could do some work around boundaries and controlling his temper.'

'Perhaps you could do your fucking job,' Elise snaps, and leaves the room, slamming the door behind her.

Driving home in her silver Lexus RX – normally she wouldn't use her car for the school run, but there is no way she's walking through the group of journalists gathered outside her gates – Elise stretches into the back and tweaks her son's foot. 'You mustn't bite, sweetheart, you know that, don't you?'

'Yes. What's a peedo?'

Elise's jaw drops. 'Who told you that word?'

'Christian.'

'Ah. I see. And did you bite him because of that word?'

'No. I bited him because I said he could come to my house and he said he can't 'cos everyone hates Daddy.'

'And then he said that word?'

'When I bited him. First he said it, then he cried.'

Elise pulls over and twists round. 'It's a very bad word, darling. Don't say it to anyone and don't listen to anyone who says it to you. Let's go home and make pancakes.'

'With you?' He perks up.

She hesitates. 'Yes. Clara can have the rest of the day off.'

This morning Clara gave notice. She can't cope with the media onslaught, hates cameras, hates attention. Elise sensed when she employed her that she wasn't going to be the life and soul, but she'd had her fill of perky, smiley nannies who quit at the first sign of trouble. When Noah had a spectacular tantrum on Clara's second day, she knew she'd made the right choice. Clara had him calmed down and playing quietly within minutes. But the downside was that she had to be allowed to live in her quiet bubble. If she doesn't want to chat, which is more often than not, they don't chat. And she can't be pushed into socialising with other nannies, so she's always at home. At first it was tricky, even a little claustrophobic, but Elise has grown used to her odd ways. And now she's going, and Elise blames that girl.

She could happily murder Amy Chilcott. She is lying for sure. She took off in a temper tantrum, making everyone panic, and then reappeared and wreaked her petty revenge on Dexter. Her Dexter, who may be flawed but is the best dad, the best husband, funny, smart, talented, quirky. She will love him until the day she dies.

195

She feels sick as she turns the corner and sees the paparazzi. How long are these vultures going to hound them? She stares straight ahead as she drives through and doesn't get out until the gate has closed again. Their muted shouts rumble through her body.

'So what happened?' Dexter asks.

'Noah's been suspended for biting Christian.' She decides not to say why, or that the suspension is permanent, until she's had time to process this latest catastrophe. 'And Clara is leaving us.'

He tips his head back and groans, then sees Elise is silently crying and pulls her into his arms. He kisses her head. 'Maybe I can persuade her to stay.'

'I don't think so.' Once her mind is made up about something, Clara is surprisingly intransigent.

'What if I go?'

'Dexter! Absolutely not.'

He scratches the side of his face. 'I've been thinking about it. I'm the reason those barracudas have set up camp and the neighbours are pissed off. It's my fault you're miserable and Clara's leaving us.' He touches her mouth to stop her interrupting. 'I'm not going far, babes. Ivo's offered me the *Liberty Rose*. I'll be doing him a favour. He wants it lived in before he puts it on the market.'

Ivo bought the houseboat after Elise and Dexter took him for a stroll along the Bute. He was recently divorced and had some romantic notion of resetting himself on the river. He quickly decided nature didn't outweigh the deprivations. The dawn chorus, though he conceded it was lovely, soon palled. He bought an apartment with a

196

spectacular view of the Thames in Vauxhall and moved out. Since then, the *Liberty Rose* has been used for short tenancies.

'You'll be lonely.'

She hasn't told him to stay. What is stopping her? She stares at her husband's face. Not a twitch.

'I'll be fine. It'll give everyone breathing space.'

'You've already decided, haven't you?' She's hurt but understands. He only wants to protect her and Noah. He won't have thought much beyond that.

'Yeah. I'm going tonight.' He lifts her chin with his finger and kisses her tenderly. 'In the morning you can tell those fuckers I've moved out and they'll leave you in peace.'

Dexter is beautiful. That's all she can think. He is beautiful, he is hers, and that little cow Amy Chilcott wants to destroy him, encouraged by her mother. Elise will not allow anyone to break her family.

Chapter 39

DEXTER

Dexter leaves at two in the morning, pushing his bicycle through the back gate and cycling across the heath with the rucksack he last used when he was on the road with D.I.G.B.Y., following familiar paths in the light of the moon until he gets to the far side, where Ivo is waiting for him.

'All right, mate?' Ivo asks. He's wrapped up in a parka and has a woollen hat pulled over his black locks.

'Fine.' Dexter's voice is hard, but only to disguise his extreme sadness. He's leaving his wife and child and going to skulk on a boat. He's never liked being on his own. He doesn't even enjoy coming home to an empty house like Elise does, in the rare event that she's given the opportunity.

They walk the quarter-mile to where the *Liberty Rose* is moored, with Dexter not knowing what to say to his old friend. Ivo talks, but it barely registers. The river is black, thick clouds obscuring the moon. Dexter finds the dark water and the faint mildewy smell oppressive.

'I wouldn't swim in it,' Ivo says, peering down. 'The currents can be very strong when the tide's going out.'

'I don't intend to, man.'

'Go easy on the booze, then; no drowning your sorrows.'

Dexter gives a humourless laugh in response.

They climb on board. Ivo demonstrates how to work the shower, gives him a file of information and shows him the contents of the fridge. 'Stocked up for you.'

Milk, sausage rolls, a pie and a six-pack of beer. 'You're a good mate,' Dexter says. To his shame, his eyes fill with tears.

Ivo pretends he hasn't noticed. 'You going to be okay?'

Dexter nods. He's knackered but also psyched. It reminds him again of the D.I.G.B.Y. days and that hallucinatory mixture of sleep deprivation and adrenaline, the not knowing how you arrived at destinations, even onto the stage, because the less memorable stretches of your time aren't getting acknowledged by your brain.

After Ivo has gone, Dexter pops the lid off a beer and sits on one of the wicker chairs on the deck. Two swans glide past in the eerie silence. He feels detached from reality; an actor in a play about someone else, some poor sap for whom everything is going wrong.

Waking up in a strange bed in a room with no double-glazing, to an outrageously loud dawn chorus, Dexter screws up his eyes. He can see why Ivo advised him to bring a sleep mask and ear plugs. Pity he didn't use them. He stares at the slatted wooden ceiling until his bladder forces him up. He pulls on his sweater, goes up on deck and pees directly into the river, yelling across the fast-moving water like he's roaring at a crowd: 'FUCK YOU, AMY CHILCOTT!'

It's not so bad. If Elise had been with him, they could have sat swaddled in the duvet, sipping coffee, watching the ducks paddle by.

After he's cleaned his teeth, he does a quick recce of the barge. It's a bachelor pad – very Ivo. His bedroom is in the main body of the boat, but there's another in the stern with its own shower room. In the main part there's a long kitchen-cum-sitting-room that houses a sofa, wood burner, table, chairs and a drum kit. The wooden floor is covered in Persian rugs, the walls in shelves containing Ivo's vinyl collection and D.I.G.B.Y. memorabilia. There's one more tiny bedroom and a bathroom. Isolated from the world, it's perfect for the man who wants to lick his wounds.

He's up on deck, smoking while he mulls over a list of questions from his lawyer, when his phone rings. His stomach churns when he sees his agent's name come up. This is not going to be fun.

'Morning, Steve,' he says.

'Dexter,' Steve says. 'How are you?' His voice oozes sympathy, but Dexter isn't deceived. The man is ruthless. 'I'm so sorry about everything.'

'You're known me a long time. You know I wouldn't do what they're saying I've done.'

'Yes, I do, and I believe you.'

'But?'

'But I'm afraid I have some bad news.'

Dexter forestalls him. '*Temporary Madness*?'

'I'm sorry. The investors feel it's the wrong time for you.'

'They don't want to be associated with me?'

Steve doesn't reply. Dexter drags on the cigarette, gazing out across the river. He's been growing his reputation slowly, avoiding using his fame to push his way into roles that would be too big for him. Two plays and a support-ing role in the hit romcom *How to Date a Friend*. *Temporary Madness*, a new film by Travis Dylan, is a high-concept thriller and would have propelled him into the big league. It's hard to move away from what you're famous for, but Dexter is determined, and there's strong evidence that audiences have begun to accept him as an actor. The pla-giarism trial was a bastard, but they'd got through it and come out stronger and wiser. And now, because of Amy fucking Chilcott, that dream is over.

'So what now?' he asks.

'We take a break.'

Dexter chews over his next question, listening to Steve breathing down the line. 'From the business or from each other?'

'You know how it is.'

'You're right. I do.' He cuts his agent off, stands up and kicks the chair. It tips over. The sound as it hits the floor scares a pair of geese into flight.

You never get better at dealing with false accusations, however old and jaded you become; he still feels the same combination of anger, frustration and hurt he felt when-ever it happened to him as a child and a teenager. Always in trouble, but not always for something he'd done. Long after the anger and frustration fades, the hurt remains.

He has worked so hard for everything he has in the years since his father bought him his first guitar. Second-hand, but none the worse for it. He'd started by playing covers on Saturday evenings in the pub his parents ran. The usual stuff, 'Danny Boy', 'Ferry Cross the Mersey', 'Eleanor Rigby'. By the time he was sixteen, he was playing the working men's clubs, doing gigs for a drink and a meal and the chance to be seen. Putting the band together and blagging their way into O'Neill's and the Cavern. D.I.G.B.Y. was not created by money men and reality TV. It was born through working their arses off and honing their craft the hard way.

When the end came, when Yann and George left, when the fans stopped screaming, the bottom had fallen out of his life. He sank into a black hole, drank too much, shut himself away and wanted to die. Once he turned to DJing, things had improved; he was in front of a crowd again, making them jump and roar. It filled a gap. He kept pushing, refusing to acknowledge that he was on a downward slope. Then his sister had called, and he'd found himself in the stalls at the Sondheim Theatre, watching *Les Misérables*. He isn't into that kind of thing, thinks it's naff, but Kerry had brought his niece up to London and he needed to find things for them to do. He hadn't expected to enjoy it, and he hadn't, but he'd been transfixed by the actress playing Éponine. He had found himself gazing raptly at the woman he was going to spend the rest of his life with. He'd actually thought that. Soft git.

He'd ended things with his girlfriend at the time, because he's not a complete tosser, and returned the next night, waiting at the stage door, collar turned up, flat cap on. When hanging around like a prize eejit didn't work, he rocked up the following evening and sent flowers and a note via the doorman.

Elise already had a boyfriend. Dexter can't remember his name, but he does remember that he was off-the-scale handsome. He'd never thought much about his own looks, but after seeing the other guy, he couldn't help noticing how badly put together he was: torso too long, forehead too high, nose crooked, a souvenir of an altercation outside Coopers when he was seventeen and unable to control his temper. Jutting cheekbones that made him look gaunt, veins that stood out in his neck if he got riled. Like now.

He grips the wooden balustrade and leans over. Beneath him his reflection ripples. He can't swim. He's never trusted the water, not since his sister nearly drowned on a package holiday to Torremolinos when he was four. It makes his heart race to think of that. The sight of his father charging over to the jacuzzi, beer gut wobbling, yanking two-year-old Kerry out by her arm. She had been vertical in the water, he remembered, her blonde hair floating out. He had yelled at his parents, who'd been arguing over something, their attention momentarily off the children.

He misses Elise. And Noah, of course, but Elise has been his guiding light. All through that plagiarism shit storm she was the one who kept him sane, who showed him he could laugh about it. She didn't give a rat's arse about selling that ridiculous palace of a house, a vanity purchase by a poor boy made good. She never liked it anyway.

She's said she'll talk to Amy. If anyone can get that kid to change her tune, Elise can.

He pushes himself away from his contemplation of the abyss and goes into the cabin to fetch a beer.

Chapter 40

LORNA

'Oh wow,' Lorna says, putting down the newspaper.

Matt looks up. 'What?'

He's been in such a difficult mood, she's glad to have something mildly amusing to tell him. Although she shouldn't laugh. It's actually really sad.

'The body they found in the lake. They've identified it. It's one of the elderly twins rattling around in that huge old house in Gladwell Grove. I'm sure I've told you about them.'

Matt grunts non-committally.

'Never mind. It seems one of them died sometime last year and the other never reported it. She put the body in the lake.'

That gets his interest. Matt is all about logistics. 'How the hell did she manage that?'

'Apparently she paid her Albanian gardener to do it. She's been collecting her sister's benefits but hasn't spent a penny. She just didn't want to be taken into care. Poor thing. She must have been so lonely. She's ninety-one and terribly frail, so I doubt it'll go to trial. I wonder if she'll sell the house now. It says here that there's a nephew.' She sighs. 'I would do anything for that sale. I'll put a letter through the door today.'

Matt frowns. 'Haven't you had enough of Gladwell Grove?'

She links her hands behind his neck. 'Don't be so grumpy. We've got Amy back, haven't we? The commission would really come in handy.'

'I suppose so.'

She strokes his cheek. 'Are you still angry with her?'

'No. I'm angry with myself. She's just a kid. She didn't think. I should have gone round and decked that man.'

'The courts are dealing with him. You'd only have made things worse. Can we just forget about it? Amy seems to have. She went off to school cheerfully enough this morning.'

'I bet she did. She'll be enjoying her fifteen minutes of fame.'

'That's not fair. She's been through a lot.' Lorna studies his face. His moods don't usually play out like this. Normally they're over quickly.

Matt rubs his fingers across his scalp. 'I don't like Coleridge, but he doesn't strike me as the type.'

'Are you saying Amy's lying?' She can feel her body heat rising, sweat prickling. 'Because if you are—'

'I'm not,' Matt says hastily.

'You barely know Dexter.'

'Yeah. That's true. But my first impression was that he's okay.'

'Your first impression was when he made a speech at the housewarming. Of course he was okay. He's probably okay most of the time. But men can make bad judgement calls

205

when it comes to women. He was alone with our daughter.' She stresses those last two words and sees Matt flinch. 'Who knows if he's done it before?'

She doesn't really believe he has. What happened with Amy must have been an aberration. She might hate Dexter, but that doesn't make her insensate. As an estate agent, she knows people. In the same way clients instinctively *get* a house from the moment they walk through the door, she instinctively *gets* her clients from the moment they walk into the office. She's rarely proven wrong. Dexter might be selfish, insensitive and a pig, but he isn't evil. So why not say that? Coming from her, it would make all the difference. She grits her teeth. Because she can't. Because she's nailed her colours to the mast. Because Amy will always come first. It has nothing to do with her own pride.

Once Matt and Jack have left for nursery, she sets off at a brisk walk to her first viewing of the day, a bay-fronted Victorian house. It's been exquisitely renovated and sits comfortably in the catchment for Alverley School so should be no problem to sell. And that's the spiel she uses on the woman with the toddler in her arms, even though her heart is breaking. Jack should be starting there in September, not Noah. Thinking about Noah reminds her of her ruined friendship with Elise, and she wants to cry.

'Do you think they would leave the curtains?' the woman asks.

Lorna smiles. *Ker-ching!* 'I'm sure anything can be negotiated. It's a gorgeous house, isn't it? I wouldn't mind living here myself.'

Chapter 41

AMY

Amy notices Elise watching her from among the students milling around the cycle racks at the end of the school day. She stops in her tracks, thinking she could run back inside and hang out in the library until Elise gives up and goes home. But then she'll come back the next day, and the next.

Lily, who has only just noticed Amy is no longer with her, calls out, 'You coming?'

Amy shakes her head. 'Forgot something.'

'I'll wait.'

'No, don't.' She improvises swiftly. 'I need to find Miss Talbot.'

'Okay. Message me when you're free. Stuff to talk about!'

Argh, Amy thinks as Lily bounces off and insinuates herself into another group of girls. She doesn't need another deep and meaningful with Lily. She takes a steadying breath, then walks towards Elise, the absolute last person she wants to see, but, weirdly, also the person she most wants to be close to. They don't speak until they've peeled away from the crowd of children ambling and slouching through the gates. Elise turns off the main road, and after a few metres the noise of chatter and traffic subsides.

Amy's palms are sweating, the drag of her heavy rucksack on her shoulders agitating her skin. A thin strand of hair, escaped from its clip, tickles her nose. She tucks it behind her ear and uses the breathing exercises Elise once taught her to calm her racing pulse.

Everyone stares at her these days. She's been called a liar to her face. If she'd known what it'd be like, she'd never have said what she did, wouldn't have run away either. When she thinks about that lonely, smelly little flat covered in a dead old lady's skin cells, she wrinkles her nose in disgust. She glances at Elise. She's going to have to be careful what she says.

She shoves her hands deep in her blazer pockets, the tips of her fingers meeting sweet wrappers and fluff. She is so muddled. Has she turned a small thing that was awkward and a bit ick into a gigantic mess?

Chapter 42

ELISE

Elise has spent the entire day working out how to approach Amy Chilcott, what she's going to say and how she's going to say it. She is by nature a diplomat. She believes in talking things through, listening to other points of view. She doesn't get angry, she gets quiet. She's a kind person, but lately she's felt a hardening at her core.

She is desperately worried about Dexter. It isn't public knowledge that he's periodically suffered from depression. It wasn't the reason his management gave when he abruptly quit DJing only five years after pivoting from boy-band stardom. The hours, the hops between countries, the waking up in anonymous hotel rooms and the manic nature of the job took a heavy toll. When Elise met him, he was still pretending everything was okay. Nine months after they got together, she'd had to fly out to Ibiza to bring him home. He retired from the circuit citing burnout and exhaustion. For her, it was a crash course in mental health.

Acting, though an improvement on DJing, still isn't the best space for someone like Dexter, but the years he's spent in the entertainment world mean that being in the public eye is his oxygen, so she supports him. What would he do otherwise? She had her own stage career, but she gave it up to coach, making the sacrifice so that her boys could flourish and be happy. It has to have been worth it. If Amy makes a mockery of everything she's achieved, Elise will come for her. She is not going to let that spoilt brat destroy her family. No way did Dex touch her.

'We're not supposed to be talking,' Amy mutters, her face sullen.

Jesus. Teenagers.

'Yet here I am and here you are, so I'll get straight to the point. Why have you done this?'

'You know why.'

'I know what you say, but I also know my husband. He is not the kind of man who makes passes at young girls.'

Amy shrugs. 'Well, this time he did.'

'So you keep saying. But it doesn't make it true.' Elise sighs. She hasn't witnessed this obstinate side of Amy before, though Lorna has hinted at it. 'Don't you care about honesty and integrity?' She rushes on before the girl can protest. 'Listen. I understand. You were upset by what Dexter said and thought you'd make a point by running away, and because you were embarrassed to have caused such a fuss and upset your mum and dad, you made up this story so people wouldn't be angry or laugh at you. That's it, isn't it?'

'No. He listened to me sing, then gave me advice, and then he touched me to show me how to breathe and moved his hand onto my breast. I was there, you weren't.'

Elise looks at Amy until she flushes. If she gets down on her knees and begs, if she grovels and appeals to Amy's vanity, if she weeps, will the girl see sense?

She adjusts the pitch of her voice, to a lower, more authoritative tone. Kind but firm. 'If you tell the truth, it will be uncomfortable, but it will blow over. If you continue with this lie, it will be with you for the rest of your life. Knowing that you hurt a good man so badly, that you ripped his family apart, will eat you up inside. Think about how you felt when your stepdad was getting all that nasty publicity; how bad it was for him. Losing respect, losing clients. Do you want that to happen to Dexter? Because it's already begun. He's been dropped from his movie, and his agent doesn't want to represent him any more, all because he criticised your singing. That's bad, Amy. You need to be better than this in life. The world does not owe you anything just because you're a pretty girl. You have to fight your corner, not blame your failures on others.'

Amy's eyes well up, and after a hesitation, Elise puts an arm around her shoulders, hoping she hasn't gone too far. She feels sorry for her. She hasn't forgotten what it's like to be a teenager. She wonders, as Amy cries into her sheepskin coat, whether dry-cleaning will get the tear stains out.

'Amy,' she says, disengaging herself. 'You can get through this. I'll come with you, make sure people see I'm supporting you. I'll help you tell the police. It will be bad for a few days, then something else will happen and it'll be forgotten. I know it's scary, but you are brave. And after this is all over, we can be friends again. If you want lessons, that's fine, and if you don't, that's fine too. Maybe we could do something else together.'

Amy appears to be considering it, but there's a group of kids in uniform approaching, crowding the pavement, and the opportunity is lost. She turns on her scuffed heel, jostles through the group and hurries back to the main road, shoulders hunched so high it looks as though her head is buried in her neck. Elise stands like a statue as the kids part like the Red Sea and gather again behind her. She hears one of them say, 'That's the paedo pop star's wife.' His friends laugh and Elise almost loses her cool.

Then Amy looks back at her and gives her a shy smile, and Elise feels some of the weight lift off her shoulders. Maybe it's going to be all right.

Chapter 43

LORNA

Jack is being a little monster, galloping from one end of the house to the other pretending to slay dragons – Lorna watched *George and the Dragon* with him at the weekend and it's been a bit hairy round here ever since. Worried about Amy, she is aware more than ever of her attention being stretched to breaking point between her two children. It's not surprising Amy is moody and withdrawn after what's happened. She ought to talk to her, and if Amy baulks at that, suggest seeing a therapist.

She finally gets Jack bathed and into bed, and is about to read him a story when Amy puts her head round the door.

'Can I read to him tonight?'

'Would you?' Lorna smiles, relieved. It feels like a chink of light. 'That would be wonderful. I'll start dinner.'

'What time's Dad back? Budge over, Jacko.' Jack obliges, and Amy wriggles under his stars and planets duvet and tucks him under her arm.

'He said about seven thirty.'

'Read,' Jack says, pulling the book open.

Lorna descends the stairs to the sound of Jack's giggles,

and the tension in her shoulders dissolves. If anyone can put Amy in a better frame of mind, it's her half-brother.

Today has been tiring. First there was the morning drop-off to be endured, with stares and questions disguised as faux sympathy. Then she had to deal with a buyer who emailed her during the night with a low ball so low it's practically scraping the ground. The seller said no, but it's the first offer and the property, a beautifully renovated flat in a slightly dubious area, has had too much money spent on it, although she won't tell the seller that. Then there was a viewing where the seller's cleaner forgot she was only supposed to lock the top lock, and locked the bottom one, which Chetham & Church do not hold a key for. Luckily the cleaner was working in the next street so was able to run round and let them in, but that kind of event, which happens often enough to make her skin prickle every time she approaches a front door, is embarrassing and stressful.

She pours a generous glass of red wine. None of that is important. What is important is that Amy is back safe and unharmed.

She hears something and turns round. Her daughter is hovering in the doorway, looking young and vulnerable in pyjama bottoms and a pale pink hoodie.

'I need to talk to you,' Amy says.

'Okay. Good.'

Two large tears brim and overflow. Amy wipes them away with her sleeve, then looks at the wet smears as if she's surprised. She pulls her hands deep into her cuffs.

'I don't even know if it's true.'

'Know if what's true?' Lorna asks, feeling a chill crawl down her backbone.

'If Dexter touched me on purpose. I said it because I was scared. But I don't know any more. I might have exaggerated a little, so Dad wouldn't hate me so much.'

'Oh Amy . . .'

'I want to tell the policewoman. Do you have her number?'

Lorna takes a gulp of wine. 'Let's think about this first.'

'Mum. I just want to get it over with.'

This is going to look really bad. It's going to frame Amy as a lying and manipulative little madam. Dexter will look like a victim and have sympathy heaped on him. Lorna is not going to stand back and allow that to happen. She understands him better now. He is one of those people for whom everything comes easily, for whom consequences don't really matter and rules do not apply. He gets what he wants and doesn't care who is broken in the process, whether it's her or her daughter. Let him, for once, be the one forced into an awkward position.

'Darling, please think very carefully. If you change your story, you'll be known for ever as someone whose word can't be trusted.'

'I know that.'

'Then you'll understand that a wrong decision now will affect your career and your future. No one will want to employ you. When anyone looks up your name on the internet, that's what they'll see.'

'But that's what's happened to Dad, and it's what Dexter's getting now. People looking them up and seeing unfair and hateful things written about them. It's gone too far. It's hurting Elise and Noah.' Amy snivels.

215

Lorna checks the time. Ten past seven. She needs to sort this out before Matt gets home.

'Far better that they're hurt than you ruin your life.'

Amy looks at her in surprise, and Lorna can understand why. It's a mother's job to instil an understanding of right and wrong in her child. She's turning everything on its head.

'Please don't do it, darling. You don't know whether it was deliberate or not, but I think you just don't want to admit the truth because you admire Elise so much. I don't want you to be defined for ever by a mistake you made when you were too young to know better.' Inside her head a voice is clamouring to be heard. *This is about you, Lorna. Why don't you admit it? This is revenge.*

'I'll have to live with it whatever,' Amy says.

Lorna reaches for her daughter's hands, but Amy crosses her arms.

'You'll move on. You'll go to sixth-form college and university and have a fantastic career. You want that, don't you?'

'No, *you* want that. It's what you've always wanted because you failed. I hate maths. I've only pretended to like it to make you happy.'

Lorna feels like she's been struck. 'You didn't have to. I was only trying to help.' She refills her glass and steels herself. 'I didn't tell you the whole truth about what happened when I met Dexter for the first time. I've never even told Matt or Daddy Pete, or anyone actually, but he ... er ...'

'He what?'

This is humiliating, but needs must. 'After the gig, I went back to his hotel room with the rest of the band and

216

a couple of other girls. I drank too much and then suddenly we were alone and he was all over me. I was in love with him, but I also knew it wasn't real, it was just a fantasy. Getting physical felt all wrong and I didn't want it. I told him, but I probably wasn't clear enough.'

Amy looks like she wants to run away, and Lorna inwardly concedes that it's too much information, but she presses on, repackaging the past to suit the present crisis.

'Let's just say he didn't back off, and to my shame I gave in and—'

'I don't want to know any more.' The words come out in a hot rush.

'I'm sorry.'

She tamps down hard on her guilt. She did kind of consent at first; she was definitely into it. That muddied the water, made it hard for her to cry rape, because he was beyond stopping once she asked him to. It was too late; he was inside her and lost to the moment. And he'd been so puppyishly affectionate afterwards, had acted like it really meant something to him. Looking back, she wishes her instincts had been better, that she hadn't been so overwhelmed by him, because of the way she'd been forgotten. He had loomed large in her mind for months. She guesses she hadn't figured in his. Another gig, another girl. For Christ's sake, she even reminded him of it, as if it was some silly teenage misjudgement. She shagged the lead singer of D.I.G.B.Y. So what? So it derailed her. Love can do that. Unhealthy love, at least.

She might as well be honest with herself and call it by its name, not hide behind the narrative of looking after her daughter's interests. There might have been an element of ambiguity, but Dexter pushed her when he must have realised she didn't want it. He was carried away by the moment, but he wasn't deaf. This is payback. Revenge served cold.

'I just wanted you to know that you wouldn't be upsetting a perfect human being. Underneath the charm, Dexter Coleridge is a predator.'

'Mum.' Amy's tone is tinged with scepticism, but she looks hopeful.

'If you let that man get away with it, not only do you change your entire future, but you allow him to carry on abusing women.'

'He loves Elise.'

'Yes, he does.' She's winning. She works to keep any sign of triumph from her voice, instead sounding deeply saddened to be the teller of such disappointing tales. 'Elise has kept him on the straight and narrow for years, but sometimes men can't help themselves. Promise me you won't do anything tonight. Sleep on it. I only want what's best for you, darling. That's all I've ever wanted.'

The front door opens. Amy swings round, looking terrified, as though it's the police at the door, but Lorna grasps her hand.

'It's all right. Dad's on your side.'

Chapter 44

LORNA

Number 37 Gladwell Grove stinks. The house is cluttered with Victoriana, dimly lit and airless, and boasts disintegrating carpets and moth-eaten rugs. The curtains have been shredded by the sun, the ceilings stained by damp from neglected gutters. The kitchen is yellow and fly-blown. The bathroom functions, but the bath is full of junk. An accessible shower has been installed at some point, but that too is revolting. There is evidence of mice, and the loft has been colonised by wasps' nests of breathtaking size. Lorna can barely breathe due to the dust and the throat-catching odour of decay, but beneath the dilapidation lie the bones of a once gracious home.

There is ornate coving, and the marble fire surrounds gracing the two large reception rooms are early Victorian and baroque in style, with carvings of fruit and flowers. When she gingerly lifts the carpet in the hallway, she finds perfect tessellated tiles crawling with silverfish.

'My goodness,' Basil Brooker says, taking it all in.

Eileen and Ann's nephew lives in Matlock, in the Peak District. He is a friendly, talkative man, and Lorna learns that his wife has dementia, that he has three daughters living all over the world, and that he hasn't visited his aunts in ten years, not since the funeral of his father, their older brother, who died at the age of ninety-seven. He feels bad, but caring for his wife on his own has made doing his duty by his aunts impossible.

'People in the street think I neglected them,' he says sadly. 'One of them told me to my face that I should have done more.'

'I know the people round here. I'll put them straight.' She'll phone Sophie Meadows. Word will get round quickly enough. 'How's Ann doing?' she asks.

'She's all right,' Basil says. 'Being taken very good care of and as happy as Larry. Except she still misses Auntie Eileen. They were funny old things.'

There is apparently nothing wrong with Ann Brooker's mind. From what Lorna has been able to glean from Basil, his aunt made the decision to sell without recourse to anyone else and has voluntarily entered a nursing home. When asked why she did what she did, she simply responded that it had been the right thing to do. They had lived here all their lives and swum in the lake until ten years ago. She wants her own ashes thrown into it when the time comes.

'So it won't come to trial?' Lorna asks.

'No. Thank goodness. The CPS decided it wasn't in the public interest to pursue it.'

'I'm so pleased. That would have been awful for her, and for you. You can move on now. Sell the place to a lovely family who'll appreciate it.'

'And its history.' Basil's eyes twinkle, then he grimaces. 'The notoriety won't hurt, will it?'

'Not at all. People love the story. It's uplifting when you think about it.'

Lorna has outlined how they would market the house and talked him through the process. She's shown him the glossy brochure for number 55 and hinted that he could get just as much for this place, though actually she thinks it will eventually go for less because the survey will turn up so many horrors. Now she lingers at the bottom of the stairs, reluctant to leave, because if she's lucky enough to get the commission, next time she's here she'll be with a potential buyer. She wanders back into the sitting room, where Basil is inspecting the contents of the bookshelves, and gazes out of the sash window. The garden is lush, bursting into colour.

'I'd better get back to the office,' she says. 'If you decide to go with Chetham & Church, I can organise a photographer in the next couple of days. The details should be ready by the weekend. Hopefully we can put it on the website and the platforms by Monday, but of course we'll phone round any suitable buyers already on our books the moment you give us the nod.'

'There's no hurry,' Basil says, walking to the door. 'I've got another two agents booked in to take a look. But thank you for your time. You've been very helpful.'

She feels deflated as he drives away. She'd had the distinct impression that it was in the bag. Chetham & Church's long-standing relationship with the local solicitor who is also Ann Brooker's solicitor is excellent. Lorna's boss plays golf with him. Perhaps Basil is cannier than he looks and is keeping her on her toes, possibly even hoping to cut a deal over their fees.

Chapter 45

ELISE

Elise has ridden her bike off the pavement and into the road before she sees Lorna. She brakes and puts her foot down. Startled, the corners of Lorna's lips lift, as though she'd forgotten everything that's happened in the last few days. Elise jumps off the bike and pushes it up to her.

'The house? Is it good?'

'In a state of disrepair, but beautiful.' Lorna's manner is circumspect, the smile gone.

'I thought it would be. And you're handling the sale?'

'I hope to.'

'How much?'

'How much?'

'That's what I asked. What is the value you put on it?'

'I need to discuss it with my boss, but probably in the region of six point five.'

Elise raises her eyebrows. 'Wow. Less than we paid for ours.'

Lorna is immediately on the defensive. 'That reflects its condition. Yours required bringing up to date, but it had been well cared for. This one is in a much worse state. It needs a new roof for a start.'

'You're back then.'

She whirls round. He's on the path. Oh God, he must have seen her this morning. Did he tell Elise? Probably not, if he wanted to make love. Nothing like a peeping Tom to kill the moment.

'To what do I owe the honour?'

She shrugs.

'You'd better come aboard.' He climbs up ahead of her and sits on one of two wicker chairs, moving the other towards her with his booted foot as she steps up onto the deck. 'Welcome to my gaff.'

Amy sits primly, pressing her knees together and pulling her skirt down over them. Dexter shows no sign of interest in her legs.

'Guilt getting to you?' he asks.

'No.'

He folds his arms behind his head. There is something odd about the way he's moving. And then she sees the cardboard box full of empty lager cans. He follows her gaze and smiles before lifting his face to the thin sun. Amy is warm enough under her coat, but Dexter's only wearing a shirt. He's also wearing leather flip-flops. Yuck. His toenails are worse than her dad's.

'I hear you've got a crush on me.'

'No I haven't.' She feels the blush and dips her head. That's gross.

'So does your mother.' He grins suddenly, and Amy is struck by the crow's feet that fan out from the corners of his eyes, by the gleam of his teeth and the flare of his nostrils. There is something magnetic about him. She can't drag her eyes away. 'Some women go a bit weird when they

It seems strange to be talking like this, as though everything is normal, but an idea is already forming in Elise's mind. She can see the light in Lorna's eyes, smell the desire in her blood. You can't see through the windows because of the filthy old nets, but she can imagine what the house is like. When she first walked into hers, she felt like she believes Lorna does now. The place is a diamond. Lorna Chilcott would kill for it.

'You want it.' It's a statement, not a question.

Lorna looks confused. 'Well . . . of course I'd love a house like this, but it's pie-in-the-sky.' She gives a nervous laugh. 'I'd have to win the lottery.'

'No,' Elise says softly. 'You wouldn't. All you'd have to do is persuade Amy to retract her accusation and go on record saying that she lied and my husband came nowhere near her.'

What has she just promised? They can't really afford it – their bank account is by no means the bottomless pit everyone assumes it is – but on the other hand, Dexter has just come through one court case; another would break him emotionally and financially. Would she pay six million plus to have the charges dropped and everything go back to normal? Yes, she would. It's only money, after all.

'Do you have time?' She indicates the house. 'Just a quick look round.'

Silent with shock, Lorna nods.

Chapter 46

LORNA

'I can understand why the old lady didn't want to leave,' Elise says, turning in a circle to take in the reception room. With her long auburn hair and Pre-Raphaelite looks, she perfectly suits the decor. 'This house must have felt like part of her family. What she did was not so very wrong, was it? It's not as though she was spending the money on diamonds and fast cars. She just wanted to keep her sister in the place they loved.'

'I suppose so.' Lorna can discern Amy in her own voice, that hint of truculence.

'I know people in the street have visited her in her care home. I haven't been invited to go with them. But still, it's kind. If a little too late.' Elise wanders over to the window. She tries to open it but gives up. It's stuck fast. 'Lovely, isn't it? A sleeping beauty.'

A gardener, organised for Basil by the next-door neighbour, has been in and cleared the worst of the brambles and nettles. Somewhere close by, one blackbird responds to another. The roses are in bud, bluebells and daffodils sway in a gentle breeze while primroses and forget-me-nots splash the ground in blue and pale yellow. Lorna feels a tug at her heart. Her garden is dominated by Matt's shed. The rest is laid to lawn with narrow borders containing mostly shrubs, since they're less trouble. This place would be such an adventure for her little boy. Matt could build him a tree house. He could build all sorts of things.

'Dexter is falling apart,' Elise says, interrupting her thoughts.

'I'm sorry about that.'

'Are you?'

'Of course. But his mental state doesn't absolve him. He wasn't falling apart when he assaulted my daughter.'

'We both know he didn't. I am not a woman who begs, but I am begging you now. Talk to Amy. Persuade her to tell the truth. I will make it as comfortable as possible for her. I will not complain, I will make sure Dexter's lawyers lay off. And my offer still stands. You make it go away, and you can have this house.'

'What if someone offers more than its valuation?'

'I don't care. We have enough.'

'You're asking me to lie to my family and put my daughter in an appalling position.'

'Lorna, darling, you know that whatever Amy decides to do, her position is bad. You might as well get her to do the right thing. You'll have a financial cushion. Believe me when I tell you that helps a lot.'

'Family's the most important thing, not money and houses.'

Elise's eyes narrow. 'I'll throw in an extra five hundred grand.'

The shock makes Lorna hesitate. How lovely to be so wealthy you can lob random amounts of money at your problems. 'I don't want to live in the same street as you.'

'So Dexter and I will move. I don't want to live here now anyway. This nightmare has spoilt it for me. People are so quick to judge.'

Lorna breathes in deeply. 'If I press Amy to retract, I will basically be saying that I think she's lied.'

'You know she'll be relieved to have the slate wiped clean.'

'But it won't be, will it? You've just said she can't win whatever she does. This will never be forgotten.'

'But for her, Lorna, for her mental well-being. When she's an adult, she will be glad that she was honest.'

Lorna runs her finger over the marble surround of the fireplace. It comes away thick with dust. She brushes it off.

'Think what this house could do for your family in the future,' Elise presses. 'You can sell it down the line, buy Amy and Jack their own places, give them the best start in life.'

Lorna's hungry gaze strips away the years of neglect, mentally restores the grand old room. She pictures herself standing in this spot in a few years' time, looking out onto her garden, knowing that beyond it the heath stretches out, a green paradise. Gladwell Grove is the best street in Alverley by a long chalk. They could live here until Jack leaves home, then sell it, set both children up for life and retire on a generous income. Her heart clenches.

'Let me think about it.'

Lorna sits in her car long after Elise has cycled away, her mind whirling. The house is more than triple the square footage of Bramcote Avenue, and the garden is longer and considerably wider. Even if they didn't have to pay to buy it, it would still cost more than they can afford to do the essentials to make it habitable: the roof, the plumbing, heating and electrics, new kitchen and bathrooms.

The windows are actually in pretty good nick. They could be restored; no need to spend tens of thousands of pounds having new ones made. And it's not as though they'd want to extend – there's masses of space. They wouldn't be digging out the cellar and adding studios like the Coleridges. Matt could do a lot of the work himself, building the kitchen and wardrobes, replacing rotten floorboards and damaged architraves and skirting. Sixty thousand for the roof, electrics, plumbing, replastering, floor coverings and contingencies. She and Matt could do the painting. It's a lot to raise, but they'd port their current mortgage, which still has two years to run. It isn't unmanageable. Oh my God, what she wouldn't give to own the house.

Maybe she could say something and see how Amy reacts; like confess to a change of heart and suggest that perhaps Amy should tell the truth: that she's not sure exactly what happened with Dexter, that it could have been an accident that she spun into something else because she was so upset by what he said about her singing. Amy wanted to take her accusation back anyway. If she refuses, then of course Lorna will wave goodbye to the house. If she agrees, she'll support her decision.

She feels a fluttering in her heart. If Amy retracts, their lives will change immeasurably. Whatever she decides, it's going to have to be before Basil appoints an agent, because if he chooses Chetham & Church, there is no way Lorna will be allowed to buy the house. It's unethical. It would damage the company's reputation. She'll speak to Amy this evening.

Chapter 47

AMY

In her bedroom, a 1970s loft conversion that gets too hot in summer and freezes in winter, Amy stares at the ceiling. In the dim light she can barely see the hairline crack that runs across the middle. She needs a wee but can't find the energy to get out of bed. Her mum calls up.

'Amy! You awake?'

Amy wrinkles her nose, then shouts, 'Yeah,' to stop her mum irritating her by calling out again. She's confused. First her mother insisted she stick to her story, saying Dexter was a predator and deserved everything he got, then last night she backpedalled, spouting psychobabble stuff about Amy needing to take ownership. I mean, like, *what*?

Maybe her mum doesn't want to be blamed if it goes wrong. Maybe she's worried Amy will keep rubbing her face in it, accusing her of ruining her life. Basically, what her mum didn't say but meant is that Amy has brought this on herself and she doesn't want the responsibility for any blowback for the path *she* pushed her into. It isn't fair.

Whatever Amy does, the outcome isn't going to be pretty. If she sticks to her story, she'll get away with it but will pay a heavy price in guilt. If she retracts, the price will be notoriety. Her whole family will be affected, but it'll mostly be on her. If only she hadn't overreacted. What she should have done was ask Dexter for advice, or maybe simply called him a sad old has-been and gone home for a cry. Instead, she hid.

She rolls out of bed and goes into the tiny shower room. It's built into the eaves, so anyone tall has to lean to the left when they're in front of the sink. After she's relieved herself, she opens the mirrored cabinet. She could take an overdose. Not die, but need to go to hospital. People would feel sorry for her and stop asking questions. There's ibuprofen – only four left in the packet, though – some antibiotics she forgot to finish, and antihistamines. She rolls her eyes. The good stuff is in the family bathroom downstairs; nothing here would do much damage.

'Amy!'

Jesus. Why can't she leave her alone? She puts the pills back, opens the door and shouts, 'I'm getting in the shower, okay?'

'I'm off, Jacko.'

Her little brother races over and hugs her hard. The one person who doesn't judge her. Amy scoops him up and smothers him in kisses, making him squirm. He smells of Weetabix and milk. 'See you later, cowboy,' she says, putting him down and ruffling his hair.

'I'm a knight!'

'So sorry! See you later, Sir Jack of Bramcote.'

She goes round to the side gate and keys in the code. Her bicycle is propped up against the wall, under the lean-to her dad built. She squashes her things into the pannier bags and sets off, but instead of heading to school, she cycles to Gladwell Grove. She's not sure why, or what she intends to do, but it feels necessary.

Stopping at the corner, she sees the gates to the Coleridges' house slide open and Elise push her bike out, followed by a woman holding on to Noah, who is bawling. Elise bends to kiss him, and the woman, who must be a new nanny, has to peel his hands from round his mother's neck. Amy wonders what's happened to creepy Clara. At least she knew how to control him. Elise cycles off, leaving Noah lying on the pavement having a massive tantrum. The new nanny hesitates, then looks right and left before grasping him under his arms and dragging him back through the gates. His screams can be heard the length of the street, but Elise keeps going. She turns into the alleyway leading to the heath. Amy cycles after her.

They cross the heath and cycle along the Bute until Elise stops near a houseboat. Amy swerves into the undergrowth in her haste to hide, grazing her shin in the process. She clamps her lips between her teeth to stop herself crying out and lowers her bike to the ground. By the time she peeks, Elise's bike is chained to the pontoon. The boat is longer and wider than a traditional houseboat and looks industrial. Dutch barge Amy thinks that type is called.

She approaches with stealth. Elise's voice rises through the partially open galley door, though it isn't loud enough to catch what's she saying. She sounds like she's pleading, though. Amy hears Dexter too. He must have moved out. She feels sick. This is down to her.

She peers through the chink in the curtains covering one

of the circular windows. Elise has her back to her. Dexter is on the sofa. Elise drops to her knees and puts her arms around him, and they hug, Dexter nuzzling Elise's neck. His hands pull her white shirt out from her cropped trousers and then slide under it. They're going to make love. Amy is transfixed. Then Dexter moves his head and his eyes are open. Amy tips backwards and scrabbles to maintain her balance, grazing her knee and the palm of her hand before she's on her feet and running back to her bike.

Did he see her watching them? She doesn't think so. But what if he did? No, he didn't. She's sure he didn't.

The remainder of the day goes by in a blur of lessons and break times. Amy must have appeared to be listening because no one calls her out on it, but when she tries to remember what she's learnt, she doesn't have a clue. When it's time to go home, she's too unsettled, too antsy. Instead she goes back to the river. She's never really appreciated it before. It's always been a question of being dragged out on family walks and forced to enjoy nature, humouring Jack by shouting 'Quack!' at the ducks. Dappled sunlight caresses her face; the water reflects the overhanging foliage. A mother duck appears with eight cute ducklings. Amy continues on her way, until she gets to the bend in the river and can see Dexter's boat.

There's no sign of Elise's bike. Amy pushes hers against a tree and straightens her skirt. There's music playing. She makes a face. That's one of his old albums. Her mum has it, used to play it in the car when they were little. Is he some kind of narcissist? Or is he just depressing himself because he's getting old?

police and the court. My lawyers will eat you alive. Don't do this to yourself just because you're scared of what'll happen if you tell the truth. You're embarrassed about your behaviour, because you're the one who touched me.'

'In your dreams.'

He laughs, but it's more like a bark. 'You're kidding, right?' His voice is suddenly clear as a bell. 'Listen to me, you're very young. You have your whole life ahead of you. Do not be influenced by your mother over this, because she has her own agenda. Do what's right. You've said something because I made you feel small. Do not make things worse. You cannot win this.'

A tiny drop of spittle lands on the apple of her cheekbone, and she swipes it away in disgust. She won't cry. 'You're a prick.'

Dexter rakes a hand through his greasy hair and rocks his head back, his face twisted. 'Jesus. What is wrong with you?'

She steps onto the ladder. 'Nothing. It's you who's got a problem.' She scratches her knee clambering down onto the pontoon. She rubs it and gets a smear of blood on her thumb. God, her legs are a mess. Dexter looms over her.

'You okay?'

'I'm fine,' she snaps, glaring up at him. For one excruciating moment she thinks he's going to cry, because his cheeks and eyes have reddened like his son's do before he goes into meltdown. But then he laughs.

His laughter follows her as she cycles away, filling the air, skimming the river until it fades, and even then she thinks she can still hear it. It's weird and it scares her. She is crying so much she has to stop once she rounds the bend. She has no tissue, so she uses the sleeve of her jumper, tugging it out from under her blazer. He's a wanker. Creep. Shithead. Tosser. She can't understand what Elise is doing with him, except that he's rich. How dare he suggest she fancies him? Just because he used to be a pop star, he thinks he's irresistible. Twat. Sad sack.

Miriam leaves as soon as Amy arrives. She's full of apologies for dashing off and seems not to notice anything amiss, though perhaps she's only pretending. Amy feels let down. She cooks Jack fish fingers, potato wedges and peas, and sits with him until she hears a key in the lock.

Her mum walks in and sends her a questioning glance before kissing the top of Jack's head. She wants to know what Amy's decided. Amy doesn't understand why she's been put in this horrible position. Why did her mum make her stick to her story if she was going to change her mind? Everyone will laugh and her life will be over.

She goes upstairs to her bedroom. Her head is literally crammed with things she doesn't want to think about. She imagines ripping it off and flinging it across the room. If she's felt anxiety before, over exams and friendships and stuff, it's nothing to this. This feels like she's on the edge of a precipice, her heart racing, stomach churning. Why did she get herself into a situation where the consequences of telling the truth will be so much worse than maintaining the lie? When she thinks back to what happened, she goes hot and cold.

Left alone in the studio with Dexter, she was self-conscious and her posture went to pieces, her legs feeling like jelly, like they couldn't support her properly. She tried to sing but her tongue felt too big and she couldn't breathe properly with him sitting there, swivelling the chair with his feet.

'Pull your shoulders back. Don't hunch.'

She'd tried again, but it was worse. He jumped up and came over, saying something like *Do you mind*? She can't exactly remember because her brain was burbling, she was so stressed. He placed one hand on her shoulder, the other in the small of her back, and applied pressure. Then he let her go and leant over the chair and restarted the music, and watching him she'd actually thought, nice bum. He joined her at the mike, and when their voices combined, hers suddenly sounded great and she felt elevated beyond anything she'd ever experienced. When they stopped, she burst out laughing. Adrenaline-fuelled, bouncing with energy, she twisted round, and before he could step back, she was hugging him. Dexter peeled her off, held her wrists and pushed her away.

'Sorry,' she said, flushing beetroot.

'You have a lot of growing up to do, love. First lesson, if you're going to survive the music business, don't rub yourself up against men. It doesn't tend to end well.'

And then Elise came back in. And he said what he said and it felt like he was punishing her for what she'd done, like he didn't want her coming to his house any more.

She steels herself. Dexter Coleridge is revolting and weird and vindictive. He deserves everything he gets. He can go to hell, or to prison. She doesn't care. She just wants this to end, for life to go back to normal. Maybe she could persuade her parents to move and change their names.

'Amy, what're you doing?' her mum calls. 'Can you come down? I need to talk to you.'

'I'm doing my homework.'

'This is important.'

Amy sighs heavily. More pressure.

Chapter 48

AMY

There's a wine glass on the table with the dregs of red in it. Amy slumps down on a chair.

'Have you thought about what I said?' Lorna fidgets with the little salt cellar. Amy wishes she would stop doing it, because it looks like a stubby penis. It's weirding her out.

'Sort of.'

'I don't want to influence you in any way . . .'

'Yes you do.'

'Amy.'

Amy doesn't apologise. Why should she when she's only telling the truth?

'I just wanted to say one thing. As a young person, it's very hard to look into the future and see yourself as older. I remember thinking childhood and adolescence would last for ever. I couldn't imagine being an adult, let alone how my actions as a young person would impact my life fifteen or twenty years down the line, any more than I could imagine ever being my grandmother's age. Amy, what you do now will affect who you are as an adult, and because people will always be able to find out about it online, you can't erase it. The days of reinventing yourself are gone.'

Amy remembers what her dad said and flinches. 'I know that, Mum. I'm not stupid.'

'I know you're not. But there's a difference between knowing and experiencing. I owe it to you to make sure you understand that you may live to regret it. You need to look carefully at both scenarios. Listen to me, darling. Accusing Dexter means court, and that will be massively stressful. Those defence lawyers are brutal. They'll dredge up anything they can: look at your messages, interrogate your friends. How do you think Lily will feel when she's dragged into it?'

'I won't mention her name.'

'You may have to.'

That silences her for a moment. She says sullenly, 'I told you I wanted to tell the truth and you told me not to.' She can feel tears welling up, her throat aching with them. 'What am I supposed to do?'

Her mother places a hand on her knee. When Amy flinches, she pretends not to notice. 'I'm sorry. Truly. Of course you must do what you think best. Ignore me.'

Amy looks at her suspiciously. She doesn't trust this new version of her mother. She's always stuck to her decisions, always helped Amy make them and backed her. She snivels and wipes her eyes on the back of her hand. 'I need to think about it.'

'Of course you do. I'll support you whatever you decide.'

There is something up with her mother. Changing her tune was so weird that Amy is sure there's another reason. She had been adamant, had told that hideous story, basically saying Dexter had raped her. Why would she then tell

Amy to back off? It literally makes no sense. Unless she's in love with Dexter and thinks she'll get to him that way. That is really cringe. If she was in love all those years ago and Dexter slept with her then ghosted her, maybe this is revenge. Her mother is playing games and using Amy to get her own back, which is not on. It's not fair on Matt either. Fuck. What if she does backpedal and the result is her mother has an affair with Dexter? She isn't as gorgeous as Elise, but at that age men don't really care, do they? Look at Charles and Camilla. Nothing will help; she has screwed everything up. She can't go backwards and she can't see a way forwards. No one is suddenly going to miraculously appear with the perfect answer, her mum least of all.

After this afternoon's confrontation with Dexter, she can believe her mother's story. He is a nasty person. The fact that he said what he did after all she did was hug him, then try to make her think it was pointless to carry on having lessons with Elise, which she loves, means that maybe he's protesting too much, and is actually attracted to her and would have done something if he hadn't been worried about Elise catching him. The room is soundproofed after all, so he'd have known he wouldn't hear her before she walked in.

She goes downstairs and tells her mother she isn't changing her mind. Her mum looks at her, then nods, and Amy goes upstairs to finish getting ready for school, grateful not to have to endure another *conversation*.

Chapter 49

LORNA

Lorna returns three sets of keys to the key safe and sits down to check her emails. It's the usual litany of requests, complaints about slow progress, difficulties finding a surveyor and anxieties about exchanges. The couple interested in the beautifully renovated Victorian terrace have put in an offer of fifty grand below the asking price. She emails the owners to inform them, knowing they'll turn their noses up at it, then switches off her computer. It's been a long day, and she's tired. And worried. This morning, after Amy made her decision known, she messaged Elise.

Amy will not retract. Please leave us alone.

She sighs. What else can she do? Nothing. As she puts her coat on, she glimpses something outside between the racks of property details in the window. The drape of a long sheepskin coat.

On the other side of Griffiths Lane there is an Italian restaurant with a row of three tables outside. Elise Coleridge is sitting at one of them. Oh Christ. Lorna does not need this. She leaves the office, acknowledging Elise with a tight smile and a cursory nod.

Elise beckons her over, friendly and smiling, and

knowing there's no point running away, Lorna waits for a break in the traffic and crosses the road. Elise pats the seat of the chair next to her.

Lorna remains standing. 'Sorry, Elise, I don't have time. Jack—'

'Your help can hang on, surely? This'll only take ten minutes. We need to settle things.'

'There's nothing to settle.'

'Sit down.' Elise's voice is cold.

Lorna sits. She's exhausted and all she wants is to be with her family. She wishes she'd never met Elise Coleridge.

'My husband is sliding back into depression because of your daughter's lies.'

'I'm very sorry, but Dexter is not my problem, and calling Amy a liar is not going to help his mental health issues.'

'What about you? Are you lying, Lorna? Do you know the truth?' Elise narrows her eyes. 'I think you do.'

'I believe my daughter.'

'And I believe my husband. So where does that leave us?'

'In court.'

'Do you really want that for Amy? Being publicly shamed for lying will be worse in the long term than confessing now. If she needs help, we can get it for her. I can pay for counselling.'

'I don't want you paying for anything. You seem to think money is the answer to every problem. This is over. I refuse to be emotionally blackmailed by you.'

'I offered to change your life. We will move. I've already talked to Andersons.'

Even at this juncture, Lorna takes the news like a slap in the face.

243

'You'll forgive me for going to the competition,' Elise adds.

Lorna shrugs.

'Jack will get his place at Alverley. You'll have number 37, the school you want, and we'll be out of your life.'

Lorna's mouth waters, but her head has cleared and she is no longer in the insane grip of that house. She is not going to sacrifice her daughter. There's a proverb her grandmother used to quote: *Better a dinner of herbs where love is than a stalled ox and hatred within.* The point is, family matters more than a big house with a view of the heath and the guilt that would come with it. She realises with a nauseating jolt that she's come very close to selling her soul.

'No,' she says. 'Amy is far more important than anything you have to offer. If she changes her mind of her own accord, fine, but I'm not talking to her about it again.'

Elise stares at her, and even though Lorna would have thought it impossible, her eyes grow colder.

'So,' she says, 'I have offered you the carrot. Now I'm going to show you the stick.' She leans down and picks up a black case Lorna hadn't noticed leaning against the chair leg. Unzipping it, she pulls out a laptop. She places it on the table, opens it and angles the screen towards Lorna.

A woman walks by pushing a pram, a terrier at her heels. The dog pulls at its lead, interested in Lorna's foot. The woman gives it a yank. Elise types in a password and clicks on a document. It's a video.

Chapter 50

LORNA

The image Elise's laptop screen presents to Lorna is black and white but remarkably clear. A woman walks into view holding a shirt. She has a furtive look round, then hesitates before moving out of the camera's sightline. It only takes a nanosecond for Lorna to realise who it is.

Her.

What she cannot see but knows is that she is checking for signs of activity from downstairs before closing the door. She reappears and climbs onto the bed. Lorna reaches over and slams the lid of the laptop down.

'Dexter and I like to film each other,' Elise says with a shrug. 'You understand?'

Lorna nods. She understands perfectly.

'There is a camera hidden above the mirror on my dressing table. Sometimes I forget to switch it off. It senses movement.'

'Have you shown this to anyone?' Lorna's voice trembles.

'No.'

'Not even Dexter?'

'Uh-uh. I liked you back then and friends don't do that to each other.' Elise laughs softly. 'I felt sorry for you, still obsessed with your teenage crush when you have a gorgeous husband who loves you to bits. Also, if you show your man a film of an attractive woman writhing on his bed, sniffing his sweaty old shirt, you risk him becoming interested in that woman.'

'So are you going to show him now? Is that what you're threatening?'

'Dexter? No. Or not yet, at least. He has more than enough on his mind. I'm going to post it on Facebook. Everyone you've ever met, and ever will meet, will be able to watch you pleasuring yourself on my bed with the shirt of the man your daughter is accusing of sexual assault pressed up to your nose. Pretty, huh? And I know Dexter told you to leave him alone. He said he had to be brutal because you'd got it into your head that there was something between you. Don't be embarrassed,' Elise adds. 'You're not the first.'

'How do you bear it?' Lorna bursts out. 'Why don't you leave him if he's like that?'

'Because I love him and I know how to deal with him.' Elise's eyes narrow. 'Do you think I didn't notice anything at the housewarming? I'm not blind. I made sure I was the last woman he thought about before he went to sleep that night. I can show you that too if you like.'

'I'll talk to Amy again,' Lorna says quickly.

Elise zips the laptop back in her bag and stands up. 'I know you will.'

'You're such a bitch.'

A soft smile plays on her lips. 'Sometimes we women have to be. You too, I think.'

Chapter 51

LORNA

Lorna had hoped she'd have half an hour with Amy before Matt came home, but he's back already. The conversation would have been hard enough with Jack around, but with the two of them, she doesn't know how she's going to manage it. Amy looks rough: spots breaking out and her hair lank. Perhaps it's all to the good. Perhaps she'll sleep better if she tells the truth. Perhaps they all will. It'll blow over.

Shames surges through her, a huge, all-engulfing wave, causing her throat, neck and face to redden. She turns away, but Matt hasn't noticed. He's too busy going through a spec.

How on earth is she going to force Amy to see reason without admitting the truth?

The atmosphere round the dinner table is grim, with Amy shovelling food into her mouth while barely looking up and Lorna tense and monosyllabic.

'How was school?' Matt asks valiantly.

'Fine,' Amy says.

'Well, I had an interesting day.'

Lorna keeps up the charade for Matt's sake. 'Did you? What happened?'

He picks up some peas on his fork and pops them in his mouth. Chews and swallows, then aims the fork at Amy. 'You're going to love this.'

There's scant interest from Amy. Just a withering glance. Undaunted, Matt relates an anecdote that isn't especially funny, but Lorna laughs anyway. Amy doesn't say a word and the atmosphere flattens.

'So what's up?' Matt asks, defeated. 'Have you two rowed?'

'I think we're both just tired,' Lorna says. 'It's been a difficult few days.'

'Difficult for me, not you,' Amy says, looking daggers at her.

'I—'

'I appreciate that,' Matt interrupts. 'But you've done the hardest bit by being brave and reporting Dexter. We can move on.'

Amy's jaw drops. 'Move on?'

'I'm sorry. I didn't mean to be insensitive. It must have been awful for you. I just wanted you to know that this doesn't need to change anything. You're young and you'll get over it.'

'You don't know what you're talking about.'

'Amy,' Lorna says.

Amy turns on her. 'Stop interfering with my life! It's nothing to do with you.'

'We're only trying to help.'

'Dad might be. You aren't. You're just making things a million times worse. My life is over.'

248

Lorna gets up from the table abruptly and starts clearing the plates.

'Will someone tell me what's going on?' Matt says.

'Ask her,' Amy says, and stomps out of the room.

'Lorna?'

Lorna can feel Matt's eyes on her back. She hears the shuffle of his chair, then his hands are on her shoulders, gentle but firm, turning her around. She looks into his eyes. She can't bear it when he's angry.

'What did she mean?' he asks.

She takes a deep breath. 'Amy told me that it might not have happened quite like she said it did.' She grimaces. 'That she might have embellished a little.'

Matt groans. 'You've got to be kidding. Why hasn't she gone to the police?'

'Because initially I told her not to.'

'You did what?'

'I told her that it would be a stain on her character, that it would follow her for the rest of her life. And that's true, isn't it? She'll for ever be the girl who cried wolf.'

'I can't believe this.' Matt rakes his hand through his hair, his eyes almost popping. He looks like he's about to have a coronary. 'Can you not see how wrong this is? Amy came clean. She should have been supported and encouraged to do the right thing, not told to bury it and let Dexter be pilloried.'

'I know that now. I knee-jerked. I was wrong. I'm going to talk to her again tonight.' This isn't so bad, she thinks. Perhaps Matt can be their salvation.

'Bloody right you are.' He walks out of the kitchen and shouts upstairs.

'I'll go up,' Lorna says.

He flicks her a glance. 'No. We do this together. Amy! Down here. Now.'

Her instinct is to reply, *Please, let me do this my way*, but she quashes it. Doing things her way hasn't exactly had a good outcome.

They listen in silence as Amy comes downstairs, painfully slowly. When she slouches into the room, they're both facing the door. She looks from one to the other, her expression closed, her body language defensive. 'What?'

'Your mother's told me what's happened. That you lied about Dexter assaulting you.'

Amy stares down at her feet. She looks as though she's about to cry. 'I wasn't sure what happened. I mean, he did touch me, but not that way.'

'Can you please explain what you mean. Either he touched you or he didn't.'

'Did Dexter sexually assault you,' Lorna presses. 'Or was it an accident that you built up into something worse because you were upset and angry?'

'I'm not sure,' Amy mutters. 'I'd been singing, but he stopped me because I wasn't breathing right. I was really self-conscious. He put his hand here.' She places a hand on her stomach and covers it with the other one. Her face reddens. 'He made me breathe from my diaphragm and told me to try and keep my shoulders still. He should have just told me how to stand, shouldn't he? He shouldn't have touched me. His hands—'

'Stop it,' Matt snaps.

They both jump at his tone.

Amy looks at him, bewildered. 'Stop what?'

250

'Lying. Stop lying to us. We're on your side and we'll help you, but you have to start telling the truth.'

Her eyes well. She glances at Lorna for reassurance, and Lorna nods. 'You don't know him, Dad. He isn't a nice man.'

'Whether he's nice or not doesn't come into it. What exactly happened?'

Amy's eyes close, and tears squeeze from under her lids, glistening on her lashes. 'We'd been singing together and I was elated because we sounded so great, and I hugged him. But he didn't like it and said something horrible. Like I was being inappropriate, when I totally wasn't. And then afterwards, when Elise was there, he told her I was crap.'

Matt releases a breath. 'I'll take you to the police station in the morning. You'll ask to make a new statement.'

'I'll take the morning off and go with you, darling,' Lorna says.

'I'm not going anywhere, and you can't make me. Dad was the one who wanted to call the police in the first place. I wish you'd just let it go, then none of this would have happened.'

'You told me Dexter molested you,' Matt says. 'I couldn't simply leave it at that. As far as I was concerned, he'd have walked free to do it again. You will tell the truth, Amy. Do you understand me? I don't want to come down hard on you, but you'll bitterly regret it if you allow an innocent man to be destroyed, his family dragged down with him. I promise you will get over this. You just have to be strong.'

'You don't understand!'

'I do. We won't let you go through this alone.' He hugs her hard, and Lorna is surprised when Amy doesn't object. She's too afraid of rejection to try it herself.

251

When Amy has gone back upstairs, Lorna switches the television on, but Matt picks up the controls and switches it off again.

'Is there something more to this?' he asks.

'What do you mean?'

'I mean, the reason you were so quick to take Amy's story at face value. I did wonder if she was lying, but you were busy making it real by validating everything she said. And now it turns out I was right. She wouldn't have taken things this far if you hadn't encouraged her. Christ, what a mess. We're going to have to move.'

He's making her feel like it's all her fault. Lorna bites her lip to stop herself protesting. She only cares about two things: that Amy survives this, and that no one ever sees the video. She couldn't live with that.

'I'm sorry. I'll do whatever you think best.'

He hands her the TV controls. 'I'm going to get an early night. Don't forget to switch the lights out when you come up.'

Lorna breathes out. Thank God for Matt. Amy will tell the truth. They'll help her face the consequences. That video will disappear. Please God, let it all go away.

Lorna's phone pings just after eleven. She reads the message, frowning, then goes upstairs.

'Are you awake?' she whispers.

'I wasn't,' Matt grumbles. 'What's up?'

'I've got a bit of a dicky stomach. I've a feeling I'll be up and down all night, so I'll sleep in the spare room. I don't want to disturb you.'

He looks at her, trying to figure it out. She knows he's

252

wondering if this is about him pretty much blaming her for everything, but it doesn't matter what he thinks, so long as he believes she needs her space and doesn't make a big deal of it.

'Yeah, sure,' he says. He hesitates, then kisses her on the cheek. 'I hope you feel better in the morning.'

Chapter 52

AMY

Before she gets into bed, Amy does something she has never done in her entire life. She gets down on her knees and prays. First she prays to God, begging him to make things right, promising to be kind, to be more patient, to work harder. Then she prays to her paternal grandmother, begging her to intercede, and ends up envying her for being dead.

Praying to Granny Thompson gives her an idea. She'll go to Devon. Her mum and dad can't stop her. She's almost sixteen. She'll live with Daddy Pete and her stepmum and go to sixth-form college in Tiverton. She could even change her surname to Thompson and use her middle name, Saffron. Or Saffy! Saffron Thompson. Saffy Thompson.

She's definitely going to Devon. Daddy Pete's house is big enough. She can help with her step-siblings, even though they're feral brats whose parents don't believe in disciplining them. Amy's all for freedom of expression, but there are limits. The walls are covered with scribbles, the youngest regularly poos in the bath, and they eat like animals. It's gross. Maybe she can turn them into human beings, sort out their problems. Like in *Cold Comfort Farm*. They'd be grateful to her and let her stay forever.

Below her, the bathroom door closes. The loo flushes. A tap runs. Probably her mum. She's usually in bed first. Amy hates her so much it hurts. She hates everyone, even Lily, who should never have given her the keys to the flat.

Tonight is no different from the last, the anxiety so acute she can't sleep. Amy opens the curtains and the windows. It's cloudy, no moon or stars, but the cool air breathes on her cheeks and that's quite nice.

Tomorrow is going to be the worst day of her life. She doesn't want it to come. It's like she's Joan of Arc waiting to be burnt at the stake. The tension inside her is making her feel really sick. She runs into the shower room and retches into the loo, then kneels there sobbing for a full two minutes before dragging herself up and rinsing her mouth.

Something has to be done. She cannot live like this.

Chapter 53

ELISE

Elise struggles to surface. Did someone ring the doorbell? She reaches for Dexter, then remembers he isn't there. He's where she left him last night, on the *Liberty Rose*, her in tears, him angry and rambling. And then to get home to find fucking Nicole's suitcase in the hall, the nanny waiting for her to get back so she could leave, but not before telling Elise what she thought of her and how she was raising her son. Noah had apparently called her an ugly fat pig and then kicked her. Nicole was an agency nanny, a stopgap until they can find a replacement for Clara. Good riddance. In the morning she will beg Clara to come back, offer her whatever it takes. Clara loved Noah.

The bell rings again. She focuses on the clock. It's only just gone five. It must be Dexter, wanting to see her without anyone seeing him. Wide awake now, she jumps out of bed, grabs her wrap and slips into it. She dreads to think what kind of state he's in. Downstairs, she opens the door and presses the button to release the gate. Pink clouds glowing with a tinge of orange stretch across the dawn sky. Two figures appear, and neither is her husband. It's the female police officers who came the night Amy went missing.

When they look into her face, she sees what they've come to tell her and presses her hand against the wall for support.

'It was a jogger who called it in,' PC Carter says.

Elise holds her cup of tea close to her chest, letting its warmth heat her skin. She feels clammy.

'Where is he?'

'He's been taken to the hospital. There'll be a post-mortem later today.'

'A post-mortem?' The image that word conjures stops her breath.

'We need to ascertain if it was an accident or deliberate. In the circumstances . . .'

She tips her head up. 'What do you mean?'

'The strain your husband was under, Mrs Coleridge,' Carter says tactfully. 'He wasn't having an easy time of it, was he?'

'My husband did not kill himself.'

She wants that to be true, but he was in a bad way last night. Even though she had insisted Amy would retract, he hadn't believed her. Deep down she doesn't believe it either. There was no mistaking Lorna's terror when Elise showed her the footage, no question the woman would use all her persuasive powers on her daughter, but as the English say, you can lead a horse to water but you cannot make it drink.

And now it's too late.

'We'd like you to come to the hospital, Mrs Coleridge. To identify the body. Do you have anyone you can ask to look after your little boy?'

Her mind races. Noah waking up to find not his mother but one of the neighbours is a recipe for a tantrum. That's if she can even get a neighbour. They've turned their backs on her since Amy's accusations. So much for their professions of friendship. Apart from that small consideration, none of them know how to deal with him. If someone did agree, it would only be out of ghoulish curiosity. There's only one person who understands her son well enough, only one person who might agree to get out of bed for her at such an unsociable hour with no agenda but to help.

'Mrs Coleridge? We could leave it till later if it's easier for you.'

'I want to see him now. Let me make a call.'

Chapter 54

LORNA

Lorna's phone vibrates on the wooden surface of the bedside table. She reaches for it, answering the call with a sleepy grunt. She looks round to see if Matt is awake, then remembers she's in the spare bedroom.

'Lorna, it's Elise. I need you to do something for me.'

'Wha's up now?' Matt is groggy with sleep.

'I have to go out. It's Elise. There's a problem.' Lorna opens a drawer, feeling around for leggings and a sweatshirt.

'What kind of problem?'

She hesitates. 'I'm not sure. I'll call you as soon as I know what's going on.'

He heaves himself up on his elbow. 'Why has she asked you for help? I thought you two were mortal enemies.'

'Look, I don't know,' Lorna says, bristling with impatience. 'Don't ask questions. I've only just woken up and I haven't had a coffee.' More to the point, she can't lie without a clear head or she'll forget which lies she's told.

'Do you want me to come with you?'

'No. Just go back to sleep.'

She gets dressed and leaves the house, driving the short distance to Gladwell Grove and parking behind a police car. She grips the steering wheel as that sinks in. A police car. And a policeman standing guard outside the gates. He peers at her as she hurries over.

'Mrs Coleridge called me,' she says, trying to get round him to ring the bell. 'I'm Lorna Chilcott. I'm here to look after her little boy.'

'One moment.' He speaks into his radio, and the gates slide open to reveal Elise on the doorstep, dramatic in an ankle-length military-style coat, flanked by PCs Carter and Dutton. Even at this ungodly hour, Carter is in full make-up.

Elise's smile is taut as she turns to PC Dutton. 'How long will I be?'

'An hour or so.'

'I'll probably be back before Noah wakes up,' she says to Lorna. 'But if not, he can have toast with Marmite, or porridge. No sugar.'

She walks away, and Lorna calls after her, 'I hope everything's okay.'

Elise doesn't turn. She hasn't thanked Lorna, who has been made to feel like staff. She shoves that thought to the back of her mind. Elise can't help it. She's obviously in shock.

It's funny being here without the boys knocking around. Lorna brews a coffee and curls up on the huge and luxuriously squishy sofa. If none of this had happened, if she and Elise's initial bond had been allowed to deepen over years of friendship, this lovely kitchen could have become a home from home.

What a fool she's been. How badly she's handled everything. Her hands shake, the coffee in her mug rippling. She sets it down and pulls her bottom lip between her teeth. She's had a thought. Where is Elise's laptop?

It isn't in here. She pads in her socked feet across the hall into the front room, where she spots it half hidden under one of Elise's cashmere pashminas. She lowers herself onto the sofa and rests it on her knees. It's password-protected, but that doesn't pose a problem. She has a photographic memory for number sequences, honed as a child playing card games with her grandmother, and as an adult at university. It has occasionally come in handy.

She closes her eyes, breathes deeply, remembers the breeze, the woman walking by pushing a pram, the terrier sniffing at Lorna's boots, and Elise's forefinger tapping out a four-figure code.

The whole operation takes less than five minutes. Lorna opens the video player, finds the right day, fast-forwards until she finds what she's looking for and deletes the file, then deletes it from the recycling bin for good measure. Is it enough? There are forensics people who specialise in recovering computer data. She'll just have to hope Elise won't want a bunch of police officers chuckling over her and Dexter's writhing bodies.

She puts the laptop back where she found it and drapes the pashmina across it, then goes upstairs to check on Noah. He's still fast asleep in his racing car bed. Lorna is fond of him, but he's going to have a tough time of it as he grows up if he doesn't manage to control that temper of his.

She lowers her eyelids, the adrenaline rush of destroying the evidence draining from her. She had to do it, didn't she? Elise asked her to make a choice and she's chosen her daughter. Any mother would do the same. It has nothing to do with the shaming fit of pique she fell into when she thought Dexter preferred Amy to her. Nothing to do with his revulsion and sneering tone when she reminded him of the kiss they'd shared, nothing to do with how her life panned out because of him. She needs to forgive herself. For everything. She's only trying to protect her daughter. That's all she's ever done.

Chapter 55

LORNA

Noah is surprised to see Lorna, but his first words are 'Where's Jack?' not 'Where's Mamma?' so Lorna explains that Jack's at home, and she's looking after him while Mummy's out, but that she will be back in a few minutes. She asks what he'd like for his breakfast.

'Toast and Nutella.' He gazes up at her with his father's hooded eyes.

'I think the Nutella is just for special treats, isn't it?'

'No,' Noah says guilelessly. 'It's for when I'm sad.' He pulls his mouth down at the corners. 'I'm sad now, 'cos my daddy isn't here.'

There's no arguing with that.

Noah still has chocolate smeared around his mouth when Elise walks in with PC Carter. Elise doesn't reproach her. She doesn't say anything at all. Lorna senses they want her to leave but are too polite to hustle someone who's done them a favour. Silently she takes Noah's plate to the sink and rinses the crumbs off, then dries her hands and pulls her jacket from the back of the chair.

'I'll be off,' she says. 'I hope everything's okay.'

'Thank you so much.' Elise speaks stiffly.

Lorna briefly touches her arm in sympathy. Elise flinches, which is hurtful. A police officer opens the front door then presses the button for the gate. Lorna steps through into the blinding light of what feels like a thousand camera flashes.

'Is it true Dexter's dead?' someone shouts, and she jerks her head up.

Another officer helps her carve a path to her car and shuts the door for her, then turns his back, his arms outstretched to protect her from the cameras as she drives away. She grips the steering wheel to stop her hands trembling.

'You're already up,' she says. Matt is dressed in his work clothes, jeans and a T-shirt under an open cambric shirt.

'I couldn't get back to sleep after you left. Jack's still asleep. What happened?'

'I'm not sure.' Lorna puts down her bag and goes to Matt, wraps her arms around his neck and presses her face into his shoulder. He hesitates, then hugs her back.

'Is it bad?'

She lets him go and moves to the cafetière. 'I think so. The press were there in force when I left. They were asking about Dexter.'

'What about him? Have there been more allegations?'

'No. They wanted to know if it's true he's dead.'

'Dead?' Matt says. 'Dead as in killed, or killed himself?'

'No idea.' She switches the radio on. The newsreader is talking about someone's talent, the way they'd put a difficult early life behind them to succeed in the music industry,

264

their influence on pop culture in the nineties. The promise they showed as an actor.

'A sad loss. Our hearts go out to Elise Coleridge and their son. In other news this morning . . .'

Matt switches it off. 'I can't believe it. Did Elise say anything at all?'

'Nothing.'

'Are you going to tell Amy?'

'I think I should. I don't want her hearing it from anyone else.'

'Shit.'

'Please don't say anything,' she says.

'Meaning what exactly?'

'Don't make Amy go to the police.'

'Lorna . . .'

'What good will it do? Everyone will assume Dexter killed himself because he knew he was going to be found guilty, but if Amy goes ahead and changes her story she'll be blamed for his death. If we keep out of it, this will all go away. Elise will leave Alverley. She's already told me she wants to.'

He puts his hands on her shoulders and gazes into her eyes. 'We can't pretend it didn't happen.'

She stares back at him. 'Yes we can. And we will.'

Later, when Matt has left, taking Jack with him to drop off on his way, Lorna breathes a sigh of relief. She's shattered. She'll go back to bed for half an hour.

Her daughter is standing over her. Lorna blinks and sits up. 'Amy,' she says. 'What time is it?'

Amy sniffs. 'Quarter past eight. Why are you still in bed?'

'I had a bad night. Dad's taken Jack, so I thought I'd try and get a bit more sleep. Why don't you make yourself some breakfast.' She needs to tell her Dexter is dead before she hears it from someone else. 'Go on. I'll be down in a minute.'

But Amy drops down on the bed beside her and bursts into tears.

'Sweetheart,' Lorna says. 'What is it?'

PART THREE

Chapter 56

THE PSYCHIATRIST

You and Yours is on the radio, with Winifred Robinson. It's funny the stuff you tune into when you don't have a job. I've learnt about scams, about heat pumps and the price of care, about hanging wallpaper and pet nuptials. Today I'm the inspiration.

'I'd love to hear your views,' Winifred says. 'Have you had experience of a romantic relationship with your psychiatrist, or have you watched a friend or relative go through it? You can contact the programme by emailing youandyours@bbc.co.uk . . .'

I listen, stunned into a state of masochistic lethargy.

My phone rings. I'm hoping it will be PC Innes. I've been waiting for a response to the message I left, telling her I intend to press charges against Ben, but I don't recognise the number. I pick up anyway. It could be legal stuff.

'Is this Dr Amy Geddes?' The voice is upbeat and female. Journalist is my guess.

'Yes.'

'Lovely! My name is Tania Boselli. I'm a news researcher for *Good Morning Britain*. We're doing a piece on patient–therapist relationships. In view of what's happened to you lately, Richard and Susanna would love to have you on the programme tomorrow morning.' She sounds breathy, as though she's conferring a great honour.

'Absolutely not.'

'I understand. But as the story's been given the green light by my senior editor, it's important for you as well as us that Richard and Susanna have the truth. Your truth. I believe your maiden name is Chilcott. Are you the young woman who accused Dexter Coleridge of sexual assault in 2009?'

'I have nothing to say.'

'There are other people I can talk to, of course . . .' She lets the sentence hang.

I call her bluff. 'What other people?'

'Dr Geddes, I know your history. I do want to hear your side of the story. I want to be fair to you as well as to Dexter's family and Ben.'

'The answer is still no.'

'You were married to the actor Daniel Geddes, weren't you? Have you spoken to him about any of this?'

I've had enough. 'My name is Amy. My maiden name was Chilcott. That is all I'm saying. Goodbye, Ms Boselli.'

I cut the call.

The next morning, still wallowing in masochism, I turn on the TV.

'Something we're going to be talking about in a few moments,' Richard Madeley says, leaning on his elbow, 'is patient–therapist relationships. From research it appears,' and here he widens his eyes, 'that seventy per cent of therapists have experienced emotional feelings towards a patient, twenty-seven per cent have fantasised about a sexual relationship and three per cent have acted on their impulses.'

'Do you know what?' Susanna Reid cuts in. 'I understand that it's morally unethical, but we're talking about human nature, aren't we? From the patient's point of view, it's impossible not to feel some kind of connection with someone whose focus is entirely on you. Not speaking for myself, obviously.'

'Exactly. The patient is vulnerable. The reason we're looking at this is because of a story that's been gathering steam in the last week or so. The case of a young man who has made a complaint of sexual assault against his psychiatrist, and the psychiatrist who has countered with an accusation of her own. I must point out that charges haven't been brought, so there is no legal embargo on our discussing the incident. Obviously, what's happened is of public interest, simply because of the ethics, but this story has its roots much further back than this year.' He smiles, the light of triumph in his eyes, and I brace myself. 'It isn't the first time this particular psychiatrist has been involved in a story about sexual assault.'

He pauses dramatically. Susanna looks eager, and my stomach flips over.

'I can exclusively reveal that the psychiatrist in question is none other than Amy Chilcott, the fifteen-year-old schoolgirl whose accusation led to the death of ex-D.I.G.B.Y. frontman Dexter Coleridge in 2009. What a tragedy that was.'

The split screen behind the presenters flashes up two images. In one, I'm striding across the car park outside my building. I barely recognise myself, I look so tired and harassed. In the other, Dexter is pictured on a red carpet, his arm around Elise. He's grinning, that wicked grin that still hits me in the solar plexus. There's a glow about him. You can tell he's a star.

'Oh my goodness!' Susanna squeals, pretending she had no idea. 'Now that is a bombshell. I was totally in love with Dexter when I was in my twenties. I was devastated when he died.'

'Like a lot of fans, I imagine. Dr Geddes has declined our invitation to tell her side of the story – viewers must make what they will of that.'

They chatter on, dissecting my life and my choices, but I barely listen. I sit hunched on the sofa in my pyjamas, chewing my fingernails. I haven't showered yet, and I can smell myself.

Susanna is speaking. 'Would you like me to share another celebrity connection to this story?'

'Please do,' Richard twinkles.

'Dr Geddes was once married to the actor Daniel Geddes.'

This time the picture on the screen is of me with Daniel. We are arm in arm. Daniel is wearing a pale green three-piece suit with a white buttonhole and I'm in a long zingy orange dress. I remember laughing that we looked like fruit. It was taken at the wedding of Daniel's best friend.

'The film star didn't want to be interviewed, understandably, but joining us in the studio is Dr Martha Greenwood, who has written a book on the patient–therapist relationship. Dr Greenwood . . .'

The camera pans right, to a middle-aged woman in a dark blue dress.

'Thank you for inviting me,' she says.

I can't say I'm surprised by this turn of events. I'd been expecting to be exposed at some point. People will always be interested in Dexter Coleridge – there's a makeshift shrine to him near where the *Liberty Rose* was moored – and my old name will for ever be connected to him online. Even if I hadn't remained in Alverley, even if Ben Clarkson hadn't made a complaint about me and I'd continued to lead a quiet life, one day someone would have come looking, and all the old wounds would have opened up. That day is here.

Anticipating it doesn't make it any easier. I still feel outraged. I don't regret not obliging Ms Boselli, but I do feel the frustration of being misrepresented. I need to do something, but I don't know what. Write it down and hope to burst a festering boil, or shut it down like I have done for years? Hope that even this will pass?

I'm still mulling over what to do when the doorbell rings.

Chapter 57

THE PSYCHIATRIST

The woman in the grey suit seems familiar.

'PC Carter?' I say in surprise.

'Detective Sergeant Carter now. Hello, Dr Geddes.'

Carter was the younger of the officers who dealt with my missing persons case. All these years later, she hasn't changed much, still wears full make-up, but there is an air of authority about her that she lacked before. She walks past me into my flat. I offer her a drink, which she accepts. I make tea and bring it into the sitting room, where I find her out on the balcony. I join her and hand her the mug. We gaze out over the heath. A lot of the trees are in leaf now but you can still just about glimpse the river.

'What brought you back here?' she asks.

'I've never left Alverley, apart from university.'

'Places can have a strong draw. Sometimes they won't let you go.'

I stay silent.

'I understand you want to press charges of sexual assault against a patient?' Carter says, going back inside.

I follow her and we sit down opposite each other. She gets a notepad and pen out of her inside jacket pocket.

There are crumbs on the table. I quickly brush them off with my sleeve, ashamed. 'Ben Clarkson. Yes, I do. Although I've been advised it won't get me anywhere.'

'Why do you think he targeted you in this way?' Carter tilts her head, questioning me with her eyes.

'Why does any man target a woman? In this case, I'm guessing it's because he imagined there was something between us and I rejected him. He raped me, and then he set about destroying me. He's been in my flat since, you know. Hiding in my coat cupboard.'

Carter raises her eyebrows.

'Before you tell me I'm paranoid, there's this.' I get up and fetch an envelope from the top of the bookshelf. It's marked *UNDERSTAIRS CUPBOARD*. I hand it to her. 'There's a hair inside it. I found it attached to the sleeve of one of my coats. I think it's Ben's. I also have the sheets from the night he spent in my bed. If the DNA matches, that means I'm right.'

'So he hid, but he didn't show himself or assault you, or steal anything?'

'Not exactly. He switched the mains off twice. The fuse box is in that cupboard. He must have come out while I was asleep because he sent an email from my computer, purporting to be from me, which has ruined any chance I had of salvaging my career.'

'Dr Geddes . . . Do you mind if I call you Amy?'

'Go ahead.'

'Amy, PC Innes has talked to Mr Clarkson and was satisfied with his description of what happened. He won't be pressing charges. He expressed regret that you lost your job. He showed compassion for you.'

275

'And PC Innes didn't wonder why that was?'

'PC Innes has enough on her desk already.'

'Then why are you involved? Surely you're busy too.'

'Before she spoke to Mr Clarkson, PC Innes did a background check on you and saw my name attached to the statement you made in 2009. She mentioned it to me.'

'So?' I say.

'So, it piqued my curiosity. I believed you were lying at the time.'

'And naturally you're assuming I'm lying now? What is the point of this? That case was closed. Dexter's death was ruled inconclusive by the coroner. It was thought to be suicide or misadventure.'

'True, but new evidence has come to light and I've asked for permission to take another look at it.'

My entire body seems to draw in on itself. I'm not good with being caught on the hop. 'What new evidence?'

She leans back and folds her arms. 'Someone has come forward to say they were near that part of the river around the time Dexter Coleridge is thought to have died. They saw a figure sitting on the deck of the *Liberty Rose*. A woman.'

'It was probably Elise.'

'It wasn't. I've read her statement. She was at home.'

'Unless she was lying.'

'Her nanny had walked out earlier that day. I doubt she'd have left her child on his own in the middle of the night.'

I concede the point with a nod. 'So why has it taken the witness all this time to speak up?'

'They were with someone. The area of the heath adjacent to the industrial estate has a reputation for late-night trysts.'

'Yes, I've heard about that. But it doesn't explain why they didn't say something earlier.'

'The person they were with was high-profile. A married man who didn't want his sexuality becoming public knowledge. He gave our source enough of a financial incentive to keep his mouth shut. The guy died last year. It's been weighing on our witness's conscience, so he made a statement. Was it you they saw, Amy?'

I look her straight in the eye. 'No.' I'm not lying. I'm answering the question put to me.

'While I've got you,' DS Carter says, 'there was some talk – I'm sure it was salacious gossip, but best to clear it up – that your mother had a thing going with Dexter.'

I stiffen. Dexter said something to me at the time. I've never forgotten it. He said some people get weird when they have crushes, that they can turn nasty when their feelings aren't reciprocated. Sneered words that turned my mother into an individual made of flesh and blood and needs, capable of falling in love, of being wounded and humiliated ... At fifteen, that's impossible to hear without feeling you're going to die of embarrassment.

'If you mean an affair, I think that's unlikely.'

'No, I don't mean an affair. How do I put this? She was possibly infatuated, and he may have encouraged her.'

'Who told you that?'

'We spoke to one of your mother's old friends. Jules Knight.'

Jules? I haven't heard from her in years. She and Keith and their kids moved to the countryside when their youngest was four, and we lost touch. Mum was hurt by that. She felt abandoned.

'Okay. Well, I don't think so, but I suppose it's not impossible.'

'If Coleridge rejected her,' Carter says, 'she could have turned on him, encouraged you to stick to your story.'

I do not want to go down this road. 'If she did, it doesn't have anything to do with what's happening now.'

She stares back, then says softly, 'I'm curious. Did you lie about Dexter touching you?'

'You have no right to ask me that question.'

'As I said, just curiosity.'

'I didn't lie.'

'Okay.' The way she says it, friendly and dismissive as she picks up the notepad she's written nothing in, I can tell she doesn't believe me. I wouldn't either, but a hard shell has developed around me in the intervening years. I can't be easily moved. The past is the past.

'Has Dexter's family been pushing to have the case reopened?' I ask.

Carter stands up. 'No. But given this new information, Elise Coleridge may well want us to do so.'

'So you haven't said anything to her yet.'

She smiles faintly. 'I need to be sure that I can go ahead before I speak to her. She's been through enough, poor woman.'

I just look at her. I can hear the three words she's left out. *Because of you*.

Chapter 58

LORNA

Lorna pays the bill, then reaches for her stick and pulls herself up. Unsteady, she waits a few seconds before setting off. It's a relief to be outside, but she's anxious, knowing this is a warning sign that a flare-up of her MS is imminent. As she walks down the street, the unsteadiness increases until she has to stop because she's too dizzy to go any further. It doesn't help that the wind is picking up. It's a blustery day. She leans against a shop window and calls Bill, the local cabbie whose services she's been using since she was forced to give up driving. That was the worst day. Losing her independence like that, when she lives in the depths of the country. She remembers when her grandmother was told at the age of ninety that she was uninsurable. She'd taken it personally, been livid with the doctor who refused to sign off on her suitability as a driver, and died within the year. Bill tells her he's in Tesco doing a bit of shopping for the wife.

'Go back to the café,' he says. 'I'll be ten minutes.'

But Lorna is unable to move. She closes her eyes, and the bag of shopping slips from her fingers, a head of broccoli and two oranges spilling out and thudding to the ground.

Someone picks up the fallen fruit and vegetables and puts them back in the bag. 'Do you need help?'

She raises her eyes to the young man's face. It's open and friendly, and she responds with a shaky smile.

'I'll be okay. I just need to sit down while I wait for my taxi. I'm meeting him at Elsie May's.' She slaps a hand on the window to stop herself falling.

He grabs hold of her. 'Steady. Here, lean on me.'

Lorna acquiesces with gratitude, and they walk slowly back to the café, her Good Samaritan supporting her with one arm around her waist, the other holding her forearm. It's intimate, but she grits her teeth. He seems to understand and keeps up a stream of chatter, outlining with some aplomb his plans for his future – how he's going to be a millionaire by the time he's thirty. In the café, he explains the situation to the waitress, who fetches a glass of water. He orders himself a cream tea and digs in. Lorna is charmed, and before she knows it, she's giggling like a schoolgirl.

She sees him glance at the clock on the wall.

'I'm keeping you,' she says.

'Not at all. But I should get going. Are you going to be all right?'

'Of course I will. You've been very kind.'

'I'm glad to have been of help. And you're good company.'

Flustered by the compliment, she pretends not to have heard and indicates his plate. 'I'll pay for that. It's the least I can do.'

They smile at each other and he gets up to go. Before the door to the café has closed, the sound of whistling floats back to her. A familiar tune that she can't quite place, but it makes the back of her neck tingle. In Bill's cab, she cannot get it out of her head.

At home it feels as though the floor is moving, or that she's been on a boat all day and her vestibular system is trying to adjust to the solid immovability of dry land. She calls Matt to let him know she's back. He worries about her. She describes the encounter with the young stranger, how engaging he was. The annoying earworm she's been left with.

Matt is busy. It's rare that he isn't up to his eyeballs in work. His cabinet design and building skills have been in demand ever since they moved here. He got his first job through a contact of Pete's – her ex has been very helpful. Matt's popularity is a blessing financially, but it means Lorna is on her own more than she would like. They've made a good life for themselves, but it can get lonely. Old friends – those few who remained loyal – visited in the first year, but it seems that once was enough, and now she's expected to make the journey to London if she wants to see them, and she's the one with health issues.

Her two sets of neighbours on the barn development are friendly, but they're much older, have known each other for donkey's years and are currently cruising the Norwegian fjords together. She should have worked harder to persuade Amy to move with them. She suggested it to Jack, too, but with less conviction. He wants to build a career in London. The thought of her son makes her smile. Jack is the one they got right. She hates to admit it, but if it had been Jack in Amy's position all those years ago, she would never have been able to manipulate him. He would have done the right thing from the off.

It distresses her to remember that dreadful time, and mostly she succeeds in blocking it, but at weak moments the memories roll in and she starts to think about the damage she's done her daughter. She'd looked for ways to get closer to the Coleridges, had been stupidly infatuated with Dexter and blind to her own vanity. She had lost all sense of reality when he rejected her. She cannot believe the way she behaved. And now, because of her, Amy is making a mess of her life. Divorced, jobless and back in the news for the worst possible reasons.

If Matt ever finds out the truth, their marriage will be over. The thought of navigating life with this horrible disease on her own is too awful to contemplate.

What a selfish thought. Her own well-being isn't the only reason. She loves him. She didn't want to lose him then and she doesn't want to lose him now. She fishes in her bag for a handkerchief and blows her nose.

A noise startles her, and she lifts her head. There it is again. A soft creak, as though someone is moving around the building. 'Matt?'

Chapter 59

LORNA

Lorna's ears ring as she tries to tune in to the sound, but it's gone. The house is silent. She shivers. Sometimes, when she isn't well, her mind plays tricks and she hears things that aren't there. Her doctor says it's probably a touch of tinnitus. Just another thing to add to her growing list of symptoms.

'Alexa. Close the curtains.'

Even though no one but the flock of sheep grazing in the field beyond the garden can see her, she feels better for being cocooned by the heavily insulated brocade.

'Alexa, play Lorna's playlist.'

She changes into a pair of soft cotton pyjamas and settles on the sofa to the sounds of Jack Johnson, Adele, Amy Winehouse, et al., and after a while the feeling that she isn't alone in the house leaves her and she becomes sleepy. That tune the young man was whistling, she's sure she's heard it somewhere before. She tries to hum it, but it's elusive and slips away.

She wakes with a sense of something not being right, and realises that the music has stopped without her say-so.

Maybe Matt came home and, seeing her asleep, switched it off.

'Matt?' No answer. She calls his name louder. Something, some change in the atmosphere, makes her afraid.

She listens intently. Again, there's nothing. She needs a drink. Normally she avoids alcohol because it can exacerbate her symptoms, but she reasons that a small glass of wine will take the edge off. She'll eat something with it. A couple of oat biscuits will do the trick. Her stick is propped against the sofa, and by taking it slowly, she reaches the kitchen without mishap. Outside it's blowing a gale, the leaves on the oak tree at the edge of their land rustling frantically. Maybe the noise she heard was the house protesting against the weather. The bones of this building are sixteenth century. It creaks from time to time. The thought fails to reassure her.

The music comes on again. A D.I.G.B.Y. song this time. They aren't on her playlist. She hasn't listened to the band, except inadvertently, in almost twenty years.

'Alexa, stop.'

The music stops, then starts again. This time the volume is higher, Dexter's gravelly voice filling the barn to the rafters. It used to be one of her favourites. A song about losing the one he loves because he didn't understand her. *You tell me I don't get you*, he drawls. *But that's your power. I like to keep it simple; you like to tie me up in knots.*

'Alexa, stop!'

Something shifts, and this time there's no blaming it on the wind. Lorna feels fear like she hasn't felt since the day they found Eileen Brooker's body in the lake and she thought it was Amy. Her stomach is taut with tension, pushing bile up to burn her throat. Her giddiness increases.

The sound goes off, abruptly cutting Dexter's voice, leaving a silence as frightening as the music. She hears a sound from beyond the kitchen door and turns too quickly, losing her balance and crying out as a figure steps into view.

Chapter 60

THE PSYCHIATRIST

I rarely use the bath in my flat, preferring the efficiency of the shower, but after the day I've had, the thought of a long soak was alluring. I've been thinking about the past and my future and I've decided to sell my flat. It's time to leave Alverley. I should have done it a long time ago. After my divorce, in fact. My phone rings. I reach for it, but it slips from my wet fingers and drops to the floor. I leave it be and don't remember to look at it until I'm out and dry and in my dressing gown and pyjamas.

The call was from Dad. It's usually Mum who phones, so I panic and immediately call him back.

'Amy. Thank goodness.'

'Has something happened? Is Mum all right?'

'I'm so sorry.' He makes an odd sound, like a stifled hiccup, then goes quiet, as though he's muffled the phone.

'Dad?'

'Sorry. Mum's had an accident. She fell downstairs.'

'Oh no. Is she all right? Did she break anything?'

'She died of her injuries. I've just got home from the hospital.'

'Died?' My tongue feels fat and useless, my brain drained of words. The silence in my head is loud and chaotic. Falls happened, but the worst-case scenario I imagined was Mum lying on the floor unable to get up or reach her phone until Dad came home and found her. Not this. 'I don't understand.'

'Neither do I.'

'What was she doing upstairs?'

Upstairs is a mezzanine and consists of Jack's bedroom, which doubles as a spare room these days, a bathroom and Dad's design studio. The ground floor was designed around Mum's needs. She had no reason to be upstairs. When the bed linen needs changing, Dad does it. If Mum's in a bad phase, he takes over the housework anyway.

'Maybe she needed something. I can't imagine what.' His voice breaks. 'I've been trying to think what she would have been looking for. I wondered if it was a bird.'

A few years ago, a magpie flew into the house. It took them half an hour to shepherd it out, by which time it had shat on the furnishings. I remember Jack's glee when he told me. He'd have been sixteen. Still a kid.

'Oh Dad.'

'They've been in the house; the police and forensics, I mean. And I was interviewed at the hospital. The policeman said that anything like that, they have to investigate. They think it was an accident, but obviously they need to be sure.'

'Have you told Jack?'

'Yes. Rob's very sweetly driving him over. He's devastated, poor boy. He was so close to his mum. Will you come down, love?'

'Of course I will. You don't need to ask. I'll leave first thing.'

I leave at seven in the morning and drive straight to the hospital, having made up my mind on the journey. This way there's no pressure and no witness. On the way, I had to pull into a service station to cry, but that was because I was thinking of Dad. If I think about how it affects me, the tears don't come, which makes me realise that for all our phone calls and care of each other, my relationship with Mum never really recovered from Dexter Coleridge's death. I rarely visit. Jack, who was thirteen when they moved here, is only an hour or so's drive away at Bristol University. That's why Dad called him first, not me.

Mum is lying on the stainless steel, a crisp sheet pulled neatly up to her neck. There's a deep cut on her head and a lot of bruising. She doesn't look like my mother; she looks like a battered mannequin. I place my hand on her arm, feel cool, firm flesh through the sheet. I force myself not to recoil, to take my time to say goodbye.

'I loved you,' I say quietly. 'I can't absolve you, but I do forgive you. Rest in peace, Mum.'

And then I leave.

Mum and Dad's house forms the largest third of a horseshoe-shaped barn conversion half a mile from the nearest village and five miles from Tiverton, where Pete and my paternal grandparents live. It's where Mum spent her childhood, so it made sense for them to settle here.

Matt opens the door before I reach it. I drop my bag on the hall floor and hug him.

'You look exhausted,' he says. 'Jack's offered to sleep on the sofa, so why don't you take your things upstairs and freshen up?'

'Where is he?' I'm desperate to see my little brother.

'Gone for a walk. I'll make you a cuppa.'

I go upstairs to the mezzanine. There's blood staining the wall where Mum must have hit her head, and fingerprints showing up in grey now they've been dusted. I open the window in Jack's room, then unpack and use the bathroom. When I come back down, I avert my gaze from the wall. In the kitchen, Dad hands me a chunky blue-glazed mug. I follow him into the sitting room and sink into the enormous dark red sofa. He sits down beside me, so I twist round to face him. He has deep shadows beneath his eyes and his face has sagged since I last saw him, the flesh around his jaw puffy.

'The police are treating it as an accident for the moment, or at least that's what they've told me. They know all about that time, though, love. They have the entire family history. Hence the post-mortem.'

'I'm so sorry.'

I'm not sure what to say that won't sound like I need to be told he didn't do it.

'I was in Bodmin,' he says in answer to a question I didn't ask. 'Small mercies, eh?'

We lapse into silence. I look around. The room is lovely; Mum designed it. She'd always wanted to go to town on a house, and she'd certainly done that. The effect of the rich brocade curtains, the wine-coloured upholstery and the huge Persian rug is one of warmth and opulence. I remember Elise's house; all that cream and white. Lovely, but I prefer this.

'We can go to the hospital tomorrow,' he says. He's leaning on his knees, his chin resting on his fists. The posture makes his voice lower. 'You'll want to see her.'

I explain that I already have, and he nods as though he understands.

'She had a bit of a turn when she was in Tiverton.'

'Oh? What kind of a turn?'

'The usual. A dizzy spell. A stranger helped her into Elsie May's.'

'That was kind of them.'

'She told me the guy walked away whistling.'

'Whistling?' The hairs stand up along my arm.

'She said that after the night you spent with . . .' A flush creeps up his neck.

'It's okay, Dad. You're right, Ben Clarkson was whistling a tune when he left my flat.' A seagull cries, drowning out the smaller birds. 'What do the police say?'

'I didn't mention it. I didn't think it was important. Do you think I should?' He looks at me keenly when I hesitate.

'Mum was visibly disabled, so it isn't hard to believe that someone kind would give her a hand. It could be a coincidence.'

'A huge one, considering that only an hour or two later she fell down the stairs when she had no business being up them.' He shakes his head. 'Getting up there would have taken an effort of will, and considering what happened earlier, it's surprising at the very least.' His face suddenly brightens. 'Ah. Here he is!'

The door slams shut and I leap up and run to the hall, where Jack is untying the laces of his muddy walking boots. I wait impatiently for him to stow them away in the cupboard, then fling my arms around him.

'How long can you stay?' I ask.

'Only till Sunday. I've got three exams next week. I could ask for compassionate leave.'

'No, don't do that. It's too important. We'll manage. We don't know when we can have the funeral yet anyway.'

'I've spoken to the undertaker. Dad couldn't face it.'

I reassess my little brother as he shrugs off his coat. The fact that he's taking charge makes me feel inadequate and ever so slightly nudged to one side. We walk arm in arm back to the sitting room, where Dad is on his feet.

'I'll give you two a minute. You'll have a lot to catch up on.'

'Dad, you don't have to,' I say.

But he ignores me and wanders out of the room, patting Jack's shoulder as he passes.

Jack gives me a look, which I return. He's twenty-two and in his final year of a degree in medicine; next year, if all goes well, he'll be a resident doctor. It's time to accept that he isn't a kid any more. He flops down on the sofa, taking the place I'd vacated. I curl into the corner, hugging my knees.

'How are you?' I ask.

'Oh, you know. Knackered, up to my ears in work.'

'But loving it?'

He smiles. 'Yeah. What about you, sis? You've had a shit time of it recently.'

I smile wanly. 'I'm sorry if you've been embarrassed.'

'Don't be silly. Water off a duck's back.'

I flick a glance at him. Jack is so nice. Why can't I be more like him?

'Do you want to talk about it?' he asks.

My arms tighten around my knees. 'No. Sometime, but not now. Can we concentrate on Mum? Let's put some music on. Something she liked.'

'We had a nineties night last weekend and they played a couple of D.I.G.B.Y. hits.'

'Not them. She never listened to them, not since 2009.'

'I know. I was only three when he died, but I still had a minor panic attack. I couldn't breathe, had to get out of the place.'

'You were young, but that doesn't mean you wouldn't have noticed the change in the adults around you. I'm not surprised you were triggered. If I'm anywhere and one of their songs comes on, I feel like crying.'

Oh my God!

It comes to me like a bolt from the blue. I sit up straight. Before that year, the three D.I.G.B.Y. albums were the backdrop to my childhood. Mum had CDs she used to play in the car when Dad wasn't with us. He didn't like the band, thought they were the worst kind of uncool, geeks who thought they were where it was at. He didn't get that that was exactly what they wanted to be. By the time I was in my teens I despised them too, but when the Coleridges moved to Alverley, I started to listen to their music, on the off-chance I ever found myself in conversation with Dexter, thinking I could impress him with my intelligent critique. That's where the melody comes from. I can't remember which one, but it's definitely a D.I.G.B.Y. track. I've been so blind.

Noah.

A little boy lost his father because of me, a little boy who will have grown up full of anger and resentment and acquired a thirst for revenge. Elise would have told him what happened, that it was my fault, and my mother's, that his father died.

'Noah,' I murmur.

'What?'

I don't answer. I'm swept back to a long-ago conversation with Mum. A conversation that led to a man's death. *Promise me you won't do anything tonight*, she had said. *I only want what's best for you.*

Noah.

I lied about his father's behaviour, made him a pariah and drove him away from the people he loved. If Dexter had felt able to stay with Elise in Gladwell Grove, he'd be alive now.

How long has Noah been thinking about doing this? Five years? Ten? More? The need fermenting deep inside him from childhood. Why have I never thought about him? I looked Elise up some time ago and discovered that a year after Dexter's death she returned to Sweden, settled on Öland, the island where she grew up, and changed her name back to Karlsson. I never thought to keep an eye on her son.

'Alexa, play "Leave Me Alone" by D.I.G.B.Y.'

'Amy,' Jack says. 'Don't.'

'Shh. Alexa,' I repeat. 'Play "Leave Me Alone" by D.I.G.B.Y.'

Nothing happens. I glance at Jack, who is shaking his head, then go to the dresser where Alexa sits and follow the wire down to the plug. She's been switched off.

Chapter 61

THE PSYCHIATRIST

Dad puts the phone on speaker so Jack and I can listen to the conversation between him and the investigating officer.

'The point is,' he says, 'this guy, this stranger, behaved the same way as the man who recently sexually assaulted my daughter. Could you at least speak to the officer she reported him to?'

'We know all about your daughter's situation, Mr Chilcott. I'm afraid there isn't any evidence to warrant an investigation into Mrs Chilcott's death, despite Dr Geddes's well-documented problems.'

'We believe,' Matt says in measured tones, 'that Ben Clarkson is Dexter and Elise Coleridge's son Noah, and that's what this has been about from the beginning.'

'Meaning?'

'Meaning revenge. And if we're right and it is Noah Coleridge making Amy's life a misery, it makes sense that he would go after Lorna as well. His mother would have blamed them both for Dexter's death. That's the narrative Noah would have grown up with.'

'Mr Chilcott, I appreciate that you and your family have put a great deal of thought into this, but it's all conjecture.

A man came to your wife's aid when she was feeling poorly. That's it. You're creating scenarios to validate your theories. There are no unaccounted-for fingerprints in your house, no witnesses to a stranger's presence inside or outside.'

Jack picks up a pen and scribbles on a piece of scrap paper. *Ask them about CCTV.*

'What about CCTV?' Dad says. 'If it was him, Amy would know.'

'That costs time and money, sir, and I'm afraid we simply don't have the budget or manpower. You may not be aware, but Tiverton has one of the highest crime rates in Devon. We've found no evidence of a crime, therefore I cannot justify putting anyone on the case. As of today, it's closed. I'd suggest you contact your local undertaker if you haven't done so already and arrange for Mrs Chilcott's body to be collected.' The officer pauses, possibly remembering he's dealing with a grieving family. 'I really am terribly sorry about what happened to your wife. It's a tough thing to deal with the death of someone you love and are caring for.'

When Dad comes off the phone, he says sadly, 'He thinks I feel responsible, doesn't he? And that's why I'm looking for someone else to blame. Perhaps that's true.'

'It isn't, Dad.' I hug him. 'You've done nothing wrong.'

Chapter 62

THE PSYCHIATRIST

Dad goes to work the next morning. He says he can't sit around doing nothing; that he needs the focus and precision to shift his mind onto a different plane, clear his head and help him think. At the last minute, Jack runs downstairs dressed in a pair of scruffy jeans and an old shirt. That surprises me until I remember how much of his life I've missed out on. When Dad and Mum moved to Devon, I lost touch with what was happening in my brother's life. I didn't know until later that in the school holidays he'd often accompany Dad to work.

The house hollows out the moment the front door closes, but I ease into the loneliness. I'm used to it. Without Jack and Dad to make me self-conscious, I move around in Mum's space, touch the things she touched, allow myself to be as sad, regretful and resentful as I like. I pull out the chair at her dressing table, sit down and scrutinise my face, looking for an echo of hers. I mostly take after Pete, but the shape of our mouths is the same. I cannot believe she's gone, cannot believe she won't call me again to fuss and probe. I cannot believe that part of my life is over. No mother, no child of my own. I am a full stop.

I shake off my bleak mood. This is not the time. We might have been blocked by Devon & Cornwall Police, but there is someone else I can speak to.

'I can't really help you,' DS Carter says, when I explain what's happened. 'It's not my jurisdiction and it sounds like a wild goose chase.'

'Aren't you interested in the fact that the man who raped me could have murdered my mother?'

Silence. Then Carter says, with a certain amount of world-weariness in her tone, 'You strike me as being a conflicted person, Amy. You think you have principles, but when it counts, you look out for number one. So now you expect me to go after Noah Coleridge, despite a lack of evidence. What's in it for you?'

'Everything! My life, my family's peace of mind. Justice.'

She turns a laugh into a cough. 'Justice? Okay. How much do you want that, Amy? Enough to restore a man's reputation?'

'I don't know what you expect me to say to that.'

'Yes you do. I'll ask you again. Did you lie about what happened in Elise Coleridge's studio?'

'And what if I say what you want me to say? Will you be satisfied? Will it be enough?' I'm holding the phone so tight against my ear, the heat is almost too much. 'Or will you prosecute me?'

'You were young and thoughtless. I have a daughter the age you were when it happened; I wouldn't want her taken to court in twenty years' time for a mistake she made in the past. Dexter could have sued you for defamation, but he didn't do so. You got away with it.'

'I didn't *get away* with anything. Look at me. My life is in ruins.'

'You have had a torrid time of it lately. Maybe telling the truth would ease your conscience.'

I hesitate. Carter doesn't fill the silence. She's using my own tactics on me. 'You won't leak what I say to the press?'

'Of course not.'

'You're not recording this call?'

'No. I'm on my mobile. It's illegal to record a call without the recipient knowing.'

'Okay.' I take a long breath. 'Yes, I lied. It's true that Dexter touched me, but not out of choice and it wasn't inappropriate. I put my arms around him. I lied about that because I was in so much trouble. I hadn't thought about what I was going to say, and it just came out.'

I've never forgotten what Dexter said when he peeled me off his body, or the acuteness of my adolescent shame. *If you're going to survive the music business, don't rub yourself up against men. It doesn't tend to end well.*

Carter emits a long sigh, part satisfaction, part exasperation.

'So please, please investigate,' I say. 'Noah has destroyed me, which maybe I deserve, but my mother did not deserve to die. At the very least could you persuade the police down here to get hold of the CCTV footage before it's too late? If he's on camera, I'd be able to tell them if it's Noah. It's worth checking, don't you think?'

'I can make the request,' DS Carter responds. 'But beyond that, I'm afraid I can't help. They don't have to give me anything.'

'I understand.'

'If it turns out to be him, then that connects the two cases and I may be able to persuade the CPS to allow me to put a couple of officers on to it. Otherwise, it'll be up to Devon & Cornwall, and at the moment they don't suspect foul play. I'll do my best, but no promises.'

Chapter 63

THE PSYCHIATRIST

DS Carter calls me back in the late afternoon. 'Okay, I've been emailed some footage. We can't identify your young Samaritan, I'm afraid. He was wearing a baseball cap. I'm sending you stills, so you can see if he's familiar. The pictures should be in your inbox by now. Let me know if they ring any bells.'

'How did you persuade them?'

'I told them I wanted to reopen the investigation into Dexter Coleridge's death, that you were tight-lipped on the subject and that helping you out in this instance might make you more open to talking to me about what happened.'

'Right. Thank you, I suppose.'

'Pleased to be of service.'

I log into my laptop and examine the grainy black and white images, the last taken of Mum. She looks so fragile, standing with her walking stick, the broad-shouldered stranger reaching for her shopping bag. It's that that makes me cry – her vulnerability.

It could well be Noah – the man I've known as Ben – but it wouldn't stand up in court. In other pictures he's captured walking down Gold Street, but again, no clear image of his face. Still, I'm certain it's him. I recognise his shape and his gait.

'Amy?'

Jack is standing in the doorway.

'You're back. Sorry. Just having a moment.'

'You don't have to apologise for crying about Mum.' He peers over my shoulder. 'That's the guy you think might be Noah Coleridge?'

I nod. 'You never see his face.'

Jack kisses the top of my head. 'There's no point trying to prove the unprovable, Amy. You'll only drive yourself mad.'

'I'll go mad unless someone can explain to me what my mother, who uses a stick to get around and falls at least once a month, was doing at the top of the stairs when she'd been wobbly all afternoon. It isn't good enough, Jack.'

'But Dad says this place has been searched. There's no evidence here. If you want to go after that guy, think about your reasons. Who are you really doing this for? Because it's not for Dad, or me.'

'It's for Mum, of course.'

'I don't think it is, Amy. I think this is for you.'

I turn my head briefly. 'I don't know what you're talking about.'

He holds up his hands. 'Okay. Fine. You're the expert.'

302

Chapter 64

THE PSYCHIATRIST

Jack goes back to Bristol the next day and I'm left on my own with Dad. I could go home until the funeral, but it's only a week away, and without a job to go to it makes sense to remain down here and help with the arrangements. I call Breda, who is looking after Dylan, and let her know.

Somehow time passes and the day of Mum's funeral arrives. Jack returns, this time with his partner, Rob, but they're not staying over so I don't have to vacate the spare bedroom.

I wear a pair of wide-legged black trousers, a cream silk shirt and a black jacket. When Dad sees me, he goes into Mum's room and comes back with a pair of her earrings in the palm of his hand: teardrop pearls hanging from delicate gold hooks. They feel warm to the touch. I go to the mirror and swap them with the jade drops I'm wearing. When I move my head, they quiver and shimmer in the light.

Pete and my stepmother and their three adult kids are among the first to arrive at the tiny Victorian church. It makes me happy that our two families have become friends. When Mum got pregnant with me, Pete was only twenty-three and nowhere near ready to be a father. He'd left her, packing a bag and spending a year travelling around South America. Now, older and wiser, lean and tanned from an outdoorsy lifestyle, with piercing blue eyes and a ready smile, he is a thoroughly nice man, and if he isn't rich in material terms, he's rich in the things that count. Family, community and purpose. My half-siblings, now well into their twenties, bring cheer and energy to what otherwise would have been a miserable experience, and I resolve to see more of them once my life is back on track. I even contemplate moving to Devon and starting over like Mum did. Then I remember that her old life caught up with her anyway.

The service is lovely. A local choir sings, the vicar knows all about my mother and the readings are perfect. I'd talked to Dad and we'd chosen a poem she loved. Dad reads the eulogy. He talks about Mum's life, about their meeting, about raising me and Jack. About her stoicism in the face of her illness, her honesty and integrity. And at that point there's a noise from behind me as someone walks back up the aisle towards the door. I turn briefly – I'm not the only one distracted – and watch as she leaves. It's a woman wearing a wide black hat and a black trouser suit. There's a tut from somewhere behind me.

Before going on to the crematorium with the members of our immediate family for the committal service, I linger outside the church. It rained while we were inside, and the floral offerings ranged along the path sparkle in the sunlight. Among them someone has left a bouquet of roses so dark they're almost black. There's no card with them. It seems an odd gesture. Everything else is pretty and colourful: single roses in pinks and yellows, brightly coloured bouquets, simple posies of wildflowers. There's even a bunch from Mum's old boss, James Chetham.

'Odd.'

I turn to find a woman with pinkish-blue hair at my shoulder.

'Maybe the card fell off somewhere,' I say.

'No, I mean, it's what the dark roses represent: hatred and revenge.'

'Really?' The skin on the back of my neck prickles.

'Their name is Black Baccara. I suppose whoever left them might not have realised their significance.'

'But you do?'

'I'm interested in that kind of thing.'

I gingerly pick the roses up, holding them by their ribbon, doing my best not to touch the petals or the thorns.

'Oh look.' She stoops and reaches for the damp card that's been trapped underneath them. She glances at the printed message, then hands it to me. 'Here's part of your answer. Ecclesiastes. My name's Debbie, by the way. I run the pottery group your mother used to come to.'

I read:

> There is a time for everything,
> and a season for every activity under the heavens:
> a time to be born and a **time to die**,
> a time to plant and a time to uproot,
> a **time to kill** and a time to heal,
> a time to tear down and a time to build,
> a time to weep and a time to laugh,
> a time to mourn and a time to dance.

I peer closely at the card, read it again, then flip it over. The other side is blank.

'Was she any good?' I slip it into the pocket of my jacket, remembering with a deepening sense of unease the woman walking out of the service.

'Sorry?'

'At pottery.'

Debbie laughs. 'She was terrible, but it wasn't really about the work, it was about the chat. I'm an art therapist. People talk more openly if they have something to do with their hands, don't you find? She was carrying a lot of guilt, your mum.'

That's a strangely insensitive thing for a therapist to say at a funeral. 'What do you mean?'

She takes the roses from me and lays them back down. 'It's intuition. When things go wrong for your children, that's what happens. You wouldn't understand.'

Mouth agape, I watch her walk away.

I glance at the card in my hand. I've noticed some-thing Debbie didn't for all her *intuition*. Bitch. I smile. She's brought out the surly teenager in me.

Chapter 65

THE PSYCHIATRIST

After the final committal, we join Mum and Dad's friends back at the barn, where two waitresses have been looking after them in our absence. Mum's sisters, Laura and Kay, are here with their husbands. One lives in Brighton, the other in Surrey. Laura complains about the journey; Kay pokes around the house and asks us if she can take a memento. When Dad says, 'Yes, of course. Lorna would have wanted you to have something,' she helps herself to a watercolour off the wall.

'I've always been fond of it. It used to hang in our parents' sitting room.'

Dad is too polite to object, but the truth is, he and Mum bought the landscape after spotting it in a flea market in Paris. I don't have the balls to expose the lie and cause ill-feeling. I leave Dad accepting condolences. I can't help noticing more than one woman eyeing him up, like barracudas after fresh meat. My cynicism alarms me. When did I become so bitter?

Later, when everyone has left, including Jack and Rob, who rumble away in Rob's ancient Saab, I meet Dad coming in from the central courtyard carrying the bouquet of near-black roses. I regard them with horror.

'Oh my God, Dad. Why did you bring them home?'

He looks at me in surprise. 'Because they're so unusual. A bit Tim Burton, don't you think?'

'Couldn't you have taken one of the more cheerful bunches?'

'I liked these.'

'They look half dead.'

'Not at all. They'll perk up if I put them in a bucket of water overnight.'

The card is in my pocket. It's nonsense, but I can feel heat coming off it. I tease it out.

'This was underneath.'

He takes it from me and reads it, frowning, then turns it over. 'No name.'

'No. Did you see the woman who walked out during your eulogy?'

'I did. It threw me a bit.'

'Well you didn't show it. You were wonderful, by the way.'

He smiles, pleased. 'You think she might have left the flowers?'

'It's possible. Walking out wasn't a nice thing to do. It felt deliberate, like she'd planned it. Mum's pottery teacher says black roses represent hatred and revenge.'

He raises his eyebrows. 'What are you getting at, Amy?'

'I think it may have been Elise. If Noah is back in England and back in my life, then so might she be. The card is a message. If you look carefully, you can see that some of the wording is in a slightly larger font.'

Dad squints and I point at it. 'Here, and here. *A time to die*, and *a time to kill*.'

'It doesn't look any different to me,' he says.

'That's because whoever left them is being deliberately subtle.'

'What's the point of that? You might have missed it.'

'I have no idea. If it did come from Elise, perhaps she doesn't care one way or the other. Perhaps she's made her point by walking out of the church and the whole hatred and revenge thing. Perhaps anyone noticing this would have been a bonus.'

'Why didn't you give it to me earlier?'

'Because I didn't want to you to be more upset than you already were. To be perfectly honest, I've been so busy I forgot all about it until I saw you with the roses. Sorry, Dad. I need a wee.'

I leave him looking thunderous. I should have been more tactful, but it's been a long and emotionally draining day.

I continue on my way to the downstairs cloakroom, where I close the door and reach to draw the bolt across, but there is no bolt. And then I know. I've been trying so hard to second-guess my mother's movements and decisions on the day she died that I missed the obvious. There are no bolts on the cloakroom and her ensuite in case she had a fall. I'm so overwhelmed by the implications of this eureka moment that I almost forget to use the loo.

'Dad!'

He walks out of the kitchen. 'What?'

'I know why Mum went upstairs. It's because the

bathroom up there is the only room in the house you can lock. She just didn't make it in time.'

We stare at each other, then his face crumples.

It would be an exaggeration to say that Devon & Cornwall police express a lukewarm interest, but they agree to come and see us in the morning. Their attitude seems to be that while Mum may well have been spooked by something, there was no evidence anyone else had been in the house so there is nothing to investigate. Dad throws away the roses. I keep the card.

Chapter 66

THE PSYCHIATRIST

The following day, I drive into Tiverton and pay a visit to the florist in Gold Street. Amid the buckets of flowers outside on the pavement, there are black roses. I gaze at them for a moment, then approach the desk. There's no one there, but in a brightly lit room behind the counter, a blonde woman in a rose-print apron is fashioning a bouquet. She wraps it in cellophane, adds a pale pink ribbon, wipes her hands on a towel and turns to me with a smile.

'Can I help you?'

'I was looking at your black roses.'

'Oh yes. Unusual, aren't they? They symbolise loss and grief.' She has a strong eastern European accent.

'Someone told me it was hatred and revenge.'

The woman sniffs. 'It depends on the context.'

'A bouquet was left at my mother's funeral. There was no name, just a card with a verse from the Bible.' I show it to her. 'I'd like to find out who sent them. Now that I know what they actually symbolise, I want to thank them for the gesture.'

She takes the card. 'I remember. Normally they'll be part of an arrangement. It's quite unusual to order an entire bouquet. It was a woman. Not old, not young. Maybe late fifties. Ash-blonde hair.'

'Definitely blonde? Not auburn?'

'Uh-huh.'

'Could she have been wearing a wig?'

The woman arches an eyebrow. 'I don't think so. You know, sometimes when they go grey, women get blonde highlights rather than go back to their original colour.' She touches her own hair. 'It's more gentle against an older complexion.'

I acknowledge the wisdom of this with a smile of understanding, but my brain is firing on all cylinders. Could Elise have made the journey to Devon, killed my mother and attended her funeral? It would have been risky, but then if Noah was here too, they would have had a plan.

'Was there a man with her? A young man.'

'No, she was on her own.'

'Did she say anything?'

'She asked if I would deliver, but I told her it was not possible. It's only me here. I'd already taken some flowers to the church before I opened. Your mum was Mrs Chilcott?'

'Yes, that's right.'

'I am sorry for your loss. She was a nice lady. A good customer.'

'Thank you.' I glance up. Above her, in the corner, is a security camera. 'Do you keep the footage from that?'

She follows my gaze. 'Yes, we do.'

'Would you mind showing me when those roses were bought? I might recognise her if she's a friend of my mother's.'

There had been a lot of people in the church, but surely

312

I'd have noticed if Elise had walked in. Then again, I'd been so busy organising everything, talking to relatives, that perhaps she could have snuck in behind other people and chosen a seat partially obscured by a pillar.

I sit in the florist's workroom, breathing in the heady scent of flowers and freshly cut stems, and watch on the small screen as Elise Coleridge buys her roses. She looks *soignée* and cool, just like I remember. The sight of her brings back powerful feelings. The last time I spoke to her, round the corner from my school, she had put her arm around me and let me cry. I can still remember the smell of her sheepskin coat.

I pull my phone out of my bag as soon as I get in the car, but it rings before I can scroll to my contacts. Coincidentally, it's the one person I want to speak to. DS Carter.

'I was just about to call you,' I say. 'I've found something—'

'Amy, I need you to listen to me for a moment.'

'Yes, of course. But first . . . I'm in Tiverton – that's where Mum had been before she was killed. Elise has been here. I think—'

'Amy,' DS Carter interrupts, 'I need you to stop talking.'

I glance out of the window as a seagull swoops from overhead and snatches the crust of a sandwich from the gutter. It turns one beady eye on me, then flaps its powerful wings and takes off vertically, hovering before flying away.

'Please. You have to listen. Elise brought black roses to my mother's funeral. They can symbolise revenge and hatred as well as grief. It's a message. And there was a card. I'm going to send you a picture—'

'Stop right there,' DS Carter says. 'The reason I'm phoning you is to advise you that you are going to be arrested tomorrow. You need to contact a lawyer.'

'Me? Why are you arresting me? It's Elise and Noah you should be arresting. They murdered my mother.'

'You're going to be arrested because you've admitted to making a false accusation about a sexual assault. You perverted the course of justice.'

'But it was off the record. I'll deny I said it. I can't . . . You can't arrest me.' I am filled with outrage. How could she betray me like this?

'The witness I told you about has remembered something else from that night. The woman sitting on the deck was wearing a beanie. From his description, it sounds very much like the one we found on the heath when we were searching for you. Pink with a cream pom-pom.'

'It was just a beanie. Everyone wore them. You can't hang a case on that.'

'True. That's why I'm so pleased you came clean about the assault, so you can be prosecuted for something. A man died. I'm doing you a courtesy by not sending officers to your door. It's an offer that won't be repeated if you refuse to cooperate.'

'You lied to me. You allowed me to think that what I told you wouldn't go any further.'

'Yes, I did, because I felt it was more important to get to the truth, even if I had to humour your delusions.'

'My . . .' I splutter. 'I'm not deluded, and that's a gross betrayal of trust.'

'I need you to calm down, Amy.'

'I *am* calm,' I spit. But I can't move. My brain has either stalled or is refusing to command my limbs. My body feels heavy, my breath isn't filling my lungs properly. They won't hold me, will they? They'll charge me and let me go pending trial. But in that time, what restrictions will be placed on me? Enough to let Elise cover her tracks?

'This is not being done lightly. It's too late for Dexter, but that doesn't mean it isn't worth doing. For his family's sake, his name needs to be cleared. For that, I will need a written statement from you.'

'And what if I refuse?'

'Then you'll have to keep running, because I won't let it go. You've lived a lie for a long time, Amy. It must be mentally exhausting.'

I take a calming breath. I'll be doing myself no favours by losing control. 'Fine. I'll be with you by lunchtime tomorrow.'

'Thank you. There will be an officer posted outside the entrance to your flat. If you need to visit your home before you come to the police station, he'll accompany you inside.'

'That won't be necessary.'

'It's just a formality.'

'In case I get it into my head to grab my passport and take the first flight to Cuba? You can trust me.' As far as I can trust you, I add silently.

'It isn't my job to trust you, it's my job to be prepared for any eventuality.'

As soon as she's ended the call, I ring my neighbour.

DS Carter was right when she suggested I was desperate

to bring this to an end. It isn't normal to live as I do, haunting the places where I caused such terrible events to unfold. I *will* cooperate, in my own time. I have something to do before I oblige her by turning myself in.

Chapter 67

THE PSYCHIATRIST

'I'm going to watch the football,' Dad says. 'It's the semi-final.'

'Okay. I'll make us something to eat. Do you want it in front of the TV?'

'Thank you. That would be lovely.'

I hesitate, watching him. I don't like to do this, but needs must. 'I have to leave early tomorrow. Something's come up.'

His face falls. 'I thought you'd stay a little longer.'

'I'll be back as soon as I can. I promise.'

'What about the police? Don't you want to talk to them?'

'You can do it. I don't need to be there.'

He frowns. 'I don't like the look in your eye.'

'What do you mean?'

'Slightly manic. What's going on?'

'Nothing.'

Telling him I've been summoned back to Alverley to be placed under arrest would only add to his stress. I hold his gaze until he looks away. Carter thinks she has me, but that isn't necessarily true. If I'm willing to risk my freedom, I can do something about this.

317

Dad roars, 'Yes!' while I'm folding my clothes into my suit-case, frightening the life out of me. I collect my toiletries together and squash them in. I'm ashamed and anxious, but it can't be helped. I am about to let him down all over again.

At two a.m., my phone alarm wakes me. I slam my hand on it and stumble out of bed into the bathroom. Barely twenty minutes later I am on the road, a coffee and a freezer bag of leftovers from the wake to sustain me.

I've never been to Daniel's house in Richmond, not even to drive past. It's within spitting distance of the Richmond Gate entrance to the park. Very desirable, as my mum would say back when she worked for Chetham & Church. The detached house is double-fronted, with a generous forecourt on which stand a Porsche SUV and an Audi hatchback. It reminds me of the Gladwell Grove properties. It's built of honey-coloured brick with rust-red detailing around the doors and windows and under the roof line. A far cry from my ex-local-authority flat. I park across the forecourt and walk up to the pale green front door, on which someone has stuck a hand-written note: *PLEASE DO NOT RING DOORBELL. KNOCK.* I knock.

Daniel is expecting me, so there's no need for nerves, but they're there all the same. I haven't seen my ex-husband since the divorce. My knees feel like jelly.

He comes to the door in his dressing gown, hold-ing the baby against his chest, a muslin slung over his shoulder. His five o'clock shadow matches the shadows beneath his eyes. This is baby number two. I think it's about three months old but I don't calculate those things.

I don't even know if it's a girl or a boy. Daniel and I were the best of friends once, and knew everything about each other, but even in those first few seconds I can see he's a different man. When I knew him, he was ambitious but still unassuming and relatively humble. With success and fatherhood, his whole demeanour has changed. It's like he's taken control. It's a relief as well as a sadness. Seeing him standing there, baby tucked into his crooked arm, like he's born to it, I know I was right to let him go.

He holds out a brown envelope. He had it ready. No need for me to come in and wait while he figures out where he put it. He never used to know where he put things, was always losing keys, phone, pens.

'Thanks so much for doing this.' I check unnecessarily for my passport. It's in there. Thank you, Breda. 'I really appreciate it.'

'I'm very sorry about your mum. Your neighbour told me. She was a lovely lady.'

'Thank you.' I immediately feel guilty. I should have let him know. He and Mum always got on well.

'So are you going to tell me what's going on? Your neighbour was very cloak-and-dagger about it. I thought I'd walked into an episode of *Spooks*.'

I manage a laugh. 'Nothing like that. I should go. I have an appointment.'

'At this time of the morning?'

I say nothing, and his eyes narrow.

'Are you okay, Amy? You look exhausted.'

'I'm fine. Nothing a caffeine fix won't help.'

'I'm sorry I can't invite you in.'

I frown. 'I really wasn't angling, Daniel.'

'No. I know.' The baby grizzles, and he shifts it onto his shoulder. 'It must have been tough since your name got out.'

I shrug. 'It's been shit, but I'm just going to have to weather it.'

If he cared at all, he would have called me, but he didn't. I suspect he discussed the pros and cons with his wife and she said, 'Do not get involved.' And because she's the mother of his children and he loves her, he did what she wanted. If our situations had been reversed, I would have reached out. But there's no point having a go at him. I need him on my side.

'Can I ask you for one more favour?'

His mouth tightens, but he nods.

'Can I leave my car on your forecourt? I need to get to the airport and I've already driven for nearly four hours on no sleep. I don't think I'm safe to drive any more. It'll only be for three days.'

'I thought you said you had an appointment.'

'Yup. It's with a plane.'

He raises his eyebrows and glances at my second-hand Polo. 'I don't know, Amy.'

'Are you worried it'll lower the tone?'

'Don't be stupid. Look, it's fine. Leave me the keys and I'll move the cars round once Helen's up. Is there anything else? Do you need money to tide you over?'

I hold up my hands. 'No. Absolutely not. Thank you very much for doing this, and . . . and have a nice life.' I walk down the steps and don't look back. The door closes.

Chapter 68

THE PSYCHIATRIST

An Uber whisks me across a city only just waking up. At Luton airport I buy a ticket for the earliest flight to Sweden. I feel like a child playing truant. Each time I hand over my passport with a forced smile or set it face-down on the scanner, I expect to be pulled over by airport security. In the departures lounge I swallow back a large cappuccino. When my flight is called, I buy two energy drinks from WHSmith and find my way to the gate. I message DS Carter to tell her I'm on the road, then I switch my phone off.

I have a stopover of three and a half hours in Gdansk airport. I find a chair and try to sleep, but I've gone through some kind of exhaustion portal and I'm craving food. A mozzarella and pesto wrap wolfed down with a hot chocolate goes some way to restoring me. There's a new baby nearby and it hasn't stopped crying since I sat down. My brain skitters from one subject to another: from Mum, to Jack, to the past, to walking into our street and seeing my mother's face – the hollow-eyed desperation, a mix of anger, joy and bewilderment as she realised it was me. How could I have done that? How selfish and thoughtless I used to be. How dearly I have paid.

I fall asleep on the plane, waking only when the pilot announces our imminent arrival. We touch down at Malmo airport in the late afternoon. There's a hotel close to the car hire offices, but I can't risk a delay. By now Carter will have realised that I've tricked her. She may even know which flight I was on. I expect she already knows where Elise lives. I can only pray that with the UK no longer being part of the European Arrest Warrant Framework, there'll be enough hoops for her to jump through before she's allowed to pursue me across Sweden, giving me time to do what I've come to do. Elise and Noah have been playing cat-and-mouse with me. Up until now, everything has been on their terms. I'm taking control by bringing the game to them. If they feel threatened, they'll attack, but that is exactly what I want. I will push them into a corner and get the evidence I need.

I set the sat nav on my hired car for the island of Öland, crack open one of the energy drinks, now at an unpleasant room temperature, and head north as the caffeine races through my bloodstream.

The view from the bridge spanning the Kalmar Strait is stunning, a sheet of gleaming silver over which the evening casts an eerie light. This is the land of the midnight sun. I've heard it doesn't get properly dark at this time of year. I'm headed east, visor down, nerves twitching, hands gripping the steering wheel. Eating up the three and three-quarter miles of straight road and smooth tarmac over still water, I have an urge to swerve the car, crash through the metal barriers and career into that gently rippling expanse of sea.

I do my breathing exercises, and slowly my pulse calms and the feeling disappears.

Öland is flat and green, a narrow tract of land shaped like the train of a wedding dress, buffering one hundred kilometres of the east coast of Sweden from the ravages of the Baltic Sea. I come off the main road at the first opportunity, pull into a supermarket car park and buy myself a bar of chocolate, a packet of crisps and a banana. And another energy drink. My mouth is beginning to feel raw with the excess of sugar, my body sick with the caffeine overload, but I'm awake enough to carry on, and that is all that matters to me at this point. There'll be time enough to sleep when I reach my destination. It's only half an hour up the coast.

The cabin I rented before I set off is in a pine forest north of Borgholm and only a short walk to the shore of the Kalmar Strait, one of those idyllic Instagrammable destinations. It's called De Gömställe, which means The Hideaway. I get out and stretch, breathing in the scent of earth and pine needles. Birdsong is everywhere, and sunlight zigzags through the ranks of conifers.

Accessed by a discreetly hidden key box, the front door opens directly on to a kitchen-cum-sitting-room nicely decked out in cosy neutrals. There's a decent-sized bathroom and a small bedroom with painted furniture. Outside is an unfenced clearing cut about thirty feet into the forest. There's a shed containing four bicycles, which guests are encouraged to use to explore the surrounding area.

It would be useful to switch my phone on at this point, if only for the internet, but I can't face the inevitable barrage of *Where are you?* messages from Dad and DS Carter. I flop down on the bed and close my eyes. I fall asleep, but keep waking up, the night haunted by the dead: by Dexter and my mother.

Sometime after four a.m., I wake abruptly, convinced I've heard something. It was a *crump*, like someone treading on a cardboard box. I slide out of bed and go to the window, lifting the edge of the blackout blind. Washed with a pale hint of sunlight, the forest at night has an eerie quality. I stay there until I grow too cold. There is no one creeping around. I let the blind drop and go back to bed. By some miracle, I fall asleep again. Until another sound has me lurching awake.

This time there's no mistaking the rhythm and weight of human footsteps. I pad quietly into the kitchen and find a sharp knife. When I open the front door, the cold hits my face, tightening my skin. I peer through the trees, but see nothing. Then I look down.

Lying on the stoop is a bundle of fur. I grimace. Whatever it is must have been attacked by an animal and left there as some kind of offering, like cats do with mice. I flick the switch for the outside light and recoil.

'Oh my God. Dylan.' I slam the door shut and cover my mouth with my hand. My heart is racing. Of course it isn't Dylan. It can't possibly be. It just has similar markings.

I open the door again and crouch to inspect the carcass properly. I gingerly curl my hand around the creature's back, and as I lift it, its head lolls back. This cat hasn't been mauled; it's had its neck wrung. A human did this. Elise and Noah know I'm here.

Trying not to gag, I ease the corpse gently into a bin bag that I find after a rummage through the kitchen cabinets, then bring it inside and bolt the door. I wrap myself in a throw, sit on a chair facing the door, the knife in my hand, and wait for morning. This is not about a swift revenge. That wouldn't satisfy the Coleridges. This is about dismantling my confidence and my sanity bit by bit. I remind myself that I've come here to provoke a reaction. And so far, it seems I'm succeeding.

Chapter 69

THE PSYCHIATRIST

According to the clip file containing useful information for guests, the police station is on the edge of town. It won't be difficult to find. I put the bagged-up corpse on the front seat, key the address into the sat nav and head into Borgholm. Helpfully, the officer on reception speaks decent English. I place the plastic bag on the counter.

'This is a dead cat. Someone killed it and left it on the doorstep of the cabin I'm renting.'

'Name, please.'

'Dr Amy Geddes.'

'Where are you staying?'

'The cabin is called De Gömställe.' I may have mispronounced it, but she seems to know what I mean.

'You are from England?'

'I am.'

She pulls on a pair of latex gloves and comes out of the office. 'Open the bag, please.' She peers inside and pokes the corpse with the end of a pen. 'Maybe it was attacked by a wild animal.'

'I don't think so. If you look at it properly, you'll see there are no open wounds. It was a human who did this.'

She gives me a look that says she's had enough of me wasting her time. 'Dr Geddes. Why would someone go to this trouble?'

'Because they want me to know that they know I'm here. I can give you names. Elise and Noah Coleridge.'

She picks up the bag and hands it to me. 'I cannot help you with this.'

'Because you're *so* busy?'

Her face shuts down. 'Enjoy the rest of your stay, Dr Geddes.'

I find a café and order some kind of fish paste on rye bread. The meal satisfies my hunger but doesn't improve my mood. It's served by a teenager who looks at me like I'm from another planet when I ask if she knows Elise.

'I do not understand.'

'Elise Coleridge? Do you know her?'

'Ah! No. Sorry.'

Disappointingly, apart from the newsagent, none of the shops open until ten. The newsagent stocks one English newspaper – *The Times*. I buy a copy, then pick another café because I'm too embarrassed to return to the first one, and sit with a cup of coffee and a pastry I don't need. There's another article about my case in the paper, but it's on page seven and is mercifully shorter than the others have been. Exhaustion comes in waves and the words swim. A man walks past the window, and my heart lurches. He's tall and skinny and has unruly dark hair and hooded eyes, and for a split second I think it's Dexter. But this guy is in his early thirties and Dexter is dead. I order another coffee.

Finally, ten o'clock comes. I get to my feet and head to

the information centre, where I try subtlety, pretending to be a culture fiend, asking the manager, a woman with a mane of long grey hair, about opportunities locally for young people interested in a career in the arts, and whether there's a choir.

'Yes, of course,' she says. 'We love to sing.'

'In the theatre?' I ask hopefully.

'Not so much. But in church, yes.'

I remember Mum saying something about Elise being churchy. 'What about singing lessons?'

'You want a singing lesson while you're here?'

'I'd be interested. Perhaps you could give me details of any teachers locally.'

'There is one,' she says, clicking on her keyboard.

I wait with bated breath.

'His name is Ulf Erickson.' She scribbles down his number. 'Perhaps you could learn some Swedish songs. We love to sing when we drink.' And then she lets rip. I don't understand a word, but I smile appreciatively and clap when she's finished. She laughs, and in that moment of connection, I throw my dice.

'You don't happen to know an Elise Coleridge, do you?'

Her laughter dries up. 'I don't recognise the name.'

'Never mind. And thank you for the song.'

She hands me a folded map of the town. '*Du är välkommen*. Enjoy your stay.'

I get a similar response at every establishment I try. If Elise is on the island, which I'm one hundred per cent certain she is, she is being protected.

I still haven't switched my phone on, a state of affairs

I realise is getting ridiculous, but the longer it stays off, the harder it becomes.

I find my way to the town's theatre, where a woman is unlocking the door. I hurry over and catch it before it closes. She switches the light on and turns, startled to find me hovering in the doorway. She says something in Swedish and I ask her if she speaks English.

'We're not open,' she says.

'That's okay. I just need to ask you something. I'm looking for a woman named Elise Coleridge. She was involved in musical theatre when she lived in the UK. That's how I met her.' I hope she'll assume I'm part of the theatre family. 'She grew up on the island and we lost touch when she moved home. I was hoping to find her while I'm here, but I don't know where to start.'

The woman regards me with suspicion. 'You are the journalist?'

So that's the assumption people are making. 'No. Elise was my vocal coach. That's how we became friends. I understand how you might want to protect her privacy—'

'Then you will understand why I won't be answering questions about her.'

I nod. 'I'm sorry to have bothered you.'

At the local library, the librarian proves equally intractable, and when I exit into the bright sunlight, I'm at a loss. I am so tired. My skin is itching, a rash developing on the back of my right hand, on my inner wrist and in the crook of my elbow. I shove my fingers up my sleeve and scratch frantically.

I go for a walk to consider my next step, trudging down to the harbour and along the shore. The wind whips up my hair and flings it in my face. I find a claw clip in my bag and secure it. For a moment, my mood lifts. The air feels healthy. The stony landscape is alive with seabirds, and wildflowers wriggle up through the rocks. It is beautiful, windswept and romantic. I lower myself onto a smooth boulder in a spot offering some protection from the wind, and hug my arms around my knees. The sea is choppier than it was when I drove across the bridge, but perhaps that's my perception. Things look smooth from far away, but up close there's turmoil.

I understand that this is retribution, that the Coleridges feel fully justified in what they've done and that perhaps they don't even care about the consequences. That makes them extremely dangerous. If it was just about me, a kind of tit-for-tat, I wouldn't care, because part of me believes I had it coming, but they killed my mother and that isn't right.

Something tickles my face. I touch my cheek and trace the tracks of tears. I hadn't realised I was crying. Memories wriggle up through my dark thoughts like the wildflowers through the rocks. I crush them down, but they keep springing back. I'm ripped back to waking in the morning to be told by Ben that we'd had sex, to the too slow realisation that I had not been part of what had happened; that I had been elsewhere, in a drugged-up dream. Violation. Rape. Malice.

I mustn't think about it.

I can't help it. I was responsible for tearing Noah's family apart, for his father's death. For his screwed-up psyche. He grew up in the aftermath. He must have thought that I'd walked away unscathed, to have come for me as violently as he has. But I didn't. I'm as damaged as he is. I'm just better at keeping everything locked away. I'm not in control; not any more.

As I look out to sea, my sight blurry with tears, a hand stretches out of the water. I jump to my feet. Someone is drowning. Even though I immediately realise there's no one there, even though a seabird has just flapped its wings and risen from that spot, I scream Dexter's name and run tripping and sliding on the loose stones, reason lost, an acute sense of urgency powering me on. My body braces against the freezing cold as I crash through the surf. I keep going, the soft floor of the ocean shifting under my feet. The sting of the Baltic brings back such an acute memory of cutting into my own flesh that I cry out and curl my hands into tight fists. I wade deeper, flinching as the water laps at my thighs, against my navel, my ribcage.

I'm petrified, but I want to feel what Dexter felt. It's my fault he's dead, my fault my mother has been murdered, my fault my marriage ended. I have no job, no close friends; my career is in tatters. Elise and Noah think I deserve this, and so do I, at heart. I've always known the past would catch up with me, always known I'd eventually have to pay for the misery I caused. It doesn't matter what I do, none of this will ever let me go. Most people would probably rather I did not exist.

The sea is all around me. My legs and stomach have grown used it. I wade further in, just to feel that stab of cold around my lower ribcage, my breasts. I'm in up to my sternum. The waves lap at my chin.

Then a dog barks, and I come to my senses. I gather my splintered thoughts and glance over my shoulder as a

331

golden retriever charges into the breaking waves, mouth grinning, tongue lolling. A long-legged man strides across the stones to the shoreline.

He squints at me, shouting in English, 'What are you doing?'

'I . . . I . . .' The trembling starts as I try to get the words out, convulsive and deep in my muscles.

He starts to take off his shoes, and that clears the fog.

'It's okay,' I shout. 'I'm coming back.' I wade towards the shoreline, pulling at the water with my hands. 'I'm so sorry. I wasn't going to do anything stupid.'

I step onto the shingle, feet sloshing, the wind chilling my skin through my drenched clothes. My teeth are chattering.

'Here.' The stranger unzips and removes his fleece. He drapes it round my shoulders, then removes his chunky woollen beanie and pulls it over my wet hair. Then he hugs me, and it's the best thing I've felt in a long time.

'Balto!' he calls over my shoulder.

The dog wheels round, splashes out of the water and shakes the droplets from its fur. The stranger rubs my arms with brisk efficiency so that it doesn't feel like an intrusion, more like a small child being towelled dry by a teacher. He reaches into his knapsack, pulls out a thermos and takes the lid off. 'Tea,' he says, helping me clasp my frozen hands around it.

I drink gratefully while he watches, his fingers looped around the dog's collar.

'You're English?' I ask.

'I am. Is there someone I can call?'

I look at him properly. He is in his sixties, tall and thin,

332

with fading blonde hair and a face full of creases. He bears a passing resemblance to Sting.

'No. I'm fine.'

'You've just walked into the Kalmar Strait with your clothes on. It's not at its coldest at this time of year, but it's the Baltic, not the Mediterranean, so it's still bloody cold. Hypothermia can cause you to go into shock, and that can be lethal. I really think I ought to take you to A&E.'

'I'm all right. Really. It's nothing a hot bath won't cure.'

'I'm serious.'

'I know, but please don't. I'll be okay. My cabin isn't far.'

'Well, if you're sure. Just get home and remove your wet clothes as quickly as possible. If you need someone to talk to, I know a very good psychiatrist on the island. I could give him a call.'

'I *am* a psychiatrist,' I can't resist telling him. 'Are you here on holiday?' I add, to steer him away from the subject of my mental health.

'No. I live here. Come on, I'll walk you back to your car.'

'You really don't have to do that,' I say, as shivers rack my body.

'Of course I do. I volunteer with the coastguard. Balto and I would be failing in our duty if we didn't see you safe.'

I yield, and we walk briskly back towards the town. My feet are so painfully cold I think my toes will break off if I don't get back to the car soon.

'You're staying at De Gömställe, aren't you? You're Dr Geddes.'

I tense. 'How did you know?'

'Sorry,' he says. 'That sounded a bit stalkerish, didn't it? I'm Gabe Lewis. Your host. Öland Cottages is my business.

I own or manage most of the holiday homes this end of the island. It's not unknown, but it isn't often we get lone females staying here. What brings you to the island?'

'My mother died recently. I wanted to look up an old friend of hers. Perhaps you know her? Elise Coleridge.'

'Careful there,' he says, catching my elbow when I stumble on a loose rock 'The name rings a bell. I can ask around if you give me your number.'

I glance at his profile. Am I imagining it, or does he look shifty. Like everyone else I've spoken to on the island. 'Okay. Thank you.'

We cross the square to where my car is parked. I pull off the beanie and unzip the fleece, but he shakes his head.

'Keep them on until you're somewhere warm. I'll drop round later to pick them up.'

He promises to get back to me if he finds anything out, then he turns away and, with a wave, strides back towards the coastal path, Balto loping along beside him. And I think to myself: you know Elise. All of you do.

Chapter 70

THE PSYCHIATRIST

I place my copy of *The Times* on the driver's seat to protect it from my sodden jeans, then turn on the engine and blast the heating. While I wait for the windscreen to clear of steam and my body to thaw out enough to be able to steer the car and work the pedals, I contemplate the blank screen of the phone on the seat beside me. With a sigh, I reach for it and switch it on. It's time.

There are nine notifications, four from Dad, the rest from DS Carter.

Amy, this is DS Carter. It's 1.15. Can you let me know if there's a problem.

Where are you, Amy? It'll be far worse for you if you run away from this.

You've put me to enormous trouble.

Do not think of approaching Elise Coleridge if you find her. That would be harassment.

Leave that family alone and come back to the UK immediately.

I can feel her fury pulsing off the screen. It isn't going to be pretty when I get back, but for now I can carry on unimpeded. I respond.

I'll be back tomorrow, when I've got the evidence you need to pursue the right people.

I'm running out of time, but there is a way to find Elise. I am certain my host knows where she lives. I have his number. I'll go back to the cabin and get showered and changed, then I'll ask him to meet me for a coffee. If he won't tell me her address, maybe he'll call her for me.

Across the road, a tall woman with ash-blonde highlights strolls out of the bank. My mouth drops open. It's Elise, stylish in high-heeled boots and a long padded coat. She folds herself gracefully into a sleek silver car.

Following at a discreet distance, I drive in the direction I would have taken anyway, passing the entrance to the track leading to my cabin before turning off the main road into a narrow lane a couple of hundred yards further along. I pull over and follow the track on foot until I reach a large modern house built of glass and weathered wood on the edge of the strait. The car I saw Elise get into is parked outside.

Concealed by the trees, I look through huge wrap-around windows that face out onto the water and the forest into a room containing a long white sofa, a table and chairs and a shelf of glossy coffee-table books. At the back are kitchen units and a long table. The contemporary interior isn't so very different from Gladwell Grove, with its creamy neutrals, comfortable cushions and fur blankets.

Elise comes into view, stepping out onto the deck, and stoops to light the fire in a shallow rust-coloured fire bowl. She has removed her coat and is elegance personified in white wide-leg trousers and a fawn-coloured cardigan, similar to the ones dancers wear. Once the fire is going well,

336

she lights a cigarette and smokes it gazing out over the glimmering water. The smoke drifts in my direction.

Further along the shore, a family of five in matching wetsuits and lifejackets launch their dinghy. They paddle out into the strait, then turn south, waving at Elise as they pass. She waves back.

Hugging myself for warmth, I watch their progress, thinking how idyllic it all is, how peaceful and clean. After a few moments, I realise the birds have stopped singing. The deck is empty. Elise has gone back inside.

There's a sharp sound, a twig snapping. Before I can turn, an arm goes round my shoulders and my cry of alarm is muffled as a wad of damp cloth is pressed against my nostrils. I breathe in something sweet and pungent, and darkness swallows me.

Chapter 71

THE PSYCHIATRIST

My head is heavy and stuffed with cotton wool, my physical inertia profound. I'm under a blanket. I move my hands beneath it and realise to my dismay that I'm only wearing my underwear. Where am I?

'You're awake.'

It's Elise. Now I remember. The forest. The house with the silver car parked outside it.

'What happened? Where are my clothes?'

'You fainted on the deck. You were soaked to the skin. Here.' She hands me a soft pile of folded clothes. 'These should fit you. Yours are in the drier.'

She's loaned me a pair of jersey sweatpants, a white long-sleeved T-shirt and a beige pullover. I put them on. The pullover is cashmere and deliciously soft. 'How long have I been out?'

'A couple of hours.'

'Hours!'

'My fault. I persuaded you to drink a mug of hot *glögg*. I thought it would help revive you, but it had the opposite effect. It's pretty strong.'

'I don't remember that.'

'You were a little delirious. Spying on me in that condition, I'm not surprised you fainted. You've made yourself ill.'

'I wasn't spying. I was working up the courage to approach you.'

'You couldn't have rung the doorbell like a normal person?'

'I was about to.'

'If you say so.'

She looks up at the sound of footsteps. 'Ah, Noah. You remember Amy Chilcott, don't you?'

He walks over and peers down at me. 'Hello there.'

Ben. If I needed confirmation, which I don't, here it is, in the flesh.

'Perhaps we can talk now,' Elise says. 'Do you want to explain why you're here?'

'You know why.'

'I'm afraid that's not true. I'm completely in the dark.'

I glare at her. 'I am here because one or both of you murdered my mother.'

'Lorna is dead? Wow. I'm so sorry. But we had nothing to do with it. Did we, Noah?'

Noah grunts. I look directly into Elise's eyes. She doesn't flinch.

'Well, perhaps not sorry exactly,' she adds. 'You and your mother drove my husband to suicide. I will never forgive that.'

'Was it you or Noah who pushed her down the stairs?'

'Don't be ridiculous.'

'You were in Devon, Elise. I have you on CCTV at the florist. You bought black roses for my mother's funeral.'

'Someone who looks like me, perhaps.'

'There's no point denying it. The florist will be able to identify you.'

Noah has been leaning against the wall listening to all of this. Now he comes over to sit next to his mother.

'Your lies killed my father,' he says.

I squeeze my hands together on my lap until my knuckles whiten. 'I freely admit that my actions may have inadvertently contributed to his death, and for that I'm truly sorry. I never meant anyone to get hurt, but I was young and confused. You, on the other hand, planned to rape me.'

Noah laughs.

'You think that's funny?'

'Yeah. I think it's funny that you'd seriously believe I'd touch you.'

I stare. 'But you said . . . I don't understand. There was semen between my legs.'

'I didn't have to rape you to do that.'

I close my eyes for a second, revolted. 'I could have gone to the police and had a rape test.'

'You didn't, though, did you? Because you're such a sad bitch, you believed what you wanted to believe.'

'I can accept that you wanted revenge, Noah. You've got it. I no longer care what you have or have not done to me. But I don't understand why my mother had to die. She was unable to defend herself. One of you watched her crawl upstairs to escape and pushed her down. What kind of person kills a vulnerable woman in cold blood? What kind of person kills a cat, for Christ's sake? You're sick.'

340

'You found my gift?' he says. 'I hope it wasn't too much of a shock.'

I glare at him.

'Enough,' Elise says. 'I don't have time for this.'

'Fine. I'm busy too. I'll see you in court.' I get up to go, but Noah blocks my exit.

Elise approaches. She speaks gently, patiently. 'It's all right, Noah. Let me deal with this. Amy, darling, you've made a lot of trouble for us. If I let you return to the UK, you'll continue to do so. The police will find out I was in England when Lorna died. They'll reopen the case.'

'They know I came here.'

'Of course. You've been asking around after me. Everyone knows, like they know you attempted to take your own life today.'

'Who told you that?'

'A friend in town. You arrived here soaking wet and very cold. While you slept, I made some phone calls and heard about the stranger who was talked down by one of our volunteer coastguards. So no one will be surprised if the next time you attempt it, you succeed. It's common knowledge you have mental health issues and that you sexually assaulted a patient and lost your job. It's common knowledge that you have a fixation with my family. The police will be given a copy of the lunatic email you sent to your place of work. You'll drown yourself in front of this house. Everyone will understand the significance of that.'

Noah takes me by the arm and hauls me out onto the deck. His nearness, the smell of him, brings back that night. Spooning my body as I lost consciousness.

I glance at the water, so still and calm. There isn't a soul in sight.

Elise is right. People will believe my death is a message meant for her, a final act of atonement on my part. Noah clamps his hand over my mouth and starts to drag me to the steps.

A dog barks.

'Gabe,' Elise says with exasperation. 'Fuck.'

Chapter 72

THE PSYCHIATRIST

A familiar golden retriever runs out of the forest and up the steps onto the deck. It comes straight to me and I instinctively put out my hand for it to sniff. I can't see Gabe, but I get the picture. This is his house. Elise is his Swedish wife.

Elise has vanished inside. She comes back out again and strides over to where Noah is still holding me. She shows me a small pistol with a mother-of-pearl handle. 'If you say one word, both of you die.'

'Mamma,' Noah protests.

'Not you, you idiot,' she hisses. 'Gabe.' She puts the gun behind her when Gabe comes round the side of the house, jogging up the steps and divesting himself of his coat.

'You found each other. That's wonderful.' His look of happy surprise would have been endearing if I hadn't been so scared. He looks me up and down. 'And I see my lovely wife has lent you some dry clothes. You didn't go home first?'

'Um...'

'Amy felt faint while she was driving,' Elise says, hurrying forward. 'Thank goodness I happened to be on my way home and saw the car veering into the side of the road. I drove it to a safer spot before bringing her back here. Amy, this is my husband, Gabe. But you met earlier, I think.' She kisses him. 'Hello, darling. I thought you'd gone for a beer with Lars.'

'He had to cancel. It's fine, I was knackered anyway. A couple of paddleboarders got themselves into trouble earlier. So you two have had a chance to talk?'

'We have,' Elise says.

'It's good to clear the air.'

I hold his gaze, hoping he'll read the fear in mine. 'You knew who I was?' Of course he did. How could I not have realised? If he was a normal human being, he'd have googled me after I took the booking. He would have warned Elise who was coming, asked her if he should cancel me. She must have told him no, possibly even said something about the healing process. And he fell for it. 'Why didn't you tell me?'

'You'll have to forgive me. You caught me by surprise and I wasn't sure what to say. Later I realised I should have mentioned it, but I reckoned Elise would come looking for you when she was ready. You found each other without me, and I'm glad. It was courageous of you to come here, Dr Geddes.'

'It's Amy,' I say numbly. 'You can call me Amy.' I still feel woozy. If Gabe hadn't turned up, I'd never have had the strength or coordination to get myself out of trouble. I'd be dead by now.

'Seeing you down at the beach today, I realised just how hard it must be. You know, yoga is very beneficial at times of acute strain. I run a wellness retreat here. I'd be happy—'

'Will you stay for supper, Amy?' Elise interrupts swiftly. 'There's plenty of food.'

Gabe puts his arm around his wife's shoulders and kisses her temple. 'I'm so proud of you, my darling.'

Is he completely blind? He must know none of this adds up. Or perhaps not. Gabe is besotted. Elise could tell him that the Easter Bunny exists and he'd believe her. 'Thanks, but I really ought to go. Early flight.'

Should I tell him that Elise is carrying a gun, that his wife and stepson are intent on murdering me? What if he's in on it? What if the woo-woo shtick is a ruse and he's actually a flint-hearted opportunist? Even if he's deluded about his perfect wife, the scales aren't going to suddenly drop from his eyes. He'll question my sanity. As Elise has pointed out, I have form.

I'll leave at the first opportunity, not stop at the cabin, get straight in my car. My passport is in my bag, along with my debit card and car key. My toothpaste and pyjamas are hardly worth risking my life over.

'You'd be very welcome,' Gabe says. 'It's nice to have a Brit to talk to occasionally.'

Noah hasn't said anything, but the rigidity in his shoulders isn't lost on me.

'That's very kind, but I won't if you don't mind.'

As I turn and take a step towards the edge of the deck, my head spins and I sway. Gabe catches me, his eyes crinkling as he smiles.

'Steady there. Noah, go get Amy some water. That settles it,' he tells me. 'You're staying for supper.'

'Sit down, Amy,' Elise says with faux concern. 'Let me get you a drink. Gabe? Beer?'

The light is changing across the strait, washing it with silvered amber. A bird of prey swoops, dives into the water with a splash and reappears with a glistening fish. Noah returns with the water. As he passes the glass to me, the tips of our fingers touch and my nerves spray sparks across my skin.

Chapter 73

THE PSYCHIATRIST

They serve baked salmon, new potatoes and sweet pepper salsa. When offered a glass of wine, I ask if they have any soft drinks, and Gabe jumps up to fetch me a Coke, to Elise's evident displeasure. Elise prepares a salad while Gabe bakes the fish in silver foil on the barbecue and chats to me. It's surreal. Gabe is charming and expansive, Elise interjecting only occasionally, Noah monosyllabic. Surely Gabe can feel the atmosphere? I glance at him as he cuts into the delicate flesh. Nope.

I avoid Noah's eyes and focus on Gabe, asking him questions about his family in England. He has an ex-wife and two daughters. He's a very open man. He admits he was still married when he met Elise and tells me his ex hasn't spoken to him since. One of his daughters recently made contact, but not the other. 'It's been difficult,' he says. 'I hate that I hurt my family, but I have no regrets.'

That may change, I think, feeling sorry for him.

Elise laughs. 'You are such a romantic, my love.'

'Anyone special in your life, Amy?' Gabe asks.

'Not at the moment, no. I was married, but we broke up

because I didn't want children and he desperately did. I loved him, I still do. There's been no one else since.'

'That's tough.'

'It is.'

'Why don't you want kids? Sorry. Is that too personal? Don't answer if you don't want to.'

'It's fine.' I feel for the right words. 'It's complicated. There are other factors, but the main reason is because I've seen how easily they can be damaged. I don't want to be the cause of anyone else's pain.'

Noah snorts.

Gabe squeezes my shoulder. 'I understand. You're talking about your past.'

Gabe is growing drowsy, struggling to stay alert. He admitted to being tired earlier, but this worries me. It isn't normal sleepiness; I think they've drugged him like they drugged me. I need to leave. I feel better having eaten and drunk, the sugar and caffeine from the Coke perking me up. Perhaps I could ask him to walk me to my car before he's completely incapacitated. I glance at Elise. She's watching Gabe, but she feels my eyes on her and turns. If I ask, she'll suggest Noah go with me instead, and that is the last thing I want.

Gabe pours water from the jug into his glass, spilling some. He drinks it all, then stands up. 'Wow. I need some air.'

Elise raises a hand. He captures it in his. 'Of course, darling. Noah and I'll clean up.'

'I should go,' I say.

'Whatever you want.'

348

Really? Is it going to be that easy? I get to my feet and look around for my bag, but I can't see it so I follow Gabe outside to look for it there. He settles himself on the cushioned sofa on the deck, and after only a few moments his head drops to his chest. The fire in the bowl has gone down, but the embers burn steadily. Balto nudges his master's thigh with his snout. Getting no response, he gives up trying and curls up at Gabe's feet with a huge, noisy yawn before dropping his head onto his paws.

Noah peers into Gabe's face. He prods his arm. No response. His stepfather is unconscious.

'I'll take you to your car.'

'That won't be necessary. I just need my bag.'

He grabs my wrist as I turn away and practically snarls at me. 'You're going nowhere.'

We stare at each other. I feel like I know him now. I'm scared of his strength and his temper, but I will fight if I have to.

'This, what you're doing, is not going to make you happy, Noah. It's just going to make things worse for you.'

'Shut up.'

'Listen to me. Elise says my mother cared about no one but herself. Well, she's the same. She's involved you in all this horror. I doubt she worries about going to prison, as long as she gets what she wants. She's had a life, but you've barely begun.'

He flicks a glance back at the house. 'I told you to shut up.'

'I don't believe that everything you said to me in our sessions was a lie. Some of it, yes, but you used your own

349

experience. Because that's the best way of convincing someone, isn't it? To stick as close to the truth as possible. You loved your father, but you were too young when he died to remember anything other than the narrative you were fed. It was the damage to her that you were faced with every day: her hatred, her need for revenge.'

Noah lashes out with the back of his hand, connecting with my cheek and knocking me sideways. 'You killed my father and destroyed my childhood. You deserve everything you get.'

I scramble to my feet and brush myself off. 'And Mum?' I say. 'Did she deserve to die?'

He can't seem to keep his eyes still. They flick from my face to the sliding glass doors and back. When I look round, Elise is watching us from the back of the room. She knows her son.

'Your mother is where this all started,' Noah says. 'She let my father take the flak for what you did. He was treated like shit by the media. Lorna could have stopped that. And so could you. A little shame for a man's life and reputation. You disgust me.'

For once, he's telling the truth. 'I disgust myself sometimes too. I've been paying all my adult life for what I did.'

'Then why do I feel short-changed?'

'That's your problem, not mine.'

I clumsily knee him in the groin. My knee doesn't quite connect, but it's enough to cause him to instinctively relax his hold and protect himself. I grab the tongs from the fire bowl, snatch up a glowing log and fling it at him. It glances off his ear and he yelps.

'You bitch!'

I drop the tongs and leap off the deck onto the soft ground. Balto comes after me as I sprint into the forest, thinking it's a game. I can hear Noah behind us, and Elise shouting at him in Swedish.

The woods look the same whichever way I turn. I think I'm headed towards the road and my car, but I should have found it by now. I make the mistake of glancing back over my shoulder, lose my balance and fall hard. The seconds lost allow Noah to catch up and drop down on top of me. As I gasp for breath under his solid weight, Balto licks my face.

'Fuck off, you stupid animal.' Noah strikes out at the dog. Balto whines.

'Balto!' Elise calls sharply. He wheels round and trots obediently to his mistress.

When Noah hauls me up, I go for him, using my nails, clawing at his face, determined to leave my mark, catching his eye with my fingernail. Elise shouts a warning. I'm ruining her plan. This is not going to look like suicide, and she knows it.

Noah is beyond reason, beyond even his own control. Locked in the crook of a muscular arm, I watch the trajectory of his fisted hand and cry out as he delivers a violent blow to my head. Light explodes in my vision, leaving stars. I hit the ground hard but I'm still conscious.

Somewhere not too far away, a car door opens and closes. Noah kneels on me and clamps his hand over my mouth, muffling my cries for help. A woman calls out, 'Elise!' Then something in Swedish. She sounds like a friend.

351

Elise swears, before responding with an equally friendly greeting, then says something to Noah. He gets off me, and before I can dodge the blow, he kicks my head, and everything fades to black.

Chapter 74

THE PSYCHIATRIST

I'm in a cold place, a blanket of snow pressing down on me, numbing my face, hands and feet. My breath is shallow, the pressure crushing the air from my lungs. I can't move my legs; my hands are pinned against my stomach. My mother is standing close by with Elise. 'Perhaps we should get her up,' Elise says, and Mum says, 'Yes, of course.' But Mum is dead. I try to tell Elise this, but I can't manage the words.

I used to suffer from sleep paralysis as a child. My mind would wake before my body did, and it would take an enormous feat of willpower to move any part of me. It happened regularly, so I knew how much determination and physical exertion it took to snap my body out of it. I channel my inner child now, concentrating so hard my entire body is involved, every muscle contracting before I jerk my shoulders and legs into sudden, violent motion. It works. I lurch up from my shallow grave into the sweet-smelling night, coughing and spitting soil from my mouth.

Everything hurts. My fingers find layers of gritty congealing blood and bruises that go deep into the bones beneath my flesh. Noah must have kept going even after I blacked out, his booted feet repeatedly meeting my ribcage and lower back. Years of rancour needed a spontaneous physical outlet, his planned acts of malice not nearly enough to satisfy him. I'm not surprised he assumes he's killed me. I shouldn't be alive.

I vomit up a mixture of what I ate for supper, along with earth and pine needles and I dread to think what else, then wipe my mouth on my sleeve and pick the dirt from my eyelids. A beetle crawls across my fingers. I lean over and retch repeatedly, the pain in my ribs flaring with every convulsion.

If I don't get help, I'm going to die. My head swims as I begin to lose consciousness again, but I won't allow myself to give in. I smack my cheeks and get to my feet. I have to move. Elise and Noah aren't going to leave me for the local wildlife to disturb; they'll be back.

Danger helps to sharpen my wits. I need to make it look as though I'm still buried. It might just give me a few vital minutes. I stumble drunkenly around the immediate area until I find a fallen branch, and drag and roll it into the hole before heaping it with earth and leaves. Good enough. In the distance, I hear barking.

'Hey!' Noah shouts. 'Come back, you stupid hound.'

Balto crashes through the forest, Noah swearing as he gives chase. I gather what little strength I have and throw myself behind a tree.

Noah arrives a few seconds later, out of breath. He grabs the dog as it starts to nose in the disturbed earth. Elise joins him.

'We can't leave the body here all night,' Noah tells her. 'Too many animals.'

Elise doesn't sound like herself when she responds in

Swedish. I don't need to understand the language to figure out that she's feeling the strain. Noah switches to Swedish too. He sounds petulant; a boy used to getting his own way with a mother he could wrap around his little finger. Not any more, apparently. I'm growing cold again, my feet like blocks of ice and my fingertips agony. I press myself into the bark of the tree, hoping to find warmth.

Finally they leave, voices fading as they trudge back to the house. I risk a glance. Elise has Balto by the collar. Noah's shoulders are hunched.

I have a dreadful headache and difficulty focusing, and there's a short delay in the messages from my brain to my limbs that doesn't help. I trip over my feet and pull myself up, using the trees as support. My mouth tastes of metal and mud. There are pine needles stuck between my teeth and in my hair and ears.

I know what injuries like mine can do. It can be minutes or hours later, but at some point, if I'm unlucky, they will strike me down. I need to reach a road, find someone to take me to hospital. I keep repeating the same thing, creating a rhythm to help me put one foot in front of the other. Get out. Keep going. Get help. Get out. Keep going. Get help.

I should have found the track by now. Did I set off in the wrong direction? I rest against a tree and try to work it out. By the shadows, I can tell I am going east, away from the water, so I should meet the track, and even if I've missed it, I'll eventually reach the main road.

I drag in several deep breaths and press on. Right foot. Left foot. Get out. Keep going. Get help. My legs are as heavy as ballast, my balance shot.

The forest ends at an unlit road. If I'm lucky, a car will pass. I have no idea of the time. It could be nine in the evening or two in the morning. The midnight sun makes it impossible to tell, and I don't have my phone. I stagger a few yards, twenty at the most, before my mind and body begin to shut down, my knees buckling. It's a miracle I even got this far. I can do no more.

Chapter 75

ELISE

So, this is it? How strange.

Amy Chilcott is dead and so is her mother. It's over. Everything Elise needed and wanted to do has been done, although it's a pity it had to end in such a mess. Still, this is where they are and she should savour the moment. She might have given up at any point, reached some form of acceptance, but for her own sense of failure. She did not adequately protect her men. None of this was Dexter's fault, and yet he was punished, and because of that, Noah has also been punished. It was Elise who invited Lorna and Amy into their lives.

The question is, have their deaths lanced the boil? Maybe. Time will tell. She never really thought about the aftermath when it came to Lorna, just the idea of taking her sweet revenge. She doesn't want to think about it now, but it keeps intruding. She has killed. She is a killer. She brought black roses to her victim's funeral.

Gabe is sound asleep and snoring. He's normally up first, so the drugs must still be in his system. She snuggles up against him, breathing in the sweet smell of his skin. He is a beautiful man. He had been so naïvely trusting when

357

he'd told her who had booked the cabin. He thought it would turn out to be a good thing, because Elise needed closure. And he was right, she did, just not the kind he had in mind. He isn't especially bright.

She misses the animal attraction that had crackled between her and Dexter, but Gabe has good instincts and a generous spirit, and he is a sensitive and thoughtful partner and lover. If the worst happens and she loses all of this, she'll still have his unwavering support. He won't be able to bear the thought of her being alone and unhappy.

Returning to Öland after a fifteen-year absence was tough. Elise never expected to come back to the place where she grew up. As a teenager, she couldn't wait to escape its confines and parochial atmosphere, but these days it is her sanctuary, like that beautifully renovated barn was Lorna's. Not that Lorna's was much of a sanctuary in the end. She isn't certain what Lorna's last words were before she died at the bottom of the stairs, but Elise thinks she mouthed, *Not Amy*.

She lifts herself up on her elbow to read the time over Gabe's shoulder. *Ah Gud*. Seven forty-five. She never wakes this late. Why didn't she err on the cautious side and set the alarm? Even with the drugs, she can't assume Gabe will stay asleep much longer, which means her plan to deal with Amy's body before he wakes will have to be abandoned.

She'll wait for him to leave for work, she thinks as she dresses in the bathroom. And then what? No one is going to believe Amy drowned, so there's no point tipping her into the lake. Öland is inconveniently flat; there are no helpful cliffs.

Noah has gone. She's sad and it's going to make it harder for her to get rid of the corpse, but it's one less thing to worry about. She can deal with things her way, calmly and methodically, without her volatile son. Downstairs, Balto greets her with a whine and a bark. She grabs his lead – she doesn't want him making a beeline for Amy's grave – and sets off, avoiding the woods and following the path around the lake. Balto keeps grabbing at the lead with his jaws. Each time, she bats his nose. The next house along from theirs is a hundred yards away and no one is staying at the moment. It's a holiday home, another one of Gabe's.

Elise prides herself on being a realist, and so she accepts the possibility that this may not work out in her favour. If that is the case, she will be sad to leave the island. When she bought the plot and built the house two years after she and Noah settled here, she thought she'd go mad without the distractions of city life, and for a while she was bored and jumpy, but it's been years since she felt that way. So, she was married to a pop star; so, life was incredible. There were awards ceremonies and parties, first-class travel and celebrity friends. So what? When they sold up in glitzy Primrose Hill and moved to Alverley, it didn't feel like much of a loss, and that hasn't changed. It had been Dexter who cared about all that glitter. What *she* cared about, and what she sacrificed, were those moments on the stage. The perfect silence as she sang, the frenzy of applause afterwards. Éponine. That was how Dexter had seen her first, as a woman who makes the ultimate sacrifice to save the man she loves. Elise couldn't save Dexter, but she will save Noah.

She breathes in the smell of pine as her feet thud along

the impacted ground. She is not the same woman she was in 2009. The Elise Coleridge who moved into Gladwell Grove that spring had it all, and was gentle and serene because she had no reason not to be. Dexter had his troubles, and Noah was challenging, but she had been on top of it. She'd revelled in her power to calm them both. Now she no longer knows who she is. Only that she's had plenty of time to weigh up the possible consequences of doing what was necessary and to decide if it was worth it. She is not scared. She lets out a shout as she runs, and punches the air.

Once they are far enough away, she takes pity on Balto and releases him. Close by on the lake there's a slumbering shelduck, head resting on its back, its brown, white and black plumage and scarlet bill gleaming. Above them a falcon glides, its shadow reflected on the strait. Her father taught her the names of all the island's birds. Balto leaps enthusiastically into the water and the duck paddles swiftly out of harm's way.

Elise bends over, gripping her knees. If she only looks at the water, feels the soft breeze cooling her damp skin, breathes in unpolluted air, she can pretend there is still a way out of this. She could drive Amy's hire car to Malmo, leave it at the airport and make her way back. Ridiculous. Come on, she thinks. Be real. She is, at heart, a pragmatist. She may get away with it, but chances are she won't. The important thing is, Dexter has been avenged. She can protect Noah at least. She turns and looks back along the shore, heaving a deep sigh. She can't see the house from here, but she can see the jetty and the tall figure standing at the end of it. Gabe is up.

'Balto. Home.'

The dog swims back to the bank and shakes himself, showering droplets over the path and her legs.

'Sleep well, darling?' She speaks English with Gabe, unless they have Swedish guests. Gabe's Swedish is functional, but English comes as easily to her as her own language. It helps that she used to sing it. Noah too is bilingual, switching from one to the other without needing to think about it. His accent is English, though. He went to boarding school there. As Noah Karlsson, of course, not Coleridge. There was no need to draw attention.

She slides her arm around Gabe's waist and leans her head against his shoulder.

He kisses her temple. 'I feel strange.'

'Strange how?' She looks into his eyes and places her hand on his forehead. 'You do feel a little clammy.'

'Must be coming down with something.'

They go back to the house. Gabe finds the BBC news on the iPad and they listen as they potter. Elise tries to act normal. She empties the dishwasher and plumps up the cushions on the sofa, performing each task slowly and with grace. She cannot wait for him to go out.

'I don't even remember going to bed,' Gabe says. 'What time did Amy leave?'

The sound of that woman's name on his lips jars.

'Oh, about ten, I think. You were out for the count.'

She and Noah had carried him into the bedroom, where she undressed him, leaving his clothes as he always did, in a pile in the bathroom. Luckily he is a slender man – but still a dead weight. She hopes there won't be bruises.

361

He frowns. 'Did I even clean my teeth? My mouth feels disgusting.'

'I don't know, honey. I'm not your mamma.'

Gabe laughs.

'You must have been more tired than you realised,' she says. 'Do you have a lot on today?'

'Yeah. Loads. Hang on.'

'What is it?'

He turns the volume up.

'. . . The injured woman has been identified as a British national, thirty-four-year-old Dr Amy Geddes, who has recently been in the news . . .'

Shock drains the colour from Elise's face. Of all the problems she'd imagined in the dead of night, this wasn't among them. She had been one hundred per cent certain Amy was dead. How can she be alive? She stays absolutely still, not looking at Gabe, focusing as hard as she can on reacting the way she should. A concerned frown, not the terrified expression her face wants to pull. Her fingers feel clumsy, her body unsteady.

'Dr Geddes is in a critical condition, having suffered repeated blows to her head and torso. Doctors have put her into an induced coma in the hope of reducing the swelling to the brain. A VW Golf, rented by Dr Geddes and abandoned half a mile from where she was found, has been traced to a hire company at Malmo airport. The off-duty police officer who found her says he assumed she'd been injured in a car crash but saw no sign of wreckage.'

'Didn't either of you see her back to the cabin last night?' Gabe, who is the least judgemental person she knows, has an edge to his voice.

'No. She said she'd be fine.' She doesn't like the look he gives her. 'It's not my fault, Gabe. She is a grown woman.'

'I'll call Nils.'

'Okay.'

'Perhaps you should get Noah up.'

'Noah's gone.'

He gapes. 'What do you mean, gone?'

'Just gone.' She tries to sound upbeat, but kind of sad too. A mother, both regretful and happy. Not someone who's just committed murder with her child. Or thought she had.

'I don't understand.'

There is still a chance she can escape this, that Amy might die. That's what *critical condition* means, isn't it? A doctor once told her that it's a way of preparing loved ones for the worst outcome without actually saying your relative is unlikely to survive.

She needs time to think. She sees movement outside and, thankful for the distraction, hisses, 'There's someone out there.'

Gabe peers out of the window. 'I can't see anything.'

'Look harder. Between the trees. Someone's moving around.'

'The police, perhaps? Poor woman. Let's hope she pulls through.'

Elise hopes not. She doesn't relish her new identity as a killer, but she only has to remind herself of what brought her to this point. The wilful destruction of a good man by two stupid, selfish women who thought more of saving their own damn faces than the life of another human being.

She's glad they've paid.

Chapter 76

ELISE

Detective Nils Palmquist's smile is boyish and goofy. He's always had a soft spot for Elise. They were at school together many years ago, and for one summer holiday when they were ridiculously young, they were girlfriend and boyfriend. Elise guesses from the way he's looking at her that it still counts for something.

They are both returnees. Nils moved to Stockholm when he entered the police force, and wound up back in Öland, overweight, weary and divorced, two years before Elise. Stress, he told her when she bumped into him that first time. Since returning, he's quit alcohol, remarried and trimmed down. He's almost attractive to her.

'This is dreadful,' she says. 'I can't believe it.'

He knows about her connection to Amy Chilcott. Most people on the island do. She is going to have to say something.

'You know who she is, right?'

'Yes,' Nils says, looking at her with sympathy. And something else. Doubt? 'I do.'

'I saw her in the water yesterday, up to her neck.' Gabe says. 'I knew something was wrong. You've got to be pretty hardy to swim here in May. She wasn't in a wetsuit, she was fully clothed.'

'Thank God you were there,' Elise says, thinking the opposite.

'Balto rushed into the water barking and distracted her,' Gabe continues. 'I called out and she came back to the shore. I gave her my fleece and hat and we talked for a while. I walked her back to her car and later she turned up here. Elise invited her in. She seemed in better spirits.'

'What did you talk about?'

'She told me her mother had recently passed away and she wanted to look up an old friend. She was looking for Elise. Of course I knew who she was because I'd taken the booking and done an internet search on her.'

'Did you tell Dr Geddes you were married to Elise?'

'No, I didn't.'

'Why not?'

Gabe clicks his fingers, like he does when he's searching for the correct word in Swedish. 'Instinct, I suppose. I didn't think she was a fit mental state to be confronting Elise. When she asked me straight out if I knew her, I said the name rang a bell and that I'd ask around. I just wanted to get her somewhere warm. I tried to persuade her to go to the hospital, but she didn't want to and I couldn't force her, so I accompanied her back to her car. She promised she would go back to the cabin and have a hot bath, and I let her go because I thought it would give me time to talk to Elise.'

Nils tilts his head, his eyes narrowing. 'Strange that she should have attempted to kill herself before she found Elise.'

Gabe pauses. 'She had a moment of deep despair, I guess. But I think she was relieved Balto and I appeared when we did.'

'Poor woman,' Elise says.

He smiles lovingly at her. 'I'm just glad I was there.'

Palmquist glances at her. 'Did you know she was coming?'

'Yes. Gabe told me. He offered to refuse the booking. He knows I don't like to be reminded of that time.'

'But you let him go ahead with it. Why was that?'

'Do you know,' she says, giving him a conspiratorial look, 'I'm not entirely sure. My instinct was to say no. But if Amy really wanted to see me, one way or another she was going to do it. I thought I might as well let her get it off her chest, then we could go back to normal.' She smiles. 'I didn't expect everyone here to circle their wagons around me, but our neighbours are very protective and for some reason have taken me to their hearts.'

'It's because you're a daughter of the island, darling,' Gabe says. 'They love you.'

He is protecting me, Elise thinks with a surge of love. But he doesn't know what from.

Palmquist looks from one to the other. She can see the cogs whirring. He wants to believe in her and so does Gabe, but he's sceptical and Gabe is confused.

'And that was all?' he says, speaking to Gabe.

'Not quite. About five minutes later, I happened to be walking that way again and saw Elise pull out in her car, followed by Amy. I was concerned, so I decided I'd head home. But then I had a call-out from the coastguard. I reasoned that Noah was at the house, so Elise wouldn't be on her own. I didn't think Amy was a danger to her, and certainly not in the state she was in.'

Elise picks up the story from there, explaining how Amy came to be at their house. 'Then after she woke up, we talked. She wanted to say she was sorry for everything that happened, and to finally take responsibility. I didn't realise how profoundly that period of her life had affected her, but she was crippled by guilt. It was hard for me to recover from my husband's death and the accusations levelled at him, but it was hard for her too, I think. Imagine living with that all your life, knowing your lies caused such a terrible tragedy.' She pauses, allowing Nils to appreciate her empathy. 'I'm guessing that either she couldn't say it while her mother was alive, or perhaps Lorna's death was the final straw and she lost her mind. Either way, she came here.' She sighs. 'I wish she had found me sooner. It wasn't very satisfactory for either of us. You have to establish ground rules, you know? I didn't trust her. The apology was welcome, but I felt it was more for her benefit than mine. She clearly has mental health issues, whereas I've been able to work through the trauma, with the help of this wonderful man.' She smiles fondly at Gabe and notes his bewilderment. 'She was about to leave when Gabe arrived, but he insisted she stay and eat with us, then he fell asleep.'

'It was a long day,' Gabe says.

'What happened with Amy while Gabe was sleeping?' Nils asks.

'Nothing. It was her cue to go, so she went.'

'Alone?'

'Well, yes. This is Öland, not Stockholm. There is no

violent crime here.' She pauses. 'Until now. But you're right. Noah or I probably should have accompanied her. To tell you the truth, I just wanted her out of the house. I'd had enough of . . .' she uses air quotes, 'making her feel better. She said her car was parked along the track, so I assumed she'd be fine.'

'You should have woken me,' Gabe says. 'I'd have made sure she got back to the cabin safely.'

'I didn't think of it, my love. The thing is,' she adds. 'I don't hate her any more. I find her pathetic. She's lonely. Did you know her husband left her?'

'What about Noah?' Gabe asks, uninterested in trivia about Amy's private life. 'Why did he leave in the middle of the night?'

Irritated, Elise turns on him. 'Noah has nothing to do with any of this, and it wasn't the middle of the night. Once you were asleep, I told him to go. It was difficult for him, breaking bread with the woman who ruined his childhood. He was jumpy. I didn't want a scene.'

'Where did he go?' Nils asks.

'Off the island. He has a flat in Stockholm.'

'It's a five-hour drive,' Gabe says. 'Couldn't he have waited till morning?'

'You know what Noah is like. What did you expect me to do?' She puts her hands to her cheeks and turns to Nils beseechingly. 'I am so sorry. I've been under a lot of strain since I found out Amy was here. It's been upsetting to say the least.'

She risks a glance at Gabe. He's looking at her like he's never seen her before. He knows she isn't making sense. 'How is Amy?' she asks more calmly. She has a thought.

368

She could make sure the woman doesn't wake up. The hospital is small, security minimal.

'She's being airlifted to a specialist trauma centre in Stockholm this morning,' Nils says. 'We're hoping to speak to her when she comes out of her coma, but we may have to wait a while.'

Elise feels her options melting away. 'You know, there are many people who still hate Amy Chilcott. They have never forgiven her for what she did to Dexter. Female fans can be so obsessive. They never let it go. I would not be surprised if one of them . . .' She falters. She's seen another officer emerge from the trees.

He climbs the steps onto the deck. He's wearing dirty latex gloves, and there are pine needles stuck to his knees and cuffs. He shows Nils an evidence bag. Nils holds it up to the light, and through it Elise recognises the teardrop pearl from one of the earrings Amy had been wearing. They've found the grave. Next they will find the spade, which she has not yet had a chance to thoroughly clean. Never mind. She will simply keep saying Noah had nothing to do with it. Maybe now he's kicked the shit out of that woman, he will be happier too, his thirst for revenge finally quenched. She must make sure he understands that she gave herself up of her own free will. She doesn't want him wreaking any more havoc trying to avenge her.

'Amy was at fault. She may have only been fifteen, but she knew what she was doing when she accused my husband.'

Nils turns away from his colleague and looks at Elise. 'Sorry?'

'He hurt her feelings.' She swallows and goes on. 'And

instead of working extra hard to prove him wrong, she destroyed him. What kind of person does that? She was old enough to understand the consequences of her lies. Her mother backed her up. They deserved everything they got.'

'Elise,' Gabe says. 'Darling. We'll call your lawyer. But for now, please don't say any more.'

She looks at him as though he's a stranger, and eventually he lowers his gaze. Gabe has brought her happiness and peace, but he has never come close to Dexter. His attraction has been in his willingness to look after her, believe in her and protect her. He can't do that now, so she has no further use for him. She wonders whether she will even need him once she's in prison; whether this stage in her life has come to an end and she ought to draw a line. And it's not so bad. Swedish prisons focus on rehabilitation, not punishment. Elise is open to being rehabilitated. She's always been queen of whatever place and situation she's found herself in. She was queen of Gladwell Grove until Lorna ruined it for her. And judging by the way her fellow islanders have been behaving over the last twenty-four hours, she's queen here too. Perhaps she can help her fellow inmates. Song creates harmony and social cohesion; it brings laughter, forges friendship and creates hope. She likes to be admired and needed. She smiles sweetly at Nils as he leads her out of the house. She will plead guilty and get it over with quickly. She has done what she set out to do.

Chapter 77

THE PSYCHIATRIST

Six months later

I reach for my bag. 'Sorry.' I've barely opened my mouth during my therapy session with Dr Fierz. It happens like that sometimes. My mind doesn't work the same since the attack. I'm slower to recover thoughts, to form sentences, and I have a slight stammer. And when I get to the uncomfortable parts, the words scatter like confetti blown in the wind.

'There's no need to apologise. You can talk when you feel like it. You know there's no pressure.'

I walk out into the sunshine and make my way to the car park, where Pete's wife Sally is waiting in the clapped-out Range Rover that smells of vegetables from her allotment. My extended family have rallied round me. I've been staying at Matt's since I left hospital, unable to drive, still prone to giddy spells and headaches. Sally organised the therapist and almost always takes me because I won't allow Matt to turn down work. If she can't do it, Bill picks me up in his taxi. He was fond of my mum and likes to talk about her, disturbingly proud of being the last person to see her alive.

'How was it?' Sally asks.

'It was good.' She doesn't need to know I spent forty of my allotted fifty minutes in silence. She'd understand, but she'd want to talk about it, and I don't. I can't.

I think about Noah as she drives. He still takes up a lot of my headspace. That first time he came to my office, what did I miss? I picture him entering the room, his coat and woollen scarf folded over his arm, a swagger in his step. He seemed more expectant than nervous. And curious? But maybe that's hindsight. I desperately want something to have felt wrong, some tiny clue that all was not as it seemed. To me, he was simply a young man with bipolar disorder and related issues, and I was there to help him manage his emotions, rebuild his confidence and get on with life; to listen and prescribe. Only after the rape and accusation did I look back and accept that there was a lot that jarred. Was it vanity that blinded me?

One time, I'd been noting the odd thing down, more to ease the tension than to record – sometimes when the focus is on them without a break, patients can find it too much – and when I looked up, I caught him staring at me, eyes narrowed. He averted his gaze and we moved on. Nothing and everything. Another red flag I ignored at the time.

My recovery has been slow. I was airlifted to Karolinska University Hospital in Stockholm, where I spent nine weeks, after which I was transferred to the recovery unit at the Royal Devon.

I am reasonably happy down here, and for now that's enough. I'm taking it easy, doing my physio, keeping myself occupied. Since my ribs have stopped hurting, I've started singing. Pete has a barn where he and his band of grizzled middle-aged men rehearse. They play the pubs and clubs, singing country and western and sea shanties. I hadn't willingly sung since Dexter's death. The act was too connected with shame. When I was young, I dreamt of stepping out onto the stage, blinded by the lights, deafened by the roar of applause. Sometimes I even dreamt about being the underdog, the poor pathetic loser who takes over at the last moment and shocks everyone with the power and beauty of her voice. When Dexter Coleridge arrived in Alverley, I took it as a sign. Meeting him would be my big break. I spun stories and created meet-cutes that felt real. He would spot my raw talent. He and Elise would want to polish me until I shone. When Mum became friends with Elise, my imagination ran wild.

And then he said, *I don't think a singing career is for you, love. Better to know now*, and my bright little bubble burst.

Singing with Pete and his mates is better than therapy. When I sing, the stammer disappears. The first evening we played live, I was so overcome I wept and had to walk off the stage.

I've made myself think about the night Dexter died. It's like forcing my eyes open when I don't want to see, but without going back there, I cannot move on. It's not that I want to look at it then box it back up, never to be revisited. I want to stop making excuses and face it. It is who I am. It happened and I can't pretend it didn't. I want to make a life for myself that's honest and clear-sighted. Thirty-four-year-old Amy Geddes is not so different from fifteen-year-old Amy Chilcott.

Chapter 78

AMY

Then

My life is crap.

After vomiting my guts up, I sit on the loo in the shower room holding a Stanley knife Dad's left lying around. I press the blade against the soft skin of my inner thigh. I've never done anything like this before, but I've persuaded myself it might stop the feeling that my head is going to explode if my situation doesn't improve – which it won't. I lift the blade and inspect the impression it leaves, then try again, using the tip to break the skin. It's like going into the sea one step at a time rather than diving straight in. A tiny drop of blood blossoms, and I angle the blade down a bit.

When Mum peels an orange, she uses a sharp knife to slice off the end, then cuts through to the pith, curving the blade in four swift movements from top to bottom. I grit my teeth and jerk my hand, stifling a cry of pain. I've made an incision a centimetre long, and it's bleeding badly. I tear a length of toilet paper from the roll and wad it against the wound. It isn't really doing anything apart from stinging, though maybe this is like the first puff of a cigarette. I've tried that, and it was horrible, making me cough and my eyes water. The things smokers talk about – the dopamine hit, the feelings of pleasure – apparently come later, when you're used to it, but I haven't bothered again.

I lean back against the cistern and look up through the Velux window at a pinkish sky, the hand holding the blade resting on my lap. Come on, I think. You can do this. The second time is a little better, but it makes me feel like I'm losing control, and I don't like it. I have Elastoplast to hand, taken from downstairs. I open one, staunch the bleeding again and stick it on. Blood blooms through the pink fabric. I find a couple of larger plasters and slap them on top. There's blood on my pyjama legs, drips on the bathroom floor. Never mind. Mum rarely comes up here. I clean up, rinse the pyjamas under the tap and hang them over the towel rail to dry.

I wake with a start. My digital clock says 11:45. I close my eyes, but as I start to drift, I remember, and the cycle starts again: wide awake, heart racing. The implications of confession bombard me. Notoriety. Taunting at school, being cold-shouldered or told to my face that I'm horrible. All those school mums who used to scream at D.I.G.B.Y. concerts and who now go on about what a great actor he is. They'll crucify me because they'll think I crucified him. But it wasn't my fault. I would have told the truth ages ago if Mum hadn't intervened.

I'm too hot, and the place where I've cut myself hurts. I fling off the duvet and switch on the bedside light. There's blood seeping through. I ease my jeans on carefully, slip my arms into my dark blue hoodie and put on my pendant for

375

luck, even though I don't really believe the world is my oyster now. The house is quiet. I'll go for a bike ride and work off the annoying adrenaline rush. Maybe then I'll be able to sleep.

The door to the spare bedroom is closed, a rare occurrence that momentarily confuses me. It's only a small thing, but it jars. I open it. The curtains are closed, the air stale, and there's someone in the bed. Have I driven a wedge between my parents? I'll never forgive myself if they break up.

It isn't the first time I've done this, although the time before I was staying over with Lily. I didn't want to, but she coaxed me into it and I had to admit afterwards that it was a real buzz. Cycling through the deserted streets, my body cooling, the wind in my hair, I feel a million times better. It's exhilarating being out alone at this time of night. It feels like I'm on the prowl, like a cat, doing something I shouldn't, my parents tucked up in bed asleep, unaware their daughter has gone rogue.

There's a police presence on Griffiths Lane, an ambulance and two squad cars, their blue lights flashing. Even though the incident has nothing to do with me, I still feel hunted. I wheel round and cycle to the entrance to the heath on Gladwell Grove. I've never been on the heath after dark on my own before. When I was younger, like nine or ten, my parents used to take me and my friends on spooky Halloween walks here, and later, with Lily, it was so much fun scaring ourselves silly; we'd had hysterics. This is different. I stand at the top of the alleyway, uncertain, the darkness yawning back at me.

If I do this, tomorrow I'll feel braver.

I grip the handlebars and push off, pedalling as fast as I can. The paths are well maintained by the council, so it's reasonably smooth going, but by the time I reach the other side, my thighs are burning and the cuts are agony. I cycle until the bend before Dexter's boat, then jump off and push my bike out of sight. The boat is strung with fairy lights. It's so pretty. Elise probably put them there. It's the sort of thing she'd do.

One step, and then another. It reminds me of playing Grandmother's Footsteps as a little girl, standing as still as a statue, barely daring to breathe, desperate to be the one to tap Grandmother on the shoulder. I step silently across the pontoon and peer through the same window as before. The only light comes from the digital clock on the oven. As my eyes adjust, a black hump resolves into a sofa. I'm still looking through the window when the boards beneath me lurch. I jam my right hand against the hull to regain my balance.

'You came.'

'What?'

'Ah. Shit. I thought you were someone else.'

Chapter 79

AMY

Then

Dexter squints at me. 'What are you doing here, kid?'

He's off his head on something. Either drunk or high, his words distorted. I can't move my limbs or drag my gaze from his face.

'I wanted to talk to you.'

'You've been spying on me.'

'Er . . . no.'

'Well, here I am.' He flings his arms out like he's been crucified. 'Come on up. *Mi casa es tu casa.*' He reaches down, and after a hesitation, I allow him to wrap his hand around my wrist and hoist me onto the deck. It's weirdly thrilling.

I lift my chin. It's now or never. 'I made a mistake.'

'You what?'

'I didn't know what I was doing. I'm sorry. I lied.'

I wait, and something grows in the silence, something dark and hateful. There's no relief in his face, no softening, no effort to take some of the blame, no *don't worry, love, I was being a jerk.* Just a cold, black nothing, as cold and black as the water behind him.

'I've got to go now. My parents don't know I've gone out.'

'Do you even understand what you've done, you stupid bitch?'

'Don't call me that!'

'It's what you are, isn't it? Your mother's the same. Peas in a pod, the pair of you. I can't believe I didn't realise what was going on. It's why she's encouraging you. Because I knocked her back.'

'I hate you.'

'You don't hate me. You can't keep away. Have you come to lure me into doing what you accused me of? Because I hate to disappoint you, but I'm not interested in teenagers. Seriously, kid, grow up. Jesus.'

I must not cry. I'm here to make this stop, and I need him on my side because that might make people less vile towards me when the truth gets out, which it will.

'Give me a chance to explain. Please.'

'Leave.' There's a warning note in his voice, and I feel a bolt of fear, but I'm not backing down.

'Not until you listen.'

Dexter comes right up to me, inserting himself into my personal space, his eyes icy, his mouth set in a thin line.

'I do not need or want to talk to you. You're a lying, manipulative little narcissist. Now get the fuck off my boat.'

It hurts my neck to look up at him. I can't stop shaking. 'I wanted to take it back, but Mum wouldn't let me.' My throat aches from keeping the tears at bay. I give up and let them come. 'I know you're angry, and you have every right to be, but . . .' I'm young, I'm pretty and I'm crying. It should work, but it doesn't.

He takes hold of my upper arms and swivels me round. 'You're pathetic. Go home to Mummy and Daddy. It's not my job to make you feel better.' His mouth is so close to my ear I feel its heat; his breath so stale I have to work hard to suppress my revulsion.

'That's not why I came here,' I insist.

'Course it is. Off you go.'

He jabs his finger in the space between my shoulder blades, and I can't bear it. I spin round, bat his hand away and shove him with all my strength. Taken by surprise, he loses his balance, his heel colliding with the raised edge of the boat. He makes a grab for me, pulling at my collar, catching the chain around my neck. It briefly and painfully digs into my flesh, and then snaps. With a cry, he catches hold of the chair, but it's too flimsy to stop his trajectory and he topples into the water. He sinks, then rises, his arms slicing ineffectually at the surface.

'I can't swim!'

'Shit! Roll onto your back. Try to float.'

He drops out of sight, then bobs up again, spitting water, arms flailing. 'Help me.' This time, when he goes under, he doesn't resurface.

'Oh my God. Oh my God!' I pull off my trainers and leap in after him.

The river is freezing, black and depthless. I'm a decent swimmer. Daddy Pete, sensible in this respect if not in others, taught me when I'd stayed with him in Devon during the school holidays. I know to work with a strong current, not against it. I swim to where I last saw Dexter, dive down and move my arms in a wide arc. He must be here. He must.

I surface and doggy-paddle, rotating my body and yelling for help. No one comes, and eventually I'm so exhausted, I'm forced to give up. Using what strength remains in my arms and legs, I swim to the bank, drag myself out and run, following the river in the direction of the current, my feet in their wet socks so cold I can barely feel them. There's no sign of Dexter. I stand half buckled over, panting, my head lifted as I stare downriver. The water is flat, there isn't a breath of wind and the only sounds are distant. I retrace my steps to the boat, gripped by the irrational hope that somehow he's made it back.

'Please let him be there. Please let him be there. Please. I'll be good. I'll never tell another lie in my life. Please God, let Dexter be okay. Please let him be there. I'll be kind. I'll work hard. I'll never ask for another thing. I will go to church. Please just let him be there.'

Despite the fact that he obviously isn't, I check inside and out, calling his name through choking sobs. I'm freezing cold and soaking wet and so shocked my breath is coming in shallow gasps. There's a jumper slumped over the arm of the sofa. I run my fingers across the nubbly wool, tempted to put it on. I don't. Instead, I drag myself up the steps onto the deck, stuff my feet into my trainers and cycle home dripping wet and shaking so hard it makes my bones hurt and my teeth chatter.

Chapter 80

THE PSYCHIATRIST

Eight months after my return from Sweden, I meet Jack at Alverley station and we go to Chetham & Church, where I hand over the keys to my flat. They have a list of keen prospective tenants. From there we walk to Bramcote Avenue.

'Wow. Plantation shutters,' Jack says when we reach our old front door. 'The house has finally arrived. Shall I ring the doorbell?'

'No,' I say. 'This is enough.'

'Where to next? The heath?'

'Gladwell Grove,' I say firmly.

We don't hang around for long outside number 55. It hasn't changed at all; the gate is the same tasteful battleship grey. There's nothing to see really. It's anonymous, just another ultra-smart family house in an ultra-smart road. I try to picture the gates sliding open and Elise stepping out to greet me, but I can't. All I can see is the version I met in Sweden. The one who wanted me dead. The case hasn't come to court yet. I'll see her when it does.

'Are you all right?' Jack asks.

'Not really.'

Jack was only three when Dexter drowned and has no idea of the depths of my self-hatred. He loves me, but I think he's bemused by all that's happened and I don't want to overburden him. What I need right now is someone to yell at. Myself, actually.

We cut down the alleyway onto the heath. Walking across it eases my anxiety. It hasn't changed. Even the people we pass seem the same, though I recognise no one and no one appears to recognise me, despite the recent publicity. We walk until we reach the far side and come out by the Bute. I take a deep breath and turn left. When we reach the spot where the *Liberty Rose* used to be moored, there's a different boat there, a traditional narrowboat with a herb garden on the roof and a pair of bicycles clamped to the side. I remember everything that happened as though it were yesterday.

The bench close to the mooring has become a shrine, adorned with shrivelled flowers in cellophane wrap. There's a laminated sheet cable-tied to one arm. I pull it forward and read it.

You know who you are
But you don't know who you wanna be.
So, baby girl, go right ahead
And take your confusion and delusions out on me.

I drop the page so that it flaps back against the side of the bench. Nineteen years and yet it feels like nothing. And now Mum's gone too. I look down into the water and my reflection resolves into Dexter's face. I step back from the edge, startled.

'Amy?'

'Sorry. I'm seeing ghosts. Block your ears.'

'What?'

'Block your ears.'

He shrugs, but does as he's told. I turn to face the river, curl my hands into fists at my sides, and yell, not words but sounds. Somewhere between Tarzan and Lady Macbeth. Primal. Several birds break cover and fly to safety.

'Jesus, Amy,' Jack says, glancing around nervously. 'Was that really necessary?'

I smile beatifically at him. 'Yeah. It was.'

On the train back to Devon, I open my laptop and the search engine. These days I type with my forefingers. It's slow and painstaking but allows me time to think. I type D, as I have so many times before. Then I delete it. Chewing my lip, I start again. *Dexter Coleridge. Images.* I scroll through a raft of them: Dexter with D.I.G.B.Y. Young, lean and hungry. Hunched over his decks. Stills from his not very good first film, the one Mum used to watch when we weren't around: *How to Date a Friend.* I only knew because she occasionally left the DVD in the machine by mistake.

Elise has already intimated that she will plead guilty to my attempted murder and to manslaughter for my mother's death. Detective Palmquist did not believe her version that Noah was not involved, but she is sticking to it. The way they both tell it, all Noah did was take revenge on me by destroying my reputation, my career, my peace of mind – such as it was – and my sanity. The rest was Elise, who, provoked beyond bearing, lost control of her pent-up anger and attacked me with the spade. If we can believe her, Mum's Good Samaritan was just that; and Noah has an alibi, which I don't believe is real. I can't help admiring her – she is a lioness when it comes to her men.

She went to my mother's house to have the conversation she'd been waiting to have for years, things got out of hand and my mother died. That wasn't the outcome she'd expected or wanted, and she regrets it.

I am both yesterday's news and the future's titillation. I care, but it is entirely out of my control. I'm not on social media, so it's hard for the trolls to spit their venom in my direction. I have more than enough challenges in my life.

As for Noah, I don't think he'll ever be satisfied. But I believe Elise is, and I trust her to control him with the sheer force of her personality, even from prison. I'm still looking over my shoulder, though, still occasionally think I hear that whistling. There is no guarantee of my safety, but I'm better off here than in London. In Devon, I'm more likely to see him coming. In Devon, there are people who look out for me.

There's an A4-sized brown envelope waiting for me when I come home from a visit to my therapist. Inside is a letter from Mum's solicitor and a sealed envelope with my name on it in her handwriting. The solicitor writes that my mother wanted me to be given it in the event of her death. I leave it on the table for an hour before I can bear to open it. I'm scared of the contents, scared that it will be an outpouring of emotion, an apology, along with self-justification over the way she behaved when I was fifteen.

Eventually, though, armed with a glass of wine, a

shop-bought chicken arrabbiata heating in the oven, I open it, tease out the three sheets of typewritten paper and smooth them flat in front of me. I start to read.

Chapter 81

LORNA

Then

The radio comes on with the bongs of the midnight news. Lorna fumbles for the buttons to turn it off, then reaches for her phone and reads the exchange from earlier.

Need to c u tonite. Houseboat midway between entry to heath and ind. estate. Liberty Rose.

Why?

U know why

I don't. I'll try but not promising. Won't be before 12

Not going anywhere

Who does he think he is summoning her like that? And who does *she* think she is even considering it? She must be mad. She shoves her phone under her pillow and closes her eyes. Fuck it.

Half an hour later, Lorna is still awake, her body clamouring to move, to go to him. She shuffles up and hugs her legs, pressing her face into her knees. If she hears him out, she risks being drawn into defending him. If she doesn't, then what? He rots in jail for the sake of her child's reputation. She wishes there was some way of finishing this where no one loses face, but she cannot imagine what that would look like.

Maybe there is. What if Dexter made a statement publicly forgiving Amy and taking the blame for her behaviour? He could say he gave her false hope, not realising how fragile the teenage ego is, that he dismissed her with insensitivity because that was how he was treated as a child. The two families could be seen together out and about. She, the mother of the alleged victim, would show him support and make her own statement, taking his part, hand in hand with Amy. Or even Amy between her and Elise, holding both their hands. Then the fuss would die down and they'd be able to put it behind them. She doesn't want the house in Gladwell Grove now. That was a brief and irrational infatuation, like her brief and irrational infatuation with Dexter. There is no such thing as something for nothing.

It occurs to her that the same goes for him. He slept with her when she was young and naïve and walked away without a care in the world, and now he's paying the price. It gives her little satisfaction. What a mess. She will go to the rendezvous. It's worth a try at least.

She zips up her black puffer coat in the dark and feels around for a woollen hat. Outside, it's cold and silent. This truly is the dead of night. After ten p.m., Alverley is pretty quiet anyway, because the streets are colonised by young families who go to bed at a sensible hour and rise early. After midnight, it's a ghost town.

The closest Lorna can park is in the industrial estate. Beyond the units is a footpath leading through about thirty yards of undergrowth to the river. Hers isn't the only car parked there, but she can't see anyone hanging around. She gets out and wrinkles her nose. The night air reeks of fox. She reaches into the car for her hat and sets off, using her phone as a torch.

Downriver, she can see the boat because of the lights strung around the deck area. She walks towards it, sick with nerves. It'll be difficult because he's so angry, but she'll stand her ground, refuse to leave until she's said her piece and he's at least agreed to think about it and talk to his lawyer.

The *Liberty Rose* is much larger than she expected. She steps onto the pontoon and calls Dexter's name softly. There's no response, so she climbs aboard, feeling for a light switch as she negotiates the steep staircase into the galley. The smell of takeaway curry invades her nostrils.

The place is a mess. In the kitchen area, the work surface is littered with detritus. There's a greasy brown paper bag, a scraped plate with a smear of yellowish sauce and rice, broken poppadoms and small tubs of raita and chutney. Cartons poke out of an overfilled bin. Dexter is such a man-child and the complete opposite to Matt, who if left on his own would be perfectly capable of cleaning up after himself.

Lorna has negotiated on many houses that have been put on the market after an acrimonious divorce. They have their own peculiar signature. It's hard to describe, though perhaps *desolate* comes close. There's a sense of this on the *Liberty Rose*.

She explores, not bothering to be quiet; finds a bathroom and the bedroom Dexter is obviously using, but no sign of him. She goes back upstairs, through the cockpit and down into the stern, but he isn't there either. Outside on the deck, one of the wicker chairs is lying on its side. She gazes at it for a few seconds, trying to work it out, then sits down on the upright one and waits. This is ridiculous. Where the hell is he?

She starts to type out a message, then her finger stops moving and she pricks up her ears. She's heard something. She stands up, expecting to see Dexter coming along the path, but no one materialises from the darkness. She's getting cold; the chair cushion was damp and so is her bottom. The adrenaline that brought her here has worn off, leaving her tired and anxious.

What was that?

Spooked, she spins round. The sound came from the direction of the industrial estate. A groan carried on the breeze, audible in the deep silence of the night. She climbs down and hurries along the path, past the alleyway and on for another twenty yards, urgency tightening her chest.

'Dexter?'

She remembers the torch on her phone and switches it on. As she swings the beam, it catches a dark shape on the ground, an arm outstretched, the upper part of a torso. From the waist down, the body is in the water.

'Dexter!' She throws herself down beside him and tries to get her hands under his arms.

His eyes are glazed with exhaustion. He mutters something unintelligible.

'It's me,' she says, then wonders why she's whispering. 'It's Lorna. Can you move if I help you?'

But Dexter isn't answering. His head is in the mud, his

arms have gone slack. She presses her fingers against his neck and feels warmth and a pulse. Oh thank God.

She means to call emergency services, but her attention is caught by the gleam of something tangled around the button on his cuff. It's a chain. She unwraps it and holds it up. A familiar gold disc with an inscription winks in the light from her phone. *The world is your oyster.*

'Was Amy here?' she demands, instinctively looking round.

When Dexter doesn't respond, she shakes his shoulder hard. 'Dexter! Was Amy here? What have you done to her?' She jerks his head up, digging her thumbs into his jaw. 'Where is my daughter?'

'Help me.'

He grasps her wrist. His fingers are cold, wet and gritty with mud. He uses her to haul his body out of the water. Her heart is beating so hard she can feel it in her veins. She lashes out at him, smacking the side of his head, her hand colliding with his ear. He lets her go with a groan.

Lorna rubs her wrist. 'I'll help you if you tell me why you've got my daughter's necklace.'

'Don't know. She was pushing me.' He starts to cough.

'Into the water?'

But she's lost him. She shakes him again.

'She tried . . . she wanted to . . .'

'Wanted to what?'

To kill him?

He slips away, into some other place. His eyes are vacant, his mouth slack. What should she do? If Amy was so desperate for it all to go away that she came here and fought with Dexter, it's Lorna's fault. She's been inconsistent and has put far too much pressure on her. There is a lot to think about, so she tries to focus on one thing: what is needed right now? That's easily answered. What's needed is for Lorna, as a mother, to protect her daughter, no matter what. Amy will not be tried for the attempted murder of Dexter Coleridge.

Dexter's fingers move up her hip, get hold of her belt. She recoils, shoving him away. He grunts and reaches out again. He's gaining ground, his hand clawing up her body. She grasps his shoulder and with all her strength forces him back into the water. He is gripping her coat and won't let go.

'You fucking bitch,' he growls. 'I'll kill you.'

Crying, Lorna clamps her hands over the back of his head. His hair is slick and wet between her fingers as he pushes back, then something gives and he goes under. Lorna is half in, half out of the water, Dexter struggling like a beached fish, arms and legs scrabbling, body jerking, bubbles rising and breaking around her fingers until he goes still. Her head drops between her shoulders. She waits until she's sure he's dead, then gives the corpse a shove with her foot to send it on its way, and crawls off the grassy verge onto the path, where she crouches dripping and muddy, wiping her mouth and nose on her upper arm, the only dry part of her.

Lorna covers as much as she can of the driver's seat with bags-for-life from the boot, then gets in, turning the fan up high to stop the windscreen fogging up. She drives home racked with convulsions. It feels as though she's been away for a lifetime, but it's barely been an hour. She strips off her soiled clothes and puts them in a carrier bag, which she conceals at the bottom of the washing basket, to deal with once the house is empty tomorrow – tomorrow which is actually today – then showers the dirt off her skin before crawling into bed, still damp.

Chapter 82

THE PSYCHIATRIST

I'm reeling with shock by the time the oven timer beeps. I lay down the sheets of paper and get up to deal with it, transferring the sizzling arrabbiata from its container to a bowl. As I force down food that I no longer want, I reread every word. How could she? I trusted her, believed her. Dexter was still alive, and she killed him. I slam the pages down and leave the house, pacing the lanes for an hour, before I break and come back, drawn to the rest of her story because I cannot not know.

I sit down, pull the chair in and pick up the next sheet, in which Mum is woken by her phone ringing and it's Elise. She covers it briefly, barely a paragraph, because she's told this story before: how Elise phoned in a panic, and she raced over to hold the fort while Elise identified Dexter's body. *The rest you know, my darling*, she writes. *Because you were there. But I want to explain how I was feeling, why I said the things I did. I know it's a lot to ask, but I need you to put yourself in my shoes.*

Everything she tells me from now on, I recollect with painful clarity.

Chapter 83

LORNA

Then

Lorna sees Dexter's pale face in the light of her phone. She has to help him, but he's slipping away, beyond the reach of her outstretched hand.

'Mum. Mum?'

Uh? Her eyelids are so heavy, but she feels instant relief. It was only a dream. Amy is in the room.

Lorna blinks and sits up, wincing as pain darts through her arms and back. She hopes her bruises don't show, but just in case, she pulls the duvet up to her shoulders before she switches on the bedside light. After being summoned to Gladwell Grove by Elise, she got home at half past six aching with exhaustion, and went straight back to bed,

'What time is it?' she mumbles. She sits up and reaches for her glass of water.

'Quarter past eight.' Amy sniffs. 'Why are you still in bed?'

'I had a bad night. Dad's taken Jack, so I thought I'd try and get a bit more sleep.' Lorna pulls her hair away from her

395

face. She's heard the quiver in Amy's voice. 'Why don't you get yourself some breakfast.'

But Amy drops down on the bed beside her and bursts into tears. 'I tried to save him, Mum. I really did.'

A chill grips Lorna's spine. Did she get it wrong? 'What do you mean? Amy, stop crying, please, and tell me what you're talking about.'

Amy wipes her eyes, but her tears keep flowing and she chokes on her words. 'I went to see Dexter because I couldn't decide what to do and I thought if I agreed something with him before I talked to the police it would be easier. We argued and it got physical. He was pushing me around, so I pushed back. He lost his balance. I jumped in after him, but I couldn't get to him in time.' Her shoulders are shaking, her nose running, eyes red, her fingers constantly tweaking at the fabric of her sweatpants. 'What's going to happen to me? I've killed him. I've ruined everything.'

Lorna doesn't hesitate. She speaks urgently. 'No one need know you were anywhere near him.' She cups her daughter's face in her hands and looks her straight in the eye. 'Listen to me. You were not there.'

'But I was! It's my fault he's dead. All of it is my fault!'

Lorna's thoughts spin and then crystallise. Her daughter needs her. Jack needs her. She cannot go to prison, therefore she cannot tell the truth about what happened last night. Amy will get over it in time. Lorna will make sure this new horror doesn't blight her life. Instinct kicks in. Save Amy. Save herself. 'You mustn't feel guilty, darling. It was an accident. It's happened, it's over. We move on.'

'I want to go to the police station.'

'Oh no, Amy. That isn't possible. Let's just allow things to run their course. If you tell them you were involved, it'll turn into a monster. Just keep quiet.'

She reminds herself she's doing this for both of them. If they are going to survive, no one must know. She might have destroyed the video, but that won't stop Elise rocking the boat.

'First you tell me I need to tell the truth,' Amy says with a flash of temper. 'Then when I decide I'm going to, you change your mind. I've told so many lies I can't remember which they are. I just want to tell PC Carter everything, right from the beginning. I'll take whatever shit comes at me.'

Lorna's frustration mounts. 'But shit sticks. That's the reality. Please don't do anything impulsive, because you won't be able to undo it.' She softens her voice. 'I only want what's best for you, darling.'

'You don't. You only want what's best for you. You're ashamed of me when you should be proud that I want to be honest. Well I'm really sorry I'm so embarrassing, but it's my life, not yours, and I can do what I like.'

'You're too young to understand the implications.'

'I am not.' She stomps out of the room and Lorna throws back the duvet, pulls on her dressing gown and follows her.

'You're behaving like a toddler. Don't be stupid.'

And then Amy goes mad. Lorna has never seen her like this and it's terrifying. She screams at her, calls her a bitch, tells her she's fucked up her life, that all this is her fault, that she's old and ugly and pathetic, that she's been following Elise round like a pet dog, trying to be best friends, that she had an embarrassing crush on Dexter and used Amy to get

397

close to him. She goes on and on, while Lorna stands there, buffeted, going hot and cold, furious and mortified, until she cannot take any more and slaps her daughter across the cheek.

While Amy is momentarily silenced, Lorna lets rip. 'Do you want to destroy this family? Do you want Jack to grow up knowing what you did? To be ashamed of where he's come from? Do you want to break up my marriage? Dexter is dead! He is not coming back. You shut up and you move on. Do you hear me?'

Amy's voice is mutinous. 'You can't stop me.'

'Can't I? Do you want to spend the rest of your teens in a young offenders' institution? Really? How easy do you think it'll be to build a career with that on your CV?' She makes herself take a mental step back and breathe. Losing her temper is not helpful. Amy is highly strung and understandably stressed. 'You have so much potential,' she continues, in a softer, more maternal tone, 'but it's not going to get you anywhere if you insist on saying you killed Dexter.'

Amy whimpers, but at least she's stopped snarling.

'I'm sorry I shouted at you. Of course it's your choice and you must do what you think is right. But please, Amy. Wait until this afternoon. Sometimes you have to give yourself a chance to absorb things. You've had a terrible shock. You were brave trying to save Dexter. I think that's incredible, but it's best that only me and you know about it. If you'd got him out, it would be a different matter. But you didn't, and he died. I need you to be able to forgive yourself and move on.'

That was horrible, but she had no choice.

Amy's eyes well, and Lorna presses home her advantage. 'Making a public admission of guilt is not going to bring Dexter back or undo what you did. You're very young and you have such a bright future. I'll support you in whatever you want to do, now and later in life, but I urge you to think very carefully before you limit your options and your brother's. You'll tear this family apart like you . . .' She can't quite bring herself to say it, but it's there.

'Like I what?' Amy's expression is dangerous. 'Like I tore Elise and Dexter's family apart?' When Lorna doesn't answer, she adds, 'Okay. I won't say anything.' Then she turns on her heel and rushes out of the room, slamming the door.

The air leaves Lorna's lungs in a rush.

84

THE PSYCHIATRIST

I'm so very sorry, Amy, Lorna writes at the end. *Everything I did was for you, but I got it dreadfully wrong and you've carried the guilt all these years. If it hadn't been for me, Dexter would have lived. I killed him because I mistakenly thought you had attempted to, and that if he survived he would destroy you. But you tried to save him and I allowed you to believe he'd had no chance. You were so brave. You deserve better than a mother like me.*

All these years and she could have spoken, could have made things a little better for me, but she didn't, she waited until she was safely beyond recrimination.

I fold up the sheets of paper and slide them back into the envelope, but they refuse go in properly. There's something stuck in the bottom. I tip the envelope up, shake it, and the gold chain and pendant I lost when I fought with Dexter slithers out. *The world is your oyster.* I hold it in the palm of my hand, then put it on. Maybe it isn't too late to find that life.

There are envelopes in my father's office. I choose a large one and slip Mum's letter inside it, address it to

Elise in prison, stick on a stamp and take it downstairs. I put it on the windowsill beside the front door. One day I might post it.

Acknowledgements

I would like to thank Consultant Psychologist Dr Fiona Bailey who read and commented on scenes relevant to my character's career and swore she didn't roll her eyes at her less than professional behaviour (without which there wouldn't have been a story). Apologies to any health professionals I inadvertently annoy.

I'd like to thank Daphne Prentice for answering questions about estate agents, the author Chris Bridges for insights into living with MS, and my dear friend, author Nicola Rayner, who talked to me about her choice not to have children.

At AM Heath a huge thank you to my agent Rebecca Ritchie and her assistant Harmony Leung. At Corvus and Atlantic, a million thank yous to my editor Sarah Hodgson, to Creative Director Felice McKeown, Senior Publicity Director Kirsty Doole and Sales Director Dave Woodhouse for making sure my books get a wide audience and a fighting chance. To Publishing Assistant Mayura Uthayakumaran for coordinating copy-editing and proof-reading. Thank you to Jane Selley for spotting my errors and bloomers. I am so grateful to you all.

To my friends in the writing world. Thank you for the companionship, advice and encouragement. I couldn't do this without you.

To the book reviewers, book bloggers and readers, thank you for accepting ARCs, for buying the book, for borrowing it from libraries, for reviewing in print and online and telling your friends. After ten years of being published, it still means the world to me.

To my growing family. Love to you all!